Elias Brook

by

Jared Topalian

About the Author

Jared Topalian is a lifelong Connecticut resident. He is quiet and easy to miss, but thinks deeply, speaks quickly, writes faster, and reads voraciously. He loves words, history, swordplay, dragons, mythology, quiet grey days, and his family. After deciding to be a writer at age eight, he has pursued storytelling ever since.

Dedication

for Mom and Dad
who were there at the first steps
and stayed with me the whole way.

CHAPTER 1

The battlefield lay quiet as the sun began to set. The dead from both forces lay where they fell, virtually indistinguishable in the growing gloom.

The ground had been a flat, open field when the day had dawned on it, but now it bore greater resemblance to a small, stinking bog. Grasses had been torn up by armored feet and hooves or burned in showers of fire. Blood, sweat, oil, and viscera crushed into the ground by the relentless pressure of the battle had churned soft earth into putrid mud; thick, clinging, and heavy with the stench of gore. Bodies and weapons had already begun to sink slightly into the mess. Perhaps with time and a few good rains, the field would grow back stronger off of the bodies left to the muck.

The earth's tribute would be slow in coming, however. Tonight, the spoils of war belonged to the insects feasting on both armies, the vultures descending on the horses that had grown soft in the sun, and the men, like overgrown jackals, quietly picking through the battlefield, helping themselves to the meager treasures the dead left behind.

The men they robbed were not finely dressed nor equipped, but the robbers were an even more ragged, threadbare lot. Filthy from picking through the messy aftermath of countless battles, many had thin hair, hard, heavily lined faces, and a hunted look about them. They twitched nervously as they rummaged among the dead, disturbing the scavengers' feast, but unnoticed by any living humans.

The only fire still burning as the sun set belonged to them, and as it became too dark to see, they drifted back to it one by one with anything of value they had managed to gather. By prior arrangement, the disheveled scavengers laid their findings together in one large pile; some

1

good boots, some perfectly fine blades, hats and jackets that had escaped the worst of the fighting, and any coins, jewelry, or armor that had kept enough of a shine to catch the setting sun. As the pile was put together, the men regarded it grimly.

They didn't consider themselves to be bad men, on the whole. They had all been raised knowing that the dead ought to be treated with some respect, not stolen from, but each of them had come around to conclude they could be forgiven for this. The dead wouldn't miss what they'd lost, after all, and between all the warlords, bandits, and self-proclaimed protectors of the realm, life was hard enough for the living without leaving things of use to rot with their owners. Still, none of them would be doing this if there was a better way to survive, and they all knew it. Without much guilt or satisfaction, the scavengers inspected their haul.

"Not that much this time," one ventured neutrally, prodding the pile a little closer together with a foot.

"Seems like there's less every time."

"Big bloody surprise, that!" one of the men spat, rolling his eyes. "All of the good fightin' and loot was at the start of all this. The *proper* warrin', mind you. This is just the bastards too stupid to quit hackin' away at each other. There's no more proper armies. Just beggars with crap iron killin' each other."

"You'd think they'd run out of men," another remarked, sitting down heavily. "They can't be eatin' much better'n us, and we don't die gettin' our bread."

"There's always a man ready to let someone else tell him what to do, until he marches into a grave," one of the scavengers said quietly, but this comment unexpectedly killed the conversation dead. As one man, the others all turned a cold stare on the speaker.

He was a man in his mid-twenties, as weatherbeaten as his companions but not as disheveled. His hair was a tangled black mess with some twigs and dirt smashed in, while an untidy black beard, mostly ill-maintained scruff, covered the lower half of his face. His clothes bore some signs of having once been quite fine, but now they were mostly patches of various colors and not far off from being dishrags in any respectable house. He was tall and skinny as a beanpole, but his lazy, crouched posture made him seem shorter than he was. There wasn't much to draw a second look to him except for his eyes. Contrasting the threadbare, dirty look of the man, two bright eyes, sharp as knives and a pale blue that seemed to radiate cold, gazed out at the world. There was a chilly cunning in that gaze that leant an unpleasant edge to everything else about the man. To meet his gaze was to distrust him on instinct, and there was more than distrust in the undisguised dislike the other men regarded him with. They were all scum to decent folk, they knew, but there are some folk that make even the lowest company feel lower.

"That's worked out well for you, eh, *Brook*?" one of the men grunted, throwing out the name like a punch. "You've done well for yourself off loyal folk dying."

The man they called Brook shifted, his facial expression not changing much but his casual air suddenly becoming a lot more forced. He wasn't by any means a stupid man, and he could see well enough that the atmosphere was not getting any friendlier than this tonight.

"What other folk do is their own business. We're all here because we didn't fancy dying for someone else's fight," he pointed out, trying to shift things. "Loyalty doesn't come into it, just living against dying."

"*You're* here 'cause you didn't fancy dyin', Brook," another man muttered, and Brook could feel the icy air of the gathering thicken. His attempt to step closer to the group had been a mistake when they were in this kind of a mood. "I reckon if you had, none of *us* would be here at all."

"I didn't put all these warlords here, if you were wondering!" he growled, changing tactics. There was no being ingratiating, the best he could hope for was making them back off again.

"No, King Morys dying in the woods with an arrow in his neck put them here," one of the scavengers agreed, glaring at Brook. "But who put the arrow there, Brook?"

A boy who had recently fallen in with the group stood up sharply. "I knew it was you!" he said. "*Elias* Brook! You're the one that shot King Morys!"

"That's a damn lie," Brook shot back, gut clenching as he saw the others' faces harden. "Wasn't my arrow that did him in. I wasn't even *there!*"

One of the older men drew closer to Brook, eyes narrowing. "Everyone knows the story, Brook. Lots of folk made sure everyone knew what you done," he growled. "Wasn't you that shot him? The king was still shot 'cause of you," he spat contemptuously. "Bah! I believe you didn't shoot him. You wouldn't have the guts for that."

There's five of them, and if one moves, so will the others, Brook thought, taking a step back. *Not enough loot for six men. They've all got to be thinking about it, or why else would they turn on me now?*

They know Elias Brook's a coward. **Everyone** *knows that about Elias Brook. These bastards aren't long on courage themselves, but they think I'll go without if they threaten me.*

I can probably kill this one before the others come help him. Threaten back, get my share, and run.

Brook's hand slid easily and imperceptibly towards his knife as he held his closest accuser's gaze. It was his good luck he'd fallen in with folks that didn't know much about fighting, he reasoned. They'd stand and glare and threaten, but when you were trying to threaten a fellow who knew when it was time to stop talking—

"Bastard!"

Brook had never paid much attention to the boy. He was younger than any of them, green as grass, and never found much worth keeping. He'd been some farmer's brat, the sort of people you stepped over these days.

If he'd paid the boy more mind, perhaps he'd have realized the farm boy knew what he was doing with that pitchfork he'd carried all this way. That he was green enough to be much braver than the old men he'd fallen in with. That he didn't waste much time mincing words, either.

Brook heard himself make a guttural, animal noise as three points of agony punched through his stomach, smashing the breath out of him even as he tried to scream. The man he'd been watching stepped back, surprised, but before Brook could even come to grips with the wound he'd taken, the boy had twisted his weapon, throwing Brook to the ground like a rag doll as the three prongs slid free. Brook's knife fell in the dirt, and he saw surprise turn to murder in his companions' eyes as they realized he'd been reaching for it.

"Kill 'im!"

Elias Brook hadn't lived this long by being slow, and even short of breath and in incredible pain, he was able to scramble to his feet and be five long strides away from the others before they'd even finished going for their weapons.

The farm boy hadn't outlived his parents by being slow either, however, and his pitchfork took Brook in the back. Brook felt one of his lungs burn as it was punctured, and felt it was a miracle the prongs sliding out again didn't throw him uselessly to the ground. If he fell, he would certainly be chopped to pieces and fed to the buzzards.

He staggered, and his blood spilled on the ground, but he stayed upright and he kept running for all he was worth, not even bothering to look behind him. There was only death in a glance over his shoulder, and he was done for if the farm boy got him again.

Brook also hadn't lived this long by being unprepared when things went bad, and reached shakily into a hidden pocket under one of his shirt's many patches.

The thing he dropped on the ground behind him looked like nothing more than a big brown walnut, but when it touched the ground, a small, complicated symbol carved into it briefly flared white.

Brook closed his eyes and put on another burst of speed as behind him, the sun appeared to briefly shine out of the ground into his attacker's eyes. He could hear them cry out in alarm and curse as the short, blinding flash seared their eyes and left them flailing about disoriented in the dark.

On a different day, the man Brook used that trick on would never see the light again, but Brook was unarmed, wounded, and in a lot of pain. He couldn't kill one of them now, let alone five. He had to settle for outrunning them. Better men than them had failed to track him down in more lawful times. This lot wouldn't have the will to waste time and food chasing him further. He didn't doubt they hated him enough to kill him when it was easy, but everyone whose hatred Brook had truly feared was cold and dead already. He'd outfoxed this lot. He was safe.

It felt like hours before Brook stopped running, but when he did, the exhaustion and pain, the desperate, self-preserving terror that he had kept at bay came back with a vengeance. Brook could only grunt stupidly as he tried to catch his breath and wound up coughing blood instead. His knees folded under him treacherously, and Brook couldn't even curse as he lost his footing and fell forward.

It wasn't the falling that concerned him, but once there, he was unable to summon the strength to stand back up. Brook finally became aware that he was covered in blood, all of it his.

That boy killed me before I even started running.

The realization was like an iron bar between the eyes. It left him stunned, dizzy, too stupid to think ahead. There wasn't any reason to, he realized, he was finished. There wasn't any desperate trick that would see him through another day, not anymore.

Elias Brook. The most cunning, vicious coward since the last basilisk died. Lord and master of all cheats and liars. The most famous traitor in all the land, a sneak-thief turned assassin. Killed a king, buried an army, caused a drought, started wars, all without picking up a weapon.

Killed by a boy with a pitchfork. Died alone in the woods. Mourned by no one.

Brook's eyelids twitched, and then slowly started to descend as the chill in his eyes faded and their edge dulled.

"Yeah...that sounds about right," he muttered, before darkness took him.

CHAPTER 2

Elias was confused when a faint rumbling cut through the blackness that had consumed him. When darkness took him in the woods, he hadn't expected anything afterwards, though a small part of him worried he'd wake up in the vast, lonely, and torment-filled expanse of Valka. But this couldn't be Valka. Valka was supposed to be oppressively hot and dry, blistering skin and searing lungs, and strewn with razor-sharp rocks that tore and cut as you moved. He didn't feel any kind of heat, or any ground at all.

It took Elias a moment to notice he wasn't breathing, either. His eyes snapped open in panic, and when they did, what was waiting did nothing to dispel his fears.

He was floating in darkness, with no way to control himself, but the darkness was uneven in a way that took him a moment to understand. Most of his surroundings were simple darkness as the absence of light, the darkness you found on starless nights or in deep caverns away from the sun. But there were…Elias struggled to make sense of what he was seeing. There were formless *things*, almost like small wisps of fog drifting in this night, only visible because they were even darker than the surrounding gloom. Elias had made his way through every form of darkness known to man in his life, but this was new to him. It wasn't shadow, just a place where light wasn't. It was the *idea* of darkness. Darkness you only saw in your mind's eye. Looking directly at the deeper darkness proved to be a mistake, as Elias saw lights like live coals suddenly ignite in its mass like furious eyes snapping open. This was followed by a cracked, dry, hissing noise, like wind through barren wasteland weaving its way through dry bones.

That wasn't the only sound Elias heard, however. Somewhere beyond the dark haze currently consuming all of his attention, there was a tortured splintering noise followed by what sounded like a scream. Below them, Elias could see crimson cracks appear in the empty gloom, and suddenly there was a blast of foul, scalding air as the fragmented cracks opened up like a massive, fanged maw. Elias felt an unspeakable dread pass through him as the boiling wind knocked him back, sending him pinwheeling helplessly through the murk. Elias could feel air flowing again, but this time it wasn't flowing out from the great rend but into it, like some monstrous creature inhaling deeply. Wordless, blind fear descended as Elias realized he was being drawn closer to the horrible gash, like a swimmer to a whirlpool. The *thing* that had been next to him when he opened his eyes seemed to mirror his panic, shifting into a form vaguely resembling a human and flailing with utter desperation to try and get away, but it was too close. Its foot slipped into the crack, and suddenly the air drew in even faster, like an excited breath. If the creature had a mouth, Elias imagined it was screaming as it was dragged down into the red light below, trying futilely to grip at anything to pull itself out. When nearly all of it was drawn in, the jagged opening suddenly slammed shut, like jaws closing, and the ungodly heat it had been releasing vanished with it.

Elias was left spinning in the dark, sure he was falling down but not at all certain there was an *up* to be falling from. There was nothing around him; he was lost, with red eyes and hungry red mouths opening to devour them as the only light. The boiling air roared loudly as it escaped from the cracks, battering Elias and the dark creatures with him about like leaves in a gale, while each gaping maw seemed to close with a sound halfway between a deep, eager breath and a death rattle. Elias was hurled about wildly, the wind scorching his skin and clawing the moisture from his eyes and throat until even blinking was agony. There was no sense of time, or direction as he spun from terror to terror, surrounded by panic and desperation.

The dark creatures trying futilely to escape being devoured knew he was there with them, and when the terrible wind battered Elias too close to one, it leapt on him furiously. Elias tried to scramble away, but his fingers and feet found no purchase in the empty air, and the creature descended upon him, blocking out all sight with its indistinct form and the angry little lights. Elias was no stranger to being stabbed, slashed, and cudgeled, but the pain when this—*thing*—attacked him, and it was certainly attacking him, was a new form of agony. The stumpy ends of its limbs, where a human would have hands, stabbed through his clothing and flesh as though they were air. It was like being torn apart from the inside with blades made of ice; there was no impact, no stab or blow, only a rapidly spreading, biting pain. It was cold and burning all at once, eating away at his insides. Elias scrambled, grappling vainly with his assailant, but he could no more move from his position than fly, and his desperate flailing found nothing to oppose him. It was like trying to fight smoke, or run away while falling off a cliff.

He ought to be dead. Everything he remembered told him he should be dead right now, but Elias was certain the pain he was in was not the eternal torment of Valka, and he had a very real feeling he was going to die *again* if he didn't get away. The creature seemed to be trying to force Elias down as it tore into his innards, and as he heard splintering noises below and felt the first hint of hot breath on his neck, he realized why.

He screamed desperately to the hostile, painful void he'd found himself in. He couldn't run, and he couldn't fight. The darkness closed in on him, malevolent and cruel, torturing and terrorizing him. And in a moment, those horrible red jaws would open to swallow him whole. In his pain and panic, all he could do was to cry for help and hope something was listening. "HELP! ANYBODY, PLEASE, *HELP ME!*"

As you wish.

Elias barely had time to process the strange voice that appeared in his mind without bothering to pass through his ears before he felt *something* grab hold of him and haul him out of the clutches of the thing attacking him. He supposed he should be relieved, but that was rather hard when he saw he was being held just out of reach of his attacker, and that it wasn't alone. Indistinct dark forms with glowing eyes had gathered around it and reached for him with lumpy, twisted limbs like clouds of smoke drifting upwards. Elias was far too terrified to feel any sort of pity for them as the maw below opened to devour them one by one, the creatures vainly flailing and fighting with each other to escape it. As the closest of them began to be drawn in, it reached for Elias, as if hoping it could throw him down in its place.

What exactly was holding him just barely out of its reach was not clear to Elias despite his eyes searching for it, and this did not comfort him at all.

They are going to Valka, Elias Brook, the voice came again. It was hard to describe, neither male nor female as far as Elias could tell, but powerful and full of command. *They want to drag you there with them. Or perhaps send you in their stead. One cannot take company on the endless road. Shall I let them?*

"No!" Elias only refrained from screaming because he was still trying to get used to the fact he wasn't breathing. "No, please! Anything but Valka!" That attack had been quite bad enough, but having to walk the hellish roads for the rest of eternity? If this nightmare was merely the *prelude* to the endless road, eternal punishment held more terror than Elias was capable of imagining.

*Then listen **closely** to what I have to say,* the voice replied sharply. Terrified as he was, Elias recognized a display of power when he saw it. Whoever or whatever he was speaking to, it had probably been letting those things attack him just so he would understand how badly it would go for him if he angered it.

"W-Who are you?" he managed, still unable to see anything at all holding him up. There was the faintest hint of light, but surely that couldn't have lifted him up...?

I am Mibotha. And I will spare you, if you do as I say, the voice replied. Elias started to speak, but the force holding him up suddenly gave away. Elias fell back towards his eagerly waiting assailants and felt the eager breath of the gaping maw. He had enough time to scream in terror before he was hauled roughly upwards and out of their reach again.

*Understand this, Elias Brook. I am not here to strike a bargain with you. This is not a negotiation. It is an ultimatum. Accept my terms as they are presented. If you attempt to barter, I will throw you back and think no more of you. **Understand?***

"Absolutely! Crystal-clear! No haggling!" Elias screamed, raw terror speeding the words out of his mouth so swiftly they practically blurred together. "I'll do whatever you say! Just don't drop me!"

I have a use for you, Elias Brook. Refuse it, and I will drop you. Attempt it and fail, and you will be back here. Your only hope is to succeed.

Elias knew without needing any details beyond its introduction that he was not going to like this job, but since his options were accepting the job unconditionally or being hurled to eternal torment, he nodded as quickly as possible.

Elias Brook

You have brought great suffering down upon yourself and countless others with the life you have lived, Elias Brook. In your twenty-five years, you have cheated, lied, stolen, killed, and betrayed. The punishment for that life hangs below you now. It would be easy, and quite likely just, to leave you to it, but that will not assuage the torment you have brought down on others. I am giving you one chance to attain a different kind of justice. I will bring you back to life, and you will save your land from the nightmare it has become. You will save Yivyn, Elias Brook...or you will die trying.

Elias couldn't see Mibotha, but he whimpered slightly as a light began to grow around him. The one relief was that the dark creatures below seemed to recoil from it before Elias was no longer able to see anything.

Steel yourself, Elias Brook. You cannot afford to fail.

When the light faded, he was standing upright in the place he'd fallen, looking around as his vision cleared. It was day now, but he seemed just as he'd been the night before with the exception of his wounds. The only blood to be seen was dried on his coat, and its stench was awful. Elias managed to stumble over to a nearby stream, his legs apparently as surprised as he was to still be alive, and took off his coat and clothes to wash the blood from them and then his body. They weren't very good clothes, he'd be the first to admit, but they were all he had. After he'd washed, he inspected his torso, to find that all that remained of his wounds were six new scars.

The temptation to dismiss the nightmare he'd just been through as a hallucination brought on by blood loss was enormous, but Elias couldn't bring himself to do so. It had been too *real* to be the work of a fevered brain, and having looked at himself, Elias was quite sure he could not possibly be alive after losing that much blood, much less already healed to the point that his wounds looked like scars he'd had for years. No, his experience and Mibotha had been real. He'd been brought back to life to try and carry out the ultimatum it had given him. Elias was certain of this, and wished he wasn't.

Save Yivyn. Aside from various threats, and terrified whimpering on his part, that had been the long and the short of his conversation with Mibotha. He hadn't had a chance to ask *how* he was supposed to do that. Everywhere he went, he was reminded how everything bad that had happened in the last five years was the fault of Elias Brook. People didn't curse the warlords for the endless fighting, or the dying animals for the disease in poor towns, or the clouds for the lack of rain, or just plain bad

11

luck when crops withered and died of blight. They cursed *him*. How was he supposed to put a stop to all that? Where did he even *start*?

"What, am I supposed to turn back the clock five years on the kingdom? Stop all the warlords, end the drought and bring Morys back to life?" he muttered darkly to himself, shaking his head as he shook some of the dampness from his coat. "Or am I supposed to pay reparations to everyone I've ever wronged out of my endless supply of *nothing whatsoever?*"

The evil you've done with your life is not something simple to undo. Elias yelped loud enough to put several birds to flight and jumped a straight foot in the air as Mibotha's voice filled his head, and he looked around in a panic. *But you can make recompense by helping to fix the problems you created.*

"Mibotha?! Where are you?!"

Your body died before we had our…conversation, Mibotha remarked. *I needed to return to it with you to heal your wounds and restore your life.*

"You're possessing me?"

If I was possessing your body, I could have simply swatted you into Valka and taken your corpse for my own purposes. Your actions are still your own, but you've been released from your fate to fulfill a mission. I will be with you every step of the way to make sure you do not forget your life belongs to me…and to keep you from being tempted by your old habits.

Elias grudgingly realized there was nothing he could say to that. He had outwitted a great many people over the years, but he was certain there wasn't a single trick he knew that would get him out from under Mibotha's power while the spirit was inhabiting his body. Mibotha had all the power here, and Elias was certain even with life back in his body, Mibotha's use for him was the only thing standing between him and wandering Valka, with only unbearable pain, hunger, and thirst for company, forever.

He was equally certain Mibotha knew he knew this. It likely wanted him to. The threat of eternal damnation was hard to beat for holding all the power in a relationship.

"N-No worries there," he said quickly. "I've seen the error of my ways! I'm here to save Yivyn, just as you said!"

There was a silence, and Elias could tell Mibotha was waiting for him to fill it. Normally Elias was content to leave a perfectly good silence alone, having no desire to converse with others anyway, but this time, he willingly stepped into the trap.

"Since you're here..." he added, trying and failing not to sound wheedling, "I don't suppose you could give me a hint about where I start?"

The land is sick, but worse than that, it is lawless, too mired in violence to begin recovering from the damage. If it slides any further into chaos, Yivyn has no future. If the land is to be made whole again, you must first restore the rule of law.

"It always comes down to bringing King Morys back to life, doesn't it?" Elias muttered, shuddering. "Well, I hate to tell you this, but he's been dead five years. I think that's harder to fix than you patching the holes I had in me."

Morys is dead, and beyond recall. Mibotha said. *Your revival is more unusual than you know. Believe me, if I had a better person for this mission, you would not be here right now.*

"I can already tell traveling with you is going to be a real treat," Elias grumbled mutinously. Mibotha's annoyance came like a red-hot stab, so sharp Elias fell to his knees, gasping and clutching his head.

SILENCE. *Morys is dead, but his children are not. His heirs still live, in hiding. Restoring the royal family to power will create a foundation on which stability can be rebuilt. This, Elias Brook, is what I need* **you** *for.*

"Restoring the princess and her brother to power," Elias whispered, sheer disbelief at the impossibility of his task overcoming even his fear of Mibotha for a moment. "You want me to find the two best-hidden people in the country. You want me to find them, while they are guarded by a number of people who would probably dedicate a holiday and several golden monuments to the boy who stabbed me to death last night. You want me to convince the two at the very top of a *long* list of folk who want me dead, who will never trust a word that comes out of my mouth, to let me attempt to put them back in power. Then somehow subjugate several warlords, who would kill them and me on sight, and restore a monarchy that's been dead for five years?" Elias looked down. "That's your plan?"

No, that is **your** *task, or you will wander Valka forever,* Mibotha replied. *I've watched you a long time, Elias Brook. You are one of the worst men I have ever seen, but I reluctantly concede you are also one of the most cunning. A number of brave, wise, and just men have been killed in this war* *trying to save the land. You are none of these things, but you know how to survive. Perhaps you can provide what this kingdom needs, with my guidance...but if you fail, neither you nor the kingdom has truly lost very much of value.*

Why did this become my life, Elias wondered to himself. I could deal with being a nobody if it meant people left me alone, but somehow I'm a nobody with everyone out to get me. That's not *fair*. You weren't supposed to be unimportant *and* a target!

"You really think this can be done? You think that I can do this, or are are you just having one last laugh at my expense before I go to Valka?" Elias asked, unable to hold his tongue. Complaining about the abundant unfairness of his life had never changed anything before, but for some reason he had never given up hope that it might. "Because at the moment I'm not seeing a great deal of difference between the tortures of the damned and what's going to happen to me here."

I could show you the difference, if you like. It shouldn't take you too long to figure out, Mibotha said sharply, and Elias could suddenly feel Valka's skin-searing winds on his face. For a moment, a road of staggering length, filled with pits and rocks like primitive blades, stretched out before him under a deep red sky. It was all but silent except the faint hissing of the wind between the rocks, and it was empty in a way the darkness between stars was. No otherworldly tormentors could be as terrifying as being left to wander that emptiness alone, forever. Elias had only been there a couple of seconds, but he could already feel his skin starting to burn, and his eyes and mouth had again become so dry they hurt.

The sight of it congealed all of Elias's mutinous feelings into utter, cowed terror, and he realized complete obedience to Mibotha's demands was the only thing standing between him and this horrible place. He had to try, no matter how impossible or painful the future seemed. Getting hacked to pieces and having his head put on a spike for his troubles was something Elias had spent his life avoiding, but the endless road of sharp rocks and boiling heat that stretched before him was another story altogether.

"No! I'll take you at your word! I'm on the job!" he cried, and the horrible vision faded away. Elias took a moment to steady himself, and then quickly started to walk. "Do we at least know where they are?"

I was able to watch you because you never made much of an effort to conceal yourself. The prince and princess have been significantly more cautious than you, and so I'm sad to say I only have a vague idea of where we should start working. You're clever enough when it suits you. You should be able to handle the rest.

Elias didn't say anything as he started to head out of the forest. He'd heard two sayings as a boy that came back to him now. His father had once told him that hell was other people, and his mother had been fond of saying that everyone, from kings to peasants, got the help they deserved.

He was beginning to suspect that before all this was over, he would know just how right they were.

CHAPTER 3

Elias was very cautious as he peered out of the underbrush towards the road. Staying in the woods was not a very appealing idea to him, but Elias had developed the habit of never assuming anything was safe to do without thinking carefully first. The habit had, with one unfortunate recent exception, gone a long way towards keeping Elias among the upright and breathing, and he wasn't about to abandon it now just because he could tell Mibotha was getting impatient.

You are a widely traveled man, Elias Brook. Is there a reason open road fills you with trepidation?

"Of the two of us, I'm the one who got stabbed to death once, and I'm not eager to go through that again. I want to be sure I don't walk right into the people that killed me the other night. Your mission involves enough walking right up to people who want to kill me as it is."

I don't understand you, Mibotha remarked. *I know quite well your attachment to your own life is the only bond you hold dear, but you have lived your lifetime closer to danger and violence than many ever come. Surely a coward would not continue to trail after marauding armies and fall in with dangerous men, as you've done?*

"I'm a real enigma, aren't I?" Elias muttered absentmindedly, checking his surroundings again and then stepping out onto the road. It seemed blessedly free of other people, and Elias took advantage of that to get a move on quickly. "So, you said you had a hint of where our young monarchs might be? You might as well give me the clue now."

There is a town not far up the road from where we are. The prince and princess are not there, but one of their retainers is. If you can earn their trust, this task will become a great deal easier.

"Oh, good, so we're starting right off with walking up to someone who has probably been told to kill me on sight. I *like* this plan!" Elias groaned.

It's really rather remarkable that you managed to stop whining about every little thing long enough to ruin an entire country. Imagine what you'd be capable of if you'd ever done anything useful with that energy, Mibotha sighed. *Yes, you'll have quite a difficult time earning their trust. What of it? You must change your ways, Elias Brook, and becoming a man worthy of anyone's trust is the greatest change you can possibly make in yourself. Besides, I believe an opportunity to prove your sincerity will present itself soon if you are quick enough.*

Based on the events of the past few days, Elias decided to regard that bit of news with significant suspicion, but said nothing. Lamenting his situation wasn't going to get him out of it and he did need to keep in mind he was going to go to Valka if he didn't somehow make all this work out.

"How far to the town?"

Not far at all if we hurry. Let's waste no more time, shall we? Mibotha asked, seeming pleased there weren't more complaints to deal with.

"At least we can agree this ought to be done as quickly as possible," Elias said, starting to run. He was pleased to find his healed wounds didn't hurt at all, and whatever mental baggage Mibotha might have brought to his body didn't seem to cross over into the physical; he felt great! If anything, he was a little faster than before!

"Listen, Mibotha. This deal of ours...is having you around going to do anything for me?" he asked.

I am merely making it somewhat more difficult for you to die before you complete your task. Anything else you notice is merely your own abilities being put to better use than normal, Mibotha said. *I'm here to advise you, not empower you.*

"So you're mostly here to be a second conscience," Elias concluded, disappointment setting back in. Not being dead was a neat deal, but he'd feel a lot better about this forced partnership if Mibotha could do more than preach in his ear while he ran headlong at certain, and likely very painful, death.

We wouldn't be here if your first conscience was functioning properly, now would we?

"It was working just fine for me until yesterday."

Yes. That's rather where the problem comes from, I imagine.

17

Elias had met kings, and far too many men that held their personal sense of worth equal to a king. He'd talked to some very powerful, very important, and above all, very arrogant men. But even among all of them, Elias had trouble thinking of the last person he'd spoken to that seemed so absolutely certain they were always correct as Mibotha. It was like trying to argue with a self-righteous landslide.

Even so, Elias was not left to brood on his unpleasant company within the confines of his head for long, as he spotted the town up ahead.

It wasn't really much more than a village. Five years ago, it probably had indeed been a sleepy little village, but not a single one of those had survived the famine and years of conflict intact. The town looked poor and the buildings of low quality, but it had a very sturdy-looking defensive wall, and Elias imagined he could see some sentries with crossbows stationed on it.

A couple years earlier, when the fighting was really at its peak, towns like this could change hands three times in a month as would-be warlords rose and fell too fast to leave their names to history. After that, they were mostly left alone except for brigands testing for weak defenses and ragged remnants of the old armies trying to find supplies and new recruits. In the last year or so, it had become nearly impossible for most townsfolk to tell the two apart. Usually the only important difference was the brigands were more organized.

An environment like that meant sleepy, accommodating people did not live in towns anymore. Elias knew, without needing to know a single thing about the town's experiences, that it would be filled with a number of hard-eyed, bitter, suspicious folk, and about as likely to welcome him as welcome a plague.

"Mibotha, if you're going to be advising me," he muttered as he got closer, "what was your plan for this, exactly? They've got sentries and I don't look like a champion of justice. If they see me run up, they'll probably shoot me on general principle, and if they find out who I am, they'll probably shoot me so that I die slow enough for them to lynch me."

It has occurred to me that our partnership would be a much easier one if you weren't so infernally good at making enemies. Did it never occur to you at some point you might want SOMEONE in this world not to wish you dead? Mibotha sighed.

"I didn't do anything worse than make a few bad decisions," Elias said defensively. "Nothing more, and nothing less. No man goes through life without making a few huge mistakes. It was just my bad luck that those decisions meant all the other disasters that came about got laid at my door. People went out and made enemies *for* me, including the folks you're so eager for me to help out."

A man has something more than bad luck and a few poor decisions to blame when every hand in the world is raised against him, I would imagine.

"Yes, I suppose unhelpful friends bear a certain portion of the blame as well."

You're being obtuse now.

"I don't know the meaning of the word."

It would not surprise me to discover that is true.

"Are you going to help me or not?"

Very well. Approach them with your hands held high, very slowly. Shout out that you've come to deliver a message. A warning.

"Messengers are not highly thought of in this day and age, and sentries are not known for handling bearers of bad news with immense courtesy, Mibotha."

Elias Brook, if you do not learn to trust me when I tell you something this is going to be a very short and very, very painful last chance for you. If I am wrong, I will not allow a crossbow bolt to kill you again. But I will not be wrong.

"You sound awfully sure about that."

Spirits are never wrong. We have a lot longer to learn these things than humans.

Elias gritted his teeth, slowly raising his hands and doing as Mibotha had instructed. He would get Mibotha for this one day, he promised himself. One day, Mibotha was going to be wrong, and Elias was never, ever going to let it forget that when the day came.

"That's far enough, mister!" one of the sentries shouted, aiming his crossbow at Elias. Elias looked up, ignoring every instinct that told him doing anything but turning and running right now was going to get him shot.

"I'm a messenger! I come with a warning!" he shouted, sweating. Mibotha was going to be wrong sometime soon, he was sure of it. Nobody that sure of themselves could be *that* smart, he reasoned.

He just really, really hoped Mibotha wasn't going to be wrong about something like "I'm sure you won't die from this."

"We can hear you just fine from there!" the sentry called, and Elias counted his blessings that he'd gotten this far without sprouting a few feathery shafts.

"Now what?" he hissed under his breath.

There's a bandit group on the move. They came down from the mountains a few days ago, and they're picking up momentum now that they're on the flatlands. You happened to outrun them this far, but they're going to be on the village by sundown, Mibotha dictated, still infuriatingly calm.

"I-I've been on the run all day!" Elias said, as quickly as he could. "Bandits! They came down out of the mountains, and they're on the move! I only just managed to get away from them, but they're headed this way! They'll be here by sundown!"

"You're a field hand, are you?" the sentry asked cynically, and Elias cursed under his breath. "You don't look like you fled any farms recently, mister."

"All right, I'm a scavenger, damn it!" Elias said, not needing to fake his growing panic. "I just go over the battlefields for a few coins and some supplies! I don't hurt anybody! Don't leave me out here when they catch up to me!"

The sentry did not appear impressed with Elias's confession, but he did regard him thoughtfully for a short time, before glancing at the horizon. A couple hours yet to sundown, if Elias was any judge.

"You could run on a fair ways before they overtake you, I imagine. What's got you so concerned you need to stop here instead of moving on? If these bandits of yours are real, you could just go around us and I don't think they'd chase a scrawny thing like you." Elias could hear the cynicism and suspicion in the sentry's voice, and his unease grew again.

"They're not swallowing this one, Mibotha, don't you have a better story?" he whispered.

Keep at it. He will let you in, Mibotha replied easily.

"I've been running all day, sir, and it's been a bad couple of days!" Elias tried, hoping his genuine sincerity as he lamented the latest turn in his life was not lost on the guard. "I'm beaten all to pieces and you know past sundown's an evil time for one man on the road! There's wolves, and thieves, and horrible evil spirits from the woods!"

You cheeky son of a bitch.

"Let's say I believe you. How many bandits are we to be on the lookout for?"

"Forty! Maybe more!" Elias shouted, Mibotha dumping the words on his tongue without consulting his brain. They came out so suddenly and rang so true even Elias believed it for a moment. To his astonishment, he saw the sentry's expression change, before he looked down gravely at Elias.

"Forty? That's the biggest band that's come our way in years..." he said. "You'd better come to the gate, we could use the extra hands when they catch up. But no funny business, or we'll skewer you and leave you out as a warning to 'em. And if you're in league with these brigands, boy, I promise you'll die slow."

Elias nearly sagged with relief as he headed over to the gate. He'd been so sure the sentry was about to prove Mibotha was indeed wrong and shoot him in the face, but they'd been granted entry. The hard part was over, now he just needed to do the even harder part with someone who likely would need a lot more convincing not to kill him then and there.

"Forty? You knew the right number to scare them. Good job, Mibotha," he muttered, heading for the gate.

While I dislike enabling your reputation as a liar, sometimes facts must be changed in the name of expedience.

"Still, that was a good story to feed them. I should've realized they'd open their gates to someone claiming forty bandits are headed that way."

They probably would have told you to take your chances in the flatlands if I admitted there were only twenty-five, but by the time they get here it won't be possible to count them that well anyhow.

Elias froze.

"You...weren't making that up? I thought we just needed to talk our way in to find this retainer!"

I can alter facts slightly, but I can't make new ones up. That would be wrong, Mibotha replied, sounding offended. *These people live in fear of brigands because of YOUR poor decisions, and they have as much right to hate you as the one we're seeking. You'll have to start making amends early to earn yourself some trust going forward, and being the hero of this town's defense will accomplish that nicely.*

"WHAT?!"

I'm aware you're not much of a swordsman, but you know how to use a bow. If you save the day this evening it will be a perfect first step on the road to redemption. You probably won't need to defeat more than twelve yourself to come out of this looking like a man worth trusting, Mibotha said, and Elias realized that the spirit actually meant that reassuringly.

So there was another hard part before the hardest part of his task here in town. Mibotha, in its infinite wisdom, had volunteered him to be the "hero" of a nighttime battle against a group of bloodthirsty mountain bandits. And if he lived through that, *then* he could go talk to the person in town who would want to kill him on sight.

Elias had been on the road to redemption for less than a day already, and he was starting to suspect going to Valka might have been the easier option.

CHAPTER 4

Elias tried to get a grip on himself, taking a few deep breaths. So the dangers of his mission were coming at him a little earlier and a fair bit more intensely than expected. That was fine, wasn't it? He'd adapt, and he'd survive it, like he always had. He had walls, other people fighting, and a spirit watching out for him. There was no reason to panic.

...No, he conceded, as his knees continued to shake, it seemed that the rest of him was not buying that for a second. He would be extremely lucky if he ever left this town alive, and thanks to Mibotha, his reward for surviving his business here would be more opportunities to risk death.

He barely noticed the sentries at the town's gates checking carefully to make sure that he wasn't armed or carrying anything suspicious before they grunted and ushered him inside. Behind him, the gates closed with a very final-sounding clang. The knowledge there wasn't any way to get out of this but to do it properly did very little for Elias's mood, but he tried to hold onto that anyway.

"There's nothing for it but to go forward," he muttered under his breath. "It's not like it can get worse." He strongly suspected he would regret saying that a great many times in the not-so-distant future, but it at least helped him calm down a little.

Show some spirit, Elias Brook. These people are hardy, and I'll be with you the entire time. This part will be quite simple, truly.

"Compared to everything else, you mean?"

Obviously, why?

"Just thinking out loud. Tell me, what exactly happens if someone runs me through before this is all done?"

I can assist you in that regard. It will still HURT, of course, so I advise you not to rely on me.

23

"Trust me, that's the last thing on my mind," Elias muttered grimly, going to the stairs that would lead him up the wall. He was a little startled to find the sentry that had grilled him earlier there, waiting for him.

"Do you know anything about fighting, boy?" he asked bluntly.

"I'm good enough with a bow to look after myself," Elias replied without thinking. "Never been in a siege, though."

"Not likely to be much of a siege. If they're tough, they'll try to climb or knock down the walls while we kill as many of 'em as we can. If we don't, they'll kill us all in the night," the sentry grunted, glaring out at the horizon. "If they aren't tough, and I hope for all our sakes they aren't, they'll camp out and make some threats before our arrows convince 'em to leave. In either case, another archer is handy. Can you shoot in the dark?"

"I've had some practice with that, yes," Elias muttered. Nobody ever sang any songs about his skill with a bow. The only shot ever mentioned in relation to his name these days was one he didn't even make. The fact remained that while he only rarely needed the knife he'd lost the other night and had considered any job where weapons of any kind were not required the sort of job for him, being able to hit targets in the coming night with a bow was one of the only things he WASN'T worried about.

"Thank the gods for small blessings, I suppose," the sentry sighed. "How far off did you say these men were?"

They'll be visible in less than an hour.

"We probably have less than an hour," Elias passed on. "Erm...how many of *us* are there?"

"There are ten sentries in this town, plus you and one other volunteer," the sentry replied, and Elias paled as he understood the man's grim demeanor.

Even if he was to admit he'd added fifteen imaginary bandits to his report at Mibotha's behest, the defenders were still outnumbered two to one, and the guard thought that a force four times the size of his would descend on the town before the hour was up. Elias was surprised to find he felt bad for the man. He was scared as it was, and he knew the score. He didn't want to imagine what it was like for the other fellow.

If you change the number now, he'll probably conclude that eleven against twenty-five is just as good as eleven and one liar against twenty five and throw you over the wall, Mibotha warned.

Self-preservation immediately quashed Elias's small desire to lighten the situation somewhat, and he had to admit he was better off leaving the defenders frightened and able to call on the strength of desperation in the fight. Even though they had a better position and weren't nearly as badly outnumbered as they thought, these were not strong walls, and Elias suspected brigands surviving in these times might know a thing or two about winning in a situation like this.

"Where should I stand guard?" he asked.

"If they're on your trail, they'll probably come into sight in front of this wall. Here's where you'll be when that happens," the sentry replied, patting the ramparts by where he was standing. He then pointed down to a little shack by the closed gate. Elias had been so distracted coming in he hadn't even noticed it was there. "Report down there for your weapons...but remember, we're watching you." Elias gulped as the sentry's glare turned back on him. "We let you in, and we expect you to pay us back for not leaving you out there. You run, or try to turn on us, and one of us will stick an arrow in you without batting an eye."

"Such *charming* people," Elias muttered under his breath, excusing himself quickly to do as the sentry had said. "I really feel like sticking my neck out for them."

It is your fault they are the way they are. The ten men standing watch here would likely have lived much more peaceful lives if it was not for the consequences of your actions. The least you can do is help them now, Mibotha scolded.

"And the other volunteer?"

The retainer you'll need to speak to. That's why demonstrating heroism is important in this battle. You must be the champion of this town!

"How about I just shoot three of them and count on each of the others to hit two, instead of getting myself killed trying to look gallant?" Elias grumbled.

You have hidden behind better men when there was fighting to be done your entire life, Elias Brook, and it ended with you dying alone and friendless in the woods. Your time of being a coward is over, whether you like it or not, Mibotha replied coldly. Elias couldn't help but flinch at the raw contempt in the spirit's voice. *The man you were deserved that death, and probably quite a bit beside. But I did not make this bargain for you to remain the man you were. You are here to find redemption, and the first part of that is changing who you are. If you hide and avoid responsibility like you have done so often before, our link to the prince and princess will be precarious indeed. You need to convince a retainer whose opinion of you is even lower than you imagine that you are a changed man, and doing only what you have to in order to live through the night will just convey that you are still a rat in a tight corner. You have to change EVERYTHING tonight. You need to convince them you are a new man. A heroic man.*

"So you want me to lie to them," Elias cut in bluntly. "Because that's more convenient."

If that's what it takes, Mibotha said calmly. *You'll find shedding your evil reputation will make much of the danger you are so concerned about far more manageable going forward. I'm confident you'll thank me for this opportunity with time.*

"I sincerely doubt that," Elias muttered darkly, ducking into the little shack where a disheveled old man, bald as a bean and just as clean-shaven, was waiting with a bow and quiver.

"Ah, you must be our new volunteer. Got chased here by bandits, eh?" he remarked, looking Elias over. "Well, you look like a man who's quick on his feet, true enough."

"Not quick enough, obviously," Elias sighed, scratching his head but accepting the bow and arrows as they were offered to him.

"Not quick enough or not lucky enough. There's few enough that have any kind of luck at all these days," the old man said, shrugging. He gave Elias a surprisingly canny glance. "You don't look like a lucky fellow to me...but there's something to you besides quickness, I imagine. Hopefully it'll last you through the night."

Elias considered replying to that, but after a moment, he just left quickly, trying to ignore the shudder that had gone through him. He was used to brief, contemptuous glances or a suspicious stare-down, but for some reason the old man looking at him without either had been mildly unsettling.

You seem troubled. Has it been that long since you've talked to someone that wasn't certain you would let them down? Mibotha asked, immediately replacing Elias's unease with his familiar sullen resentment of his new partner.

"I have a lot to be troubled about, Mibotha. Bandits coming to tear down these walls. Sentries ready to shoot me if I put a toe wrong. A loyal retainer somewhere in this town that will gut me if they hear my name before I've pulled off a minor miracle. Oh yes, and a spirit determined to make every damn thing that happens just a little worse to teach me a lesson in morality," he whispered harshly.

My sympathy for you is boundless, truly. Mibotha's voice was solid ice, and for a moment, Elias was afraid again. *But you are a clever man. You managed to pull off a number of minor miracles to escape the consequences of your actions before, while good people were dying or having their lives ruined. I'm sure you can find a way through this, if for no better reason than to save your own skin a while longer.*

Elias took his position, shivering a little. Mibotha had been annoyed with him a number of times already, but now it sounded truly angry.

*If your life is all that matters to you, Elias Brook, then you will fight for it every day we are together. And if your life that is all you have to fight for, I assure you, you **will** lose that fight eventually, and I do not envy what will become of you when you do.* There was no threat in Mibotha's voice. Each word was a statement of bald fact, almost a promise. *If I were you, I would consider how similar I am to the man who got what he deserved in the forest one night. I would consider how different I would want to be so I would not end up the same as that man. And if I were you, Elias Brook, I would recall that the men who are most tormented by their consciences are the ones who need conscience the most.*

With that, Elias was left alone in his head as the sun began to set, staring out at the horizon. It was the beginning of a warm night, but he did not remember ever feeling quite so cold in his life.

CHAPTER 5

Elias shivered slightly as night fell, although it was far too warm on the wall for him to claim it was anything but fear.

He could hear them out there now, getting closer, and even seeing them wasn't hard. The band approaching the town had torches of their own to match the ones he was seeing by on the wall.

Not even bothering with trying to move stealthily...these were either very stupid bandits or very, very confident killers, and Elias had a sinking feeling he knew which one was more likely. Sometimes luck favored the stupid even in rough times, but anyone whose luck had saved them from their stupidity had probably run out of luck long before now. What was left were those too determined to give up and those skilled enough to kill everyone weaker and stupider than they were.

Only twenty-five, Mibotha had said. That sounded great at first, especially compared to forty bandits attacking a town of this size. But they outnumbered the defenders two to one, and as the force got nearer and nearer, Elias couldn't help but think these sentries and their moderate fortifications were not each worth two of those men down below.

He would have to pray he was wrong about that. Mibotha had led him here, and there wasn't any chance he was going to sneak away when the fighting started. If he tried to bolt now, he'd be the first casualty, plain and simple.

Maybe another solution would present itself if he was lucky, but Elias had never been long on luck he hadn't stolen from someone else. He knew in his gut his only chance of seeing sunrise was to win this.

"That's far enough, my lads!" the sentry called out, his crossbow ready to fire and aimed at the mass of bandits. There didn't appear to be a leader, Elias realized. If they had one, he wasn't drawing any attention to himself. He could see the sentry's face as the older man was realizing he'd need to get very lucky to cut the head off this snake before it could bite.

"And who might you be, friend? The one in charge of this little dung heap?" a voice called from the crowd below.

"No friend of yours, bastard. I'd move right along if I was you," the sentry warned grimly. It did not, Elias noted with some dismay, seem to do much besides amuse the bandits looking up at him.

"Now, now, old man, there's no need to be like that. You could at least answer my question: Are you in charge here?"

"I've got a crossbow and thirty men ready to fire when I do. As far as you care, I'm a god!" the sentry snarled. Elias, no rookie to bluffing, was impressed how smoothly the sentry spat out the bald-faced lie. People underestimated how special a person you needed to be to lie that big that smoothly.

Despite the threats to shoot him earlier, Elias almost liked the man standing next to him.

"I do believe that's blasphemy, friend," the voice replied, with a pleasantness that made Elias's blood run cold.

There was no warning, no sudden movement in the crowd. A bow twanged, and Elias saw the sentry pitch over backwards with an arrow in his eye, never making a sound.

"You see, gods take at *least* three arrows to drop," the voice went on, cheerful as a knife was sharp. "You lot...maybe ten will do it for the rest of you? A little more? I'm not honestly sure, but I'm keen to find out."

They're going to kill everyone here, Elias realized, staring at where the sentry had fallen. They're not going to make any demands because that would suggest they won't kill us all for fun before they even think about loot.

"Even if there is a god up there with you, friends, I'd start praying now even so. We've got enough for him, too—"

Elias had been watching the stillness of the bandits while the words had washed over him. It had provided an excellent backdrop to notice movement, but he hadn't realized he'd even readied his bow until the bandit who had moved slumped over with an arrow in his throat. For a moment, there was a stunned silence on both sides, before the voice resumed with a laugh utterly divorced from the notion of humor.

"Watch out, boys, someone's keen up there. Let's kill him!"

"Oh, crap," Elias muttered, as the bandits rippled. Seconds later, a small swarm of arrows was hurtling at the battlements, and Elias threw himself to the ground. He could *feel* several whistle by overhead where he'd been standing seconds ago, and he saw three more men fall.

"Twenty-four against eight. I've seen massacres with better odds than that," he whispered, heart sinking.

This will BE a massacre if you don't carry the day, Mibotha warned grimly.

"You should know by now how much experience I've got saving the day," Elias grunted, coming up and firing off a shot of his own. It was hasty, as he expected retaliatory shots, but another man crumpled.

*There's a first time for everything. I would suggest you learn **very** quickly.*

"I hate you."

The other defenders were apparently not intimidated enough by losing four of their own to be lax in their counterattack. Elias was incredibly relieved to see seven more men fall when the bows on the wall with him sang out, and to his surprise, one of the defenders further away managed to get an eighth before ducking down.

"Only fifteen now," he whispered.

That might still be too many.

Elias was about to question Mibotha's grim pronouncement when two little black balls sailed up out of the dark. Elias's eyes widened as he recognized them, and he scrambled away.

"Get away from them!" he called desperately to the others, but two men still died when the little balls exploded with a force that seemed impossible for their size, shaking the fortifications, tearing a hole in the wall, and sending a blast of blazing hot air across his face.

We're being attacked by men with Demon Dust, he realized with dim horror as he tried to clear his head from the ringing the explosion had caused. The materials for those two little bombs had probably the equivalent worth of most of the loot they'd find in the town, and yet these men had detonated them without hesitation.

The men swarming at the walls were either hungry enough that profit meant nothing to them, or they were devoting themselves to the destruction of this town purely because it was *there*. Either way, Elias's last fragile hope of holding off the gang from his comfortable spot atop the wall until they lost heart and fled came apart. It had never been a strong hope, but some bandits had lived this long by learning to pick their battles. This lot would keep coming at them until all of them were dead.

The defenses won't hold much longer, Elias Brook. If you're planning anything, I'd recommend doing it now, Mibotha said. Elias didn't even bother thinking about it as he stumbled awkwardly to his feet, taking aim at the rapidly advancing bandits and firing.

He felt like the world was spinning, but he'd been in worse situations and gotten his mark. A man fell, tripping up several of his comrades, and Elias managed to shoot another in the throat as he tried to rise. Thirteen left now...

The remaining sentries showed rather less self-preservation than Elias would have in their situation, piling in towards the gap and firing valiantly into the bandits stubbornly climbing up the now much-shorter wall. One fell, then two, but while the sentries had a better rate of fire than the dazed Elias, they seemed to lack his accuracy. The dead didn't fall fast enough to push the bandits away, and those that collapsed provided a shorter climb for their heedless companions.

If they make it over that wall, a great many people will die. We can't let that happen! Mibotha said, and Elias felt his disorientation after the blast suddenly burned away by Mibotha's urgent command. *STOP THEM!*

Mibotha's voice brooked no disobedience, but Elias knew he was fighting for a lost cause as he fired as quickly as he could, taking out two more. Even less than ten bandits getting up to where the wall had been blasted and spreading out would be the end of it. The sentries were no match for them and Elias knew his reprieve from the afterlife was over if one of them got close enough to engage him.

His great quest of redemption was over before it had started for reasons beyond his control, with a lot of people who probably didn't deserve it dead, himself among them. It seemed so utterly typical for the last significant event in his life it made Elias want to puke.

His growing despair meant his next arrow missed, and Elias's heart sank as he realized the bandits had their foothold. His attempt to make peace with the vengeful gods he would likely be facing momentarily was interrupted when one of the defenders, wearing a fine dark hood and cloak quite in contrast to the sentries' lackluster armor raced past him, discarding his bow and drawing a sword. An impressive flying leap made Elias's jaw drop as the first bandit to make it up to fight them on the walls was neatly decapitated, and his fellow following after him caught an armored boot in the chin, briefly breaking the bandits' foothold in the wall.

Elias was the only one close enough to see the would-be hero take half a second and a breath for courage before leaping out to tackle the next man climbing the wall, throwing the men below him into disarray.

"He's out of his mind!" Elias gasped. That man may have saved them, but he'd just landed himself headfirst in the striking range of every remaining bandit.

He's stopped this from becoming a massacre. He's a hero. But those seven left are going to kill him just the same if you don't get down there NOW! Mibotha said, with a level of desperation that surprised Elias. Elias looked down, seeing the would-be hero's valiant tackle had killed the bandit he'd intercepted, but left him unable to get his sword up as the last of the group rose up around him, ready to kill. Even if he and all the remaining sentries shot like champions, their savior would be dead. Mibotha was asking the impossible of him.

In the space of a second, his brain had hit upon the only way to appease the growing, desperate wrath of the spirit he could feel in the back of his mind, and unsurprisingly, it was the stupidest thing he could imagine doing.

"I *will* get you for this, Mibotha, if it takes me a thousand years," he groaned, before swallowing all sense of self-preservation and diving off the battlements as he fired his last arrow.

Moving as he fired meant Elias missed his shot by a mile, but it did momentarily distract one bandit long enough for another sentry's arrow to take him in the back of the head.

Six.

It was not a terribly long fall. For all their importance, the walls were pitifully short compared to actual castle walls, and Elias could recall taking a spill off a similarly tall ladder. It was still a long enough fall for him to contemplate the dozens of ways this was the worst idea he'd ever had. He landed on top of the bandit he'd been aiming at when he jumped, bringing them both crashing to the ground in a confused mess of tangled limbs. Elias punched blindly at what he hoped was a throat and brought his knee lashing out as brutally as he could manage, expecting to hit the man in the stomach but taking no small satisfaction when it connected with his groin instead. As his victim made a strangled noise and curled up instinctively, Elias managed to scramble to his feet...

And found himself staring down five bandits, just as murderous as before but now focused on him as the sixth man tried to recover, vengeance burning plainly in his eyes.

...What exactly was your plan from here? Mibotha asked. Elias was rescued from admitting he'd been very surprised he'd been the one that got up when he landed on the bandit in the first place by the stricken man's companions charging him as one. Elias narrowly ducked an axe-stroke that would have taken off most of his face, but met a rock-hard fist coming the other way and was sent sprawling by the punch. If he'd needed to think about rolling aside before he did it, another axe stroke would likely have killed either him or his unborn children, but fortunately it merely crashed into the dirt.

The man Elias had gone to rescue was struggling with the bandit Elias had landed on, trying to finish him off before he could rise again. Elias knew he should not like anyone whose idiocy got him in danger, but it did warm his heart to see the bandit who probably wanted to kill him the most right now meet his end on the man's sword before he could recover enough to stand.

Five.

Elias was able to avoid a swinging fist this time as he got back to his feet, but he moved too slowly on his next dodge and felt a blade brush his side, close enough to open a white-hot line of pain and further ruin his coat, but far enough that he had few concerns about bleeding out. Yet.

He would have been a lot happier in this situation if he'd had his knife, but sadly Mibotha had not been concerned with providing him with a replacement. Still, a part of him was relieved to be in a five-man brawl, crushed in on all sides. It brought back a number of happy memories of other times he'd been pressed this close to people he hated with his arms free while they had to focus on their weapons.

The man who had cut him was close enough that Elias was on him before he could start to bring his sword back, and Elias made all the use he could of the space.

It all came back so easily, the feeling of thrusting your arm with all your power behind it before someone could finish winding up. People had laughed at him in scuffles, saying he didn't know how to throw a punch. He'd learned the hard way in one of his first fights that the heel of an open palm could hit harder than a fist, and had since been happy to pass on the information as demonstratively as possible. You didn't get good with a longbow by having weak arms, and Elias's strike had his entire arm behind it as it smashed into the bandit's face, flattening his nose. The man took one step back, on instinct. Elias doubted he could even see in the second he'd done it, but doing so had opened up a little more room that wasn't soon to be occupied by blades.

Elias stepped forward as the bandit stepped back, and his other arm shot out to smash the already-flattened nose as deep into the man's face as it would go in one hit. Already moving backwards, the man lost his balance entirely, and Elias tackled him to the ground to avoid being cut down from behind. As they fell, Elias scrabbled desperately, and found the dagger he'd been hoping for in the man's belt.

They said Elias Brook was a coward. He'd never denied it. He liked to fight from far away, and he liked even better not to fight at all. Danger made him nervous, no matter how familiar it got. Dying scared him, and what came after terrified him.

Killing was the scariest of all, and so he preferred to deal with it very, very quickly. The bandit was dead before he hit the ground, and Elias moved along the ground-line like a snake, taking the next man in the calf with the blade to leave him howling and off-balance as Elias rose up like a geyser and drove the blade up through his chin.

Three.

He couldn't get the blade free in time to do anything about the axe stroke coming towards him, but he was able to push the dying man in its path and dodge around a stroke from a second man who'd *almost* gotten in his blind spot. His would-be surprise attacker was quicker than Elias expected, and his heart stopped for a moment as his enemy's thrust nearly caught him in the ribs. Counting his blessings the man's ability to gauge distance didn't match his speed, Elias slid around it with no more than a little cut and connected one palm, then the other, with the man's nearest ear as hard as he could. The man staggered, but the hits just made him angry, and Elias narrowly avoided being decapitated by a vengeful slice of his sword. He dove in with all the speed his desperation could give him, managing to hit the man in the throat before going for his eyes with rather less finesse than he'd laid out the last bandits. The bellowing was terrible, and the man wasn't afraid to use his knees to help as he tried to use his sword this close up, but Elias found his target and *pressed* until the enraged bellow turned into a squeal. The man flailed blindly as Elias danced away, catching him with a kick but missing him with a sword stroke.

"You bastard!" Elias barely had time to react before the axe almost split his head in two again, but the man who still had his eyes wasn't nearly as quick or as skilled as the one now screaming and flailing around. Elias was able to get behind him easily enough and kick him in the fork of his legs with all his remaining strength. The bandit astonishingly managed to stay upright, turning with an extremely wobbly swing. The sheer surprise of it almost ended Elias's second chance at life, but fortunately his instincts didn't bother to consult his brain in dropping him to the ground.

"I'll kill you!" the man wheezed, but Elias rose up and hit him in the stomach with both hands as hard as he could. It wasn't much, but the bandit staggered back one step, then two.

Right into the man still swinging his sword like a lunatic in an attempt to hit Elias.

Two.

The blind man had been quick, and he'd been deadly. In a fair fight, he would certainly have been more than a match for Elias.

Blind, against Elias with a knife retrieved from his comrade's body, the fight was over before the man knew Elias was there.

One.

"Easy now, friend!"

Elias stared in surprise as the last remaining bandit stood over the unconscious form of the man he'd come down here to rescue, his sword ready for a killing strike. He recognized that voice.

"After all that, nobody managed to hit you before you ran out of men?" he remarked, standing very still as he thought.

"Ah ha...what can I say? I've got a charmed life."

"I've known a few men like that," Elias said evenly, staring at the dirt and blood-streaked face of the man across from him. He recognized a kindred spirit looking him in the eyes, this man was a coward the same way he was. While twenty-four strong proved a very capable barrier to fear, one possible hostage between you and oblivion did not. He might well kill just because he was that scared now, even though he was trying to be the same arrogant bastard who had opened the night's festivities. Elias knew what it was like to bluff for your life with no hand, but he found his sympathy in very short supply. The bandit seemed to know this, licking his lips and grinning in a way that made Elias's skin crawl.

"Look, I've—"

Thunk.

The bandit pitched over backwards, that awful look still on his face despite the knife between his eyes. Elias wondered if the bandit even noticed his wrist move before it hit him.

And then there were none.

Elias looked around at the assortment of corpses lying outside the walls with him, most slain by arrows but a few unlucky bastards nearby all killed in nasty ways. He didn't want to know what was on his fingers, and his hands were covered with blood, and shaking. He suddenly realized he was incredibly tired, incredibly sore, and had a lot of painful wounds he'd been ignoring.

"...So this is being a hero, huh?" he asked Mibotha, taking a look at the carnage around him.

Then he passed out.

CHAPTER 6

The cot Elias woke up on was a strong contender for one of the most uncomfortable things he'd ever slept on, including the ground in midwinter, but his relief to wake up in the world of the living was so profound he didn't care a bit.

He was in a small, dimly lit cottage now, and a quick glance around indicated nobody was about. Taking advantage of his time alone, Elias checked himself, and was surprised to find none of the painful injuries he'd taken had been untreated. Not a one looked bad at all. None of them even hurt, which was a definite first for him.

"Huh. I could've sworn..." he muttered, frowning a little.

The people treated your wounds. Once they'd applied what they could, I stepped in afterwards so no one would think they had healed on their own.

"You healed me?"

*You're no good to anyone too injured to go on, me least of all. I **did** mention I would make injuries you received on this quest easier to bear, even if I wasn't making you stronger,* Mibotha reminded him, a touch reproachfully. *You are completely fine. All you have taken away from last night's battle is a few new scars, and they will merely be a small reminder of what you accomplished.*

"I don't know that I want the reminder that badly," Elias muttered, remembering the mad, bloody scramble beneath the walls. If that was heroism, he had to wonder what sort of lunatic would ever want to be a hero.

*Truly? You defeated eleven men last night, protecting this town. The other defenders that survived the night cannot claim nearly so many without combining their achievements, and each of **them** was lauded as a hero last night. People know you saved this village by leaping from the walls* *last night to protect a comrade. You have done a fine, brave thing, the sort of deed the old Elias Brook would never be associated with.*

"I only did it because there wasn't any other way to last the night, and I still thought I might get killed doing it. I wasn't chomping at the bit to save the day and you know that," Elias muttered.

I do. They don't, and they're the ones you need to impress, Mibotha replied simply. *I had hoped this incident would bring an end to your constant concerns about self-preservation, Elias Brook. They are a liability to you now.*

"Casting aside a lifetime of instinct isn't that easy, Mibotha. If you had a life to threaten, you'd know that," Elias snapped.

Those instincts served you when you were alone against the many enemies you'd made in life. That life is over, and you must accept things have changed. Look at yourself! You fought to the death with a great many men last night, and certainly not so flawlessly none of them could touch you. But the following morning, you are no worse off than before you ever caught sight of those brigands. Threats to your life should not be your primary concern anymore. A man in your position might want to think more about his soul than his neck.

The point was valid, and Elias suspected the veiled threat he perceived in it was completely intentional. He hated to admit it, but Mibotha was right. If he healed like this, and if indeed Mibotha was correct that his primary concern about getting stabbed was how much it would hurt, injury to his person was more to be avoided for comfort and convenience's sake than to protect his newly-granted life.

Even acknowledging this did not make him any more eager to face the possibility that living through things that would normally kill him still left him with a very painful future if he put one foot wrong. He found he was still not able to trust that Mibotha would save his life if the prince and princess sentenced him to death when or if he found them.

Be ready. Our friend the retainer is coming to speak to you alone, Mibotha warned suddenly. *You have an opportunity now, thanks to last night. Don't waste it.*

Oh, yes, back to business, Elias thought, getting up off the cot. He'd prefer to be found standing, if for no other reason than that he might need to dodge something soon. He would probably be the type who *was* eager to be a hero, this retainer. Elias had met a number of men like him, the sort that thought heroic, suicidal attacks were so gallant they should be attempted immediately when things looked grim. Elias had some respect for the man's abilities after last night, but he'd had enough encounters with young men who thought leaping into action was the solution to everything to last him a lifetime.

It wrong-footed him somewhat, therefore, when a young woman opened the door and let herself in. She seemed equally wrong-footed to find him awake and standing up, and for a moment, they stood there in surprise, staring at each other.

There had been women in the Royal Guard before, of course. Elias had known a couple of them, and been vaguely aware King Morys had encouraged the inclusion of female Guard for his daughter's sake. King Morys had held very specific views about retainers getting ideas above their station where the princess was concerned. Even some of the warlords that had risen up had been women. But despite knowing all that, Elias was not expecting the retainer he needed to impress to be a woman, especially not after this much fighting. Many of the remaining armies wouldn't even take women anymore. At a time when each carved-out province dwindled in size with each new battle, losing potential mothers necessary to keep the provinces alive was a risk few warlords would accept. Elias wondered if Mibotha had simply not bothered to correct him when he assumed the retainer was male last night or if he now had proof the spirit was not always right.

Even with the darkness and the chaos of last night, however, there was certainly no mistake that this woman was the same person he'd gone to help. He recognized the fine dark cloak, although the hood was now down, but took some time to study the features he hadn't been able to observe. She was a little shorter than he was, tanned from a great deal of time in the sun but not as weatherbeaten as Elias often looked. Her hair was short and nut-brown, almost boyish in how short and untidy it was, but that was nothing unusual for a woman who wanted to fight. A freckly, honest-looking face, but very wary brown eyes were observing him even as he studied her. She'd foregone the heavy plate armor many of King Morys's protectors had preferred, but the light armor she wore, particularly the gauntlets, greaves, and breastplate, were the distinctive silvery-blue Elias remembered. It was a whipping offense five years ago to wear those colors without proof you were a direct servant of the king or his children, not that it had deterred some opportunists from trying their luck.

Elias's primary concern, however, was the long, elegant sword hanging easily on her belt in a white scabbard, and the fact she was clearly quite ready to draw it.

"...You're awake," she said after a long, awkward pause, evidently withholding judgement for the moment whether that was a good or a bad thing.

"Much to my relief, I feel quite refreshed now that I've rested," Elias said, forcing some levity into his tone. "If whatever you came in here for requires me to be lying down, however—"

And in a single graceful moment, there was the sword at his throat, suddenly making Elias very reluctant to swallow. He supposed that answered the question of if his new friend had a sense of humor.

"I know who you are, Elias Brook," she said coldly, glaring at him. "If you were still asleep when I came in here, I would have needed to think very hard about if you ought to wake up at all."

"That's odd, I don't remember ever meeting you in the old days," Elias said, speaking very delicately. Mibotha might have advised him to stop caring so much about his neck, but he liked it free of holes and wished to keep it that way. "Do they have a portrait of me you all throw darts at so you can recognize me?" Immediately the sword point moved just a tad closer, and Elias concluded the next attempt at humor would probably prove whether or not he had to worry about someone killing him with a sword while Mibotha was inside him.

"No matter how long you run away, I'll never forget your face. No Royal Guard ever will. A man with as many enemies as you is never anonymous," the woman said, the blade not wavering an inch. "Give me one good reason why I shouldn't send you to face King Morys's justice in the afterlife, Brook."

If she cuts my throat and I don't die, they're probably going to burn me next, Elias thought, a bead of sweat trickling down his forehead. How *much* exactly can Mibotha help with before they find something that kills me?

"I saved your life," he said, as nonchalantly as he could manage. "Twice."

"And you think that balances out what you've done?"

"Don't be an idiot. Of course not," Elias growled, surprised Mibotha did not need to prompt him at all. "I didn't have a choice about staying here to defend the town. I'd certainly have been dead on my own with those bandits. But saving you? I was running out of arrows but I had enough I could have killed most of those men from safety while they hacked you apart. I didn't have to risk my neck saving yours. That used to mean something to the Royal Guard."

Ah, there it was; a little flicker on her face. He might still have this under control after all.

He could feel Mibotha pressing suggestions to him, but they all sounded too earnest and fake to be coming from him. Mibotha had been right that this woman's opinion of him was even lower than he'd imagined, and he'd been expecting a sword in the throat already. Owing him her life wasn't going to mean a damn thing unless he could be very persuasive in the next few minutes, and if anything Mibotha gave him to say sounded false, she'd chop him into pieces.

The point didn't waver, but the response had at least prevented it from pressing any closer.

"You knew who I was, then? Is that why you saved me instead of one of the sentries that lost their lives last night?"

I had a good idea you were my only chance not to spend eternity in Valka, he thought.

"I've never met you in my life, and all I knew last night was you had better gear than the sentries," he said instead, trying to keep the lie as sincere as he could manage. "If I'd known all I'd get for my trouble was your sword at my throat, I'd probably have left you to be the hero down there instead of me. But hard as it might be to believe, I didn't want somebody to die right after they took a risk for me. That doesn't happen enough in my life to waste."

"I didn't do it for *you.*"

"And I didn't pay it back because you're special. We can do this all day," Elias said bluntly, looking her in the eye with more courage than he felt. "So are you going to cut my throat, or can we talk? Pick one before your arm gets tired or I cough."

The point lingered where it was a few seconds too long for Elias's liking, but eventually the sword was lowered but not sheathed. Opportunities now existed if this went sour, but Elias was pretty sure he and Mibotha were through if he took any of them.

"People have compared your sense of gratitude to the cool of the summer sun. They mention a lot of things when your deeds are recounted, but helping someone that helped you? That's a new one," the woman admitted, still looking at Elias with no small amount of suspicious dislike. "What's your game, Brook? I don't believe for a second you just happened to come here and decided to volunteer instead of just running for it when you saw the bandits."

Well, at least she's not honestly shocked I didn't join the bandits for the looting, Elias thought. It's always been easier to win over people that think you're a coward than the ones that think you're a monster.

"There is no game, lady," he responded, running a hand through his hair. "Most of what you were told about me is true, but the part that this is all some kind of game to me, or that I'm having a good old time out here while decent folk are miserable, that's a load of crap. I've hated the last five years more than you can imagine. My "game" didn't get me anything but the most miserable period of my life."

"Do you have a point, Brook, or am I supposed to pity your actions having consequences?" the woman asked sharply.

"The point is I had a scare recently," Elias said, and the woman seemed quite surprised to hear Elias sound completely sincere for once. "I nearly got my guts spilled one night, and I saw death, too close for my liking. It got me thinking about what comes after." Elias sat down weakly on his cot, and lowered his head. He didn't need to fake his distress for this part.

"Look, you can hate me. I'd imagine that's well within the rights of the folk loyal enough to stick with the crown after all that's happened. And you can think I'm a liar and a bastard. I'm both, and there's no denying that. But I'm a man. I might be worse than other men, but I've got the same feelings any of them do. I can bleed. I can get scared. I can feel guilt, whether you believe that or not. I nearly died that night, spent the evening under a tree in agony with a fever like you wouldn't imagine. I saw everything I'd done, and then I saw myself in Valka for it." Elias's voice shook, but he looked up at the woman.

"I'm not a good man. I know that. But I'm trying," he whispered, "Right now I'm trying as hard as I can to be better. Trying to make things right."

"It might be too late for that," the woman said quietly.

"I know," Elias replied. "But I've gotta try, even if that means all I get is you lopping my head off right now."

A minute passed, then two. It seemed like an infinity elapsed before the woman sheathed her sword and started to turn away.

"I saved your life once, and you saved mine twice last night. That *does* still mean something to me," she said, her voice tight. "I'm giving you your chance to leave here and do what you have to do to live with yourself. We're even now. But I don't ever want to see your face again, and I won't stop my brothers and sisters from killing you if they find you."

If she leaves without you, we'll never find the royal family.

"I can help you."

"I don't *want* your help. I don't want your good intentions!" the woman shouted, rounding on him. "They're five years too late for me to care you saw the light! I don't want *anything* from you! If you're well enough to travel, leave here as fast as you can and never look for me again!"

"I know where the Regalia are hidden!" Elias blurted out, filling the room with a sudden, shocked silence. It took him a moment to realize Mibotha had forced him to say that, but he was certain it was going to end in violence if he took it back now.

"You *what*?" the woman breathed, paling. "What did you just say?"

"I know where to find them. If you let me help you, I can help put the royal family back in power," Elias said. He was fairly certain Mibotha was making most of this up, but his desperation to keep her attention made it ring true. "I...I have a plan, but I can't do any of it all by myself! Please! I need to work together with the Royal Guard, or it won't work!"

"If you're lying—" the woman threatened, and Elias raised his hands.

"You can do whatever you want to me if you think I'm trying to trick you! I'm out of angles to work! I'm not playing any more games! I'm trying to do something right for a change, and I can't do it unless we work together!"

"This is insane. The others will never accept your help," the woman sighed, but Elias's plea had rattled her. "Gods only know why I'm even listening to you right now."

"They'll listen to you. You know that the Regalia will go a long way towards re-establishing the throne's power. The Royal Guard can end all of this if you just let me help you!"

"Why don't you just tell me, then?" the woman put her hand on her sword's hilt. "If you really know, then I want you to tell me where to find them!"

"No. There's too much for me to just tell you. I have to be with you," Elias insisted, cursing Mibotha.

"Why should I believe this isn't some kind of trick? What do you get out of this?"

"I'm the only chance you've got, that's why!" Elias shouted. "You said it best, I'm doing what I have to to be able to live with myself. I can't just drop you a hint. I have to make up for what I did. I have to *be* there. And if you won't let me help, then I can't do anything more."

Distrust, fury, desperation and indecision all warred on the woman's face, and Elias could see every muscle twitch with the desire to end all the conflict with one clean swing of the sword. But desperation won, as Elias found it usually did, and the woman offered him a hand.

"...I must be insane, but I'll accept your terms, Brook," she muttered reluctantly. Elias gratefully took her hand, but she yanked him close when he did, her grip like a vice.

"I'm not interested in your need for redemption, Brook. I'm not interested in what you feel you have to prove to yourself to sleep well at night. I don't trust you. I'll *never* trust you, and no one who knows you ever will. But whatever's in your head might save my lady's birthright and this land, and I cannot in good conscience throw that away. You are bound to us until my lady and her brother are restored to their rightful place. If you change your mind, or lead us astray, I will personally send you down to Valka, and I pray the spirits will rend your soul there until the end of time," she whispered. Elias swallowed, but smiled nervously.

"Fair enough," he conceded, trying to hide the shiver going through him. "Then if we are indeed bound together, could I at least know your name?"

There was a pause, and then the painful grip loosened. There wasn't anything friendly in the woman's gaze, but at least it wasn't pinning him to the wall with hate at the moment.

"Cecily," she replied, releasing him.

"It's a pleasure, Cecily."

"For you," she sighed, turning to go. "Make whatever preparations we need. There's no time to waste."

With that, she left the room as quickly as she could. Elias slumped against a wall, relief overcoming him.

That went surprisingly well, Mibotha remarked, sounding happy. *I like her.*

"So you did know she was a woman, then? Or did you make a mistake earlier calling her "he"?" Elias asked.

Of course I knew she was a woman. I merely saw no reason to correct you earlier while her life was in danger, Mibotha huffed, sounding rather miffed by the question. *Treat her right, Elias Brook, and Cecily may be the greatest friend you will ever have in this life or any other.*

"I believe you," Elias sighed, starting to get his few belongings together.

It wasn't exactly like the competition was stiff.

CHAPTER 7

Elias didn't have enough belongings that it took very long at all to be ready to go, but while Cecily had not been impressed with his actions, the townsfolk certainly were. After five years of people primarily reacting to the sight of him with cries of "hey, you!" and "don't let him get away!", it was a very, very strange experience to have people shake his hand and thank him profusely for protecting the town, and try to offer him food and gifts.

Strange, but not at all unpleasant. Elias wasn't used to people thanking him for anything, but he could understand how other people would get used to it.

Elias would have happily stalled his trip to celebrate in the town, but the burning presence in the back of his mind let him know hanging around was not an option.

Still, when Elias departed town half an hour later with Cecily, he was up a horse, some food, and a few coins the surviving sentries had been able to gather for him and Cecily. It had, on the whole, been a better turnout than any of the scavenging he'd done for the last year.

There was a long, awkward silence between Cecily and himself as they left the town behind. The horses ambled along without care, but even Mibotha seemed reluctant to disturb the tense quiet that settled upon them. Eventually, Cecily blinked first.

"So, can you tell me where the Regalia are *now*?" she asked, hiding her impatience poorly.

It won't do any good with just the two of you. Regroup with the rest of the Royal Guard.

"We're just going to be killed if we go after them ourselves. Where are the rest of your companions?" Elias passed on.

"I don't know if I should tell you that." Cecily's suspicion was back in force, and it was not a kind eye she turned on Elias. "The other Royal Guard are protecting my lady and her brother. You claim there's no ploy here for you to get near them, but you have no way to prove that until you can show me any of this is true."

"Don't be ridiculous!" Elias protested. "You saw perfectly well I'm unarmed and I'm not eager to try taking on the best swordsmen in the land with my fists! What evil scheme do you think I've got that involves getting close to the Royal Guard instead of staying far away from them?"

"I don't want you near my lady or her brother. Making amends or not, you killed King Morys," Cecily replied bluntly.

Elias bit his tongue to avoid screaming in frustration. Sometimes he hoped the damn bard that thought the tale of Elias Brook, assassin of kings, would make good lyrics to an infernally catchy tune he'd cooked up had lived through all of this. At least he sincerely hoped the man was still around and maybe even playing his thrice-damned song when Elias finally caught up with him. Elias wouldn't even need to be armed when that day arrived.

"You may be the ten thousandth person I've said this to, but I'll repeat it until someone unblocks their ears and listens. *I did not kill King Morys*," he growled. "I was not anywhere nearby when he died. I did not make the plan that led to him dying. I did not make the damn shot they wrote that damn song about! Sometimes I *wish* I'd killed him since nobody ever believes I didn't!"

"Why would they? There were dozens willing to testify that you assassinated the king," Cecily replied, not looking impressed.

"Not one of them was there. Bloody Captain Thurgood was with me while Morys was dying in the woods, and he still swore up and down I bested him in a fight and then sat in a tree for hours and fired that shot. Because it sounded better than me finding him stinking drunk in a tavern and trying to join him," Elias groused.

"Captain Thurgood had a number of troubles, but he was an honest man. I would not blame anyone but myself that his word carries more weight than yours," Cecily said, not bothering to hide her disbelief.

"Raulin Thurgood cultivated a reputation as an honest man because it was the easiest of the virtues he lacked to fake convincingly," Elias countered, glaring at the horizon. "He wasn't that bright, or terribly brave, or good at holding his drink, or even all that honest, but he could fake honesty well enough. The one thing I will say for him was he was loyal as a dog. Although I've known dogs that could've led soldiers better than him, so I'm not sure why Morys bothered with him at all."

"So you had nothing to do with his death at all, was it?" Cecily said mockingly. "It was just an accident that a great number of respectable men and women linked you to his death, and it was all a big misunderstanding? Or are you saying everyone who bore witness you were involved is a liar? That they just *made up* finding your arrows?"

The urge to exclaim that every last one of them had bent the truth because it was easier that way boiled through Elias, but he gritted his teeth. Cecily would just remain as she was if he answered like that, convinced he was making it all up.

Good old Thurgood had been cleverer than him in one way, he had to concede, if *only* in one. Cultivate a reputation for honesty and people will believe any damn thing you say, but when people call you a liar, defending yourself becomes an exercise in futility. Of course a liar will *say* he's not a liar, but who could believe him? If he'd had a lick of sense, he'd have made people think he was a truthful man, too, but then, Morys hadn't entered his life because Elias was trustworthy.

"What I did was make a mistake," he whispered, knuckles whitening on the horse's reins as he said it. "I made a mistake, and Morys died. That's all there is to it. If he died because of that mistake alone, then fine. It was my fault. But I didn't hold the bow. I didn't make the shot. I wasn't there when he fell."

"Then who did kill him?" Cecily asked, but she sounded different this time. She hadn't been expecting him to say that. Elias rode in silence for a few minutes, suppressing a shudder at the question, but the returning suspicion plain on Cecily's face forced him to reply.

"...Oliver Bones," he muttered, unconsciously making a small gesture to ward off bad luck. Cecily studied him in silence for a moment, but it gradually dawned on her that Elias was either a tremendous actor or his trepidation to even mention the name was wholly genuine.

"Oliver Bones? "Basilisk Eye" Bones?" she asked, looking incredulous. "I thought he died years ago."

"He was very pleased to hear that when I said it five years ago," Elias groaned. "If you don't believe anything else I say while we're together, take this as fact. Oliver Bones is still around, and I'd bet my right arm he's still in business in spite of all this. He might even be thriving."

"Or you're blaming a crime you were accused of on the best assassin you could think of, and one too long dead to protest the claim he's alive and in hiding," Cecily pointed out. "You must admit that's a very convenient story for you."

"If I'm any good as a liar, I'd come up with a more plausible lie," Elias snapped. "I know perfectly well how it sounds saying he did it, and if I didn't think he was miles off I wouldn't have answered your question at all. I can't change the facts, and if you need an act of the gods every time I say something to believe a word of it, you might as well kill me now."

This is going to get tremendously difficult for everyone involved if she takes you up on that, Mibotha warned.

Thankfully, Cecily did not draw her sword, and appeared to concede the point to Elias.

"...All right. If old Basilisk Eye really is still alive, or there's even a chance he is, we might as well treat that as a fact. He's certainly a bigger danger to my lady and her brother than you," she admitted. "How did you get mixed up with a man like that, anyhow?"

"It wasn't like I fell into circles he moved in or sought him out!" Elias protested quickly. That one had hit a little too close to home. Ugly memories stirred, and Elias wondered if Cecily had the faintest idea how often Elias had asked himself that question in the last five years.

How had he managed to get mixed up with that monster? How could he have been stupid enough to let the Basilisk-Eye into his life? How, how, how, could he have made such a terrible mistake?

Elias had gotten good at answering his own questions comfortably enough in the last five years, however, and he told her what he'd told himself many times before at the end of a bad day.

"I don't *know* why it was me, but he showed up in my room one night with a big damn knife and a couple of questions! I answered them. That's *all I did.* The next day, Morys was dead."

"You told him what he had to do to kill him." It wasn't a question, but a statement.

"Bones knows everything there is to know about killing people. He didn't need any of that from me. He just wanted absurd little details I knew! He didn't even ask anything that sounded like it would make it easy for him to get near the king!"

"You *had* to know he wasn't paying you a social visit in those circumstances."

"You're damn right I knew. *You* try waking up with a knife an inch from your eyeball and see how composed you are when questions start."

"Oliver Bones was the deadliest man in the world in his prime. You didn't think of how many lives you could have saved by not telling him anything he wanted to know?"

"I was thinking about how many I was going to save by saying what I had to to get him to move his hand a couple inches up instead of down," Elias snapped. "The Royal Guard would have held their tongues until he killed them, I know. *I'm not a Royal Guard.* He never implied he'd kill me quick if I stayed quiet."

"That was your mistake, then?" Cecily asked, seeming to understand. "You told him what he wanted to know, and Morys died because of it."

"A lot of things they say about Morys are true. That anyone in the land except me would have died for him is not one of them," Elias said. "Morys was the hardest man in the world to get anywhere near, wore armor most of the time he was awake, had a good taster and the *best* bodyguards in the land," he added, shooting Cecily a mildly accusing look to see how she liked it. Her face reddening slightly brought him some mild satisfaction, but not as much as he'd hoped. "I was alone, naked under a blanket, and staring down a knife while some questions were presented to me and answers required. Nobody was coming to help me! Nobody ever stood watch for *me!* I liked Morys's chances of survival better than mine if I tried to protect him! I thought he'd be safe!" Elias realized he was starting to shout, and took a deep breath before turning his attention out to the road. "I thought he'd be safe," he repeated, mostly to himself.

Cecily was silent for a little too long, and Elias glanced at her again. She was looking at him, still without any compassion evident in her gaze, but something that resembled pity had come into her eyes. The sight of it made Elias's blood boil, and he gritted his teeth and glared down the road. He remembered when he'd gotten looks like that. Thinking they understood it all and congratulating themselves silently for seeing the real Elias Brook when all they were really doing was looking down on him.

"We're getting off-topic," he managed through clenched teeth. "This venture of ours will fail if it's just the two of us, as I said before my supposed crimes sidetracked us. We need your companions, even if it's not all of them. We need to regroup with the Royal Guard. Are you going to lead us to them or not?"

"I can lead us there, but you should be aware I might not be able to convince them bringing you there is good for anything but seeing you die," Cecily said. Somehow the suggestion in her voice that she was weighing whether or not he deserved it if they killed him set Elias on edge more than all the hostility that had come before it.

"I've been very lucky in that regard so far. I'll have to trust in that to see me a bit further," he sighed, forcing a casual tone. "I'm lost without the Royal Guard, and if they won't help me I don't have anything to live for anyhow."

"You won't be murdered at the gate. I can guarantee you that much," Cecily said, frowning.

"Truly, you are an angel of mercy made flesh."

"I mean my brothers and sisters will likely give you a fair trial once we arrive. Then it's up to my lady to decide what to believe."

"A fair trial," Elias repeated, not bothering to hide what he thought of that. "Considering I'm defending myself against a lot of dead, respectable witnesses to people who think I am the lowest kind of scum, how exactly is my trial going to be *fair*?"

"Having a chance to convince my lady that you deserve a chance to redeem yourself more than a quick beheading is roughly as fair as a man in your position has any right to expect," Cecily pointed out.

...Ah.

"What?" Elias asked, forgetting Cecily was paying enough attention to notice if he tried talking to Mibotha.

"My lady generally considers execution barbaric, but she *does* hold you responsible for her father's death, and the order the Steward presented, that you be brought back to the castle and beheaded for your crimes, has never been revoked."

This may be a problem, Elias Brook.

"Explain, please," Elias said quietly, hoping that Cecily wouldn't think it odd. He didn't know exactly what was going on, but Mibotha's voice was not filling him with courage.

"It's fairly simple. If the order was never revoked, it is still the lawful way to deal with you unless you are granted a pardon by the crown. No pardon has been given, so unless my lady sees fit to offer one now, my comrades will be obligated to behead you," Cecily said, blinking. "I'm sorry to say, Brook, but there's nothing for it. If you have to be with us to do all this, you will have to impress my lady *very quickly* at your trial."

I had not been told you would not be sent to the gallows if they found you guilty. I can fix your neck if you break it, but I can't put your head back if it comes off!

Elias felt all of the blood drain from his face, and he began to wobble involuntarily in his saddle. He gave Cecily an extremely fake, brittle smile as an all-too-familiar sweat of absolute terror began to break out. It took self-control he never knew he had not to turn his horse and ride like there was no tomorrow away from Cecily.

This, at least, could lay to rest his suspicion Mibotha was as close to always right as he was. He just wished it had come under any other imaginable circumstance. His mind raced furiously as he tried to find the loophole in his situation.

If he ran now, he would fail his mission. Mibotha would likely send him to Valka on the spot.

If he tried to avoid going to trial, he would probably be cut to pieces by the Royal Guard, dying if any of them cut off his head, and then off to Valka he would go.

If he was found guilty at a trial that would almost assuredly be a farce to confirm what everyone living on the planet already knew without any need for facts, his head would be cut off and he would go to Valka.

In fact, everything seemed to point to the idea that Mibotha's bright idea to have him redeem himself had just made the process of him dying and going to Valka a little more lengthy, painful, and humiliating than the pitchfork might have been, with more chances for people to smugly nod to each other that he got what he deserved before they danced on his grave.

All of this, unless he impressed a girl he hadn't seen in five years, who had been told in no uncertain terms that he had murdered her father, and that he was the sole reason she was hiding under some gods-forsaken rock with her brother instead of ruling the land.

Elias wondered if he'd be able to tell the difference when he died and the eternal suffering part of his fate really began.

CHAPTER 8

He worried too much about self-preservation for someone who'd died once already, Elias seemed to recall being reprimanded. The fate of his neck shouldn't mean as much to him as the fate of his soul, or so Mibotha had told him. It had seemed a reasonable enough point.

It would have seemed less reasonable to Elias if he had been informed earlier that something severing his neck would seal the fate of his soul in the same stroke. Now he rode mechanically toward almost certain doom purely in the hope some god that had not been paying attention before would now look down and take pity on him. It wasn't much of a hope, but it beat the alternative of just accepting there was no way he could talk his way out of this one, much less fight his way out of it.

Mibotha and Cecily were both quiet at a time when Elias would honestly have been grateful even for their most irritating prattle as a way to take his mind off things. Elias wasn't sure if they were soberly contemplating his chances and drawing the same conclusions he was or merely leaving him to stew in his fears with no distraction. In his panicked, spiteful depression, Elias was willing to assume the latter first. He had little enough reason to believe either of his unwanted companions in this suicide mission would be greatly distraught if he was declared guilty almost immediately and slain.

He wondered how it would be, if things followed their usual pattern in his life and a sudden miracle of good fortune failed to come to him when he was at his lowest. An unnecessarily violent arrest, no doubt, before he was clapped in chains and dragged before the royal children as a prize. Then a short trial, likely conducted entirely without him, or anyone for that matter, to speak in his defense. He would probably be accused, yet again, of personally slaying King Morys, and in all likelihood would be linked to the ensuing drought and warfare. Nobody would be willing to suggest it was merely bad luck and poor timing that caused the rain to stop and blight to set in right after the king died. They would probably call his mother a whore again, and somewhere amidst his fear and self-pity that was one of the things that rankled Elias the most. He didn't care that judging him and blaming him for things he hadn't done quickly became the favorite pastime of everyone he met these days, but his mother had been a kindly washerwoman who had quite a normal relationship with his father and really did not deserve such slander. As for stories told about his *father,* equally believed and untrue, the less said the better.

He'd be found guilty, of course, long before the trial actually started, but they'd make a show of it before they sent him to the headsman. Elias couldn't imagine them *not* taking their time to torment him and congratulate themselves before ordering his execution. They wouldn't torture him, unless the Royal Guard had changed quite a lot over the last five years, but the self-righteous posturing he'd need to endure before they killed him might well qualify.

Not to worry about torture, of course, as there was plenty of that waiting for him when his life was done, his second chance nipped in the bud. Maybe having the time to do one good deed before he died again would help him get an eternity in some kind of purgatory instead, but Elias wasn't exactly hopeful.

It was in this dark mood that he followed Cecily, paying no attention to his surroundings, while mentally jumping desperately between trying to figure a way to get out of this and already beginning to despair. Cursing Cecily, cursing Morys, cursing Mibotha, and most of all cursing his luck within the confines of his mind. The scrambling for ideas helped very little and only deepened Elias's fears. He despaired of any hope of earning amnesty from the princess in exchange for what Mibotha knew about the Regalia. The despair helped even less, leaving Elias with nothing useful to think about beyond his imminent death. He'd heard it said that a coward had to die a thousand deaths while the brave only knew the one. True or not, his coward's mind was certainly trying to render it truthful.

"We're almost there, Brook," Cecily spoke up, glancing over at him. "Are you ready?"

"As ready as I'll ever be," Elias muttered, surprised his voice wasn't just a squeak of fright. He gripped the reins tightly, and tried to fight down all the useless feelings clamoring for his attention.

There *was* a way out of this situation. It was nearly impossible, he was fully willing to admit that, but it existed. He was not buried yet, and he had spent most of the last five years wondering every few days how that was so. Deserved or not, he was an extraordinarily lucky man in his own way, and a rather clever one in his own estimation. The way out of this was singular and remarkably difficult, but at least it was obvious; convince the princess not to cut his head off. Since he didn't need to waste time figuring out some other way out of this, he could bend all of his thought towards how he was going to make this one goal possible. It occurred to him that even if he just convinced her to have him executed in some way that kept his head attached, he might be able to turn that in his favor and walk out of this alive.

It was not a very comforting thought to know it was a big "if" just to convince her to hang him instead of beheading him, but it was about as comfortable as Elias felt he should get with this mission. As long as he always expected to survive in the worst way, even the second-worst thing happening to him instead would be a pleasant surprise.

Just keep your head attached, Elias Brook. I can see us through everything else, Mibotha said, and Elias wondered, not for the first time, if the spirit could see his thoughts or not. It might have been more convenient if it could. With Cecily around he couldn't exactly talk to the spirit without looking deranged. Still, Elias didn't reject the cold comfort offered. It might be deeply unpleasant for him, but he was going to be counting on Mibotha if the very likely came to pass and he was not pardoned.

Strangely, accepting he had only one tiny chance to survive and no possible way to influence his situation beyond it helped quell the panic. He ought to have been as tense as a bowstring by this point, but he actually felt almost calm. At the very least, for a moment he was able to stop thinking about what would happen to him shortly and just watched a small flock of birds fly by overhead.

Cecily brought her horse to a stop, and it took Elias a moment to spot that they were indeed at their destination. When he did see it, he almost wanted to laugh.

They had come to a stop in front of several hills, but Elias could see the gate concealed in the nearest one. No wonder nobody had been able to find the royal family or their protectors, they had retreated from their ancestral castle into one of the "Invisible Castles!"

Elias remembered Morys talking about it, back when things had been much safer for both of them. The previous king, his father, had been the unfortunately common sort of ruler that had visions of his line reigning a thousand years, but rarely considered what might happen to his descendants fifty years after his death. Elias knew there were a number of fanciful rumors that blamed him for the curiously depleted castle coffers when things had gone bad, but the truth was King Symond had been the actual culprit in Morys inheriting a rather poorer kingdom than he deserved. Elias remembered Morys complaining about it when he was in his cups, lamenting how many grand ideas he had to do without because his father's obsession with an immortal legacy had not left his son with very much to build one of his own. He had been canny enough to make do with what he had, but in some ways, being assassinated at the very beginning of the greatest catastrophe to strike the kingdom in centuries had been the best way for King Morys to be remembered after his death.

The invisible castles had been King Symond's one saving grace, the one good idea amidst a dozen doomed but costly vanity projects Morys had been left to pay for. The king had railed at his father's arrogance and idiotic spending habits, but he had blessed the old fool more than once in Elias's hearing for leaving him not one but three secret fortresses, hidden with great cunning and a little magic across his lands. Even if the castle fell, he'd boasted once, his line would not want for strongholds to hold off their enemies.

It was just bad luck on the king's part that *his* enemies had come for him while he was outside his usual stronghold hunting, Elias supposed. But either the princess was a very canny young woman or the Captain of the Guard was a wily one, for they had wasted little time making use of this fortress hidden beneath the hills. To the warlords that had sacked and squabbled over the castle, it was as though they had vanished into thin air.

It made Elias want to smile and frown at the same time. Someone in there was sharp enough that they were not going to be easily swayed, and that person was likely going to be making most of the decisions. On the bright side, if he failed, at least he'd know he hadn't been brought low by a simpleton.

Cecily dismounted, withdrawing a small silver bell from her robe and ringing out a short, specific pattern before the gate. After a moment, a large glyph across the doors glowed blue, and they seemed to become somehow more *real* than they had been a moment ago. One of the doors opened slightly, and several of the Royal Guard stepped out, looking surprised.

"Cecily! We hadn't expected to see you for another month!" a woman with long blonde hair, exclaimed, hugging Cecily. The others, however, had taken stock of her companion, and Elias's heart sank as recognition dawned and the three Royal Guard looking at him drew their swords.

"I don't believe it..."

"You captured him, Cecily?"

"Wait," Cecily said quickly, stepping away from the woman who'd embraced her to stand between her comrades and Elias. "This is Elias Brook, but things aren't as simple as we thought."

"What's so complicated about it? You finally caught him! We can finally bring him to trial before he gets what he's had coming for five years!" one of the Royal Guard spat, glaring at Elias.

"Normally I would agree that was the proper course of action, Boors, but I found him when he helped me save a town a few miles from here from a bandit raid in the night. He saved my life," Cecily replied, looking rather embarrassed to admit it to her friends. "O-On top of that, he volunteered to come here with me. He claims he knows where the Regalia are hidden."

The resulting silence this brought about as the incredulous stares turned from Cecily to him made Elias pray quietly that Mibotha had not been making him lie when he'd said that. It was the only reason Cecily hadn't left him behind with the promise to kill him if she saw him again, but he could tell that if they even *suspected* he was playing them false after making a claim like that, they would do what they could to make Valka seem like a vacation afterwards.

"*He* knows where they're hidden? You must be joking!" one finally accused, although without much heart in it.

"He probably knows because he stole them himself!"

"I did *not*," Elias insisted, but this only got him more glares. He'd forgotten for a moment that his version of events was not popular among friends of the crown, even, perhaps especially, when it *was* the truth. Elias met the hostile gazes as coolly as he could manage, but he was a little surprised when it was the one woman among them besides Cecily that the others turned to for a decision. She did not blink as she stared at him, and Elias decided he did not like the look of her eyes. They were a very fetching green, true enough, and there was the same mix of the vigor and honesty Cecily's gaze possessed, but there was also something rather darker and more experienced in them. Elias was decent enough at reading people to know from Cecily's glare she'd been considering killing him as righteous retribution for all the bad things she'd heard he was responsible for. It was a simple, honest look, dangerous as it was. This one looked like she was calculating something very complicated as she regarded him coldly, and that worried Elias.

He'd rather be done in by a worthy opponent than a simpleton if he had to be done in at all, he'd admit, but until that time came, he would much rather be at the mercy of someone simple and honest than someone that calculated more than he did before acting. Royal Guard weren't supposed to do that. It was one of the things he'd prized being able to do that they couldn't. That the blonde woman had both the strong, certain, upright air of a typical Royal Guard *and* a worryingly cunning look in her eyes seemed somehow like cheating.

"Maybe he did, and maybe he didn't," she said at length. "It might be a lie, but if it isn't, we'd be foolish to ignore it. We'll find out soon enough. Bind him and bring him inside."

Elias would have preferred to stay on his horse, but he wasn't given much room to argue. The large, bearded man Cecily had greeted as Boors stepped forward sharply and pulled him from the saddle to the ground without any visible effort. A Guard on either side of him pulled a small silver orb from their belts, and Elias resigned himself to whatever fate had in store for him as the orbs glowed. Without any chance to avoid it, Elias found himself bound hand, foot and neck by glowing blue chains, leaving rising a rather difficult prospect in his current position. Boors took a hold of one of the chains and started to drag him inside like a sack of potatoes.

"Is that really necessary, Boors...?" Cecily asked, falling in alongside him.

"Yes," Boors said simply, and Elias became keenly aware from the hint of amusement in his tone that he and Sir Boors would not be friends.

The blonde woman brought up the rear, still watching Elias as he was dragged across the rough, uncomfortable ground, across the threshold, and into the castle. Elias suspected Boors would likely ensure he looked like someone had scraped him off their boot when he was presented to the princess and her brother. Not, perhaps, the best way to look the part of a man who deserved a second chance.

Look on the bright side, Mibotha spoke up as Elias became keenly aware King Symond had not chosen the floor of his hidden castle for the comfort of human faces. *Your bindings include one around your neck. Nobody will cut off your head unexpectedly while you're trapped like this.*

Ah, Mibotha's comforting words, Elias thought to himself. Truly, he would be lost in these dark times without them.

CHAPTER 9

Elias did not merely look like a large boot scraping when the horrible dragging finally stopped, he felt like one, too. On the bright side, he supposed, the demons that would claim him if he failed would have to get rather creative to make an eternity with them less pleasant than some of the things he'd experienced in life, particularly of late.

"On your knees, Brook," the blonde woman said calmly, finally catching up to him and giving him a surprisingly gentle prod with her boot. If Sir Boors had not made an earnest effort to spread him across the castle floor for the last ten minutes, it probably wouldn't have hurt at all. But finding a spot that wasn't bruised to prod would have required time and deliberation his captors didn't care to spend on him.

He wouldn't need any gold or thanks if he ended up saving the kingdom, he decided. Sir Boors and Mibotha in a big burlap sack and ten miles of gnarled road would be all the thanks he required.

Still, if he didn't respond sharply to a command to be on his knees, he suspected he might have his first interview with the princess on his face instead. He wasn't sure he could make a worse first impression on the person whose goodwill was imperative to his survival at this point, but he wasn't keen to try. Up he got, from lying on his side to kneeling on the floor, trying as best he could to wipe off the castle dusting that had been performed with his face while his arms remained bound.

He'd been brought to an audience chamber, not that different from the one he remembered from Morys's castle. Of course, he'd never been the one in the center of the chamber, he'd always been off leaning against one of the walls. His audiences with Morys tended to be in less conspicuous places, and certainly not in ones where everything sounded quite as loud as it always seemed to in these big, round rooms. The Royal

Guard stood around him, all quite ready to leap into action if he made a false move. Elias wondered exactly what they thought he was going to try when the arrangement of his chains meant he would probably strangle himself if he tried to move faster than a shuffle, but he'd found it best not to question the need of a man with a sword to look ready to use it. Cecily and her blonde friend withdrew to stand on either side of the entrance opposite to the one they'd come in through.

"Announcing Her Majesty Queen Amira, by grace of the gods ruler of Yivyn and guardian of its dominions," the blonde woman declared, and Elias shifted a little. *Queen* Amira? Well, he supposed she wasn't the princess anymore if her father was dead and Prince Elindri was eight years her junior, but it was strange to hear her called that. People had been so respectful of little Amira that it was like pulling teeth to get anyone to say her name, and risk dirtying it somehow with their common tongue. Morys had approved of that, Elias remembered, perhaps because nobody had ever shown his name that kind of reverence.

Still, without the Regalia, Elias was aware the title of queen was mostly wishful thinking on the Royal Guard's part. Amira would be a princess until the day she died without Elias's (or, perhaps Mibotha and Elias's) help. He could use that.

Seeing her come into the room after five years was a very strange experience for Elias. He'd met Amira a number of times before things went bad, but the person stepping into the audience chamber was still a complete stranger.

Morys had been a distinctly plain man, although Elias had always respected his beard. Being king would make any man handsome. However, "plain" had never been a word anyone used to describe his wife, who had been compared to a goddess even at her funeral. As the father in any such union would hope, Amira had taken after her mother in looks, but the sight of her still chilled him.

Little Amira, the princess he remembered, had been an irrepressible, charming girl of thirteen, spoiled beyond belief, but surprisingly polite for a girl who had been raised to believe the sun rose and set for her. Tangled red hair, darting blue eyes, and a grin infused with the surety that nothing would ever go wrong in her life. That was what he remembered of the princess.

This Amira was a beautiful but grim young woman of eighteen, her hair a straight crimson waterfall down her back, her eyes guarded and distant, and her face set in a mask of stoic unreadability. She had grown into her mother's elegant frame, and her bearing seemed to carry the promise she would only grow more beautiful, more queenly with each passing year. But she seemed to have aged much more than five years to Elias, and perhaps not for the best.

It was not a merciful gaze she turned on him; it promised neither mercy nor cruelty. She just looked right through him, seemed to find something, and then turned away, dismissing him. Amira instead turned to Cecily, her face softening briefly into a small, reserved smile as she embraced her.

"It is good to see you back among us, Cecily," she said softly, and Elias could hear some of the old politeness in her voice but very little of the cheer or certainty of her youth.

"I am honored to be by your side again, my lady," Cecily murmured, bowing as Amira released her. Elias had heard less reverence in churches, but then, he guessed Cecily had probably been younger than Amira was now when she first swore loyalty to her, and her absolute respect was hardly unique to her. The entire room had seemed nearly at prayer since Amira had joined them. He felt like a heathen peering in on a service in a language he didn't understand.

I had feared she may have begun to wither in such seclusion, but look at her! She's stronger than ever. Every inch a queen! Ah, we are fortunate, Elias Brook... Mibotha murmured, and the sheer admiration in its tone took Elias by surprise.

Even so, he frowned slightly. This Amira was more queenly than the coddled child he remembered, he would concede that, but it was like someone had spent five years drawing the vitality from her like water from a well.

For a moment, feeling like an outsider in what had once been familiar surroundings, Elias felt guilty.

The moment passed quickly when a hand pressed against the back of his neck and made him bow low from his kneeling position.

"Cecily has not returned alone, my lady," one of the Guard spoke up. "After five years, she has brought us Elias Brook."

Peering up from where he was pressed to the floor, Elias wondered briefly if the announcement of who he was would get a reaction, but Amira took it quietly, turning her attention back to him as unreadable as before.

"I had not expected to ever see him again," she murmured, speaking like Elias wasn't there even as she looked right at him. "Did you capture him, Cecily?"

"No, my lady, our paths crossed at random defending a town not far from here. He saved my life," Cecily admitted, sounding even more reluctant to admit it to her queen than to her friends. "I would normally never have allowed him to accompany me here, but he claims he knows where the Regalia are hidden."

"Did he suggest why he was telling you this?" Amira asked, dismissing Elias from her attention again to focus on Cecily.

"You could ask me," Elias spoke up, straining to make himself heard. He did not feel his last chance was going well so far.

"Sir Boors, if he speaks again before I ask him to, please beat him," Amira said without even glancing at Elias, and this time he heard the frost in her voice.

She had looked through him while other people glared, but Amira recognized him, and Elias was willing to bet she hated him more than anyone else in this room.

"With pleasure, my lady," Boors said, stepping closer to Elias.

"I've been thinking about that the entire way here, my lady," Cecily said, glancing at Elias before returning her attention to the young queen. "It is certainly true beyond a doubt that Brook is an accomplished liar, and I'm not eager to forget just how many people have suffered because of his tricks. But even so, I haven't been able to hit upon any scheme Brook would risk certain death for. Before we departed, he told me a near-death experience had opened his eyes, and he was trying to undo the evil he's done. It was the reason he'd stayed to defend the town, he claimed."

"Do you believe him?" Elias was surprised to hear Amira's question was absolutely sincere. It sounded to him like she would believe Cecily's word without hesitation. If Cecily said something nice on his behalf, he had a chance.

"No, I don't," Cecily sighed, crossing her arms.

Ah, well, Elias thought, maybe eternal torment isn't as bad as it's cracked up to be.

"But I do believe that his desire to help us is genuine."

"Explain, please," Amira requested, cocking her head slightly.

"I don't believe Brook has repented everything he's done and sought us out purely to atone for his crimes. I'm not sure that he had a near-death experience at all. But I do believe that he's survived five years with many enemies and no friends, and I believe he regrets that his treachery in the past has left him in such a state in the present. He might even genuinely be afraid of the fate that awaits his soul." Cecily sighed, glancing at Elias. "I think his attempt to make amends is sincere, but his motives for restoring you to the throne are less pure than ours."

Elias gritted his teeth slightly. It had been unsettling enough to see one of the Royal Guard give him a look that suggested actual cunning, but now even Cecily was proving cleverer than he'd guessed. In Elias's extensive experience, a day someone proved smarter than he'd realized had never been a good day for him, and it had happened twice already today.

"...I see." Amira turned to Elias, and then took a few small steps closer to him. "I will speak to the prisoner. Cecily, Blanche, you will remain here. The rest of you, leave us."

Reluctance warred with respect amongst the Royal Guard, but it wasn't a very long war. Elias was bound as tightly as ever, although he was able to sit up now, and the capacity of the two women remaining to protect the queen was apparently not in doubt among their comrades. Soon enough, Elias was alone with them, Boors glaring at him as he withdrew. Elias turned to meet Amira's eyes as she took another step closer to him, and for a moment, nobody spoke.

"Blanche? The sword, please," Amira said after a moment, not taking her eyes away from his. Blanche stepped forward smartly, bearing a long blade with a golden hilt and a silver scabbard. It looked quite ornate compared to the practical one she wore on her belt as a twin to Cecily's, but Elias had little doubt it would kill him just as dead in a situation like this if his bindings were removed and it was taken to his neck.

Blanche knelt to let the shorter girl draw the sword forth from its scabbard. Elias recognized it when the blade that emerged was a pure, milky white. He'd never seen Morys use it, but the High Priest and the executioner had both wielded the sword in his presence, and knights had sworn oaths on that blade. He wondered which purpose Amira had in mind as she drew the sword free. It was a little too long and a little too heavy for her, he could tell, but it did not wobble when she pressed the point to his chest.

"You recognize this, don't you?" she asked quietly, focusing on Elias in a way she hadn't before. She wasn't looking through him anymore, but Elias wasn't sure he appreciated the change. "This is the Sword of Absolution. Not a part of the Royal Regalia, but a treasure of the kingdom all the same. It is the only piece we managed to save, and that was purely because Blanche happened to be near it when the time came to flee the palace." Elias shifted uncomfortably as the point dug slightly into his skin. For a treasure-sword, it was kept uncomfortably sharp.

He wasn't in a whole lot of danger unless she tried to use it like the executioner had, but he couldn't imagine he would enjoy having that blade shoved through him, and what came after would probably be even worse.

"The sword was forged with powerful magic. It's the reason the blade is always white. Do you know what the magic in it does?" she asked. Elias shook his head. He'd tried to avoid thinking about the thing when he'd seen it used, if he was honest.

"No falsehood can be spoken to the one who carries the sword while it is drawn. It is a blade that every Royal Guard and Knight of the Realm swears their oath on." Amira tightened her grip on the sword. "It is also said it breaks all enchantments and sweeps away the regret and the grudges of those it slays. Their attachments to this world are severed along with their life, and their spirit does not linger to haunt the living. So it is said. I know the first spell exists. It has been tested extensively since my family attained this sword. If I do not like what I hear when it makes you answer truthfully, we will find out together if the second spell really exists."

Well, now there was a coin toss's chance that the blade pressing against his chest had the power to kill him if she pushed it forward a few inches, even with Mibotha to help. If Elias wasn't aware he was doomed anyway if Amira ended up rejecting his help, he would probably be back on the verge of panic.

"That sounds fair," he said hoarsely.

"Did you kill my father?"

"I did not." No burns, no flare of magic, no condemning voice stripping it bare...Elias savored the look on Blanche's face as the sword did not challenge his claim, but Amira wasn't done.

"Were you involved in his death?"

That blade's power is genuine. Do not attempt to bend the truth when you speak while it's drawn. Mibotha warned.

"...Yes. I was," Elias whispered.

"Who assassinated my father, if it wasn't you?"

"Oliver Bones." This time both Blanche and Amira looked stunned, but the sword remained at peace.

"Did you hire Oliver Bones? Do you know who did?"

"No, I didn't hire him, and I'm not sure who did. I only have guesses," Elias admitted.

"Did you steal the Regalia from the castle?"

"No, I didn't!"

"Do you really know where they are?"

And Elias was stuck, he couldn't answer that. He *didn't* know. Claiming he did had been a lie. It was one Mibotha had made him tell, but he could not truthfully say he had the faintest idea where they were. But if he admitted that, he had a keen feeling Amira would run him through before he could explain himself. It might already be too late, as he saw the fury build on her face.

"Do you really know where the Regalia are?" she demanded, getting ready to stab.

"Yes!"

Elias was shocked to realize Mibotha had not made him answer that time. It had spoken directly through him, and he could see on the faces of the three woman watching him they had all heard something strange in his voice. Amira paused for a long moment, and Elias could see a lot of questions fighting to get out next. Was Mibotha nervously twitching in the back of his mind, or was that merely his own nervousness at the magical sword aimed at his heart?

"Why are you doing this, Elias?" Amira finally asked. For a moment, she sounded less like the rightful sovereign of all the land and more like the girl Elias had remembered. At the same time, he could feel Mibotha gently urging him as he opened his mouth. The sword was not so clever that he had to tell the *entire* truth. For a moment, he considered exposing the whole thing then and there. It galled him that Mibotha had the audacity to demand he admit to any guilt he had before the sword but try to hide the truth in order to protect Mibotha.

"When Morys died, it ruined a lot of lives," he said, hiding his distaste as his courage failed him. Mibotha had done very little to make him fond of it, but he felt compelled to hide the spirit's involvement. His confession would sound pathetic enough without him mentioning he'd been blackmailed into doing this by a spirit, and despite everything, he feared Mibotha's vengeance if he crossed it now. "You know that well enough, you're hiding under the hills being hunted by people who ought to be helping you rule the land. But while you've been hiding out here with your servants and your Guard in a castle for five years, I've spent five years stealing from battlefields to eat. Five years without a friend in the world and a lot of people, yourself included, who wished me dead. Five years knowing that life was going to be nasty, hard, and short. I needed to do *something*, or I really would end up dead in a ditch somewhere." Elias looked at Amira, clearing his throat before pressing on. "I don't want to die, your Majesty. I don't want to spend whatever's left of my life scraping around in the mud for enough loot to eat one more day. I don't want to always be sleeping with one eye open for the day someone comes to take revenge on me. I'm a dead man if nothing changes in this kingdom. I hoped I might be able to change my luck if I helped you take it back. You need my help, and I need yours."

Amira had expected very little from him when this interrogation had started, he was sure of it. And yet, somehow his answer had still managed to disappoint her. For a moment, the young queen closed her eyes.

"Do you regret betraying my father?" she whispered.

"Yes." He hadn't needed to hesitate that time. He would almost be proud of himself if he didn't feel like trash listening to her voice.

"Do you regret that you're alive instead of him?" And this time, he couldn't hesitate, even though he wanted to.

"No."

Amira wasn't a very strong girl, but it still hurt when she dropped the sword to slap him. The second slap, coming the other way as the first jerked his head around, hurt more, and Elias's entire face stung as she took a step back, on the verge of tears. She stood there for a moment, breathing heavily but waving Cecily away when she came to her side.

"You are a despicable man, Elias, and I wish I'd never seen you again," she whispered. "I ought to take that sword and *make* you tell us where the Regalia are. Then I would cut off your head, only because I don't think your heart is big enough to hit. Let *that* be your atonement to offer in the afterlife." Elias shuddered; he knew that Amira was trying not to cry, but her tone was becoming more measured and regal, not breaking down. She was putting her mask back on even while admitting how she felt. "But my father wasn't a cruel man. My brother won't grow up to be a cruel man, no matter what this world does to us. I am...I am *not* like the ones outside that raze the land and butcher my people. So I will give you a chance to help me yourself. You will atone for what you've done with your life, not your death." Amira picked up the sword, but this time she held it before her like a cross, the blade pointing downwards. "You have told the truth so far. Now I must ask you to tell it again. Will you aid me and my Guard in reclaiming my Regalia?"

"Yes," Elias said quickly. He wondered how they would react if they understood how much helping them was his only chance.

"Will you remain with us until the task is complete?"

"I will."

"If I ask it of you when all is done, will you give up your life to atone for your crimes?" The last question bent suddenly and sharply, much like a hook, and it snagged him just as efficiently. Looking her in the eyes, Elias was sure she was testing him. But the truth was the truth.

"You'd have to catch me first."

After a moment, Amira smiled slightly, before sheathing the sword and clapping her hands.

"Fair enough, Elias Brook. Blanche, gather the others. There is work to do."

CHAPTER 10

He would not have believed himself if he'd been able to send an account of his recent exploits back one week, Elias reflected to himself as he was grudgingly released from his bonds by the Royal Guard.

Died in a forest thanks to a random farm-boy with a pitchfork. Recruited forcibly by a spirit to come back to life and try to clean up the mess the world had become. Hero of a small town besieged by bandits. And now he had walked into the lair of some of his most determined enemies and emerged unscathed, one step closer to completing Mibotha's quest.

Even though he was aware Mibotha was not done with him by any stretch of the imagination, Elias felt almost cheerful he'd gotten this far in one piece. Every step of the journey so far had seemed so absurdly impossible that actually managing to pull it all off meant the equally impossible steps still ahead weren't bothering him nearly as much as they ought to. Even Mibotha seemed less intolerable lately.

You did well to get us this far, Elias Brook. I will admit I had my doubts you would make it, Mibotha admitted. *But still, don't celebrate yet. Now that we're here, the true work will begin. You must see the young queen reclaim her Regalia and become a ruler in fact as well as name. It is absolutely imperative you do not allow any harm to befall her!*

Elias just nodded vaguely, as if he didn't know that already. If Amira came to harm because he showed up claiming to know where her Regalia was, it wouldn't matter if he'd done his best to protect her, Sir Boors and his friends would carve him like a turkey. Still, he didn't understand Mibotha's worry. This "invisible castle" had kept Amira hidden all this time. It was unlikely attackers would somehow find their way here before he and the Guard fetched the Regalia and returned.

His heart sank slightly when he realized Amira was only a few steps behind Cecily as she rejoined the other Guard.

"Cecily, why is she here?" he asked, hoping he didn't know the answer already.

"I will be coming on this expedition," Amira replied simply, giving Elias a look that dared him to challenge her decision in the midst of her retainers.

"With all due respect, Your Highness, that is quite possibly the worst idea I have heard in my life, and I'm including your grandfather's projects," he replied bluntly, finding some petty enjoyment in the outrage of the Guard. He should have expected this. The Royal Guard had not been picked to think about the sovereign's decisions, just to carry them out sharply. Even if one or two of them had displayed rather more insight than he'd come to expect from Royal Guard, he would not be surprised if Boors and his ilk eagerly supported every foolish idea that entered the head that wore the crown and thought themselves fine men for doing so. Loyalty made people so *stupid* sometimes, even the people it was given to.

"You believe I should remain here in safety," Amira guessed, seeming to take his objection in stride.

"Yes, I do. I don't think I need to point out that you have very little to gain and a lot to lose by putting yourself in harm's way," Elias insisted. "There are warlords stomping around right now that would love to see you dead. We may well run afoul of them in the process of retrieving your Regalia. The Royal Guard and I are capable enough of defending ourselves if they come for us, but this whole thing is meaningless if you are killed."

"With the size of the force moving with you, I'm just as safe among you as I am inside these walls," Amira said simply, before holding up a hand as Elias tried to respond. "Secrecy, I know, but if the worst should happen, our enemies might track your path back here anyhow. My brother and his protectors will be awaiting news in one of the other castles. I, however, will be joining you."

It's risky, but probably a wise decision. She can put the Regalia to use immediately if we reclaim them, and she will show the land she is a brave leader. A female sovereign has a great deal to prove. Mibotha muttered.

Elias didn't care for that line of reasoning at all. Brave kings ended up just as dead as any other kind when they marched into danger and their guards weren't good enough. Even with Mibotha's approval of this foolishness, Elias didn't follow its apparent belief that becoming queen officially would mean more if Amira assumed her rightful place in the middle of her enemies instead of in the safety of her castle.

"I can't guarantee your safety, Your Highness, and if the Guard say they can, they are misleading you," Elias tried one last time. "This is a mistake, and it's one that could get you killed."

"I understand that it is dangerous, Elias," Amira said, looking mildly annoyed. "That doesn't change the fact that I need to take charge of my destiny if I am to rule after the land after five years of decay. Your knowledge has provided that opportunity."

She will have her way in this, Elias Brook. You will simply have to take particular care no harm comes to her, Mibotha added unhelpfully. Elias didn't know why he was surprised. It wouldn't be his life if there wasn't an unreasonable condition attached to his latest endeavor to make it that much harder.

"Fine. But I want you to remember if you change your mind a little down the road that this was your idea, not mine," Elias muttered.

"I will," Amira said simply, walking past him with Blanche following her. Elias couldn't say he thought much of her reasoning in this, but he supposed it was admirable in a way that she did not second-guess herself after making a decision. She'd likely inherited that from her father.

"The queen will not want for protection, Brook. If I were you, I would merely concern myself that she received good guidance," Sir Boors warned, glaring distrustfully at Elias.

"I already answered the queen's questions to her satisfaction with the Sword of Absolution pointed at me. Is that not enough for you not to be watching me for betrayal every time I do something?" Elias sighed.

"It isn't," Boors said simply. "I'm not privy to what exactly you told the queen, but if any man could lie in the face of the Sword, it's you, Brook. Until the Regalia are in our hands and the kingdom is restored, I'll be watching you."

"Wonderful. It's not me you'll have to explain yourself to if your queen gets killed on the road because of her decision to come along and your decision to watch me instead of her," Elias said sharply, turning away.

Despite her being instrumental to him getting this far, Elias had not cared very much for Cecily's company on the way to the castle. And yet, when he set out with Amira and the selected Royal Guard from the hidden castle, he found he liked the change of company even less. There were perhaps fifteen Royal Guards alongside him now, Blanche, Boors, and Cecily among them. Nearly all of them regarded him with a look that assured Elias that the shaky trust Amira had extended to him was not one they shared. He was tolerated here, never welcome, and things would only get worse unless he was very lucky.

All in all, it almost put Elias in mind of the good old days at court.

"Are you going to share where we're going with me any time soon, or are you just going to speak up when everyone starts getting suspicious I'm making this up as I go?" he muttered under his breath, riding a bit ahead of the company to consult Mibotha without being overheard.

Now that we've gotten this far, there's no reason not to share the information. The Regalia have been hidden underneath an abandoned Traveler's Shrine four days' journey north of here.

"Four days' journey north...doesn't that lead into...?"

It is an occupied territory. Duke Hache and his wife hold dominion over it.

"Of course it would be Hache, why should this be easy?" Elias lamented, as quietly as he could manage.

You and I both know that Duke Hache is the furthest thing from a friend our young queen has, but I don't anticipate great difficulty. The shrine is in a neglected area of a wide territory, and Hache has depleted his armies fighting other would-be usurpers. He has no idea that the Regalia have been hidden this whole time in a province he conquered and promptly forgot some time ago, and with so many ragged armies fighting against his, the arrival of seventeen travelers will not draw his eye.

"You sound very confident in that."

Hache is a vicious man, but very little of his power comes from himself, and his obsession with conquest has rather blinded him to important details these last few years. If he is a threat at all, it is the concern that his wife may be more vigilant than he, or that your friend Oliver Bones may be in his employ.

Elias nearly came to a halt. He hadn't considered that possibility at all.

"I knew Amira shouldn't have come! He'll slaughter her if he's still around here!" It was hard not to shout, but the last thing he needed was people who distrusted him hearing half of a loud conversation with himself.

She is surrounded by fifteen of her finest and a man empowered by spirits.

"That's not anything close to enough if he sees us before we see him."

Perhaps you should voice this concern, then. He may not be there at all, or employed elsewhere fighting Hache's enemies, but at least the others will be on the watch.

Elias sighed, letting his horse slow so the others could catch up. Mibotha had a point, although Elias took little comfort in it. If this war had not killed Oliver Bones, and he would not believe for a second that it had, then it would never be over until someone did slay him.When Amira became known to the world again, Elias was keenly aware that sooner or later, her path would cross with Oliver Bones, and unless someone very brave, very skilled, and very lucky was there with her, that would be the end of Queen Amira The First. In some ways, it would be better if Oliver was the obstacle to overcome on their way to the Regalia. At least then they wouldn't have to worry about him coming at a time of his own choosing after the quest was over.

"Your Highness, I have some concerns..." he murmured, falling in beside her as they rode. He was relieved to see Amira had left the protection of her castle quite sturdily armored from the halfhelm on her head down to the armored greaves on her feet, with dark steel plate everywhere in between. Even her long hair was braided and coiled away nicely to avoid flowing out of her helmet. It was more practical than Elias had hoped, but it also wasn't likely to protect her from an assassin of Bones's caliber.

"You may speak them, Elias. I want to hear what you think while we're following your lead out here," Amira replied calmly.

"The Regalia are a four day journey from where we are, due North," Elias reported, glancing up the road. "You may know, but that will take us into Duke Hache's territory."

Amira was quiet for a moment, and her expression hardened slightly. It seemed she was not oblivious that Hache was one of her worst enemies at the moment. "I knew I would have to confront him eventually, although I had not anticipated doing so so soon. His army might be depleted, as they say, but it's still fighting."

"This is why I considered it acceptable to venture here. He's fighting so often a force this size won't draw much attention when he's watching his rivals like a hawk," Elias explained. "The duchess, however, is a great deal cleverer than her husband, and I have to warn you, Oliver Bones may be taking Hache's coin."

"You think he was the one who employed Basilisk-Eye?" Amira asked, glancing at Elias.

"He's one of the ones who could afford him. I have no proof. Bones has never been sloppy enough to leave any clear proof of any of his dealings. We have to assume he'll come after you if we want to see him coming," Elias warned.

"I've heard a great deal about Oliver Bones. I don't know how much of it is true," Amira murmured. She looked curious now, more than scared. "Do you know him well, Elias?"

It was a good question, and a very pertinent question. Elias sidestepped it like a champion. Of course he hadn't known Oliver Bones well. Things might not have turned out like this if he had.

"I don't think anyone knows him well. I...I only met Oliver Bones twice in my life, and that's two times more than I'd have liked," Elias said, shivering. It wasn't a lie, but Elias was relieved when Amira did not press on the comment for details.

"They say such strange things about him. They say that he made love to a gorgon in exchange for her knowledge of the killing arts. That he can walk up walls and slip through the narrowest crack. That his right eye has a curse in it that withers whatever it sees. That he uses...basilisk venom to kill his targets."

"You can take some comfort that none of that is true, at least," Elias sighed, shaking his head. "People get superstitious about men that dangerous, and Bones certainly started at least one of those rumors himself to bolster his reputation. Gorgons aren't real, and no one uses basilisk venom for anything. It's too corrosive, for one thing, and even if you could forge a blade that wouldn't *melt* being coated in it, just picking the blade up would probably kill you even if you wore gloves. Your father used siege crossbows to hunt basilisks for a *reason*. That poison is cursed. It can't be used for anything unless you have a death wish." Elias sighed, looking thoughtfully at the sky. "I don't know him well enough to answer for sure, but I suspect Oliver Bones is merely an extremely agile, quiet man who exaggerated his prowess to scare people. There are plenty of mundane poisons that kill just as dead as basilisk venom, and it wouldn't surprise me if he was skilled in their uses. But basilisks are mythical, terrifying. Borrowing their name and claiming to have some of their power makes *him* seem more mythical than he really is, and in his business that's worth a lot of gold."

"You make him sound quite ordinary, underneath all that," Amira remarked.

"That's not my intention," Elias said quickly. "The man's dangerous enough as it is without attributing supernatural powers to him, that's all.

He's patient as a stone, and about as merciful. His accuracy with a bow isn't exaggerated, and if he poisons his arrows, that just means he can kill someone before they're even aware they're in danger. If anything or anyone in the world scares him, I don't know about it, and killing's not just about the money for him. He has a taste for it. He enjoys watching people die." Elias shivered again. "He's not a monster, Your Highness, he's a man, and that by itself is quite dangerous enough. We'll never really be safe until he's dead."

"I think you're right, Elias. But if what you say is true, then we simply need to take away the element of surprise to turn the tables on him," Amira said.

"Easier said than done, Your Highness, but I suppose," Elias sighed.

"Forewarned is forearmed, as my father used to say," Amira shrugged, beginning to ride a little quicker. "As you say, these are merely concerns you have. With any luck, we will pass unnoticed and reclaim the Regalia without any great trouble."

Elias frowned slightly, but kept his peace as he rode back to the head of the party to lead it onwards.

That was what worried him, if he was honest. He didn't know about his new companions, but he'd never had any luck with things being easy.

CHAPTER 11

Despite Elias's concerns, it seemed that someone in their party was luckier than he was. The first day of the journey passed without incident, although Elias personally felt he would not start to relax until things were certainly over.

Still, the Royal Guard did not seem at all out of their element as they made camp for the night, setting up with admirable swiftness and efficiency. As someone who had endured more nights than he cared to count on a lousy jacket and a prayer, Elias appreciated their work even though the majority of it was clearly meant to shield Amira from the elements. Even so, a good fire was soon built up, and Elias sat down next to it. None of the Royal Guards allowed him to sit too close to them, but Elias didn't mind. Considering his company, he preferred some space.

He depended on these people, but he didn't feel for a second like he belonged among them. He hadn't when Morys was alive, and he certainly didn't now that Morys was dead. They were tolerating his help because he had something they wanted, but when that was done with, Elias was not optimistic about how far their gratitude would stretch. He'd felt the hostility even while he was guiding them to their goal. Sometimes he imagined that they might *want* him to fail, even though that would hurt them even more than him. It would at least give them an excuse not to change their minds about him.

They were ignoring him now, pointedly, with the exception of Cecily and Blanche. In his younger days, Elias would have thought it obvious why two of the five or so women in their group besides the princess would pay attention to him, but he wasn't stupid enough to assume anything of the sort now. Cecily was simply not ignoring him. Like her mistress, she seemed to be treating him like a normal person while their mission lasted, even if she did not make any effort to resume conversation with him as they rode.

Blanche, however, had been staring at him regularly, and it was starting to unnerve him. There was a time not too long ago he would have (and had) spent good money to get a girl that looked like Blanche interested in him for a while, but since setting out, he had wished increasingly that Blanche would lose interest in whatever she was looking for. She was pretty, a good deal prettier than Cecily, but Elias had been thinking for the last few hours, trying to nail down exactly why her eyes set him on edge.

He was starting to think it was because he couldn't recognize their look.

Cecily's looks had been very easy to read. People with honest, expressive faces were never that tricky to figure out. Righteous anger, deep suspicion, grudging acceptance...even muted pity had been clear as day when it was on her mind. Most of the others, like Boors, didn't even need to be read. Their faces, and their body language, practically shouted everything they thought to him. Some were so lacking in subtlety Elias would probably have been able to pretend to hear their thoughts if he didn't think it would be an invitation for them to shut him up quite bluntly. But Blanche was a blank, and that worried him. He'd met people that were trying very hard to keep their thoughts and their emotions inscrutable, and he'd gotten the better of most of them in one way or another. She didn't seem to care if her thoughts were visible, but they didn't *look* like anything to Elias. All he had were scraps, which seemed contradictory when he put them together. Calculation, experience, cunning...but also zeal, friendliness, and that quiet air of hopeful, serene purity that Elias found so bloody irritating. It didn't add up to Elias. If Boors or Cecily lived to be a hundred, he still doubted they'd ever have the little glints of cynicism Blanche's countenance contained right now. But there she was, talking quietly with her friends, with no indication she felt at all out of place or was thinking about something they weren't. It was only when she looked at him that the ordinary Guard seemed to mix with something else.

Elias had some very happy memories of beautiful, crafty women that had wanted to use him like a dish rag and kept all the cunning under a carefully prepared mask in the belief he wouldn't pick up on it. He would have felt quite at ease if he could convince himself that was Blanche, but he couldn't quite talk himself into it. He got the feeling there was something more complicated in the woman across the fire from him, and complicated people were dangerous.

She wanted something from him, that was plain enough. The others were tolerating him, but Blanche was making plans. Perhaps it would be in his best interest not to stick around when Amira was crowned queen, but with Mibotha in his head he wasn't sure if he'd be able to run if he had to.

When Amira was crowned...there was a thought. If he did manage to pull this entire quest off, "redeem himself", and be granted pardon by Mibotha, what was going to happen to him then? Would Mibotha simply withdraw the aid it had given to bring him back to life, send him to his eternal reward, whatever that had become? Or maybe he'd be left alone to live out the rest of his life without a spirit breathing down his neck? Elias privately hoped for the latter. Even if Mibotha assured him Valka was no longer waiting for him, Elias was not eager to quit this world just yet.

"Elias."

Elias looked up in surprise to find Amira standing close by, still armored. He stood up quickly, not wanting to offer some kind of insult in front of most of her Guard, but Amira just cocked her head.

"Walk with me, please," she said calmly, starting to walk away from the fire.

She had a strange way of asking for things, Elias thought to himself as he followed her. So often she phrased things like requests, but it was always a command at its core. Polite, but not really allowing for disobedience. Perhaps it was a product of growing up always being obeyed, but knowing her vassals were only with her now because their loyalty had outstripped their self-interest enough to stay and serve. He wondered what kind of queen the land would be getting if this mission actually succeeded.

Amira was clearly cautious enough she didn't venture very far at all from the campfire, but it was enough that she and Elias were alone when she sat down on a rock to look up at the bright full moon overhead. For a long time, she didn't say anything. Elias got the impression she wasn't all that aware he was even there.

"...You wished to speak to me, Your Highness?" he asked uncertainly, after a long silence. Amira still didn't look at him.

"I've never slept without stone walls around me. Not a single night in my life," she said, almost to herself. "There were always walls, defenses, enclosures. I've never been...out in the open like this. Even with this armor, and all my Guard, I feel," she struggled for a minute, "exposed. Like I'm naked."

"If it's any consolation, you certainly don't *look* naked," Elias remarked, although Mibotha's disapproval was like a whiplash to the back of the head. Wincing slightly, he sat down next to Amira. "And you certainly don't lack for defenses with that many protectors."

"I know that, but it doesn't seem to change anything," Amira sighed. "It feels so strange to think about, how much more open it is beyond the castle walls. I've been inside castles so long that I feel like my fortress is a part of my body. Is that...how a queen should feel?" she turned to Elias, and he realized Amira hadn't just called him here to listen to her talk to herself. She was so afraid of saying what was on her mind to the people that upheld her crown that she was talking to *him* of all people as a way to let it out. "My father wasn't afraid of anything beyond his walls."

"Or in them, for that matter," Elias sighed. "With all due respect, Your Highness, your father might have lived a lot longer if he had been. Fearlessness isn't a virtue."

"It is for a ruler," Amira said sharply, looking at Elias. "A queen cannot be afraid when the time comes for her to do her duty. No one will bow for very long to a throne that seats a coward."

"Fear has its good points, you know," countered Elias Brook, well-known coward. "Fear makes you aware you're in danger and you need to respond. Your Guard might not be afraid, even when they ought to be, but that just means they won't run or back down when they should. It's the same with a crown. You ought to be afraid, so you don't walk right into danger."

"You sound like you're speaking from experience," Amira murmured, glancing over. "But you don't seem nearly as cowardly as I've heard."

"I'm not. I'm a much bigger coward," Elias said bluntly. "I've lived this long because everything scares me enough that I don't let it catch me by surprise."

"I can't see fear driving a man to submit himself to the mercy of his enemies in hopes of improving his lot."

"That's because you're a lot braver than I am," Elias replied, phrasing it as a criticism. "Never forget this. A man who's scared enough to die and desperate enough to live can do *anything*. That's not bravery. That's fear at its strongest."

Amira didn't reply, seeming to consider this. Elias started to get uncomfortable again. While he appreciated someone that didn't wince with contempt every time he spoke, and was privately impressed Amira had the strength of character to be that person after what they'd been through, he always hated it when someone seemed to be trying to understand him. It felt too much like condescension, even when it was well-meant.

"I think I can see your perspective better out here than I could at home," she murmured after a while, looking up at the sky. "No walls...no home...nothing between you and the world but what's on your skin and in your head. This is your world, isn't it? We're just passing through it trying to get me back to mine, but you *live* here."

That had not been something Elias had expected Amira to say, but he managed a shrug.

"Some people are meant to be out, not in. I'm just one of them."

"I don't think anyone lives outside of everything by choice."

"Tell it to Oliver Bones," Elias snapped, suddenly angry and not sure why. He stood up. "Listen, if you want advice from me, don't forget how naked you feel without walls around you. Remember the feeling. Treasure it. Knowledge of your vulnerability is worth more than the best armor in the world out here. People and walls will let you down, but fear will keep you alive if you let it."

Amira just continued looking up at the moon. In contrast to Elias's sudden restless irritation, she seemed more serene than ever, and somehow that just made Elias more irritated.

"I think I understand you a little better now, Elias. Thank you," she said quietly, not looking at him.

You don't understand a thing, little girl. You and all the others just think you do because it gives you a warm feeling thinking you know what goes on in my head.

The words fought to come out, but Elias had the self-preservation to swallow them and leave quietly with all the dignity he could muster even as he fumed.

Gods save him from the people that thought they understood him. He could take the hatred, or the distrust, but every condescending attempt to pity him because someone thought they had magically seen his inner workings in the space of one candid conversation made his blood boil.

It was a lovely feeling, wasn't it, to pity someone? To think to yourself that you knew all you needed to know about them, and that wonderful warm feeling you could get thinking about how much worse they were than you. You could hold it over them in your mind forever. '*Poor Elias, I've seen the pathetic core of you and understand it all!*'

Sadists loved the feeling of having power over people, having the capacity to diminish them until the feeling of superiority set in. Elias didn't see how pity was any better. It was just a way for the great and the good to diminish others into nothing and think themselves fine people for doing so. At least tormentors *meant* to hurt you when they cut you down to size to feel powerful.

He'd take Blanche and all her mysterious, frightening analysis over that. He'd rather be scum or prey than something pitiful.

I don't understand you.

It was a strange experience, halfway back to the fire, to hear words he was far more comfortable with coming from Mibotha. Elias came to a stop, his anger suddenly fading.

*She tries to see what little good there is in you, and to comprehend what makes you what you are. She may be the only person in the entire world who cares **why** you are Elias Brook, and you recoil from it in a rage. Is compassion so hateful to you?*

"I've never known compassion, Mibotha, so I can't tell you," Elias replied, gritting his teeth. "That wasn't compassion. It's the same old garbage I've dealt with my whole life. You have one honest conversation with someone, say one unguarded thing, and they think they know everything they need to know about you. I've been hated, and I can take that, but I can't stand the people who think they understand me. It's just another way to look down on me." Elias spat. "She can keep her pity, thinking she's got me all figured out. I've got no use for it."

I see. You look at pity and see others making you less than you are in order to feel better, is that it?

Mibotha was surprisingly in tune with his views for once, it seemed. He nodded slowly. Mibotha was quiet for a while.

Perhaps it does make sense, then, that you devote so much pity to yourself. Few indeed could match you at making yourself less than you ought to be in order to feel better.

The analytic, curious tone turned to pure, cold venom at the end, and Mibotha fell silent.

Try as he might, Elias couldn't find anything else to say for the rest of the night.

CHAPTER 12

Elias kept to himself when the expedition resumed the following morning, merely scanning the road ahead and saying nothing to anyone.

It wasn't about what had happened last night, he told himself. Mibotha's contempt and the misguided pity of his betters were things he was well used to by this point, and certainly not enough to leave him shaken. He was simply ill-at-ease traveling among this many people. Going it alone had its advantages and disadvantages, but Elias had never found he had any place in groups this large and organized, and he certainly didn't have a place in this one.

He wanted to be done with them. With Cecily, with Blanche, with Boors, and especially with Amira and Mibotha. As dangerous as a world without friends might be, Elias was starting to crave some solitude, especially within his own head.

He didn't bother asking Mibotha what would happen when the Regalia were reclaimed, if they got that far. He knew at this point all the spirit would have for him was an unhelpful answer. There was simply no getting around the fact that the spirit would consider their bargain completed and release him to whatever remained after he'd found "redemption" at its own convenience. If Mibotha wanted Elias to stick around and serve Amira in restoring her kingdom, he didn't doubt it would hold eternal punishment over his head until it was done.

Where did that end, he wondered bitterly as he rode slightly ahead of the group. Where did Mibotha lose its right to keep asking more of him? There wasn't anyone to judge how fair their bargain was besides Mibotha itself, and Elias had no way to assert influence over the spirit. If he rejected its orders, it would likely withdraw its aid from him as punishment. That would happen if he decided he was done with all this today, and for all he knew that would happen if he decided he'd done enough ten years from now. It had all the power in their abrasive partnership, and Elias reflected, not for the first time, that he was stuck with Mibotha until the spirit was satisfied. His only hope was that Mibotha had some interest in fairness and would eventually leave him alone and intercede with the afterlife on his behalf once he'd finished helping Amira in this matter. He wouldn't be expected to stick around for the Royal Guard trying to finally rebuild the land, would he?

"I've got some work for you, Elias my boy. I'm afraid this is something only you can do for me."

Morys's words came back unbidden, and Elias shivered a little hearing the dead man's voice in his memory. That was right, though...Morys had work he needed a good thief for in the good old days. Sometimes kings needed swords and armies, other times they found the service they required related more to some inconveniently locked doors that needed to be opened without much fuss.

Hah...he had been busy in those days, thanks to Morys. Their first meeting should by rights have been the end of Elias's life. Amira or her grandfather would certainly have laid a heavy, maybe fatal, punishment on a peasant boy who had broken into the temple reliquary in search of treasures. The priest, certainly, would have been within his rights to kill him on the spot if he could catch him.

Morys, on the other hand, had considered how a boy with the dirt of the streets stamped into him head to toe had managed to get into the very heart of the king's personal temple without being noticed and broken into a chamber whose location was a secret to most. Elias was sure anyone else would have seen a blaspheming thief and put him to the sword, but Morys had seen talent, and put him to work instead.

He wondered sometimes if Amira knew anything about why he'd really lived at court. Certainly the nobles didn't believe that he was an advisor, but Amira, guileless as she'd been, had always assumed he was there because her father took an interest in what the people on the street had to say. To be fair, it hadn't been a lie. Morys was the successor to an unpopular king, and such men tended to take a keen interest in what others thought of them. But that had been a fairly minor use of Elias's talents, and Morys had seen much better ones.

A king with shallow coffers sometimes needed more than his richest would give. A king mindful of being well-thought of sometimes couldn't move overtly against someone powerful giving him trouble. But, if a thief was to help himself to some of a noble's stores after he avoided his taxes, or a nobleman or cleric with a little too much ambition should find a secret of theirs exposed...well, that was hardly Morys's doing, was it?

He had never, and this was important to Elias, ever killed someone on Morys's orders. He had been asked to find things out in secret, and he found them out. He had stolen from people who had a lot to take. He had used information against people stupid enough to have secrets that would ruin them. He'd delivered bribes on the sly, and sometimes made sure other bribes never reached their destination. He had occasionally quietly reminded someone that people with a great deal of power had so much to lose if their fortunes changed. Sometimes he had heartily advised someone to take a very long holiday elsewhere, for their health. He had–just a few times, of course–left a few doors open and windows unlocked, and not asked any questions afterwards. He did what was asked of him, and he'd done it well.

It was funny, none of that ever seemed to get written down when people eulogized Morys these days. He wondered if anyone around him had the slightest idea what he'd done for their sainted king, if they'd have the gall to ask him to do it all again for their precious queen.

He'd normally have taken comfort that this lot, parading around on their high horses, would be only too happy to see the back of him. But only some of the Royal Guard these days were as...simple as he'd remembered. He worried it would only be to his own cost if he underestimated them and what they stood to gain by keeping him around. Where would he be if whatever Blanche was considering when she studied him started to come to light right at the moment Mibotha abandoned him? The promise his soul would be safe would not make being volunteered for service at sword-point any more pleasant for him, and then he'd still be stuck, for however long his life lasted.

How long was he going to have to pay? Yes, he would grant he'd done some things wrong with his life. Hell, he would reluctantly concede the vast majority of his life was riddled with things he wished he hadn't done. But he held like a drowning man to a steady rock his belief that his punishment seemed disproportionate to his crimes.

He had lied, cheated, and stolen; what of it? He had done no more than many in that regard, and less than a fair few. He had killed, but never anyone that wasn't trying to kill him first. He'd blackmailed, and he'd threatened, but that only worked on people with something to hide. The world was full of men like him, he told himself, and most thought them no worse than rascals while his reputation was poison.

He had betrayed Morys's trust, and bad things had happened because of it, everyone was so keen to remind him. They seemed convinced that this made everything else that happened his fault as well. Everything from the famine to bad weather was the treachery of Elias Brook. He wasn't even sure he'd be free of that if Mibotha strong-armed him into fixing every last bit of it, not if he didn't bring Morys back to life in the process.

He pitied himself too much, Mibotha insisted. Elias preferred to think of it as being the only one willing to ask if his situation struck anyone else as just a tad unfair.

He would likely have gone on in such a mood for the entire day if he hadn't spotted movement up ahead and held up a hand to alert the Royal Guard.

"Company. Looks like soldiers," he said, looking over his shoulder. The Guards nodded, and in a moment Amira was completely out of view behind a grim wall of steel and horse. Elias let his horse shy to the side a bit as they began to advance again. He might have gotten the better of those bandits in hand-to-hand combat, but he had not gotten into that mess willingly and if he could let the Royal Guard take care of this fight entirely, he would not hesitate to do so.

Get your bow ready. I think you might need it.

Elias tried not to sigh. He'd been expecting that, but wasn't any happier when he heard it. Reluctantly, Elias fingered the bow and quiver the Royal Guards had reluctantly provided him with. They were fine work, better than any he'd actually owned in his career, but he didn't feel particularly safe with them when he suspected he was about to be firing into a chaotic melee. It would not do wonders for his future if he had to convince someone that it had been an accident he'd shot them instead of the enemy.

Still, his bow was ready but tucked aside subtly as the two groups met. The soldiers were about what Elias had been expecting in this day and age, weatherbeaten armor, ragged uniforms, and second-rate weapons. Their thuggish, determined faces marked them among those that had been too stupid or too desperate to stop fighting but not stupid enough to join the front. They were recruitment officers, if Elias was any judge, which after five years of war translated to slightly more stubborn, less intelligent bandits in matching shirts. On the other hand, there were a fair number of them, enough that Elias did not look forward to the part where the two sides ended the pleasantries and started killing each other. He hoped the time in hiding had not made the Royal Guard slow.

"Well now, what have we here?" the leader of the soldiers grunted, leaning forward on his horse and regarding them suspiciously. "A well-armed bunch, I see. Deserters? Bandits?"

He's actually too stupid to recognize these are Royal Guard, Elias realized. They're wearing their armor, but he didn't even notice. We might be just fine after all.

"Well, I know what you are now. You're new recruits in the army of his grace Duke—"

"Be silent and stand aside, oaf," Blanche cut him off, glaring coldly at him. "We do not fight for Hache or any traitor army, and you would do well to let us pass and forget you saw us."

"Not happening, woman. One way or another, you're coming with us!"

There didn't seem to be any need to announce the battle had begun. The lead soldier punctuated his ultimatum with a thrust of his spear, but Blanche batted it aside and spurred her horse forward, cutting the man down and plowing into the surprised foot soldiers behind him. Boors gave a mighty bellow, and seven of the Royal Guard followed him in a charge just behind Blanche, smashing the surprised soldiers back even as they tried to rally and counter-attack. The remaining Guard held back, protecting Amira on all sides.

Elias had not been expecting so many Royal Guard to stay back and protect Amira, but he was also frankly astonished to see how little their absence seemed to matter. The Royal Guard had been excellent fighters in his day, but he would not have thought eight of them more than a match for a larger force. Yet the duke's soldiers were still being pushed back by their charge. Blanche had cut a line dividing the unit in two with her first push, and each half had four Royal Guard smashing their way through it. Swords and lances flashed, and Elias winced as he saw one man on horseback after another challenge Boors and his mace and lose, many of their mounts perishing along with them. Despite Mibotha's warning, Elias found there was little reason for him to fire into the melee. The soldiers were dregs of an army that had spent years depleting itself of its best fighters in one battle after another, but the Royal Guard who remained had clearly been the pick of a well-regarded lot. When the dust cleared, only one of them was among the fallen, but the soldiers had all been routed.

There! One's getting away! Mibotha alerted him, and Elias turned to see one soldier had played dead long enough to take his chances and run.

He didn't need Mibotha telling him to know that a man running off to raise the alarm would make their task a great deal harder. He drew back his bow, took aim at the fleeing man's back, and fired.

The arrow found its mark, and the last soldier fell. Elias lowered his bow, realizing the bloodied Guard were all looking at him, and shrugged.

"You missed a spot," he said casually. Blanche gave him a small, curt nod before riding over to the Guard who had fallen and dismounting. She knelt by his side for a few moments before looking up at Amira.

"I'm sorry, my lady. Darin is dead," she said quietly, and Elias had to admit he was a little surprised to hear how genuinely sad Blanche sounded that even one of her men had fallen. She'd certainly been cool enough cutting her way through those men that she had to be familiar with death in battle.

Another reminder he didn't understand her, and that perhaps he didn't want to. Her mood seemed shared by the rest of the Guard. Elias felt like he was the only one who thought one man falling in the process of utterly routing the enemy was a pretty good result.

"He was a good man. We are sorely diminished by his loss," Amira murmured, sounding like she sincerely believed what she said.

"We should bury him...do something to hide these bodies, as well," Blanche said, standing up. "Darin shouldn't be left to the beasts, and these corpses will alert someone we're here eventually if we just leave them."

"We'll lose traveling time that way," Elias warned. "We might sacrifice half a day or more of this journey if we stop to clean up this mess."

"The exact time required to complete our mission is of less concern to me than maintaining its secrecy, Brook," Blanche said bluntly. "I wish to be done with this quickly and quietly, but without covering this up Hache might learn he has enemies on his land quite sooner than I'd like. If we take five days all told to pass through this place unnoticed instead of four, I will take that over being discovered in our haste and losing more time and men in battle."

Amira nodded in agreement with Blanche, and that was the end of any attempt to argue with proceeding. Darin was buried by the side of the road, only a small stone and some flowers indicating anything was under the disturbed earth at all. Elias got down from his horse to help deal with the soldiers' bodies, spotting a pair of decent daggers among the corpses and helping himself. He'd thought they would try to dig a pit to bury the dead soldiers in, but surprisingly the Guard seemed content just to pile them all up on one side of the road. Before Elias could ask what the purpose of such an effort was, Blanche walked quietly to the bodies, regarding them impassively for a moment before clasping her hands and beginning to whisper quietly.

Elias nearly fell down in shock when Blanche opened her hands and blew a sharp breath over her palms. As she did, a pure white flame shot forth as though she'd been cupping it in her hands, striking the pile of bodies and sticks and beginning to burn without smoke or heat.

"A mage," he finally said, unable to hold himself back. "You're a bloody *mage?*"

Blanche turned to look at him for an uncomfortably long time after the question slipped out, seeming curious, then mildly amused. When Elias proved unwilling to hold her gaze, she shrugged and turned away.

"I don't have any idea what you're talking about, Brook."

Elias looked around, but most of the other Guard had apparently been quite absorbed in making camp as the light began to fail. If any of them had been surprised, or even all that interested, in the white fire quietly disposing of the evidence of their battle, they gave no indication. Blanche rejoined Cecily, as she usually did, leaving Elias alone by the white bonfire.

He watched it collapse down into nothing but some ash and dirt as suddenly and strangely as it had begun to burn, reflecting on a dozen stories he had never previously had any reason to expect would have any relevance in his life.

He was immortal, mostly, while he remained bound to this cause and Mibotha's will. Even so, he was now more certain than ever that becoming Blanche's enemy would be the last mistake he would ever make.

CHAPTER 13

If Elias had avoided Blanche before that evening, he redoubled his efforts now. Don't go near her, he thought to himself. Don't look directly at her. Try not to *think her name.*

You seem quite shaken, Elias Brook, Mibotha said curiously. *What troubles you so?*

"You saw what she did!" Elias whispered, ducking behind a tree to have the conversation in private. "She's a mage! She set those bodies on fire!"

I am aware we witnessed this. I am more concerned with why it appears to have alarmed you to such a degree.

Elias was brought up a little short by how unbothered Mibotha seemed to be about all this, but he wasn't about to let that go unchallenged.

"Maybe you don't know this, Mibotha, but most people go their entire lives without ever seeing things like we just did," he muttered. "I've got some familiarity with magic myself, but it's got its own place. In stones, in trees...magic belongs out there, in nature, where it's not doing any harm unless someone calls on it. It's not right, magic being *inside* someone."

It might not be the usual dwelling-place for magic, but your fear is largely unwarranted, Mibotha commented. *Blanche's ancestors likely interacted more closely with my kind than their fellow humans did. A mage is not some aberration upon the face of the world. They are humans whose blood carries a boon from the spirits. Nothing more, and nothing less.*

"Most people who gain a boon from their friends can't set things on fire with a wish to see it burning," Elias grumbled, not comforted at all.

Mages!

Despite what Mibotha told him, Elias was quite convinced that magic belonged where most people brave or stupid enough to tamper with spells found it; great thrumming stones in the hearts of the mountains. Ancient trees deep in the forests, too deep to have ever seen an axe. Bound to the earth by monolithic structures to keep the strange power from flowing wildly and causing harm. Magic never caused much trouble when it was kept there, far away from normal people and only drawn forth a bit at a time to empower the glyphs on magical devices. It might be abused sometimes, but it was still mostly safe, stable and controlled.

Not three words Elias would use to describe anyone that was carrying a similar power around in their chest.

The gift was more common in the old days. More humans were in harmony with us then, Mibotha sighed, sounding disappointed. *Mages, as you call them, were a symbol of that era.*

"Just because something was around in ancient times doesn't mean it was a good thing," Elias countered. "Basilisks became common during the "old days" too, because one man couldn't stop himself from abusing his magic. Do you want to tell me *that* was nothing to get upset over?"

Basilisks were a horrible disruption of the natural order, but...

"Disruption? They were natural disasters with *teeth*, every last one of them!" Elias hissed, shaking his head. "Monsters, worse than any you hear about in stories. And they were born because of mages using their "boon". There's no good that can come of humans having that kind of power."

The Royal Guard seems to disagree.

"Desperation," Elias said quickly, not entirely satisfied with his speculation about why the Royal Guard would allow a mage to lead them but deciding not to let Mibotha know that. "They're in a tight corner right now. I doubt they'd have let one lead them in the old days, but they need all the power they can get their hands on right now. They probably know they can't afford to be too choosy."

Or perhaps the woman best-suited to be their captain also possesses a gift that further improves her capacity to defend the queen. Mibotha countered. *I would not let myself be blinded by superstitious fear, Elias Brook. We may have cause to be very grateful for Blanche's power before this is done.*

I'm hiding behind a tree from a mage while a spirit tells me not to let superstition mislead me, Elias thought to himself. When did this become a normal day for me?

"Doesn't mean I have to like it. I've heard the stories. Having magic at your fingertips does things to you," he muttered.

Power is neither good nor bad. Power is, Mibotha said simply. *If magic is misused when bound to human bloodlines, that is the fault of the human, not their power. Consider also that your benefits from our partnership are not so different than Blanche's abilities.*

"She can cast spells from a power in her blood. You knit me up when I'm hurt if you feel like it and talk my ear off. That's different."

Would your abilities seem any less mystical to an outsider than hers?

Elias bit his lip. Actually, his would probably be worse. Blanche could play casting spells off as having a subtle magical device on hand. A man that didn't die when you stabbed him was probably going to get burned before he could figure out a way to explain himself. It did sound like he was in the same boat as Blanche after all, if a bit lower. This did not make him any happier to be linked with her in any way.

"Our deal...Mibotha, *I'm* not going to be passing on magic to my descendants when this is done, am I?"

Judging by your current level of success with the opposite sex, Elias Brook, I would not spend much time speculating on the nature of your descendants.

"I'll have you know I'm quite popular with ladies who didn't grow up in castles," Elias said, sounding a little more defensive than he'd meant to. If he wasn't sure Mibotha had no sense of humor, he'd suspect the spirit was ribbing him.

Recently?

"I've had other things to take care of, as you might have noticed," Elias mumbled, gritting his teeth.

Ah. I'm sure you'll be quite a terror once you've had some time to get back into practice, then.

"...I'm going to start ignoring you now."

Yes, I can see how you would want to save your skill in repartee for the future mother of your mage progeny.

Elias sighed, but let the whispered conversation die out. There really was no talking to Mibotha about some things, he decided. Especially not until he figured out something to fire back when the spirit started fighting dirty.

Still, the spirit might have a point that Blanche having powers beyond her fellow Guard might be vital to their success. If Oliver Bones didn't know one of the Royal Guard had magic, that might be the piece of information that finally let someone get the drop on *him* instead of the other way around. But this did not change that Blanche was not his friend and he did not intend to associate with her any longer than he needed to.

"Brook."

Oh joy, Elias thought to himself as he turned to see Boors had left the campfire to come over to the trees. *More of my favorite people coming to talk to me.*

"Is my absence so keenly felt you came to invite me back?" he asked sarcastically. Boors glared at him, and Elias was only too happy to return the favor.

"Being spared your company is quite pleasant, Brook, but no one cares for you skulking about when night falls where nobody can see you," Boors replied.

Elias sighed, shaking his head. "Boors, I understand you and your brothers and sisters dislike me, but this is really starting to get tiresome. You don't want my company, but you don't want me somewhere you can't see me. It galls you to ask me for help, but you're wandering blindly outside your castle without me leading the way. You have *no choice* but to trust me or you wouldn't be here at all, and yet every single moment you expect me to betray you. What is a man to do with all that? Would it put your mind at ease if I sat in chains and shouted directions to the rest of you as we rode?"

"I would find it preferable to leaving you to your own devices," Boors replied, either not noticing or ignoring Elias's tone. "I can't help but imagine a man like you might be fool enough to try turning on us not far down the road in an attempt to curry favor with Duke Hache."

If I fail, and go to Valka, I wonder if conversations like these will be part of my punishment for a life of wrongdoing, Elias wondered, eye twitching.

"Wonderful. On top of everything else, I'm a fool to you now?" he said, unable to stop himself. Having his intellect insulted by a man like Boors goaded him, even though he knew Boors could swat him like a fly if his response was too sharp.

"If you were a clever man, Brook, you would not be where you are," Boors said simply, shrugging. Elias seethed. If Boors knew even half of the times he'd made it this far purely on his wits when his luck and every other skill he possessed failed him...

"You're right. If I was at all clever I would not have come crawling back to you lot to give you a chance," he hissed. "I'd have left you all to sit under those hills without any hope until you died if I had any sense."

Boors laughed in his face, which surprised Elias so much he took a step back. Boors shook his head, giving him a contemptuous glance.

"Returning and managing to convince the queen not to behead you within the hour is the only clever thing you've done in your life, Brook. If I thought it meant you'd learned anything, I'd be less wary of you."

Elias's fists clenched. He dearly wished he had the guts to take a swing at Boors, but he'd seen the man's strength was not any sort of bluster, and he knew he would regret trying to wipe that look off his face. He'd beaten some very capable men with nothing but his hands and his wits, but Boors would not be one of them.

He was back at court, even here in "his world" as Amira had put it. This wasn't the pity he hated so much, it was just the more honest way of looking down on him that he'd learned to hate *before* he found out about pity.

*We need you, Brook, but we don't accept you. We never will. You're not our equal. You don't **belong** among us. But we'll tolerate you, while there's something in it for us. Isn't that generous enough?*

"You don't think I've learned anything," he repeated, keeping his voice even. "So that means I might do something as stupid as leading you all this way only to sell you out to a power-mad wreck of a man who can barely keep one province under control? I'm a pragmatist, Boors, not an idiot."

"Pragmatism. Is that how you describe letting cowardice guide your actions?" Boors asked. "Never thinking about anything but yourself at that particular moment?"

"*Everyone* acts for themselves. Call me a coward for protecting my life if you want to, but don't act like I'm the only one not thinking of the realm's health every waking moment," Elias snapped.

"You've been closer to the Royal Guard than most people ever have, and you still hold that belief?" Boors asked, sounding incredulous.

"I see nothing that challenges it," Elias shot back. "Look at you! Loyal to the queen and country, sure enough. But you're out here fighting for *yourself*. I saw you out there today. You love to fight. You probably live for the chance to use your strength on the queen's enemies." Elias sighed, shaking his head. "You think you're so selfless? This path simply is the one that gives you what you want, a chance to fight and be respected for it. If you weren't a Guard, you'd find some other battle. Defending your town, maybe, or even being a bandit or a soldier. You fight for your own satisfaction, Boors. Don't talk to me about acting for myself."

He'd been expecting some sort of spluttering denial, but Boors merely maintained his glare, arms crossed.

"Is that truly how you see the world? When a man takes up arms to defend his home, you think he does so merely for his own satisfaction?"

"Not everyone loves to fight like you do, Boors, I didn't say that," Elias said, glaring back. "But every man, living or dead, fights for themselves. You do it because you love battles, using all that strength to be a hero. Others do it out of ambition, or greed for a reward. Nearly all of them fight because they want to live, you and me included. Each man's reasoning is his own, but everyone in this world, *everyone*, acts in their own interest. Every man with a thought in his head will look to his own needs when the time comes. Don't you look down on me for that! You're not any different!"

Boors listened to Elias talk with a quiet intensity he had not previously shown. It was agitating Elias, and his voice rose slightly as he continued throwing words into the judgmental silence. When he fell quiet, Boors raised one hand, and Elias jumped back on instinct only to realize it wasn't even threatening a blow. Boors lowered it, seeming satisfied, and the look he gave Elias made him wish Boors had just punched him.

"Maybe you're right, Brook, though I don't believe you are. I have always believed my strength required a purpose, and I found it here. With my brothers and sisters, in my duty to the crown," he said quietly. "Perhaps I have come this far fighting for myself, as you are so quick to claim. But my love of battle has saved many that would otherwise have been left to the tyranny of evil men. My love of battle has led my friends to put their lives in my hands each time we draw steel, because they know I will not fail them. If I love playing hero, then I have played it well enough to spend five years of my life protecting my queen from those who would do her harm. If I am called upon to do so tomorrow, I will lay down my life for my friends and my liege, and face my creator with a clear conscience. If we are not so different, Brook, can you say the same for yourself?"

"I've made my mistakes, Boors, and my creator knows damn well I've been paying for them in my own way," Elias growled, shaking slightly. "It's easy to criticize when you've never had to doubt your path in life. I don't owe you an apology for the way I've lived, and if you're expecting one, you'll be disappointed."

"Of course. Why should you apologize when it's so simple to point at others?" Boors said, shaking his head. "Perhaps that's why you say the world is so full of selfish men. You stand out less that way."

"Don't you start with me, you pompous bastard!" Elias hissed, losing his temper and his fear in a moment and closing the distance with Boors. The conversation was beginning to be noticed at the campfire, but Elias was no longer aware of them as anger narrowed his vision until all he saw was Boors, looking down on him from on high. "I've dealt with you and your kind my entire life! All of you strutting peacocks from court looking down your damn noses at me! Thank the gods for you, Sir Boors. Without you I might have thought things would *change* when Amira is crowned." His fists itched, every remaining fiber of self-preservation Elias had was struggling to stop him from doing something, *anything*, to shove Boors from his high horse to the ground that very moment. "Nobles, Royal Guard, knights of the realm...I was never good enough for any of you pissants unless Morys needed something from me! You think I was a fool to turn my back on you lot when the time came? *I* think I was a fool to throw in with any of you in the first place! Don't talk like you know anything about my life. You don't, and you never will!"

"And you think you know anything of ours?" It should have been a bellow, Elias thought. It should have been a wave of hot air, Boors shouting. But it wasn't. It was cold, hard, and far more terrible than any roar. Each word was a metal fist punching out, measured and merciless. "What do you know of *any* of us, besides your resentment and your envy? What do *you* know of a life of service, when you turned on the one man in court who gave you a chance? *Five years, Elias Brook!*" The steel punches rained down harder and harder as Boors towered over Elias, anger shining like a primeval sun in his face and eyes. "Five years every man and woman sitting at that fire has served knowing in their hearts there would be no reward for their loyalty but a grave and a clear conscience! Five years we waited without hope for a sign it wasn't all for nothing, that our queen would have something more than this! What do *you* know, *coward*? What did *you* learn in those five years, *thief*, clinging to your life and stealing from the dead? What have *you* done, *traitor*, that you stand here among us and demand our respect now?"

"Boors!"

A third voice was like a bucket of ice water over both of them. The fury and the terror that had been roiling inside Elias's gut drained away and Boors's wrath broke as they turned, together.

Amira had come away from the campfire, without her armor, with Cecily hurrying behind her. For the first time Elias had seen, she looked scared...frightened and so very young...

"My lady..." Boors said quietly, seeming to forget Elias was there as he faced her. As much as he despised him, Elias had to admit he was like a different man.

"Leave him be, Boors," Amira said, trembling as she stepped closer. "Please...just let him be."

And the giant knelt, without hesitation, before a frightened young girl in her nightclothes and bowed his head.

"Forgive me, my lady," he said gravely. "If you wish it of me, it will be so."

Amira extended her hand, and Boors solemnly reached out to take it with gentleness Elias would not have expected from a man his size. Cecily remained behind as the two walked slowly back to the fire together. As Boors receded, Elias found it easy to breathe again.

"Are you all right?" Cecily asked, and surprisingly it even sounded like she meant it. Elias took a deep breath. He would never be able to know with certainty, but a part of him had been sure that without Amira, his argument in Boors would have ended in blood. *His* blood.

And yet it was a callous, nonchalant smile he gave Cecily, cocking his head a little.

"The big bastard's not quite as stupid as he looks. Who would have thought he could put that many words together in the right order?" he asked, chuckling lightly. "You lot aren't half the idiots I thought you must be to still be doing this after five years."

Some sympathy bled away in Cecily's eyes, and something in him was savagely pleased to see it go.

"You should come to the fire. It's going to be a cold night, and no one will trouble you after overhearing that," she tried.

"What, can't Blanche change the weather, or can she not do that when anyone else is looking?" Cecily did not deserve the acid in the question, but she was the only person listening. Elias could see from her expression that one had stung more than he'd intended.

"You shouldn't say things like that. Blanche is different. That doesn't mean she's your enemy."

"That doesn't make her my friend, either!" Elias could hear a voice urging him to shut up right now. At first he thought it was Mibotha, but even realizing it was his own couldn't seem to stop his mouth. "Not her, not Boors, not Amira, and not *you!*" Cecily took a step back, looking hurt. "I know why I'm here. And I know what you all think of me. Boors was just a big enough idiot to say it out loud while you all still need me." he spread his hands, laughing mirthlessly. "Well, you've got me, still! Coward, thief, traitor! And it's all yours to use as you'd like! I'll help you all the way to your damn crown, and maybe I'll even stick around for whatever plans you cook up once Amira's actually a queen! You don't need to worry about that! You don't need to be the one that has to be my friend!"

"I don't understand you." Most of the women Elias had known would probably be near tears, or started to get angry. Cecily was neither. Some of that had hurt, he could see that plainly, but she seemed to be bearing it as stoically as she could manage. "Not even a little. What do you *want*, Brook?"

I want Boors to know what it feels like scrabbling in a pit of mud and blood for five years knowing you'll starve if you don't. I want Blanche to be able to imagine what it's like hearing singers try to rhyme every line about every disaster that's happened in the last five years with your name and for people to consider beating you half to death in the street a restrained, merciful response to hearing who you are. I want you to stop looking at me like I'm some mangy, pathetic dog you nonetheless feel obligated to leave food out for. I want Amira to realize she doesn't know anything about anything and should never have left her comfortable hole in the ground. I want to be able to go through life without magic and spirits and the company of people who despise me. I want to leave you, Mibotha, and all of this a thousand miles behind me in the dust!

But out loud, he said, "I want to do this job and be left alone," and turned away. "I want the slate cleaned so I can be done with all of this for good."

She was tempted to say something, or hit him, he wasn't sure which, but he almost wanted her to. She did neither, and simply nodded curtly.

"Fair enough, Brook. Good night."

And with that, Brook was left by the tree, watching Cecily walk back to her seat at the fire without a backwards glance while he stood alone except for the shadow of Mibotha's disapproval looming over him.

...That was—

"Shut up." Something in Elias's voice struck even Mibotha silent, and Elias felt something akin to relief as the spirit's presence withdrew.

He was alone. For an evening, at least...

He was completely, utterly alone.

95

CHAPTER 14

Elias did not stand apart from the fire the entire cold night, but he made a spirited effort to do so. He only gave in when he started to lose feeling in his hands, and many of the Guard had fallen asleep. Those that were awake when he took a place by the flames paid him no mind.

There was conversation when they set out the following morning, but none of it involved him in any way. No one spoke to him. No one spoke about him. Nobody even *looked* at him, as far as he could tell. They just followed the route Mibotha pointed him on when the time came to start riding again.

Mibotha's presence had gradually stolen back into Elias's mind, dark clouds with lightning crackling inside them, but the spirit was blessedly quiet, merely offering certainty the path he was on was the right way still. Elias tried to enjoy the sullen silence, but it was a little too bitter for him to relax into it.

Two days of an eight-day journey down, he told himself. Probably half-way to their destination at this point before the return journey began. In the course of two nights, he had managed to re-affirm his hatred for every single person riding behind him, and those that might have been considering rethinking their views of him were almost certainly right back where they'd started. Boors might have hated him more than when they'd started, but he didn't notice any glaring or grumbling.

Let him be, Amira had said. And so they let him be. Just a sign to follow, not a person to acknowledge or hate. Hadn't that been what he wanted of them? To leave him alone and not bother him with their judgements or attempts to figure him out?

Boors had been in the wrong last night, he reminded himself. There would have been no argument if the big idiot hadn't opened his stupid mouth and let Elias come back on his own. It hadn't been Elias that had gone looking for a fight last night. He'd thrown the bastard's contempt back in his face, what was the matter with that? Nothing at all, he told himself. Coward he might be, but at least he wasn't a hypocrite or an elitist.

Thoughts like these had been extremely comforting to him over the years, but they didn't seem to be working today. Elias grumbled slightly, glaring down the road.

It would be stupid to lament any kind of rift between him and the Royal Guard. The less they wanted him around, the sooner he'd be free when they were done with him. He wasn't here to make friends, and they weren't out here because they cared a fig for him. He was using them to save his own skin, he reminded himself, and they were using him right now because it was of greater profit to them than killing him. There wasn't a relationship there to be salvaged or developed. He hadn't cared when the other groups he'd drifted with over his life had fallen apart, and he wasn't about to start caring *now*. There was nothing in it but pity and contempt, and he'd had enough of both to last him ten lifetimes. He'd see them safely to their destination and back, to please Mibotha and spite Boors, but beyond that they could all go hang as far as he was concerned.

Good arguments, he reflected. Who did he need to convince with them when not even Mibotha was talking to him?

He heaved a sigh of irritation, spurring his horse a little harder. Naturally, when everyone else finally shut up, he couldn't even have a pleasant conversation with himself. It seemed like there was no getting away from tiresome company these days.

It would seem last night's argument did not help our cause enormously.

"Shut up, Mibotha," Elias muttered, not in the mood to be moralized at. This was shaping up to be a bad enough week already.

Is that your answer for everything? Demanding to be left alone?

"Unless you have something helpful to say, I don't want to hear it."

...Very well. Elias was a little surprised Mibotha was willing to let it go instead of browbeating him, but he didn't question his good fortune to be spared another lecture. *The path will remain quite steady, but there may be trouble up ahead. One of Hache's armies won a costly victory earlier. Their return journey might bring them across our path. There's a lot more of them than the men the Guard defeated yesterday.*

"How far?"

I would anticipate coming upon them in half an hour's time, maybe a little more, if your paths cross.

Elias nodded, but he rode in silence a while longer. Mibotha informing him of danger up ahead was useful, but he'd have to be cautious in actually applying that information. It'd look very suspicious if he somehow became aware of a potential confrontation down the road from no evidence whatsoever. He'd need to be closer first before he warned his companions, at least close enough he could play it off as the good senses of a scout if the others couldn't see any evidence of incoming enemies. There wasn't enough trust in this group for him to seem too prescient, even if one of them *was* a mage.

Still, after fifteen minutes of riding, Elias got the break he wanted and held up his hand, bringing the company to a halt.

"What's going on, Brook? Why have we stopped?" Cecily asked, looking puzzled. Elias pointed, oddly glad to see the cloud of dust not far off which made proving his point a lot easier. Thank the gods the duke's armies were subtle as a caravan full of anvils. Unlike bandits, you always saw bands of soldiers from a long way off these days.

"We've got company coming to meet us up ahead," he pointed out. "I can't get a good view from here, but a little group like the one we fought yesterday isn't that easy to spot. Could get nasty if they see us."

"We might be able to simply outpace them," Boors suggested. "They're likely to be on foot, mostly, and forces that big are sluggish compared to our company. We might be able to ride hard and avoid crossing paths with them."

"I don't care for our chances of doing that and keeping the horses in good condition to keep going if they follow us," Blanche muttered. "They look like they've got the numbers to make any fight ugly, too. It seems like our best option is to go around them. Brook, any ideas?"

Elias was a little surprised that Blanche turned to him for suggestions, before realizing that the entire group must think he'd been this way before if he knew where the Regalia were hidden. Not wanting to hesitate too long, Elias started to think about his previous encounters with the armies during the years of war. A solution quickly presented itself, and Elias nodded confidently.

"Most soldiers these days stay very firmly set on established paths, from what I've seen," he explained. "The group of scavengers I fell in with was able to avoid ever being set upon by sticking to the trees. The soldiers have grown too superstitious to venture into the woods. A lot of the armies are afraid of spirits and whatever else might be living there. If we head into the woods and proceed that way, they'll stay on the road and never come near us."

"Are you sure of that? Men on foot might gain the advantage if we take a path through the trees. Our advantage of mobility will be gone if they don't behave as you expect," Blanche said, looking uncertain for once.

"That is true, but like you said our advantage of mobility isn't really going to help much in a chase, and we can't meet them head-on. I don't expect this lot to be that different than the armies I've gone around before. If you want my advice, that's it."

"...All right, Brook," Blanche sighed. She didn't seem happy with this option, but Elias could tell she was aware there weren't a lot of better ones available. "We'll do this your way. Everyone, proceed into the forest, and stay close together! We want to pass by that army without being noticed!"

Had the instructions come from Elias, he suspected there would have been much grumbling and reluctance, but from Blanche the words brought swift action. Soon enough, the open road had been left behind, and Elias now found himself leading the party through the thick, tangled woods along the side of the road, trying to keep out of sight.

The horses did not care for the change of path, but he had to admire how well the Royal Guard trained their mounts. After a moment of reluctance, the beasts trooped on obediently, making a much slower pace but not resisting the urging on. He felt oddly content as they made their way forward, branches and bushes crunching slightly under their hooves, but he wasn't sure why. He had hidden out in the forests before when he needed to, but he'd always felt most at home in towns with lots of places to climb and hide, not out in the wild. He realized it was bleeding over from Mibotha. While he'd normally just been aware when the spirit was angry or displeased with him, now its mood drifted through him carrying a deep-seated contentment.

I had feared the forests here would be crippled or burned, it said conversationally. Elias did not reply, aware the others were now sticking far too close for that. *It is good to see they still grow strong. With any luck, we will be successful and end these pointless wars before these woods feel their spite.*

Elias chose to file that under "very interesting". There was something odd in Mibotha's relief the woods had not been disturbed. Was Mibotha a woodland spirit, then? That would mean its natural home was likely in some giant stump back in the forest he'd died in. He might have just gotten a glimpse at what Mibotha was really after in all this, and the thought comforted him. Knowing what people want is like having power over them, if you're clever enough.

Still, the army began to become more and more visible and pressing as the group proceeded, and Elias gave them a worried look. They didn't seem to be anything special, but it was a big force. Routing them would not be a possibility unless half of them died of shock when the Royal Guard drew their swords, and outrunning them would be difficult and risky after taking to the woods for cover. If he'd been wrong, and the soldiers weren't afraid to come into the trees after them...

Wait, what was that?

Elias's breath caught in his throat, and he frantically scanned the oncoming army again, trying to confirm what he'd seen.

He didn't see it again, but that didn't give him much comfort. The army was an almost monotone mass of beat-up metal and the threadbare vermillion uniforms every fighting man sworn to Hache wore, faded after five years of constant battle. But for just a second, he'd thought he saw a spot of green among them, and there was only one person Elias knew of that would be among Hache's soldiers without wearing a uniform to match theirs.

Calm down, Elias, he told himself. You're in a forest, and leaves fall all the time under the trees. You might have been tricked by an insect, or some light, or a whole number of things. It might even just be his imagination providing what he dreaded to see.

Any of that. Not *him*. Not *now!*

"How far does this forest go, Brook?" Blanche asked quietly, glaring out at the army as they started to draw level with each other. If they were on the road, a fight would be imminent, but Elias was relieved to find the soldiers paid the trees and anything moving around in them no heed.

The forest will not follow the path we must much longer, but it should be sufficient to slip around these men unnoticed and proceed up the road again.

"Far enough," Elias supplied, shifting uncomfortably in his saddle. He didn't want to cause a panic, but...no. If there was even a chance he hadn't been seeing things, everyone needed to be on high alert. "We need to get around them quickly, and without being noticed. I think Oliver Bones is with them."

"What?" Blanche jerked around to look Elias in the eye, clearly understanding his distress. "Are you sure?"

"No, I'm not, and that's what worries me. That army is dangerous enough with just their weapons and numbers against our own, but Basilisk-Eye being with them means we're dead if they become aware of us. If he's there, that little glimpse I got was probably all the chance I had to confirm it. We need to proceed as if it's a sure thing he's there. Oliver Bones is a lot keener than your average soldier, and he's not afraid of going into the woods to get us." Elias shuddered; from what he'd heard, the forest had been a home to Oliver Bones as much it was to animals and spirits. He was quite sure Bones's famed ability to climb and move silently were not exaggerations, and these thickly growing trees would give him as fine a vantage point to attack them as the one he'd surely had the day Morys died.

"You're right. We can't take that risk. Lead on, Brook, as fast as you can. We'll increase the protection around the queen," Blanche muttered, fading back to rejoin Amira. Elias wondered vaguely if having a mage on their side would help balance out the other side having Oliver Bones. He certainly wasn't confident having him and Mibotha on their side would.

Running with the fear of attack crushing his chest was familiar territory to him, but not ground he'd wished to tread ever again. The ongoing struggle between speed and stealth, the inability to relax, or even swallow...Elias had great difficulty concentrating when his eyes darted ever upwards, and side to side, trying to spot death creeping towards them under a leathery green cloak. He would not have expected the Royal Guard to understand what he felt, but he could see similar feelings in their honest faces, mingled with concern for Amira's safety above their own. Amira, he was oddly pleased to see, finally seemed to understand being truly afraid. He hoped, if they lived through this, that she would remember in days to come how fear, not courage, muted their steps and quickened their pace. A queen needed to know you couldn't fight death, but you might be able to run and hide.

The woods broke far too early for Elias's liking, but the army was a ways behind them as they emerged quietly from the trees back onto the road. Far enough that the army was little more than a big reddish blob in the distance. No sudden attacks, no soldiers surging to meet them...they had avoided disaster today, and with night a few hours away, they could leave the soldiers far behind before they made camp and got ready for the fourth and hopefully final day before their return journey.

Just as he'd finished thinking this, however, five tired-looking soldiers walked out from behind a couple of large rocks on the other side of the road, and Elias's heart sank as the two groups stared at each other in momentary silent surprise.

Scouts. Of *course* they had scouts. In days like these, even a big army would often be harassed all the way back home by bandits in both victory and defeat. These five unlucky bastards had probably been ordered to check the road ahead, and probably another group was searching back the way Elias and his group had come. They'd been taking a breather behind the rocks, out of the wind, just as the Royal Guard had emerged.

Elias was the first to break the interminable moment of surprise by drawing back his bow and shooting the nearest soldier dead in one quick movement. The spell broken, another tried to shout an order or call for help but only managed to open his mouth before Elias's second arrow found his throat. The Royal Guard did not dither, surging forward immediately to silence the other three. Blanche decapitated one while another met an unfortunate end under Boors's mace. The fifth soldier managed to survive an ugly cut from his assailant, however, long enough to dig something out of his belt and hurl it into the sky. Elias took aim, trying to shoot it down, but the object burst apart before he could, releasing a shower of crimson sparks. While it was clear the sparks were harmless little lights, Elias paled as he realized they'd been unable to stop the fifth scout from signaling the army.

There was no way the army they'd evaded hadn't seen those lights, and other men in Hache's employ might have been alerted to their presence as well. Elias turned quickly to the others, seeing dawning comprehension on all their faces as well.

"*Ride,*" he shouted, realizing he was shaking. "Don't worry about pacing your horses, *ride!*"

Nobody in the group needed to be told twice, and Elias took off as fast as his horse could go, his companions not far behind him. He already imagined he could hear the boots of the duke's forces, closing in...

CHAPTER 15

Elias rode as though all the basilisks that had ever been were behind him, terror giving his horse wings. He'd never be able to keep this pace up, not without killing the horse, but he prayed to the gods that had never heard him before that he could keep it up long enough the soldiers would lose them.

The soldiers knew someone was here. If they were able to discover this was not routine bandit activity, then Hache and his wife would soon know an enemy was on their soil, and more men would be combing the countryside looking for them.

Worst of all, if Oliver Bones really was among the men chasing them now, then the danger in the forest they'd so narrowly avoided would catch up with them all too soon. One way or another, Elias realized, that scout had trapped them by holding on long enough to signal. Elias knew, bone-deep, that this mission would now bring him and the Royal Guard face-to-face with the duke's soldiers before all was done.

His horse served him better than the dozens Elias had stolen over the years. Its hooves ate up mile after mile long after he would have expected it to stop, but as the sun set, its pace slowed, then slowed again. Eventually, the horse had clearly had enough, and Elias knew the beast would die pointlessly if he pushed it to continue. The Royal Guard similarly were coming to a stop behind him. Their flight was over for the night unless they wanted to proceed on foot.

"Do you think we lost them?" Amira asked, not sounding very hopeful.

"We were able to outpace them, but I don't think we've left them behind," Cecily said grimly. "That's a big force, mostly on foot, and we had a good head start. But they're persistent, and we know they have scouts. It could be some time, even by forced marches, before they're close enough to bring their whole might to bear on us, but scouts...mounted troops...that army might have some that are fleet enough to catch up to us in the night while the rest of the army follows at a distance. If they slow our flight down, or attack us often enough to tire us too much to fight or flee, they've got us. They'll know that. This can't be the first time they've chased enemies with a head start."

"Cecily's right...but they still don't know exactly what they're up against," Blanche said, dismounting. "They're going to be expecting bandits...opportunists, not a huge threat worth wasting men on. We might still be able to give them the slip if they don't catch wind of who we are and why we're here."

"Hache is not famous for his concern with spending his men's lives meaningfully," Elias warned, hopping to the ground and stretching his legs. "These men are in his army because they're the only idiots he could bribe, bully, or talk into throwing themselves at another lord's legion of sorry bastards. They may well have been through enough pointless slaughters that they'll actually dedicate themselves to hunting us down and killing us even without any idea who we are or what we're after."

"If they do, is there any hope? We can't fight an army that big," one of the Royal Guard said, frowning. "We don't have reinforcements coming, but they might."

"If they keep sending advance units out to try and catch up to us while the main body is in pursuit, they'll be breaking their forces into much more manageable numbers," Cecily suggested. "We can take out their scouts and cavalry easily enough as they catch up to us. They can't lose too many units before they catch up to us with numbers we can overcome."

"I wouldn't count on them fighting like that," Elias sighed. "We're going to have to cut down anyone that comes after us but hope we can use that big, clumsy army's slowness against it. Hit the shrine, get the Regalia, and go around them. Make for the border and get out of this territory while they're chasing our tail. Bloody their noses, yes, hit them when they're vulnerable and fade way. Fight them head on? No. Most of that force will probably be standing when we get out of here, but that won't matter."

"Hache will be sending everything he has against us once Queen Amira is revealed to the land," Boors suggested. "We might have to fight that army one way or the other."

"You'll have *castles* then, which is more than a lot of your enemies can say at this point. I don't think I need to explain the difference between that legion trying to attack you at your stronghold, where you have lots of supplies and the high ground, and them catching us out here, do I?" Elias sighed. "Listen, I know you lot are big about fighting the good fight, but courage isn't going to get us through this. Picking our battles, focusing on the objective, and escaping while the chance is there is."

"Brook has a point, Boors. We don't have the luxury of risking open combat here in Hache's territory, but after we regroup it will be a different story," Blanche agreed, her face grim. "But any enemies we *do* stand our ground against will not be there when the time comes to fight the duke's armies in earnest."

"I understand," Boors sighed, crossing his arms. "Then shall we dig in and await any uninvited guests following us?"

"Precisely. All of you, get ready to make camp and fight here if anyone catches up to us. Brook, Cecily, come with me," Blanche instructed.

Elias was a little surprised, but he followed the two ladies as the Royal Guard made their preparations near large stones by the roadside.

"What's the plan, Blanche?" Cecily asked, sticking close to her friend. Blanche frowned, bringing out a large black bag Elias had seen on her saddle a couple times.

"I don't know that we've got long enough to make any elaborate measures for our incoming guests, but we should have long enough to seed the road for their coming," Blanche said, opening the bag and drawing out something small. It took Elias a minute to get a good look at it in the fading light.

A caltrop. Four wicked little spikes, arranged so one always pointed skywards. This one was bigger than most that Elias had come across, with a slight barb on each spike. It had been painted, too. It wouldn't glitter in whatever light was available. Elias suppressed a shudder. He remembered how dangerous it was to travel down roads that had been "prepared" by soldiers for unfriendly cavalry. He'd never gotten one of those things in his foot, for which he was profoundly grateful, but he'd known people that had, and he'd lost more than one stolen horse to caltrops from a long-forgotten battle.

These ones would be nearly invisible in the dark of the night, and those barbs meant nothing good for the poor bastard who wasn't wearing boots strong enough to keep it from piercing his foot. Elias had heard of warlords leaving entire cities alone rather than risking their precious cavalry against a field of caltrops. It was the last weapon he was expecting a Royal Guard to employ against their enemies.

"The armory of righteousness has changed a little since I lived at the castle."

"Shut up," Blanche said bluntly, handing him the bag, "and help me scatter these."

"You know it's not good tactics to use too many of these on roads we might need to go back over, right?" Elias asked, although he did as he was told. He might have felt guilty scattering spiked, hard-to-see death all over the road if he didn't know most of that death belonged to people who intended to run them down and kill them.

"We've got a ways to go to reach our destination and may be taking a very different way out," Blanche said shrugging. "The people who are most likely to be using this road in the near future are the men chasing us, and anything that slows their advance gives us more time to do what we came here to do and escape before they can catch up."

Elias nodded, joining Cecily and Blanche in getting a large, dangerous stretch of the land seeded with caltrops before leaving the rest in the black bag and stepping back. It was almost night, and Elias would not willingly go anywhere near the place they'd been working again. He'd already lost sight of the metal points awaiting anyone that tried to follow their trail in the night. The duke's soldiers tended to be a straightforward lot, from what he'd observed waiting to scavenge from the battlefields. It was probably going to kill a lot of them before this was done, and if anyone caught up to them tonight, he suspected they would not remain quiet enough to sneak up on the camp if their path took them over this spot.

"Do you have anything else we can leave for them? Maybe magic up something to trap them with?" he asked, glancing at Blanche. Surprisingly, Blanche gave him a look of profound irritation, and Elias flinched away in spite of himself. Fortunately, Blanche just sighed and shook her head.

"You should know this if we're going to work together, Brook. I don't 'magic something up.' You have seen the sum total of what I can do, and I don't feel like discussing it with you." Blanche looked over her shoulder. "I don't know about their tracking skill, but we were going for speed, not subtlety. I'd be very surprised if we went the whole night without being attacked. Best get ready to fight, Brook."

With that, she headed right back to camp at a quick pace, leaving Elias coming behind with Cecily. Elias avoided looking at her. Now that night was falling, he was reminded it had been only a day since he'd shouted at her, and from how quiet she'd been, he was quite sure she remembered it, too. He didn't regret what he'd said the previous night, but he did start to hope alienating all of the Royal Guard all over again wasn't going to come back to bite him while they were on the run. They'd let bygones be bygones while he was still cooperating with their mission to get the Regalia back, wouldn't they?

"There are some things you shouldn't talk about with Blanche, Brook," she said before they were quite back to the camp, looking at him. There wasn't any rancor in her tone, but any hint of friendliness she might once have had addressing him was long gone. "She didn't *ask* to be born like that, and whatever power it's given her has also brought her a great deal of pain and suspicion she didn't deserve. She's gotten this far in *spite* of that power, not because of it, and you will make an enemy of her eventually if you don't let it go."

"It was just a *question*," Elias grumbled defensively. "I'm not sure someone who gets angered by something that minor should have the power to conjure fire, if I'm honest."

"Neither is she," Cecily said bluntly, before increasing her pace and letting Elias make his way to the camp alone.

Well, at least he knew for sure where Cecily would stand if he *did* end up becoming enemies with Blanche, not that it was an enormous surprise. All of them were likely to band together against him if their uneasy alliance fell apart. Maybe he should be glad they had a common enemy to keep them occupied for the time being...

There wasn't any campfire, and the Royal Guard were all alert and ready to fight. Elias prepared his bow and went to crouch in the shadow of a rock. While checking his supply of arrows, his other hand went down to check that his newly-acquired daggers were close to hand. It was a good feeling to have a blade on him, even if he preferred any fighting he did to be at range. It meant he wasn't in as much trouble if someone got close to him this time.

Mibotha stirred, and even though it was invisible, Elias found himself imagining it as some great beast, sniffing the air.

An attack will come tonight. We don't need to wait long.

Elias let out a slow breath.

"Can you tell who's coming?" he whispered, one figure looming in his mind.

The human you call "Bones" is not with the men approaching us. If he is here, he is keeping a distance beyond my immediate awareness.

"Is your immediate awareness shorter or longer than a good bow-shot?"

Longer.

Oh, finally, some good news, Elias thought, feeling oddly cheered despite the approaching attack setting his stomach churning. They were going to be beset in the night by soldiers, but at least the terrors that weighed most heavily on his mind would not be ones he had to confront this night.

Maybe, just maybe, the bone-deep feeling was wrong. If he was very, very lucky, Oliver Bones did not feature in his future at all.

Just lots and lots of other well-armed killers.

CHAPTER 16

It didn't take too long for a horse's scream to alert Elias that they were no longer awaiting their unwelcome guests.

Ducking out from behind the rocks revealed a scene of rising pandemonium. There were a *lot* more men on horseback than Elias had anticipated, perhaps thirty or forty at a glance, but so many of them had run into the trap he and Blanche had set that it was only serving to increase the size of the resulting panic. Horses trod on the caltrops left and right, screaming, bucking, and losing whatever control their riders had as the ground attacked their every step with merciless, clinging barbs. Several horses were lamed already. One particularly unlucky bastard had his horse fall over on its side in its panic, crushing him. His screams didn't go on very long, but they drowned out every other horrible sound in Elias's mind for quite long enough.

The horses that had not already stepped on the deadly ground were wheeling around madly, their riders bewildered by the men before them suddenly falling into a panic and avoiding flailing hooves. It was not a force ready to charge. Or to defend themselves.

Blanche's sword caught the moonlight in a signal that was hard for the Royal Guard to miss, and Elias drew back his bow and added his first arrow to a small, deadly volley that fell on the riders mercilessly.

The unfortunate souls that had entered the caltrop trap died almost to a man when the arrows fell, but there were still enough of them to try and rally rather than be slaughtered at a distance. Someone in the back took charge, and Elias was surprised how quickly the remaining soldiers were able to organize enough to charge over the bodies of their fallen now blunting the spikes. Underestimating the size of the trap still cost the five men and horses leading the charge their lives, but the remainder managed to clear the trap on a narrow bridge of the fallen. Many more than Elias had expected. Perhaps he'd miscounted earlier, but the force closing on them still outnumbered them after taking some terrible losses in the first few minutes.

The second volley scythed down the first rank again. Ten more riders were gone in a sigh of bows, and Elias fitted another arrow to kill the man behind his first target. Surprisingly, Boors rose up next to Elias, armed not with a bow but a short spear. With a low growl, Boors heaved it at the charging riders, striking a man in a fine hat with such force he was launched out of his saddle before he struck the ground.

The survivors were now nearly at the camp, and then and only then did the Royal Guard who had remained on horseback ride out to meet them. Swords clashed as the two forces finally came together in a fierce melee. Elias remained on his high vantage point, taking shots where he could but unsure of the impact he was having. Others, however, darted into the battle on foot. Elias was astonished to see Boors go up against a man on horseback, wielding a saber. The man was leaning back, getting ready to slice down, but Boors's mace took the horse in the side of the head. Elias hoped for the poor animal's sake that it died instantly, but the force of the blow caused it to stagger, then sag sideways. The saber slice missed Boors entirely, and the rider gave a wail of alarm as his mount collapsed, trapping him under it. Boors stepped forward and put an end to the fight with a single downward stroke.

Nobody shouted any orders this time. Elias suspected the man Boors had speared had been the officer who had come up with riding over the dead to get this far. Without a leader to rally them, a few more minutes of intense fighting saw the enemy division routed, the Royal Guards bloodied but still alive.

"Well...we made it..." Elias muttered, surveying the carnage uneasily. He'd combed over enough battlefields not to be sickened by the sight of them, but he was troubled to consider that so many men had been thrown at them for one attack in the night. They hadn't been expecting a foe significantly better-trained than themselves, but still...

That force was the one meant to find you and kill you if it seemed practical. There are men on foot not far behind them, and that fight made enough noise for them to know something is wrong. We haven't won the night yet.

"Another force? They certainly didn't dilly-dally..." Elias muttered.

Never underestimating an enemy makes Hache think himself clever, from what I understand. In practice, it means his armies have flung great

*numbers into the unknown time and time again in the name of "caution".
You've seen the outcome of that when they don't understand exactly what
they're charging at in your time going over the battlefields.*

"Vermillion Field, they're starting to call it now," Elias muttered,
starting to feel ill. He hoped he never saw that many corpses again in his
life. "They said the tidings were what caused Hache to crack."

Do you believe that?

"No, I believe he was always cracked. But the field didn't help any,"
Elias muttered. "I was amazed his own men didn't revolt when they heard
what happened. Morys himself wouldn't have been able to keep down a
mutiny if that had happened on his watch."

*Most of Hache's finest officers died because of that massacre. Not all of
them were present for it,* Mibotha said darkly, and Elias wondered how it
knew that. *It is a very dangerous mix of method and madness that is now
guiding the army chasing you. Do not let it catch you by surprise.*

"Right," Elias muttered, watching the road.

If Hache had just been *stupid*, that would have been one thing. Stupid,
cruel men had risen and fallen very rapidly in the last five years. But the
duke…he had been enough of a fool that his attempts to take control of
Yivyn had reduced him from one of the most powerful men in the
country to a wreck of a warlord scrabbling to hold onto whatever
territory he could with his waning army, yet clever, determined, or lucky
enough he'd outlasted many of his enemies. If new rivals didn't keep on
rising up as his old ones fell, he might have become king by virtue of
somehow surviving the losses his armies took. Privately, Elias suspected
the duchess was the only reason her husband's head wasn't long-since
rotted on a pike somewhere. Unfortunately, that meant there was still
someone that could think clearly ruling this land. Getting rid of Hache
might be a bad thing if his wife did not go immediately before him.

"There might be more coming," he called down to Blanche. Blanche
looked up at him, surprised.

"More? I wouldn't be surprised if they exhausted most of their
horsemen just now trying to catch and finish us quickly."

"I don't know about more horsemen, but I've seen the duke's way of
doing things. Unless his military strategy has changed lately, we're likely
to see a second wave before the night is done," Elias said, hoping Blanche
wouldn't ask too many questions.

She was tempted to, he could see quite plainly, but something in his
voice thankfully caused her to drop the matter. She nodded instead.

"Best to be cautious. It's possible they have scouts behind this unit to reinforce them. I don't think they expected something like *this* to befall them on the first night of the chase," she sighed, going to give orders to her comrades.

The living horses were rounded up. Their fate would be decided when morning came, but the dead were left where they had fallen. After being ridden over by their comrades, the bodies left in the caltrop trap no longer presented an appealing bridge for anyone following them. Elias was certain a number of the wicked barbs remained undisturbed and hidden. Soldiers advancing on a scene like this were likely to watch their step, but Elias imagined that little spot he'd seeded had not seen its last corpses yet.

It took some time, but when the Royal Guard was hidden again, Elias saw the soldiers beginning to make their way up the road, moving as quietly as they could. Again, there were far more than he'd have expected so soon, but after seeing how the Royal Guard fought, he was also aware that the numbers might not mean as much as they seemed.

He did dislike what this implied about their escalation, though. If he and the Royal Guard had killed this many in one night, how many would be sent to catch up to them tomorrow? Elias was aware the Royal Guard were all quite a bit stronger than any of the soldiers Hache had left, as the previous battles had demonstrated, but the duke's army had them massively outmatched as far as the capacity to take losses was concerned, and numbers and weariness could make all the difference in the end.

Hache wasn't much of a strategist, and his men were not the finest fighters in the land, but if they'd gotten good at one thing these last five years, it was winning by attrition.

Blanche made a few quiet signals from her hiding place, but it was clear the oncoming soldiers were not to be caught as unaware as the horsemen that had come before them. The dead were still clearly visible, and the sight of them lying there with the enemy hidden from view did not inspire courage in the hearts of the soldiers. Elias could see their pace falter from here, before timidly resuming as they crept forward.

These men hadn't had the luxury of horses to track a very fast-moving mounted force. They were probably all the way out here, this far ahead of the main force, by virtue of forced march if Elias was any judge. They were weary, they were uncertain what they'd be up against, and now they were frightened. They'd been expecting to come reinforce the mounted troops that outpaced them, but instead a field of their own dead greeted them. Something had gone very wrong, they were aware, and

Elias could see the soldiers struggling with their orders to advance versus the evidence doing so would invite their deaths as well.

Tired, nervous, reluctant soldiers never had good morale, and they weren't aware the enemy was so close yet. On the other hand, they still had a lot of numbers on the Royal Guard, and Elias's companions were not exactly daisy-fresh with such a small pause after their last battle. Elias could envision things going very badly if they rallied properly, if they had good orders, if they were desperate enough to live that they fought with the savage strength he knew only the terrified could find. It could be disastrous, even if the Royal Guard won.

On the other hand, Elias had seen few fighting men less eager to fight in his life, and that was including himself. If the Royal Guard gave them hell, these men would not rally properly. They'd break, and then they'd run, probably trying to return to their homes rather than to whatever punishment awaited cowardice in battle. Elias had been in battle long enough to know that the so-called strength of despair wasn't much to write home about compared to the feats a man could accomplish with a sliver of hope to desperately cling to and a lot of fear in his heart. If these men were hit hard enough, Elias reckoned they would take their chances that running would save them instead of fighting.

This is the only body of soldiers looking for us within the scope of my senses, Mibotha informed him. *Defeat them here, and we will have a sizable head start on that army. Any following advance troops will have to run that much farther just to catch sight of us.*

Elias nodded, waiting. The advance towards the killing ground where the remains of horses and men had been trampled into the dirt was particularly reluctant, but it was continuing. That would be the place to strike, after the men found the ground before them had unpleasant surprises hidden in it. Make going forward seem like suicide. Elias was certain Blanche was thinking along the same lines, so he watched the unlucky men forced to march at the killing ground intently.

The soldiers were probably quite tough men in their own way, but there are some things even a rough life doesn't prepare you for, and a barbed metal spike punching through your boot's flimsy bottom to stab into your foot is one of them. Elias saw the line ripple as dozens jumped in unison in response to the first bloodcurdling shriek. A man fell down, holding his leg and crying out loud enough that his companions were sure to realize stealth was rapidly fading as an option. More ruthless men might have killed the stricken soldier to try and keep the quiet, but these men had not been expecting the sort of battle that required them to be that ruthless, and it was confusion and not calculation that was set off.

Another man, stepping over to help, trod on another caltrop and soon joined the first man on the ground.

Now there was real panic starting to grow in the ranks. No shots had been fired, no magical glyph had ignited, but the soldiers recognized danger before them all the same. Those ignorant of caltrops in battle were likely scared on account of their confusion. No trap glistened obviously on the ground, but something unseen and certainly very painful had befallen two men, and might befall anyone that went near them. Those aware of the trap's nature were scared because of experience. For all they could tell, the road and the fields around it had been seeded very throughly with unforgiving spikes meant to lame horses. A man who stepped on one of them was going to find walking very difficult, let alone charging, or more importantly, running away if things got bad.

The advance halted, and Elias could hear, vaguely, a lot of shouting. The way forward was clearly in debate now. Every step past the men who had fallen seemed dangerous, and the enemy wasn't even in sight, but none of the soldiers liked their chances of being treated kindly if they were still standing there when the rest of the army caught up.

Elias knelt there, body full of tension, as timid attempts to calculate the size of the trap began. Ten more men fell victim to Blanche's trap, one of them unfortunate enough to fall forward when a spike pierced his heel. Elias tried not to look at him as he writhed for a time, his comrades too scared to go help him. Eventually, however, two men on either side of the trap seemed to find their path clear.

The relief was palpable among the soldiers as they quickly flowed around the trap. What little compassion Elias might have felt towards them evaporated as he saw they left the wounded where they were, even as the one who had fallen onto other spikes called out to them. They'd gained some hope now, but he was going to take it away from them. Back to fear. Back to uncertainty. One step closer to breaking and running away like anyone with sense would on this godless night.

The first man to feel certain that he was past the danger of the trap raised his spear happily and grinned at the others. Elias's arrow took him in the chest so suddenly the man probably died without ever realizing he was still in danger.

The others seemed to get the message when the Royal Guard opened fire on them from concealment, shattering the momentary relief they'd felt. The soldiers flowed together again, but to Elias's disappointment, someone did manage to call out.

"Don't retreat! Don't retreat! CHARGE!"

It wasn't a well-disciplined order, but at the moment it seemed they would have to deal with the soldiers' alarm forcing them to run forward instead of away. They had probably realized the arrows had come from the rocks. It wasn't like there was anywhere else a force of archers would be able to hide in the area.

"Here they come," he muttered under his breath, joining the other Royal Guard in firing at will into the oncoming soldiers. He was aware somewhere behind him a few of the Royal Guard were hanging back to ensure Amira's safety, but he imagined soon most of them would abandon archery to meet the foe head-on.

His prediction was correct. While the charge started from a long enough distance that two more volleys intercepted the men in front, the Royal Guard rode out with their weapons drawn not long after to counter the oncoming soldiers with a charge of their own. Elias, however, stayed where he was, firing one shot after another.

This was the biggest force they had yet come up against in battle, and it was beginning to show. Despite the soldiers being outmatched and shaken, their numbers were not making it easy for the Royal Guard to hurl them back, even with men like Boors laying waste to every man in reach of their weapon's arc. Despite a heroic effort, they weren't halting the advance, just slowing it...Elias realized his position wasn't going to remain safe very long, and he fired desperately at the soldiers.

"Break," he whispered with each arrow he fired. "Break, break, break, *break*! Run, dammit!"

These men weren't quite the sensible cowards he'd been hoping for. Maybe the thought of a battle turning into a slaughter they'd win by dint of starting with more men was so familiar it didn't occur to them to turn and run, or maybe the small amount of defenders gave them hope they'd win this battle if they held firm. Whatever the cause, they weren't giving up now, and the chances of them panicking enough to flee decreased the longer the melee continued.

And then he was out of arrows, and the enemy was too close to ignore. Half of them were dead already, but Elias was aware his time of shooting safely in hopes they'd give up was over.

"Damn it all..." he muttered, drawing his daggers. He felt like he should be shaking, but his hands knew well enough to be steady even though he felt anything but.

Closer...closer...closer...*now*.

Perhaps it was good it was a particularly dark night, or that he'd been quite still after loosing his arrows. The enemy did not realize Elias was more than a shadow on one of the bigger rocks before he leapt into their midst, bearing one swordsman to the ground with the dagger already in his throat. One turned faster than the others to try and stab his spear into Elias, but Elias was turning as well, and his foot managed to trip the man up before one of the daggers flashed out, punching into his belly twice. The soldier fell, and did not rise.

A spear blade grazed his shoulder, but not enough to slow him as Elias whirled around, bringing his other blade into his attacker's face. There was a brief, strangled cry, but Elias knew the man was already well on his way to the afterlife when he pushed him onto the man next to him, knocking both of them down long enough for Elias to find his throat and stomp down, once, twice, three times. A man with an axe came at Elias, but he kicked out from the third and final stomp to hit the man's kneecap as hard as he could. There was some pain from striking light armor, but the man stumbled, and the back of his neck was exposed for far too long for him to regain his balance before the dagger came down.

The battle seemed to blur together for Elias. He stabbed and slashed with his daggers, and kicked, stomped, and tackled as he felt he had to. He was vaguely aware he was hurt, that he wasn't dodging every thrust or slash, but either focus on the fight or Mibotha's interference meant the fact he was bleeding did not somehow seem relevant as he kept fighting.

Still, he stumbled back to avoid a spear point, only to come up against a hard, immovable barrier as he tried to avoid his opponent's pursuit. Turning sharply, he and Boors narrowly avoided taking a swing at one another. The Royal Guard was bloodied, but not slowing down at all. Recognition alone saved Elias's life as Boors stepped past him and smashed the spearman flat with a single blow while Elias darted to take down a soldier trying to attack Boors from behind, knocking him to the ground and cutting his throat.

So much blood...so many enemies...it had been a big force that had come for them in the night, but it seemed like there was no end to them here on the ground. Elias dodged a clumsy axe strike and buried his dagger deep in its wielder's armpit, but he didn't know how much longer he could go...

And then, all at once, it seemed quiet. Elias looked up in surprise to realize the only movement that disturbed the night now was a few survivors running away into the dark as the Royal Guard, wounded but mostly accounted for, regrouped not far away. Elias staggered over to join them, wincing; *gods*, he hurt. He hoped Mibotha could do something about all that.

Blanche, looking more tired than Elias had ever seen her and with blood smeared across her forehead and breastplate, counted them, her face falling.

"Only twelve of us left..." she murmured, looking crushed. Elias was privately surprised that many of them had survived, but he could see from the expressions of the others that looking on the bright side was not going to earn him any friends tonight.

"I think that will be the last of them," he said, trying a different track to add some good news to the gathering. "I'm honestly amazed they sent this many men to try and catch us right away."

"Against bandits, that measure would probably have resolved this in a single night. As it is, the rest of them will be that much fewer if they catch up to us," Blanche sighed. "Still, a smaller army will move faster. We'll need to hope winning here means we have more time than they realize to find the shrine and get out of here."

Elias nodded. For once, he liked the sound of what Blanche had to say. Blanche clapped her hands once, looking at her assembled companions.

"We have triumphed for tonight. Everybody take a rest, and we'll head out at dawn. We need to try and stay fresh," she said wearily. Elias nodded, heading back to the campsite, but he saw several Royal Guard, their armor undamaged, come past him in the opposite direction, carrying shovels. He glanced over his shoulder, seeing Blanche take one and walk slowly towards the nearest fallen Guard. For just a moment, Elias thought Blanche looked like she might cry. He looked away quickly.

He did not return to the camp alone, but he was surprised to find the one who walked at his pace back was Boors this time. Elias tried to ignore him, but Boors spoke.

"Cecily described how you fought, that night at the town," he said slowly, seeming to consider his words carefully as he laid them out. "It wasn't like anything she'd seen before, she said, and she's seen a great many ways of fighting. She described you like an angry dog, or a wolverine in a rage." Boors glanced down at Elias. "I didn't believe her."

"I wish I could say that surprises me," Elias said, a bit wrong-footed by the unexpected topic of the conversation but trying to end it as quickly and civilly as he could. He needed another argument with Boors like he needed a hole in the head, and forgetting that might get him just such a hole if he wasn't careful.

"I thought she might be exaggerating, since she knew we had to work together for this to succeed. But now, it doesn't seem so." Boors glanced at

Elias again. "I've never seen anyone fight like you, but it did the job. That was well done."

And with that, Boors seemed to bow out of the conversation, leaving Elias behind and unsure what to think of what had transpired.

Elias decided he was much too tired and banged-up to care and made his way to his own part of the camp, sitting down with a sigh. He looked out at the battlefield he'd left behind, seeing the bodies stretched out and the Royal Guard that had stayed safe and fresh protecting Amira collecting arrows for the following day.

He'd gone through more battlefields than he cared to remember, but he didn't recall ever leaving one behind like this. Battlegrounds were places you picked through, shook a few times, to see if anything valuable fell out. They weren't supposed to be like...this. You weren't supposed to look back at one and feel like a part of all that death *belonged* to you.

He'd killed people before. In fact, he would reluctantly concede that from the perspective of the average man, he had killed a lot of people. But Elias had reminded himself every day for years he had never, ever killed someone who wasn't trying to kill him first. These men were just the same as that, but...it felt different. Elias had told himself, over and over, he wasn't a killer. He wasn't a soldier. It was always them or him. This time there were just so many that he was responsible for it made him feel like he was going to vomit. Did the Royal Guard deal with this all the time? How could they stand it if they did?

No, he thought, shaking his head, he didn't want to know. He needed to sleep and hope he could make sense of it in the morning.

"Mibotha?" he asked quietly, lying down and turning his back on the battlefield.

Yes?

"If enemies enter your perception...no matter who or what they are, or what's going on...I want to know immediately."

...I can do that.

Elias closed his eyes, relaxing a little. At least while his partnership with Mibotha lasted, they wouldn't catch him by surprise.

Knowing what was coming might be the only thing that saved their lives if tonight's heroics brought Oliver Bones down on their heads.

CHAPTER 17

Dawn came much faster than Elias would have preferred, wrenching him from unusually troubled dreams straight to making preparations to ride like there was no tomorrow. Still, he was strangely comforted the atmosphere seemed a little different. The battle last night had given a lot of the hostility from the previous two days, including his own, a vent. A common enemy might be what was needed to keep their little band running smoothly.

Mibotha was not aware of any enemies on their trail, which meant the enemy was quite out of sight if not nearly out of mind enough for his tastes. Still, it was a relief to have Mibotha fill his mind only with knowledge of the path ahead instead of enemies behind.

Maybe the battle last night had been the only real consequence of their earlier mistake. They'd needed to stand and fight, but that big army had more than a bloody nose from losing that many men in one skirmish, and now the Royal Guard had a long head start on them. Plenty of space for speed, stealth, and cunning to carry the day and deliver the party to their destination and then safely home.

Elias began to understand why so many bloody people were optimists even in times like these, he thought to himself as they began riding, fast. It must be quite a pleasant life to go through your day without waiting for the other shoe to drop. He could see why it'd take more than common sense to overturn such a comfortable worldview.

Elias was not an optimist, however, so he reminded himself that celebrating now was not the action of a clever man. They were close to the shrine, but they weren't there yet, and the world had never been more resourceful in finding something new to hurl at him than the moments that he believed he had it all figured out. But...if he stayed smart, and he didn't lose his well-honed caution just because, for once in his life, he could see a genuine victory, they might pull this off. Elias Brook, coward, thief, and general ne'er-do-well, would be the one directly responsible for the rightful queen reclaiming her birthright.

Maybe *that* would get the damn bards off of his back, even if Mibotha was able to cook up something else to keep him hopping around doing good a while longer. That was the important thing. It was working. If he kept his head long enough to put a crown on Amira's, things might finally get better for him.

The notion that freedom from his quest for redemption and the hatred of his enemies might be only a day's ride away seemed to flow from Elias into his horse. His mount seemed to recover much of the spirit it had lost the previous day, carrying him faster and faster. For just a moment, Elias felt like he could leave everything behind.

It ended quickly as he saw the Royal Guard urge their horses after him at a similar pace. He wasn't done with this yet, he reminded himself. First, he'd have to hold up on his obligation to bring this unusual partnership to a close. If Mibotha let him disentangle himself from the Royal Guard after that, wonderful.

If he still needed to convince them they needed him...well, it wasn't ideal, but he'd already gotten farther making himself useful to people he'd counted his worst enemies than he'd imagined possible. He might be able to tolerate Amira and her entourage a while longer, if Mibotha required it of him. At the very least, he hoped crowning Amira would make them square. No more lectures, no more scorn or pity. That alone might make further time in their company bearable.

We've made better time than I expected. The shrine we're seeking isn't that far ahead. We should be able to reach it by mid-day. Mibotha informed him. Elias couldn't help but grin and look over his shoulder at Amira, her face set in a sort of nervous exhilaration as she tried to match his speed on her own stallion.

"We're getting close!" he called back, and he saw hope brighten the expressions behind him before he returned his attention to the road. The Royal Guard were a stoic bunch, usually, but he'd given them perhaps the best news they'd gotten in five years. They weren't his friends, Elias reminded himself, but he believed they were no longer his enemies, and their gratitude might be a resource worth cultivating in the brighter future he envisioned.

While his excitement at success being so close made him a little impatient, Elias willed himself to be calm as they ate up the miles. Before long, he could see the shrine ahead, growing bigger as they came closer and closer to it.

After so long thinking of this place as the destination of his quest, Elias had to admit that the shrine itself was something of a disappointment. He'd expected something...grander. Something that hinted, even subtly, that there was something important hidden there. Although he was aware a shrine that implied it was hiding something of value would not likely have kept it long, he still felt actually seeing it after all this time was a bit of an anticlimax.

No rich, well-decorated home to wandering gods, this. It was only a *building* because Elias was inclined to be generous to it and not call it a *heap*. It had been a lot bigger, once, but it must have been in decline for more than five years, looking at it. All Elias saw now was weather-beaten stone, scarred by wind and rain, in a shape vaguely resembling two intertwined olive trees growing out of an altar. Of this, the altar was nearly all that had endured, the two stone "branches" that had once entwined above it were broken down to two stubby pillars above the altar with a lot of rubble around it. Elias wondered, looking at it, if it had belonged to any god in particular. He noticed Mibotha did not seem elated to be here, like he expected. In the back of his mind, he could feel a strange melancholy from it as it observed the shrine through his eyes.

"*This* is the place?" one of the Royal Guard asked, sounding incredulous. Elias had to admit, it did seem somehow wrong that the most important treasures of the royal family were entombed somewhere like this.

There is no doubt. This is it. Mibotha's answer was distant and terse. It didn't want to speak, but there was no arguing with the certainty in its voice. *Approach it.*

Elias, not sure exactly what Mibotha had in mind, tried to give the appearance he knew what he was doing as he got down from his horse, walking over to the altar. Was it hidden *inside* the altar? It seemed almost too small for that...

Your ability to get into places, even secret places, is well-known. Put it to use. Mibotha said impatiently, and Elias felt his arm tingle.

So, Mibotha even knew about that? Elias would have to admit, if asked, that most of the claims he had a way with secret doors that were hard to find were erroneous. Just rumors attached to times he'd found easier windows or holes to get inside somewhere.

That did not, however, mean *all* of the stories about his knack with hidden doors were fake.

Elias started scanning the surface of the shrine. There was always a tell, with these doors. Something that was there that didn't seem to have a reason to be. Sometimes he'd thought there were doors that didn't give anything away, and sometimes there were things he'd been sure were tells that proved meaningless, but every secret door he'd ever opened had something he could spot to give him access.

This was usually long, detail-intensive work that Elias liked to have a lot of time for. Mibotha's impatience, however, was telling him he wasn't going to get to dilly-dally on this one, and he could feel the spirit looking through his eyes as well, scouring the stone with its consciousness as Elias ran his hands over it. Was that his imagination, or were his hands more sensitive than usual while Mibotha's attention was so focused?

In the end, he found three tells, things he'd assumed had just been his imagination at first. But two of the stones on the sides of the shrine could be turned, and after some testing, Elias twisted each stone until he heard a faint *click*. He then went to observe the nearly invisible pattern on top of the shrine, but Mibotha let out a little flare of both eagerness and impatience into Elias's mind, and he watched in surprise as his arm traced the pattern of subtle grooves by itself. A bit unnerved he couldn't feel his moving arm, Elias had to stand there until Mibotha was done, and feeling came back into his hand. Could Mibotha have done that at *any time*?

While Mibotha seemed satisfied, the shrine stood quietly long enough for Blanche to shift uncomfortably in her saddle.

"Nothing's happening."

"*It will work.*"

Blanche looked at Elias, and he could tell she'd heard something wrong again but couldn't put her finger on it. He *hated* it when Mibotha answered questions with his voice instead of telling him what to say, it made his entire throat feel strange.

Almost in response to Mibotha's words, the shrine began to glow, rumbling slightly. All eyes turned to the little stone structure as it shifted, groaned, and gradually came apart to reveal it had been covering a trap door. Feeling vindicated, and failing badly to contain his excitement, Elias stepped forward and smartly grabbed the handle of the trap door, pulling it back to reveal a stairway leading underground.

"Who prepared this? I'd never heard of it..." Cecily muttered, and even Amira could only shrug helplessly, looking to Elias for answers.

"*There's no time to explain. Come on.*" Elias coughed as Mibotha relinquished its hold on his voice again, but he could feel the spirit making him aware of the proper path again. *Down*, it said. *Down, down,*

down. For a moment, the sheer desperate *need* of the directive gave Elias pause, but Mibotha was as out of patience as he was to finally get what they'd come all this way for. As one, man and spirit started to walk down the stairs into the dark unknown they led to.

"Follow me. Stay close."

The Royal Guard needed to go practically single-file to follow him, but they left their horses and did so, Blanche in the lead and Amira directly behind her. As their surroundings grew darker, Elias felt more aware of his surroundings than he ever had before. He knew that the last of the Royal Guard had just begun to walk down the steps; that Boors was the source of the sound of someone in armor shifting as he peered distrustfully into the murk; that Amira held onto Blanche's hand with both of hers just behind him, and that Cecily had laid a hand on her shoulder. He was aware of everyone behind him, and felt he knew exactly where he was going even though all he knew was to walk forward blindly.

It got stranger as he descended. He was aware of a great sense of space, and his body, and everyone behind it, seemed smaller and smaller. He could feel the shrine all around them even though it was too dark to see, and it was expanding. He could feel the land above them, a breeze stirring the grass. He could feel...Elias shivered. He could *feel* emotions that weren't his. Not just Blanche, Amira, and Cecily forming a chain of excitement, worry, and hope behind him, or the other Royal Guard running the gamut from steeling themselves against one more disappointment to those radiating hope that *this* time, their faith would be rewarded. It was in his awareness of the land itself. He could feel something strange, disembodied but powerful. Sadness, and pain...and worse than either of them, a quiet, building anger.

Was this what Mibotha felt like *all the time?*

"It's black as soot down here, Brook," Blanche whispered, even though she had no reason to be so quiet. The path beneath the shrine seemed to drink in sound and light, and even her muted words were clear as day. "How are we supposed to find anything if we can't see?"

"Preparations were made," Elias replied, and felt momentarily disoriented by the impression he and Mibotha had spoken at the same time rather than Mibotha just forcing out its words on his tongue. He knew to brush the wall, almost absentmindedly, but a glyph carved in the stone glowed golden at his touch. In a moment, dozens just like it began to shine, and the stone corridor was soon glowing brightly enough that it was easy to see, even with the sun far out of sight.

The bards, the peasants, and even the Royal Guard had always been quite vague with their praise for King Morys. Typically it was his goodness the songs focused on, some sort of saintly light that shone from his every pore, keeping ill fortune and bad weather at bay before the wicked, wicked Elias Brook shot him down in his prime. Elias sometimes got the impression that Morys's most fervent admirers never knew him very well, and remembered some sort of storybook king when they thought they were remembering him.

Elias remembered his praise for King Morys very specifically. He was good to his children, knew talent when he saw it, had a very impressive beard, and appeared from his accounts of his family history to be the only king Yivyn had ever known with a head for finance. Perhaps his most unique virtue as a king, however, had been entertaining the notion of what he might need done if one day he wasn't king anymore.

The stairs ended, and a short walk on even ground saw the corridor open up into a large, five-sided chamber. Elias recognized it, a very similar chamber was in the castle. Morys had taken him to see it, once or twice, it was where he had been crowned, he'd said. There was a throne, more modest than any chair he'd ever seen Morys sit in but still carved of respectable, formidable-looking dark oak, and a large stone table before it. Five items were arranged on the stone table.

The scepter, that ponderous golden half-a-staff Elias had always thought looked ridiculous as a symbol of authority. A silvery shield, almost mirror-polished and ornamented around its edge with gold and jewels. Elias had always thought it looked like a single strong blow would shatter it, but he knew the legends of its alleged indestructibility. A goblet, which appeared to be made of the same white metal as Amira's sword, and decorated with a number of small precious stones from top to bottom. It had been the only one that ever tempted him in the good old days. The only one he'd ever wondered what it would be like to have.

The last two he'd seen far more, and the sight of them gave him pause. The ring, of course, was just as he remembered it. The silvery band that had seemed too small and simple to be a king's most prized piece of jewelry, but bearing a small symbol of the royal coat of arms. Next to it was the crown, a circle of gold with silver-white wings extending from either side. It had never been that ostentatious, not compared to some crowns Elias had heard of in other lands, but it had always seemed...right.

He was aware Amira, just behind him, was barely breathing.

It seemed like an eternity before she could bring herself to release Blanche's hand and step away from Cecily, but eventually she walked, one slow step at a time, past him without seeming to notice he was there. When she came to a stop at the table, she stared, and the silence was deafening as she searched for words.

"Father mentioned a place like this...once or twice," she finally murmured, the small words echoing with nothing to compete with but bated breath. "He always said it was a fiction. Something Grandfather meant to do but never did. He told me this place doesn't exist."

"He lied," Elias said quietly. "You never knew who was listening, in those days." He could feel several of the Guard turn to look at him, and with his awareness seeming so heightened in this place, he was aware their expressions were unfamiliar to him. He didn't care, and Mibotha did not let him look away from Amira. He could feel it behind his eyes, staring at her with an intensity that made it hard to blink. Amira didn't seem to notice, touching the ring like she was afraid it would burn her even as she stared at the crown.

"He had both of these with him when he was killed. How did they come here?" she whispered, turning back reluctantly to meet Elias's eyes. He wondered if she could see Mibotha there, or feel it in the room with them. All Elias could do was answer honestly, and so he shrugged.

"I don't know," he admitted. Mibotha did, he was sure of that, but the spirit wasn't interested in sharing that information. How *long* had Mibotha been preparing for this day, he wondered? And *how*?

"I don't suppose it matters," Amira said quietly, picking up the crown. For a moment, she rested her head against it, as though the head of her father still filled the golden circle. With Mibotha's awareness still pressing down on his mind, Elias was aware of the faint, faint noise of water dripping briefly on stone before Amira blinked furiously.

"Blanche," she said, and merely speaking the name became a command all its own. Blanche stepped forward, but for once, she seemed unsure. Elias realized for the first time Blanche herself wasn't a great deal older than Amira.

"Me, milady?" she asked, trying to sound as cool and collected as usual. Elias could feel through Mibotha that she was shaking. Too subtly to see, but quivering all the same.

"I would not be alive to reclaim any of these if it had not been for you, Blanche. This is your right as much as it's mine," Amira said, turning to Blanche and smiling at her in the artificial light. Blanche sank to her knees, bowing and averting her eyes.

"If...If that is your will, my lady, it would be the greatest honor I could ask for," she said reverently.

No priest, Elias thought. No priests for miles. Just a thief, a group of Royal Guards, and a spirit only one of them even knew was there, giving that poor thief a headache as its impatience grew. In those circumstances, of course the Captain of the Royal Guard made the most sense to crown Amira.

He could feel Mibotha's desire surging and bounding within his mind as Blanche went to join Amira between the table and the throne. He could barely hear himself think over his borrowed awareness of all the hope singing out in this room now that the Regalia were in their grasp. He couldn't bring himself to say that after they'd come all this way, he didn't understand why this had been his quest for redemption.

Why does any of it matter?

The thought seemed strange, even coming from him, but it gripped him as Blanche began to recite from memory, Amira responding where appropriate. The words drifted past him without ever developing any kind of significance.

Why did it matter that they had the Regalia? There were stories about what the king's great treasures could do, but as far as Elias knew, only one of them was *true*. They were symbols, mostly. Decorations. Stories about invincible shields and a goblet that negated all poisons aside, nothing on that table seemed likely to Elias to protect Amira from the malice of her enemies better than the sword or the suit of armor she'd had before they even started.

It marked her as the queen, recognized by the gods, but why was that important? She was already the queen, by virtue of being the King's oldest living child. The men and women that would happily kill her to avoid being branded usurpers right now would not stay their hands after Amira put on the crown. Nobody outside this room could possibly care that they'd secretly made her queenship *official* down here, could they?

And yet, the Royal Guard watched Blanche perform the rituals and Amira giving oaths identical to ones her father and grandfather had spoken as though some kind of miracle was happening. Mibotha's fierce, desperate need to see this done was so intense it *hurt*. The spirit had craved this since they joined forces, and who knew how long before Elias had died? He didn't need Mibotha to break its worrying silence to know this was more than success to it. This was an obsession becoming reality. Why did it *care*? What did it *need* so badly from Amira?

Would Amira want the circlet Blanche was lowering onto her head if she could feel the white-hot desire focused on her the way Elias could?

"—Queen Amira the First, rightful ruler of Yivyn and guardian of all its dominions, recognized by gods, men, and spirits. Long may you reign," Blanche finished reverently, her words finally making it back into Elias's consciousness as she and everyone else bowed before the newly-crowned Amira. For a moment too long, Elias was the only man that remained standing, and Amira turned to look at him.

She was the same girl he'd spoken to just a few nights before. The one that had confided in him that she felt naked without castle walls around her, and had never slept under the sky before in her young life. She was still a girl. A sad, sheltered, noble girl wearing a simple metal circlet.

When Elias sank to his knees, the only one in the room that looked at her as they honored her, it was not entirely by choice. Amira did not seem to notice, turning back to Blanche and raising her to her feet.

"Thank you," she murmured, before turning out to the room. "Thank you. I would not have been able to come here without your unfailing bravery, your loyalty in times of strife, and your friendship in a time when true friends seem a distant memory. Thank you all." Amira saw the Royal Guards raise their heads to look at her, all of them grinning with an almost delirious relief. We *made it. We did it. Things will change.* Amira stunned them all by sinking to her knees and bowing to all of them, trembling visibly. "I will never forget what I owe to all of you for bringing me this far. I swear to you, to my father, and to all the friends we lost that by rights should stand here now...it will not have been in vain. I will be worthy of your loyalty."

Elias glanced at the assembled faces. Some too happy to think about anything else, their minds already full of grand visions of how much better the future would be. Some stunned by Amira's humility. No king in history had ever bowed to the Royal Guard, but their queen, in her first act, had honored them beyond any of her predecessors. And in some faces, like Cecily's and Boors, Elias saw an immense pride for the woman before them, and a reverence that had exceeded what he'd felt from them when she stood tall and crowned.

Elias knew without needing to see into the future that no Guard in this room could ever betray Amira now. He wondered what it felt like in her world, knowing in her heart that these men and women would never, ever let her down. It was a feeling so alien to Elias he couldn't even imagine it.

"All hail Amira!" Boors shouted, rising to his feet. "Long live the Queen!"

"All hail Amira! Long live the Queen!" The cry began to rise as the other Royal Guard began to echo Boors, ringing from wall to wall as Amira rose slowly. Elias could feel an intense, savage satisfaction that didn't belong to him grip his heart as Mibotha listened to the echoing roar of loyalty.

"All hail Amira! Long live the Queen! All hail Amira! Long live the Queen! *All hail Amira! Long live the Queen! LONG LIVE THE QUEEN!*"

Amira stood before the stone table, leaning on it subtly and staring out at her guardians, celebrating her triumph with more joy than they ever had their own. Elias watched her, a spot of quiet amidst the shouting. He felt like an intruder here. This wasn't *his* triumph, not in the way it was theirs. It hadn't been him that had waited five years for this. This was his penance, as Mibotha had judged it, and now that it was upon him, he felt oddly lost amidst this joy.

As Mibotha roared in triumph, as the Royal Guard shouted their joy to the heavens, and as praise for her name echoed off of every wall, Elias felt like he was the only one watching when Amira put her face in her hands and began to cry.

CHAPTER 18

It felt like some time had passed before the celebration in the underground room slowed, and eventually quiet returned as the elation of the moment faded.

"This is a very important moment, everyone, but it's not the end," Blanche sighed, stepping forward. "We've completed the first part of our mission, but we're not done yet. The queen must be brought safely back to the castle to rejoin her brother...and from there, the real work begins."

Elias nodded, glancing back at the stairs. Mibotha was quiet now, but that wasn't reassuring him as much as he'd like it to.

"Blanche has a point. We got her here and crowned her. That won't mean anything unless she survives the return journey and manages to pull off whatever you were planning to stop the fighting," he remarked.

Attention in the room gradually turned to Elias, and he couldn't help but shiver a little under the scrutiny. He hadn't wanted to think about it, but it was staring him in the face, now. They'd crossed the threshold.

He'd shown them the Regalia he'd bought his life with at the outset of their journey, but he didn't even know where the Royal Guard were planning to go on their return journey. His time as a guide was over.

Despite their honorable reputation, Elias started to sweat as he became keenly aware Amira and the Royal Guard didn't need him alive anymore.

"Brook is right," Cecily said, briefly allaying Elias's fear for his life. "We've gotten this far, but that army's still behind us. We would do well to get out of Hache's territory before the situation escalates any further. Our advantage so far has been that the enemy is unaware of who we are and what we're doing out here. I recommend we do everything we can to keep it that way and withdraw to safety with no further bloodshed."

"Good point, Cecily. There will be battles enough when we're striking out from a place of strength," Blanche sighed. "For the time being, let's focus on not letting them see us again. We'll want to make sure they don't track us, either." she turned to Elias. "Brook, can you help us cover our trail?"

"I think I can handle that," Elias agreed, mostly wanting to seem useful. Honor and duty were all well and good, but the part he'd played in getting them all here was not something he was going to count on to pay for everything. Until Mibotha released him, Elias was never going to assume he was out of the woods or didn't need to invent a new reason for the Royal Guard to keep him around. Blanche nodded, seeming satisfied.

"Let's get to work, then. I don't want to waste any time."

There wasn't anything more to say as they geared up to go, but despite the good cheer among the Royal Guard, Elias found he didn't feel as good coming out of the shrine as he had been coming up on it.

Some part of him, he was aware, had hoped it would be over when he fulfilled his promise. Mibotha would hang some sort of sign up in the sky, telling him *Yes, Elias Brook, it's all over! You're free! Your life is your own again! Enjoy your redemption!*

But it wasn't that simple, was it? Elias was beginning to wonder how he'd ever hoped that it was. He'd helped Amira out in a big way, but people weren't just going to forget why she needed his help in the first place. Mibotha would hold that debt over his head until it was satisfied, and Elias had no honest way of telling when or if it ever would consider the scales balanced.

He was at court again, he thought, not for the first time. Elias Brook, the outsider among the elite. The sovereign's personal sneak-thief. Always waiting for the call to come down from the throne, a new justification for his presence so far from home. Bowing and scraping in the meantime, trying to find ways he'd stay useful so his betters wouldn't tire of tolerating him.

He'd done some things he wasn't proud of, living that life. He'd done much worse things to leave it behind, if he was honest with himself. Maybe it was only appropriate the punishment for everything he did wrong to leave the court in the dust was to be forced to revive it, relive the "good old days" until Amira or Mibotha saw fit to dismiss him.

It wasn't much of a life, Elias thought to himself as he started to bring up the rear of the departing band as they rode away from the shrine. But, and this was important, it still beat the *hell* out of death.

Elias looked over his shoulder as they departed, wondering if someone else would find the emptied chamber after they'd gone, but was surprised to find that it had closed up on its own behind them. Elias probed around in the back of his mind for Mibotha, but for once the spirit seemed to be avoiding him. Elias decided not to look a gift horse in the mouth and enjoy being alone in his own head while it lasted.

After that experience, he wasn't going to complain that Mibotha was suddenly keeping its distance. The spirit had never pressed on his mind, his *self* like that before, and Elias hoped it never did again. It had been eerie, below the ground. He hadn't been Elias Brook for a few moments, but he hadn't been Mibotha either. That strange, in-between feeling of someone else acting, speaking, and feeling as *him* was not one Elias was eager to remember or experience ever again. Things were bad enough already without his contract with Mibotha making him feel like a stranger in his own body.

Still, Elias wondered if he'd gained something useful by getting too close for comfort to Mibotha's thoughts. He'd seen...or at least felt...*something* while Mibotha was surging through his mind and body. He remembered all too well the emotions he'd become aware of, although he still wasn't sure if they were from Mibotha or something Mibotha could sense.

That fierce, desperate *need* had been Mibotha's, he was sure of that, and for whatever reason it was focused with obsessive intensity on Amira. If Elias wasn't fairly sure that the only human Mibotha had any power over was him, he might have felt concerned for Amira's safety, but as it was...Mibotha wanted something from her very, very badly. It was an intensity of desire Elias had never felt, and Elias knew what being desperate enough to kill felt like. What had been in Mibotha's mind watching Amira crowned could level cities. Elias wasn't sure if he could use that against Mibotha or not if he had to, but knowing what something desired had always been the surest way he could imagine to acquire power over it. He would need to keep a watch on Mibotha's thoughts, see why it was so concerned with what befell Amira.

That hadn't been the only emotion burned into his memory from the experience, though. Elias shuddered a little when he remembered the strange awareness of the land around them. It had felt like there was so much *anger* in everything. In the ground, in the trees, in the air...it had felt like the world was clenching its fists in rage, and Elias wasn't sure what would happen if whatever owned all that anger started swinging.

Still, these were abstract concerns. Elias felt he could devote more time to them once they weren't riding around in the territory of one of their fiercest enemies. Elias stuck to his duty of making the trail of the Royal Guard as hard to follow as he could. He wasn't expecting grunts like the ones they'd fought on the way here to be able to follow any trail that wasn't blindingly obvious, but Oliver Bones loomed in Elias's mind.

Soldiers like the duke's couldn't follow even partially cold trails, but Oliver Bones wasn't a soldier, and he hadn't gained a reputation like his by being a poor tracker. If he was involved in this, Elias didn't intend to make anything even a little easy for old Basilisk-Eye. They'd need every advantage they could get if he came after them before they were in the clear.

Much of the day passed without great incident. Mibotha remained quiet and distant, the Royal Guard did little to bother him, and Elias was free to ponder what came next if things proceeded in this manner. Was he going to be a part of whatever attempt Amira made to reclaim her kingdom? He wasn't much use there as far as he knew. He was a decent fighter, but war was another matter and they surely wouldn't expect the skills that kept him alive in their little scraps to be much use on a big battlefield, would they?

No, he probably wouldn't be pointed at an enemy and told to march, but he knew how to get in and out of guarded places unnoticed. Morys had seen the value in having someone like that around, and it was safe money to bet his daughter would, too. He was no assassin. He left work like that to the likes of Oliver Bones. But he was a better thief than Bones would ever be, and he might be called upon to dedicate his skills at breaking into people's houses to take things that didn't belong to him to the cause of "justice" before this was over.

Elias Brook.

Elias snapped to attention immediately as Mibotha finally spoke up. It sounded oddly tired for something with no body, but it would not have spoken up unless something important was on its mind.

The army from before. It's changing directions to try and intercept you up ahead. If they don't get in front of us before nightfall they will certainly be upon us by morning.

"How?" Elias gasped, keeping his voice low in the back but looking at his trail. "There's no way they could have predicted what way we'd be going!"

I...I don't know, Mibotha muttered, and it sounded very troubled to admit this. *Something is wrong. We need to be ready to fight, or break through. Increasing our pace will only hasten crashing into them sooner and I fear they may just gain on us if we change direction again.*

Elias nodded subtly. This was bad, but maybe being forewarned the enemy had somehow figured out where they were would give them a chance to set up a countermeasure. "Anything else?"

You...were afraid of one man being among that army, were you not?

Elias's heart nearly stopped.

"Yes," he whispered, barely hearing himself.

There is a man in a green cloak and a mask with the army now. He is directing their movements.

It took a great deal of willpower for Elias to stay steady on his horse.

He'd felt quite hopeful at the start of this day, but now it was all crashing down around him. The army they'd planned to evade had grown wise to their movements, through some trickery Elias couldn't understand. They were going to intercept them, and this time there would be a lot more men the Royal Guard needed to cut through to get free.

On top of that, it was entirely possible if the army was interested enough to be tracking them through some kind of trick, there was a decent chance they would send word to the duke. Elias couldn't imagine the enemy could know who they were and why they were here, but the enemy had been curiously prescient in their movements just now. Who knew what else they might know that they shouldn't?

Either of these things alone would not have made the situation ahead seem so very dark to Elias. While that army was big, it had depleted a great deal of its strength in the failed attack on them the other night. With their scouts, their cavalry, and their vanguard of infantry routed, it would be a much less formidable foe trying to meet them head-on in the near future. With the Royal Guard's skills and horses, it would be possible to break through them and escape into the woods.

But Oliver Bones was directing the army now, and that changed everything. A man that lethal surrounded by an army to hide in and strike invisibly from could devastate a small, elite force like the Royal Guard without any difficulty at all, and if a single one of his attacks pierced Amira's defenses, they had come all this way for nothing, Elias most of all. Bones would chase them if they got away, and any men that were still in the force would not hold to their superstitious aversion to the woods if the alternative was to try and desert while the Basilisk-Eye was watching.

One man...but so much fear, Mibotha muttered, cutting through Elias's thoughts. *He terrifies his own men as much as he terrifies you. Any ten of them could band together and put an end to him.*

"No, they couldn't," Elias whispered, absolutely certain he was correct. "That's why they're scared of him."

If this man is all you say, Amira will never be safe while he draws breath.

"Tell me something I *don't* know."

*He may be more deadly than ten men together, but you have **me**, Elias Brook. In battle tomorrow, you must be the one to slay Oliver Bones.*

"Oh, is that all?" Elias asked, hysterical terror warping his voice. "All right, then. I can't wait to get started!"

CHAPTER 19

Elias needed to wait a little longer than he was comfortable with to break the bad news to the Royal Guard, but fortunately even depleted the army did not possess any gift of stealth, and he could see the movement to intercept from a long way off.

"Blanche! The army!" he called, moving from the back of the group to join Blanche and Cecily up at the front. Blanche paled visibly as she followed his pointing finger to notice the army in the distance.

"That's impossible...how did they know to change direction?" she whispered.

"I don't know, but I don't think we can avoid them, either. If we change direction they'll be able to catch up to us faster, especially if they're tracking our movements somehow," Elias said. "I...I still think Oliver Bones might be with them, too. If he is, we're all in grave danger."

"With apologies to your tactics, Brook, we're not taking a force of that size head-on. Even depleted, they're dangerous enough without an assassin using them as cover," Blanche said, glaring ahead before surveying the landscape. "We've been pacing ourselves to run if we had to, and I'd say we have to now. Cutting through the woods to reach that path through the cliffs can give us a way around that army and a lot of rough, narrow terrain for them to follow us."

"The army might be slower, but they will have an advantage of mobility in the woods. They might catch up faster than you think," Elias warned.

"We've already observed that they are in no hurry to go near the woods. Even if they break from that doctrine to try and catch us. we'll have a good head start. In the cliffs, we can outrun them and get to safety," Blanche replied simply, angling her horse towards the woods. Elias had to admit she had a point.

"If Oliver Bones is with them, though, he won't let up even if we cross out of Hache's land, and those soldiers will do as he says."

"Only tacticians like the duke think an army more scared of the man standing behind them than focused on the enemy in front of them is a force worth sending into battle," Blanche remarked. "Forcing them to break with superstitions, chase us across rough terrain, even enter enemy territory while not at full strength purely because their commanding officer frightens them? I've been in fights, Brook. I've seen what happens when you rely on men with no morale to get the job done." Blanche glared at the army, and Elias couldn't help but shy away from the look in her eyes. "As for Oliver Bones...perhaps this is the time we must finally put that man in his grave for good."

"Don't underestimate him," Elias begged. "He's no legendary monster, but he *earned* his reputation as a killer. Even a Royal Guard should be afraid of fighting him."

"I am," Blanche said quietly, although she certainly didn't *look* it. "But if that snake tries to take my lady's life like he did her father's, *I will see him burn.*"

Elias didn't have anything more to say to that. Oddly, he found himself hoping Blanche was there, too, if this really did come down to a fight with Bones. He certainly liked her chances better than his own taking the Basilisk-Eye on man-to-man. And there was something curiously delightful about hearing someone finally say it out loud. *You didn't kill the king, Brook. Oliver Bones did.* It was no apology for the last five years, but it was a start. Blanche spurred her horse, shouting over her shoulder.

"Into the woods, everyone! We're making for the cliffs!"

Nobody hesitated to follow Blanche's instruction, Elias least of all. He wondered if Blanche was right about that army. If the fear whipping them forward might break them in the end. He'd known Oliver Bones as a figure of terror, but he couldn't imagine anyone drawing much in the way of inspiration from his leadership, except a vague relief he wasn't being paid to kill *them.*

It appeared Blanche had timed her decision excellently. They'd seen the army before the army had seen them, and so their sudden deviation from the path of collision was not detected for some time. As the darkness fell, Mibotha informed Elias that the army was sitting still in confusion while they were making good progress through the woods. It wasn't all cheerful news, however.

They're starting to scout around. It will likely take them all night looking for us in this darkness, but I imagine they will have a good idea where we went by morning. I do not believe your enemy will pursue us until sunrise tomorrow. But he is restless, Elias Brook, and he will be relentless when his pursuit begins.

Knowing this, the Royal Guard took advantage of their head start to ride through the night. Elias was expecting someone, or at least the horses, to tire, but things remained curiously energetic, and not just from terror. Despite going hard to evade the army, Elias was aware that he wasn't the least bit tired, and his horse seemed as fresh as it had this morning.

"Mibotha...? Are you doing something?" he whispered.

I have petitioned for a little aid. You and your companions will not tire beneath these trees, Mibotha answered, and once again it sounded curiously exhausted. *I won't be able to help beyond keeping you alive once we're out in the clear again. You'll have to see them through the cliffs on your own speed and cunning, Elias Brook.*

"Thank you," Elias muttered, surprised Mibotha had managed something like that.

It cost me to acquire this small mercy for you. Don't let it go to waste. Mibotha said shortly. *It will be some time before I am able to help you know when your enemies are coming again. Ride with the certainty your enemy will find you in the cliffs, and kill him there. You must do this, or everything we've accomplished is at risk.*

A feeling curiously like the one he'd experienced on the way to what he'd been sure was his execution came over Elias as they rode through the night. He was going to meet Oliver Bones in battle. There didn't seem to be any way around this now, it was simply his fate. The knowledge was oddly...liberating. He couldn't avoid it, so he just had to meet it and hope it didn't end with his head on the ground and Amira dead.

As they broke the tree line, Elias glanced over his shoulder, fear warring with a sort of resigned determination. He didn't think Oliver Bones had ever been scared of anything in his life. He wondered if the assassin understood just how dangerous a coward in a tight corner was.

"I won't be sleeping when you find me this time, you snake," he whispered hatefully, before turning and riding full-tilt for the cliffs.

CHAPTER 20

There wasn't any immediate sign of pursuit as the group made its way at full tilt for the cliffs, but Elias only took that as a mixed blessing. The army was too big to sneak up on them, even after the losses it had taken, but another advance force, particularly one marching with Oliver Bones at their back, was a different story. And if what Mibotha had told him was true, they were sure to meet him somewhere in the cliffs, likely before Mibotha recovered enough to warn Elias in advance when the assassin was coming.

Surprise was one of Bones's greatest weapons, more than any of the tools he used to kill. He might be deadly with a sword and bow, but Elias suspected much of that deadliness derived from his ability to catch those who might otherwise outmatch him unawares. Elias didn't like the sound of taking him on at a time and place of his choosing, not after everything he'd heard, but it didn't seem he had the luxury of choosing this time around.

The cliffs would at least give him less cover in that green cloak of his. The forest might have had spirits friendly to Mibotha, but it was a favored hunting ground for Bones and Elias wanted to at least have a chance of seeing him coming. Bones's poison arrows could devastate a group like this without ever presenting a target for them to strike back and Elias knew most, if not all, of the group would die without even seeing their killer if Oliver Bones was able to set up his shots in peace.

If they could get the drop on *him* though, there was a chance. Old Basilisk-Eye was not to be underestimated in close combat, but Elias liked the Royal Guard's chances in a sword fight better than he liked their odds of evading the best archer of his era.

The cliffs weren't particularly tall, but they were certainly big and steep enough to make a compelling border for the ever-shifting territories the warlords squabbled over. There was a narrow path leading down through it, but Elias knew treacherous, rocky places like this were usually left alone. Nobody wanted them enough to fight over them, and many were so full of bandits that armies actively avoided them. The soldiers following them wouldn't have a superstitious dread of the place like they would the forests, but Elias took some grim satisfaction that anyone chasing them would have to make a forced march through not one but two locations most soldiers would prefer to leave alone. Without a charismatic leader, the punishing blows to troop morale would catch up to their pursuers one way or another.

Oliver Bones was a great many things, Elias would be the first to admit, but a charismatic leader of men was not one of them. He'd likely respond to the threat of mutiny by killing a few obvious targets and letting that intimidate the others into falling in line, but any amount of time he wasted getting his force in order to chase them was time the Royal Guard got to leave him as far behind as they could. Elias was quite certain that Mibotha's prediction coming to pass would require Bones to leave the vast majority of his troops behind to pursue them. It wasn't an enormous comfort, but there was still something to be said for having only one very dangerous enemy to worry about instead of a very dangerous enemy and an army.

The horses were no longer so tireless as they had been in the forest, but Elias was pleased to see the exhaustion that had been held away from them had not returned as they went on. They could tire now, but they would not do so prematurely. Elias put his energy to work guiding his mount carefully along the rocky path and casting a glance at the river winding through the base of the cliffs. He didn't care much for the notion of falling into that if something should knock him off the path. Once he was sure his horse was able to set its feet surely on the narrow path, Elias busied himself looking around for any signs of movement in the cliffs around them, or a little flash of green. Mibotha might not have been always right, as it once claimed, but it had sounded awfully certain they would not make it through these cliffs without a reckoning with Oliver Bones, and Elias did not intend to be caught napping.

In the end, it wasn't a little flash of green that announced the end of the tense but uninterrupted ride. Vermillion uniforms against gray stone stood out a lot more, and Elias didn't need to think twice to have an arrow in the air the very moment he saw the bright red spot a little higher up the cliff.

A strangled cry echoed across the cliffs, and a dead man came rolling down from his perch, bouncing bonelessly on the path before beginning the lengthy slide down to the river. No orders needed to be shouted for Amira's guards to immediately form up around her as bows and swords came out. Elias, scanning the cliffs, was able to spot another poorly-concealed soldier moving to better cover and send him tumbling after his companion. Behind him, several Royal Guard scored kills on the scouts with their own arrows.

It was while Elias was scanning for any further signs of movement, any soldiers that had scrambled out of his view, that an arrow struck him in the side like a thunderbolt, knocking him out of his saddle as his horse reared in alarm. Elias was pitched to the ground, his vision briefly blurring in pain. He tried to force himself to focus, looking down at the arrow now protruding from his side. He had a terrible feeling he could describe it before he even looked, and he was not disappointed.

Ash shaft, made with obsessive care. He was quite sure the arrowhead he was now fumbling with his dagger to cut loose was iron. And...there it was. Black fletching. There was only one person in the world he knew of that liked to use crow feathers to fletch his arrows.

"I really hope you know how to deal with poison, Mibotha..." he whispered, sweating as he tried to widen the wound enough to get the arrow out. He was vaguely aware there was a lot of commotion, and the sound of arrowheads smashing into shields and armor, but he couldn't focus his attention anywhere until he'd gritted his teeth through several painful little slices and at last saw the evil little point come free. He'd have lived through a shot like that even if he hadn't been bonded to a spirit, and Elias didn't see anyone writhing on the ground in their death throes yet.

It appeared that Bones was in a playful mood this afternoon.

"Well, now, *this* is interesting."

The voice allowed Elias to finally pinpoint its source, and a short ways up the mountain, a tall, thin figure in a leathery green cloak seemed to step out of solid rock, looking down at them. In spite of himself, Elias felt his gut clench. It was the first he'd seen of him in five years, but Oliver Bones was as frightening standing a good distance away with his bow drawn as he had been when Elias had woken up staring up a long knife into his face. The first man that tried to go for his bow while the Basilisk-Eye talked was likely to be dead before he finished his first twitch, and everyone on the cliff knew it.

He didn't want to see their attacker any closer, but he suspected he wouldn't be able to notice any change wrought in those five years. It's not like he'd ever known what the man's face really looked like anyway. It had occurred to him more than once that Oliver Bones had become so well-known for wearing a mask that he was in disguise any time he took it off. The voice hadn't changed, though. It was deep, clipped, and flat. Unpleasant but oddly compelling, particularly when its owner was armed. Rumors of Bones's death might have been grossly exaggerated, but his voice had never allowed Elias to fully discount the notion he'd crawled out of a grave.

"Just thought you were smart bandits, maybe mercenaries, spies. But Royal Guard? Unexpected," Bones went on, surveying them from his vantage point. Elias suspected his surprise was the only reason he hadn't started shooting to kill some time ago without saying a word. It had been quite some time since anyone had seen the Royal Guard in action, Bones included...Elias felt a chill down his spine as he realized Bones's attention had shifted to him.

"Royal Guard and Elias Brook, no less," he said casually, even his dead voice managing to convey a sliver of amusement. "Patched things up with the king killer, perhaps?"

"You'd be wise just to let this go, Bones," Elias called from where he lay, struggling to get back up. His voice sounded a lot more confident than he felt. "You might kill somebody with that arrow, but there's enough of us here that the next one that flies will kill you."

"Possible. Not likely," Bones said bluntly, shrugging ever so slightly. "Don't think I'll go. Not when you brought *her*."

The Royal Guard drew even tighter around Amira, their fear for her safety evident even at a distance, but Amira stared at Bones with that guarded expression concealing any fear she felt towards the man.

"You know who I am, then?" she asked, and Elias suspected she was trying to keep him talking. They'd been fortunate he seemed interested in conversation for once instead of just killing them, but the moment he got bored enough to stop playing around Elias didn't doubt a lot of them were going to die.

"Amira," he said simply, nodding once. "Was looking for you, once. You've grown since then."

"*You* killed my father."

That seemed to surprise the old snake, but not much and not for long. Elias had always expected a maniacal laugh or some sort of rant when he imagined Oliver Bones confessing his guilt, but all the assassin seemed to feel the truth coming out merited was a little nonchalant shrug.

"Morys. His guards. His horse. His dog. All of them," he replied, as casual as if he was discussing the weather. "One shot each. It was a good day." His attention shifted again, and Elias gritted his teeth. It was creepy being able to tell when Bones's eyes were resting on you. Just knowing he was looking at you gave you a clammy feeling on your skin. "Don't you think, Elias?"

"I've had the worst five years of my life because you were able to pin that on me, Bones," Elias growled, forcing himself to meet the masked man's horrible gaze. He was a little too far away to see it, but Elias hadn't forgotten the strange, yellow-white eyes from that night five years ago.

"Credit where credit was due, friend. Couldn't have done it without you," Bones remarked. Elias didn't intend to let him continue in that vein, not when the people he was depending on knew he didn't have anything else to offer them.

If it hadn't been done to him, Elias might have found it quite clever. A man with such distinctive arrows, doing his work even though he was 'dead'? It hadn't been enough that he'd stopped using his own arrows to cover his tracks. That fateful night five years ago, he had left with Elias's quiver, and Elias had known when the time came for him to run whose arrows they'd found at the scene of the crime. The rest, as they said, was history.

"We're not friends, you lunatic!" he shouted.

"After all we've been through?" Bones asked, sounding like he was trying to feign hurt without the slightest understanding of having feelings to hurt. "We did good work together, you and I. We made each other's lives easier, didn't we? Morys's, too."

Now Elias could hear the maelstrom of questions, accusations, and denials that would be released from his companions if they weren't ready to fight for their lives. He'd steered the conversation one way, but Bones had, as usual, found some way to make that even worse.

"I never hired you! Neither did Morys!" he shouted.

"Tsk, tsk, Brook. I helped you, you helped Morys, and Morys helped me. It was a wonderful arrangement, and when it had to end, you were still right there to help me," Bones said, his voice almost sing-song. "There's no shame in that. We're all professionals here."

"Shut up!" Elias snapped, getting angry again. Only he could hear the taunts hidden in Bones's insinuations. Only he knew enough to see the bastard laughing in his face behind that mask.

"Well, if we're not friends, does that make us enemies?" Bones asked, not sounding troubled by the notion. "It's been a while since I've had any."

"You can borrow some of mine, if you'd like," Elias grunted, smiling humorlessly. "Listen, Bones, even someone like you knows the odds of you taking on this many of us and walking away are slim. I don't know what you've been paid, but–"

Bones shot him in the leg this time, and the ground came rushing up to meet Elias as his thigh burned in agony. Several retaliatory shots were fired the moment the arrow was in the air, but Bones didn't avoid them so much as he vanished.

"Some people are worth killing for free," he hissed, reappearing lower on the slope to shoot a nearby Royal Guard in the throat. The man fell from his horse without a word, but the other Guard split between defending Amira from approach and trying to rush Bones. Elias had expected the assassin to stick to his archery, trying to strike Amira down from a distance with an opportune shot, but he put aside his bow and swiftly drew a long, thin blade from under his cloak. A quick lunge from him gave one of the Royal Guard a deep cut in his side, and in a few moments, he too fell from his saddle. Elias didn't need to look at the wound to be sure Bones's sword was slathered in the deadliest poison he could find.

Bones stabbed into the second Guard to reach him with similar results, and then he was upon Elias. The temptation to freeze up was intense as he saw the ugly iron-grey mask with its skeletal grimace under the green hood coming towards him rapidly, but he couldn't run with the arrow in his leg and holding still would be the end of him.

Instead, Elias stepped forward, inside the swing meant for him, and drove the heel of his palm into the mask as hard as he could manage. Doing so sent a jolt of pain up his arm. He hadn't realized the mask was actually *metal*, but the shock went both ways. For the first time, the assassin who had seemed more snake or shadow than human...stumbled, and Elias relished the surprise that briefly occupied the horrible, pale eyes beneath the mask before their expression turned murderous.

In the time it took Elias to go for a dagger, wincing in pain as the arrow in his leg reminded him of its presence, Bones had recovered his footing, and rushed at Elias with terrifying speed. Elias's stab went wide, but on instinct he brought up his wounded leg as fast as he could. He was rewarded seeing the back of the arrow jab Bones in the gut even as a twinge of searing pain ran up his leg. Bones let out a little grunt, and Elias tried to grab him, take the man to the ground where they might be on more even terms. Bones, however, sidestepped his grip, and the sharp, jerky motion conveyed his anger more clearly than a snarl. Elias tried desperately to gouge at those horrible eyes with his free hand, but Bones was too cunning for that old trick, and in a moment, he was inside Elias's guard.

Time seemed to flow both far too slowly and far too quickly as the sword whipped out in an arc Elias could barely follow, taking him in the shoulder and raking its way down to his hip, drawing a white-hot line of pain across his torso.

Elias stumbled a step before the blade whipped out again, catching him in the side of the throat with a horrible, crimson spurt. Elias became aware he couldn't hear anything, and seeing anything but the cold, savage glee in Bones's eyes as blood—*his* blood, he dimly realized—lightly spatted his mask was similarly difficult.

The two slashes gave way to one final stab, the wicked, thin blade piercing his stomach and burying itself up to the hilt there. The poison and the wounds did not do their work gradually. Elias's strength went out like someone had blown out a candle, and he found himself on the ground, staring blankly ahead as the blade slid out.

He'd been like this once before, he fuzzily remembered; in the woods, alone and bleeding from a collection of puncture wounds...a lifetime ago.

He should have known it would end up like this. He should've tried to get out of there when the fighting started, let the blows land where they would. He should have known he'd just get himself killed trying to fight this far out of his league.

If Amira survived this, it wasn't going to be because of him. He wondered if Mibotha would bother saving him this time. If it didn't...

Elias found himself hoping inanely as he struggled not to die again that someone might write a catchier song about the lucky shot he got in on the untouchable Basilisk-Eye than the shot he never took at King Morys.

He couldn't hear much, but he had the vague impression there was a very loud noise before Boors and Cecily charged Bones together, Boors nearly flattening the assassin with his mace. For the first time in memory, Elias found himself cheering for Boors.

Bones seemed ready to take his revenge with a single stroke against the giant of a man, but surprise registered through his body language as Cecily stepped in with her sword drawn and expertly parried the blow. To Elias's swimming vision, the swords multiplied into a parade of deadly blades as Bones tried to cut Cecily down only to find every lightning-fast cut, every devious stab, and every attempt he made to press forward or move around the woman met with an unwavering blade. Moving with practiced ease in coordination with Cecily's parries, Boors nearly took Bones's head off once again, the assassin's lightning reflexes proving the only thing that saved his life. For such a big man, Boors was much faster than Elias had given him credit for.

He's...not winning, Elias realized. The Basilisk-Eye, terror of terrors, was being *driven back*.

He found himself wishing he'd gotten behind Cecily *before* Bones had gutted him, but he supposed one couldn't have everything.

You must kill Oliver Bones.

Elias wasn't sure if the thought was Mibotha returning to speak to him, his memory of Mibotha's words...or just his own thoughts echoing them. He never would be. He just knew that his numb arm moved on its own, and his body, despite being fairly certain it was supposed to be dead, shifted as close to upright as it could manage, clutching the fallen dagger.

You've seen power. Never understood it. Am I wrong? Morys has power. Great power. Power over men and armies. You respect that. Of course you do. You have no power of your own. But you can pretend you're borrowing his.

Now it was Bones's voice inside his head, as he remembered waking up to find a blade an inch away from his eye and two pitiless eyes looking down in the darkness. Time had felt as sluggish then as it did now. It was just as difficult to move, or think.

*This is a secret. Morys has no power. He just **thinks** he does, and so do his men. Kings have an invisible power. It lives in people's heads. This knife is **real** power, and it belongs to me. I have real power over you now, and **it** will be inside your head unless you help me.*

Kings, nobles, knights...assassins, brigands, and the salt of the earth...it never changed. Real power or fake, the only consistent thing Elias ever seemed to notice was that none of it was for him.

Terror had weighed him down like iron chains that night five years ago, but now rage filled his leaden limbs like a benign wind filled a sail. Pain, anger, and hate narrowed Elias's vision until nothing in the world existed but him and the Basilisk-Eye, and without a sound, Elias flung his dagger at Bones.

He hadn't paid Elias any mind, thinking him dead, but Bones was clearly very surprised when Elias's dagger missed his head by inches, sailing off the mountainside. In his moment of distraction, Bones was cut by Cecily and made a horrible noise Elias had never heard from a human before.

He finally got around her in that moment, and Elias's heart sank when he punched out savagely with his sword hand and dealt a powerful blow to Cecily's temple. She staggered, dazed, and lost her footing.

Elias was just close enough to launch himself to try and grab her before she went over the side of the cliff, but he didn't have anything near the balance or the strength to haul her back up. The ground beneath his feet just...went away.

He saw Boors do his best to reach them in time to haul them both to safety, but Bones tried to pounce to get between them so he could see all three of them dead. Judging by the look in his eyes, he was not expecting Elias's flailing arm to snag his cloak nearly so tightly.

The cloak had a legend of its own, it was so distinctive. People said it was made from one mythical creature or another, usually a basilisk (though Elias knew the tools tough enough to make basilisk-hide into anything useful did not exist), and that it was strong enough to be used as armor.

Whatever it was made of, it did not rip in Elias's dead-man's grip, and Oliver Bones was dragged off the cliff after them, Boors arriving just a moment too late to do anything but watch them fall.

Elias had only a few moments to think through what he was going to do. He would *probably* be all right if Mibotha was feeling up to fixing him after all this, but Cecily and Bones were in significantly more trouble. Concluding only one of these facts bothered him, he released the cloak, watching Bones spin away flailing and cursing helplessly in midair. His attention then turned to Cecily, not entirely conscious and in a lot of danger if she hit the water in that state.

"Damn it, this is going to hurt..." he groaned, moving as best he could to make sure Cecily was on top of him when they hit the water.

He had thought he was completely numb at this point but he was at least aware of an extremely painful *crack* before cold and dark consumed him, and he knew no more.

CHAPTER 21

...release...enough...

Elias wasn't sure exactly where he was. Everything was completely dark, and he couldn't feel his...anything. He wasn't sure if his eyes were open or not, and could not find the strength to test it. He felt as insubstantial as smoke. But there were whispers, and Elias quietly listened to them, suspecting they might be important.

...MINE ALONE...need...still, for...

...greedy...tricks and fake promises...enough! Release...

...answer to...do you deny...?

...Elias Brook...

...still...Elias Brook...

"ELIAS!"

In keeping with Elias's luck, the world became solid and he became aware of his body just in time for Cecily to slap him hard across the face.

"Agh!"

Now that awareness was back with him, Elias was allowed to go from an insubstantial but restful repose to realizing he felt like he'd been smeared across the castle floor by Boors again, with the additional bonus of being soaking wet, cold, and dizzy. Cecily, sitting bedraggled next to him, didn't look a whole lot better, and she had a bloody nose, but all in all the Guard seemed to have come through their fall into the river much better than he'd honestly expected.

"That hurt..." he mumbled resentfully, coughing.

"In my defense, you should be dead four times over," Cecily said, watching Elias like he might explode any second.

Elias realized, now that he'd had a few minutes to get back up to speed, that he had been fatally wounded three times with a poisonous sword before falling off a cliff. The fact that he was still breathing was going to take some more artful explaining than he was sure he was prepared to do.

"Ah...yes...that," he managed lamely, mind racing. He wasn't sure what Mibotha was going to do to him if he blabbed about everything now, but what other choices did he have? Cecily wasn't going to believe anything but the truth, he imagined, and she might not even believe that—

"Blanche was right about you, wasn't she?"

Elias's train of thought was cut off by the question, and he looked at Cecily in surprise. It wasn't a pitying look she had, for which he was grateful, but there was still that feeling of misplaced but well-meant understanding.

"Blanche?" he repeated, trying to figure out if this was good or bad. Had Blanche gotten suspicious of the times Mibotha had answered for him and actually guessed at its presence? If so, she was a lot smarter than Elias had realized, and he'd been taking her intellect seriously.

"She's been watching you more closely than you might realize. I thought she might just have been imagining things, but this...you're a mage, aren't you? You've got magic inside you that makes you heal!"

While Cecily's theory was completely incorrect, Elias stared at her for a long moment, realizing it was actually more plausible than the truth. Cecily was likely to greet the story about Mibotha with considerable suspicion, especially coming from a known liar, but Elias "conceding" to her own theory based on something she already knew existed might save him a lot of grief with Mibotha.

She's provided an explanation for you. Don't correct her, Mibotha advised him sounding tired even after its long absence. Elias felt a mild sting of irritation. It lectured and lectured him about being a better man, but it certainly didn't seem to mind when his lies worked for its own interests.

"Something like that," he eventually sighed, deciding this was more strictly accurate than "yes". "It sounds good when you put it like that, but in practice..." Elias looked at his ripped, soaking shirt and coat. From the looks of it, Cecily had torn them open to look at his wounds. It was a strange sight, looking at his body since all this had begun. There, and there, were the angry little scars of the pitchfork where it had pierced him, the injuries the bandits' swords and axes had carved into him permanently, and the newer, only recently scarred wounds he'd taken from the duke's men. More familiar, but no less painful, were dozens of much older scars, mostly small white things he hadn't looked at seriously in ages. He was astonished to know he still remembered how he got every single one. To accompany the crowded roads carved across his skin, he now had a long, shallow, painful-looking cut across his chest and a little hole in his stomach still faintly oozing red. Only the wound in his neck had closed completely, and Elias was aware of a sharp pain still coming from all three of the wounds. "It's not as great as you'd think. I might still be alive, but I've still got these, and..." he trailed off, shivering. "I might not have died from it, but I feel the pain just like anyone else, experience what it's like to be fatally wounded. But thanks to this power, I survive."

"That's amazing! Think of what you might be able to accomplish if you made use of–" Cecily started, not seeming to appreciate Elias's fear.

"I have. Mostly it seems to let me die the thousand deaths people think I deserve," Elias said bitterly, cutting her off. "And most people accused of witchcraft or sorcery or what have you tend to have a choice between being drowned, burned, or decapitated, all three of which would still kill me. This...magic is something that started happening to me only recently. I can't rely on it, and I don't know when it might desert me. I honestly didn't know if it'd even work when Bones cut me up." Elias tried to stand up, but the ground wobbled dangerously and he fell over. "Oof!"

A cut in your neck, a gash in your chest, and a stab through your stomach, an arrow in your leg and side, the blow you took to the back of your head and the ribs Cecily broke landing on top of you, Mibotha listed, sounding like it had been having a difficult time of its own. *I healed most of the damage from each, fixed your ribs and your head, and closed your neck wound, but that poison is a different matter. I stopped it from killing you, but shaking it off is going to be difficult. I can't seem to purge it completely. I'd advise not letting your enemies use poison on you again. Keeping your soul in your body was hard enough on both of us this time around.*

"Are you all right?" Cecily said, coming over and helping him to his feet. While grateful for the assistance, Elias couldn't help but twitch in annoyance that even with a spirit aiding him his good deeds tended to leave him tired, sore, and dizzy while Cecily seemed none the worse for wear.

"I think so, but I've never tried healing off poison before," Elias grunted. "I don't think it's working that well..."

"The fact you didn't die in seconds from the first cut means it's working well enough. We need to regroup with the others, and then they can treat you for the poison still in your system," Cecily said, supporting him.

"You'll catch up with them faster if you leave me here," Elias pointed out, wincing a little. There wasn't much point dancing around it. Cecily's priority was and always would be her queen, and Elias decided he might as well save them both time so he wasn't left behind with a promise to come back somewhere in the cliffs instead of here by the river. "You've seen what I can do. I'll be fine."

"No," Cecily said simply, starting to walk with him.

"Don't be ridiculous, Cecily, we both know the rules of this game," Elias snapped impatiently. "The Royal Guard always go to the king or queen's side immediately. That whole thing about protecting the innocent is for when the sovereign isn't in need of any protection. I'm not innocent, and we aren't friends. You're just kidding both of us right now."

"Brook, please do me a favor and shut up for a while," Cecily said, continuing to help both of them along without hesitation. "I'm starting to think Boors is right that you're not that smart."

"I'm being realistic. Amira can't wait to search for anyone, not even you, and if they move castles without you who knows how long it'll take to find them again," Elias said. "I did my job, and I," Elias fumbled for more, "...was going to ditch you all once you were over the cliffs anyway! Just let me go my own way!"

"You can heal from wounds, but you're weak and you're stranded in unfriendly territory. I don't trust in your magecraft to save you from starvation or bandits or animals finding you in this state, Brook," Cecily countered, not looking at Brook as she sought a way up they could both take. "And if you think I'd leave someone to die, good reason or bad, you don't know a damn thing about me *or* the Royal Guard. Nobody gets left behind."

"I'm nobody," Elias said without thinking. Cecily paused, looking at him without saying anything for a long, awkward moment. Just for a second, Elias was sure she was going to drop him and move on alone. She surprised him, however, by turning her attention forward again and proceeding.

"Brook, remember how I started this conversation asking you to shut up? Now's a good time to put it into practice," Cecily said, before falling quiet again as she started to make her way towards a path to the bottom of the cliff.

Despite immense temptation to ignore that, Elias decided to humor her for a while.

Even without any conversation distracting them, it was not an easy road that lay before them. The cliffs were far steeper here by the river than they had been on the path from the woods, and while that wouldn't have presented much of a challenge to Elias normally, he didn't trust much in his climbing skills until his wounds and the poison were fully healed. As it was, Cecily couldn't move very well with him in tow either, and so it was a long, difficult trudge uphill for the both of them.

"Maybe we should follow the river, instead. See where that takes us?" Elias suggested, observing their painfully slow progress.

"I don't think that'd be wise. There's a good chance without Oliver Bones driving them, the army that was tracking us won't want to risk the cliffs, but they could try to catch up by the river before Queen Amira can cross the border," Cecily said, shaking her head. She took another step forward, and stumbled slightly, nearly dropping both herself and Elias to the ground. Elias managed to help steady her despite his uneven footing, glancing at the big ugly bruise by her temple.

"That was a hell of a hit he gave you before you went down. Are you sure you're all right?" he asked. It had been a lucky escape for Cecily that Bones hadn't managed to nick her with that poison blade when he finally got around her guard, but Elias had seen a blow to the head kill people after the fact before.

"I'm fine, trust me," Cecily said quickly, touching her bruise. "It was a nasty punch, but I've shrugged off worse than that in training. Boors taught most of the recruits of my generation to be quick on their feet, but I don't think anyone completed training without feeling a blow from him once." Cecily smiled a little at the memory, but Elias wondered how anyone being asked to get in a fist fight with Boors to learn quickness didn't flee in the dead of night and never come back. "This is nothing. I'm just a little dizzy from that punch and the fall."

"Let's hope we both patch up quickly, then," Elias said, looking up the cliff. "We won't move very fast if I'm poisoned and you're dizzy, and we're not cut out to fight that army by ourselves."

"You have a point...but I'm more concerned about just catching up to the others. I wish we had a way to send them word that we're not dead, but we're just going to have to find them to let them know," Cecily said.

"They have horses, and we're on foot and injured. I'm not liking our chances."

"I don't think we'll catch them here, but I don't think we should anyway. I want Blanche to ride for the border with all possible haste, get everyone to safety. It'll be easy enough for us to sneak out and find them on our own, and two people can disappear from an army a lot easier than a whole party can," Cecily shrugged, sounding surprisingly optimistic as she began to press forward again.

"You're remarkably upbeat for someone who had a narrow escape from death, you know that?" Elias grumbled. It was admirable in a way, he supposed, but it sure got on his nerves sometimes. Why was everyone but him so certain that eventually things would go their way in life? The belief seemed directly contradicted by all evidence Elias had ever observed.

"We reclaimed the Regalia, crowned my lady, and killed the Basilisk-Eye while bloodying the duke's nose, and we did it all in secret, so he won't be expecting the queen's triumphant return," Cecily replied, grinning. "I had a bad feeling about this expedition, but we've won some important victories these last few days."

"You think he's dead, then?" Elias asked, looking back at the river behind them uncertainly.

"You told my lady yourself that he's not a monster, he's just a man, Brook, and he fell off a cliff. I imagine that's the last of Oliver Bones," Cecily muttered, seeming a little surprised by the question. Elias didn't look so sure, scanning the waters without expecting to see anything. Mibotha would have likely told him if someone was near, but...

Oliver Bones had been legendary for cheating death before the false rumors of his demise settled in. He'd used the reports he'd finally died to continue his work in secret and take his enemies by surprise. And while Oliver Bones might not have had Elias to shield him like Cecily had or Mibotha to heal him as Elias had, Elias couldn't help but think that if he was in that snake's position, waking up banged-up but alive in a river bank with everyone believing him dead for good this time would be a golden opportunity to take his revenge on an unsuspecting young queen before vanishing into the night again.

"I will believe that bastard's dead when I see his corpse. Not before," he said to Cecily, clenching a fist.

"His body could be lost. If his corpse never surfaces, do you intend to live in fear forever?" Cecily asked, although Elias could tell his words had set her thinking.

"I'd rather be afraid than dead...but I can just *feel* it. I tried to kill him up there on the cliffs, but I failed. He's probably hurt, but he'll be back, and he'll be angry."

"...All right," Cecily said quietly, appearing to trust in what Elias said. "He'll be back. But we'll be ready."

"I hope so. We were lucky enough last time that he decided to show off like that. He didn't take us seriously at all. If he gets the drop on us again, it'll be with poison arrows, not taunts. I don't know if he'd have survived a fair fight with you once it came to swords, but his bow's a different story."

"And he won't fight fair even if it does come to swords, I'd imagine," Cecily said, grunting a little as she helped Elias over a particularly steep slope onto a flatter niche in the mountainside. "But we have an advantage of our own in that department, don't we?"

"We do?"

Cecily nodded, prodding Elias in the shoulder.

"You have your gut feeling that Oliver Bones isn't done yet, but I'd bet a good horse old Basilisk-Eye thinks he's seen the last of *you.*"

Elias wanted to comment that Cecily was being rather optimistic again by assuming that tipped the scales somehow, but a moment's consideration forced him to concede she had a point. They'd seen one of the most feared men of his age stumble, miscalculate, and even fall. Elias had held onto the knowledge of Oliver's humanity as a half-hearted ward to keep the fear of him from consuming him, but the sure knowledge that the assassin was fallible was a new and comforting treasure.

Elias might not know much about power, true or fake, but he did know something about getting results, and one of the easiest ways to get what you wanted from someone was to know something they didn't.

It might well be that Cecily was right. Oliver Bones might miss his mark again because this time he wouldn't see Elias coming.

CHAPTER 22

Cecily's dizzy spell appeared to pass after a while, and while Elias still did not feel very good, he gradually began to walk with greater assurance. Their glacial pace up the cliff slowly improved, and while Elias was on the lookout for any new dangers, nothing appeared to harass them as they climbed back up towards the path.

"We seem to be in luck. Not even any scouts..." he remarked, looking around for any signs of enemy presence. Not a single uniform to be seen, and Elias doubted that any new soldiers in the area would be any better at hiding themselves than the ones he'd spotted earlier.

"It wouldn't surprise me if they're reluctant to advance any more," Cecily said, looking over her shoulder. "Bones must have driven them hard to catch up with us the way he did, and the forests and cliffs are not places soldiers like to venture in these times. They might be relieved Bones hasn't returned to order them after us, and the duke won't be able to punish them for awaiting orders."

"It'd be nice if all Amira had to contend with to retake the land were the lazy cowards that survived this long. But it's never that easy." Elias sighed.

"No...perhaps not. But we'll be able to ride out in force for the first time in years," Cecily said, leading the way as they reached a stable path. "Some will surrender to their rightful queen, either from conscience or from fear. Those that stand still will have to be met in battle."

"Duke Hache isn't much of a tactician, but the duchess is cunning and his army is stubborn," Elias mused. "Amira's still going to have a long, hard road ahead of her."

"She's had five years to plan for this day when so many merely dreamed about it. She won't fail," Cecily replied, and Elias was impressed with the ironclad certainty in her voice.

"You don't doubt her for even a second, do you?" he asked, cocking his head. "None of you seem to."

"Faith kept every man and woman at her side for five years, Brook," Cecily said. "Our generation had to show loyalty in suffering rather than valor for a long time, but it made our loyalty all the stronger. But that's not all there is to it."

"It's not?"

"Not for me," Cecily muttered, keeping her focus on the way ahead as they talked. "Blanche and I...we're not much older than Lady Amira. We were still half children ourselves when we became her guards. We began our service not long before the assassination...I suppose many of the Guard still around today did, but none at quite the same time as us. I knew my lady just before her father was murdered, and I watched her grow up in the shadows of this conflict. Most in her position would flee, or despair, or be content to dream of better times. She started making plans. Trying to become stronger, become wiser, be more than a child stripped of her rightful inheritance. My lady does have it in her to make this land great again."

It was an interesting experience, Elias reflected, to travel with Cecily. He hadn't talked to someone this...*sincere* all the time in a long while. He didn't need to wonder how much of what she said was meaningless noise or a lie. She just said exactly what she meant and felt all the time.

He was fairly certain someone like that would never have gotten far in courtly life without some sort of catastrophe, but he'd been wrong before.

"I did notice Amira seemed closer to you and Blanche. Because you were practically children together?" he remarked. He'd meant it casually, but to his surprise, Cecily's face fell and she gave him a troubled look.

"I met my lady not long before she stopped being a child forever. I don't know if Blanche ever was a child, but that time was dead for her before I ever met her," she said quietly. "I was the child, among the three of us. I was the one that had to grow up so I wouldn't get left behind."

"You make it sound like they'd have abandoned you." A curious thought, that. Even though Elias could see clearly that the assassination had turned Amira from the spoiled, cheerful girl he'd known into the subdued young woman who had come all this way with them to prove to herself she wasn't afraid, he couldn't imagine either Amira, child or woman, turning away from Cecily.

He was quite willing to entertain the notion that Blanche had sprung from her mother's womb fully grown and armed with a calculating look in her eyes, but he refrained from saying this as well.

"They would never have done that. But my lady had to grow, and grow quickly, not to despair when her life fell apart. Blanche was already beyond me when we first met. We were the same age, but she seemed... *perfect*, while all I had was skill with a sword. It was the only thing I could excel at enough to call her a peer, but even with that, our pasts separated us. I was just a silly girl at the time...I couldn't begin to understand her, even though I was trying my hardest," Cecily murmured. "There wasn't room for a silly girl or a young woman in mourning on the Guard. Blanche was ready to meet the evil times when they came, and Amira grew into them because she had to, despite our attempts to shield her. I needed to grow, too. I needed to be able to stand with them, carry my own weight and be the support they needed, or I would never have been able to live with myself these last five years."

"I can understand putting your queen up on a pedestal, but if you couldn't even understand Blanche, why did you care so much about keeping up with her?" Elias asked. Even in the present day, while the two seemed quite close, Elias didn't see much that was similar about them beyond their loyalty to their queen.

"You didn't know her back then. I can't explain it now," Cecily said simply. Elias cocked his head. Normally he'd assume it was sidestepping the question, but Cecily didn't seem to do that from what he could tell. She actually did think he wouldn't understand if she told him.

"I know a little more about decency, loyalty, friendship and all that crap than you and your friends have given me credit for, you know," he said, mildly annoyed. "It's not like I can't understand friendship just because I don't have any friends." Cecily gave him an odd look at this, but just shook her head.

"I believe you, Brook. But the matter is between Blanche and myself. It is, and I mean this as politely as I can, none of your business," she said bluntly.

Hm. Not sidestepping the question, then, so much as blocking it. Swords were apparently not the only thing Cecily had learned to deflect in her career with the Royal Guard. Elias's natural suspicion disliked that his only companion at the moment seemed to have something she wasn't willing to tell him about herself and Blanche, but on the other hand, Elias wasn't sure he wanted to know anything about Blanche besides what he needed to do to keep away from her.

"Fair enough," he conceded, leaving the matter alone for now.

Perhaps he ought to jump to Amira for this conversation, he mused. If Cecily was willing to talk about her lady some more, it might be information he could use. Learning about the new queen might give him some idea of why Mibotha seemed so obsessed with putting her back on the throne. If he just understood the reason for the overpowering *need* Mibotha had felt seeing Amira crowned, he might have something he could use against it if he had to.

"I remember Amira, from back when I was at court," he remarked. "Morys treasured that girl...I'm surprised to hear you started off as her guard. I thought most of the Guard worked their way up to positions like that."

"My lady was one of the best-guarded people in the kingdom before I first laid eyes on her," Cecily replied. "Blanche and I became her guardians *because* of our youth, not in spite of it."

"...You were also keeping her company?" Elias guessed, seeing confirmation in Cecily's expression.

"Amira already had some of our finest seeing to her safety. Boors alone would scare off all but the most brazen enemies, and my father's eyes would spot even the most subtle threats. But Blanche and I were girls not much older than the princess...a good chance for Morys to let his daughter have friends who would still follow orders and lay down their lives to protect her from danger. I believe it was my father's idea."

"Your father was in the Guard?" That explained a lot, now that he thought about it. It wasn't normal even for a highly-born girl to be admitted into the Guard that young. There was the odd prodigy every now and then, but...family opened a lot of doors at court. It was an advantage Elias had learned a great deal about, since he was forced to make do without it.

"Of course. I would never have joined if he wasn't," Cecily remarked, smiling a little. "He was my hero. I wanted to be just like him..."

Elias listened to Cecily talk as they walked, mostly to pass the time, but inside he braced himself. Suddenly Cecily was volunteering an awful lot of information about herself, and Elias knew how that worked. People tended to go on about themselves when they were building up for a trade. I've told you all about me, they seemed to think, and now you are obligated to answer my questions about *you*.

He'd figured Cecily knew just about everything she cared to about him, since he'd served his purpose to the Royal Guard already, but her sudden talkative attitude had him on edge to defend himself against any hooked questions she would toss his way when she was done giving him information about herself. Bones *had* made some insinuations in their encounter that might earn him some suspicious probing, and Elias would be ready when the talk turned to that. As a result, he didn't ask the obvious personal question, but wasn't surprised when Cecily felt she had to tell him anyway.

"...He never made it out of the castle. He stayed behind so that Blanche and I would have enough time to get the princess and her brother to safety," she said quietly. "It's been five years since that day, but it never gets any easier..." Cecily's voice shook for a moment, and she stopped herself. For a moment, they walked in silence, before Cecily shook her head.

"I'm sorry. That's not very good conversation for the road, is it...?" she said, keeping her voice light.

"It's nothing to apologize for..." Elias said, a little uncomfortable now. He hadn't *asked* her to share something that personal with him. He may have initiated the talk turning to Amira, but he hadn't asked Cecily about what happened to her father. She surely knew he had a fairly good idea already what had happened to any of the Royal Guard that weren't there to see him when they arrived at the hidden castle, didn't she? But now she'd dumped this on him...

"I'm sorry about your father," he tried, feeling awkward even as he said it. In the last five years, everyone he'd met had lost somebody precious to them except maybe Blanche and Mibotha. That entire time, Elias had never figured out what could be said to them beyond an insincere-sounding apology. Perhaps for him in particular, since so many felt he personally owed them an apology for their suffering in the wars...

Cecily, however, seemed to take the mumbled apology well enough, nodding.

"Thank you..." she replied, before an uncomfortable silence descended on the conversation for a few minutes. Eventually she looked over at him. "It wasn't your fault."

That was a new one.

"What?"

"For the longest time, we felt so sure you were to blame for everything, back in that castle," Cecily went on, sounding mildly apologetic. "That you killed the king, that you set the castle up to fall...we all felt so helpless and so angry as the world fell apart, we needed someone to hold responsible for it. We didn't have the power to do anything about what happened to the kingdom, but having someone to blame…it's strange, but at times it almost helped. To know it wasn't just chance that did this to us, but the malice of someone who could be caught and punished."

Elias kept quiet, not in much of a mood to respond to that. In his experience, things going *right* was the happenstance, and things going wrong was the basic nature of the world. Things only went well as long as luck held out, but the world coming apart was always right there waiting. It baffled him how many people seemed to feel it was the other way around.

"But it's not right to blame you for everything. You have your sins and mistakes, and we have ours. I understand that now," Cecily went on. "Until a couple days ago, I blamed you for all of it. I hated you long before I ever met you. I kept thinking that…my father would be alive, if it hadn't been for you. But he taught me that fairness is more important than just thinking and feeling what's easy, and it's not fair to blame you for everything. My father made a choice, to save my life, Blanche's life, and my lady's. He did what he swore to do when he was knighted, and I know he gave his life proudly. It diminishes his sacrifice to blame someone for it." she ran a hand through her hair, an expression that wasn't quite a smile or a frown flickering over her face.

"It's strange, isn't it? So little has actually changed. You're as innocent of the crimes I blamed you for now as you were five years ago, but…knowing you weren't really responsible, one little fact, changes *everything* I thought I knew for the last five years."

Elias fought the urge to squirm as Cecily rambled. Nobody had ever talked to him like that before. What was she even saying? That she forgave him for a death that obviously wasn't his fault in the first place? Or was it just apologizing for how they all thought of him after the assassination? Either way, he didn't understand how she could link him with her father's death at all, even in the absolving him of blame for it.

If she wanted to blame someone for those five years, Elias would have thought blame lay with the man who chose to get himself killed for his duty instead of doing everything he could to live for his young daughter's sake. What good was valor if all it did was let you die nobly?

She does you no small credit, Elias Brook.

Mibotha's voice, returned to full strength, was not a welcome intrusion, and Elias narrowly avoided flinching. He'd been getting used to the quiet of his unwanted partner in this venture, but all good things must come to an end, he supposed.

*That man gave his life because he saw no other way to ensure that his future queen and his precious daughter would escape with their lives. He died nobly. But he would not have ever needed to make that choice if Oliver Bones had failed in his mission, **and he succeeded because of you**. She does you a great kindness to forgive you, and she did so without terms or conditions. I would not forget that, if I were you.*

Elias didn't respond. It was going to be hard concealing Mibotha's presence with Cecily right there as it was, and he'd rather chew his own leg off than have this conversation with Mibotha. What was the *point* in trying to make things right if such a big portion of it was having his face rubbed in everything he'd done wrong?

"I don't understand it," he finally said out loud, unable to avoid saying something for tact's sake. "I could never do something like that. Go to my death knowingly out of duty? It doesn't make any sense."

"You say that, and yet you've courted death since we've met, if the charm on your life is as fragile as you say," Cecily remarked. "A great deal of what you've done since I met you is not so different than our actions, facing danger we might not be able to overcome to save Yivyn."

Elias was caught without an immediate comeback to that. Had his actions of late actually resembled those of a Royal Guard? That seemed impossible to him. He was blackmailed into this in the first place, and on top of that, he'd been scared out of his mind or hadn't known what he was doing for a significant portion of the trip. He would have run for it ages ago if that was an option...

...Wouldn't he?

For some reason, the image of Boors and the others vindicated as he ran with his tail between his legs and Amira saying nothing as he fled, silently judging him with every step flashed across Elias's mind instead of Mibotha's wrath if he betrayed their pact. The thought made Elias grit his teeth, feeling foolish, but unable to fully explain why.

"As a point of order, I fully intend to live through all this," he said, aware Cecily was taking notice he'd been quiet a while. Cecily laughed, but there wasn't anything mocking or dismissive in it. It was a pleasant sound, and despite being serious, Elias found himself unable to resist laughing as well. Still, he pressed his point when they had quieted down.

"I'm serious, though. I'm not out here looking to get killed making things right for Amira. But you and the Guard, you're not scared of anything. You're all ready to pay the ultimate price out here if it moves Amira forward. I don't understand that, no matter how it looks to you. I don't understand not being afraid that all doing your duty will get you is that you might die for nothing in the end."

"For most of us, to leave our duties would be to *live* for nothing," Cecily said quietly, but she saw that Elias didn't seem to follow and just shook her head. "Perhaps it doesn't make much sense...but I feel one day you'll understand what I mean."

Elias hoped he wouldn't, although he didn't tell Cecily that. Living for nothing was all right in his book, as long as it coincided with living *continuously*.

Once Cecily's musing was at an end, Elias braced himself for whatever questions she'd been brooding on this whole time to come at him, but he was rather perplexed when his companion simply walked in complete silence, not even paying him much mind.

Elias kept himself braced as they walked, knowing perfectly well that people like Cecily could be counted upon to kill a perfectly good silence with personal questions sooner or later, but he remained braced against nothing. No questions, no comments on his own past, not even a token attempt to resume the conversation.

Elias had not been looking forward to having to deal with Cecily's questions, but somehow her appearing content to just walk in silence was somehow worse, if only because it once again made him feel wrong-footed and foolish. He'd made a very decent career out of being able to guess pretty well what other people were going to do, and he had not previously encountered someone who would ramble about their personal life with no intention of inviting or pressuring the person they were talking to to do the same.

On top of that, the notion that Cecily didn't have any questions she felt the urge to ask seemed insulting, somehow. If he wasn't sure he'd make a fool of himself falling into any traps the long quiet created, Elias would have spoken up himself.

As a result, Elias resigned himself to walking in silence until Cecily said something, wondering all the while if Cecily was much simpler or much more complicated than he was giving her credit for.

CHAPTER 23

Despite Elias's expectations, Cecily did not press him for any sort of information, or attempt to re-initiate conversation with him as the day went on. The Guard's thoughts were clearly elsewhere as they walked, and Elias was forced to grudgingly admit he had been wrong to assume she was the sort to ruin a perfectly good silence.

The fact her quiet was starting to make *him* tempted to say something was rather annoying, but Elias let it be. Talking to Cecily was nowhere near as unpleasant as his encounter with Boors had been the other night, but it had still made Elias feel vaguely uncomfortable while it lasted, and he had not forgotten how he'd snapped at her after confronting Boors. Calm as Cecily acted with him, he was sure she hadn't forgotten that, either.

Feeling vaguely like he'd lost some sort of contest of wills, Elias finally broke the silence as the sun grew low.

"We don't have much daylight left…"

"You're right," Cecily agreed, seeming to easily slip out of the thoughtful silence they'd been walking in to answer him. "I'd say we've got about long enough to get out of these cliffs if we hurry, but after that we'll need to make camp…"

"I don't know this part of Yivyn very well," Elias grunted, scratching his stomach as his wound itched unpleasantly. "But we should stay off the roads when it's dark. I can't imagine this territory is any less likely to have dangerous sorts out on the prowl for easy targets at night, and we're not in much shape to fight them off right now." Between his poison and Cecily's head injury, which Elias had noted was still affecting her gait slightly, he worried the next misfortune that befell the two of them on the road might well be the last.

"We'll need to look for somewhere sheltered at the base of the cliffs, then," Cecily groaned, not sounding eager to pick up the pace enough to make that possible but gamely starting to speed up. Elias was even less enthused to drag his heavy, poisoned body along fast enough to keep up with her, but being left behind or caught by unfriendly company while he was in this state was out of the question, and he forced himself to follow quickly.

"It looks like the road or the woods are our only options if you don't fancy bedding down in the sharp rocks," Cecily said, looking ahead rather than at Elias as they spoke. "I don't know which is more dangerous."

"We should go in the woods," Elias cut in quickly. "I don't trust these cliffs, and the roads are where I've met the most people trying to cut my throat the last few years. The woods aren't safe, but they're a lot safer than the road."

Cecily seemed to trust that Elias had some idea what he was talking about, and started to head for the trees huddled in the shadows of the cliffs.

"I'd have thought bandits would appreciate the cover forests would offer them…" Cecily remarked, glancing at the road as they went.

"I gather they did, which was the start of why soldiers avoid the trees like the plague," Elias shrugged. "After a year or two, though, you stopped seeing brigands in the woods unless they were pretty desperate. Not a lot of prey for them to ambush there, and…" Elias paused, glancing at Cecily. Elias's recent experiences had by default made him a very superstitious person, but he didn't really have a good grasp of Cecily's spiritual beliefs.

"And?" Cecily asked, looking curious. Elias shifted, a little uncomfortable even without knowing Mibotha was with them.

"The forests in Yivyn have…gotten strange, over the last few years. The ones that have survived the fighting, anyway. It's easy to get lost in them, sometimes for weeks, from what I hear. Damn near impossible to hunt anything there, but at other times the animals are out in force, and they're unnaturally hostile," he said in a low voice as they approached the forest. "But sometimes it's not even that. People just…disappear in the forests, and nobody ever finds out what happened to them. The bandit gangs that didn't clear out of the forests? They're all gone. Nobody's seen or heard from any of them in years, and nobody goes into the woods to try and find out what happened to them."

"Are you trying to frighten me?" Cecily asked, raising an eyebrow.

"No," Elias said seriously, casting a dubious look at the trees as they grew closer. "I meant it when I said the forests aren't safe. They're just safer than the roads if you don't linger in them too long. No one's stupid enough to come looking for us in there, but we should make sure we don't draw any attention to ourselves from whatever's already inside."

"...All right," Cecily said, deciding to take Elias at his word. He felt some small relief seeing that she was taking his warning seriously, but he felt his wariness shift as he entered the forest with her. Whatever might be outside the forests wouldn't find and harm them now, but...despite the shelter they had given him on many desperate nights for the last five years, Elias was never wholly at ease in the woods, now more than ever. Mibotha stayed curiously quiet within him, but Elias remembered the odd relief Mibotha had felt when it saw the forests in Hache's territory had not been disturbed, and the sense of quiet, building anger he'd become aware of through Mibotha's senses. He imagined he felt some of it simmering in the air of the forest. Some of that great anger was here, Elias was sure of it, growing little by little with time. He did not want to still be here when something finally stirred that anger into explosive life.

It didn't take very long at all after they reached the trees for the gloom of the dying day to go from mild to oppressive. Elias could barely see, and his night vision was better than most. Cecily looked around, seeming troubled by the darkness.

"Too risky to build a fire?" she asked, glancing at Elias. "I know how to make sure it won't spread to the trees, but someone might see the light and smoke..."

"The smoke, not likely. Not on a night this dark or under branches this dense," Elias muttered. "And people don't go towards lights they see in the woods anymore. They're afraid they might find out what's casting them."

"It sounds like people live in perpetual fear, to hear you describe the world..." Cecily remarked, starting to gather branches.

"You've been out here with your eyes open. Are you saying they don't?" Elias countered. "There's a lot to be afraid of these days."

"...You are right..." Cecily muttered, looking troubled as she started to build a fire pit in what little light remained. "There has been a great deal of turmoil and very little hope to be had in Yivyn for years now. Perhaps it's not surprising that without anything to be hopeful about, people become more and more fearful..."

"You're big on hope, aren't you?" Elias commented, joining Cecily in trying to get the fire going. "The other Guard don't seem to have nearly so much of that as you do." In normal circumstances, Elias would have attributed this surfeit of optimism to a certain amount of willful stupidity, as he did for most optimists in his life, but it occurred to him he'd underestimated Cecily several times before. It would be helpful to try and get a better look at her thoughts before writing her off as a fool, his gut told him. Especially if he didn't want to deal with the embarrassment of being made to look like a fool by a Guard he'd underestimated at some point in the future. Cecily just shrugged, starting the flame without much trouble. Soon there was a little crackling fire giving the pair a little more light to see each other by.

"Hope is a good thing. It helps you keep going when life looks too bleak to go on. It gives you courage in hard times," she said simply. "You need skill and strength and intelligence to stay alive in a bad situation, but if you fall into despair, none of that will protect you."

"In my experience, people that trust too much to hope are the ones who get disappointed the most," Elias replied cynically, scooting closer to the flames, "and trying to be brave seems like it gets a lot of people killed when they fight instead of run."

"You don't seem to think much of bravery, I notice," Cecily said mildly, giving him a curious look. "I know you have never argued with other people's claims you are a coward, but I've never seen a man so dismissive of courage before. Doesn't that seem odd to you, with the life you've led? You have done quite dangerous work, even before you joined forces with us, and a man doesn't make as many enemies as you did by being meek."

"No. Being afraid's kept me alive," Elias insisted, but he found he wasn't explaining himself with the same defensive anger he'd felt towards Amira and Boors. There was just…something in how Cecily was talking to him. He didn't see her making accusations or assumptions about him, no pity and no contempt. She seemed…*interested* in what he had to say, which was new to Elias. Displays of sincerity usually put him on edge, especially since Elias of all people knew how easy they were to fake. But with Cecily…she wasn't *being* sincere, it was just something she *was*. It was strange to get that impression from an adult, but somehow it made Elias abandon his tight clamp on talking about himself without any cajoling.

"I've never been brave like you people. I've seen the Royal Guard completely ignore danger in order to do their duty. I'd have been long dead if I was ever like that. There might've been risks in the work I did, but I knew about them, and I was afraid of them. It helped me plan ways *around* them, not through them. I survived because I knew to avoid risks," he went on. "I always found the safest way for myself because I listened to my fears. Windows and secret doors don't endanger you, and dead men don't fight back when you need something of theirs to pay for a meal. Even when I couldn't avoid all the risks, and something managed to corner me, it was being afraid that saved my life. You can power through a lot on terror and the desperation to stay alive, and unlike courage, fear helps you do *whatever* it takes to survive, including running away when you can."

Cecily seemed to digest this for a while, poking the flames with a stick absentmindedly.

"That's interesting. You sound like my father, but all the words are turned inside out," she said quietly. Elias had been expecting a pitying look or a refutation of his words, and so this caught him completely off-guard.

"What? What do you mean?"

"You talk about letting fear guide your cunning so you stay safe, or using desperation to give you strength when you're in danger. I didn't realize it earlier, but…you think that courage is not being afraid of anything, don't you?" Cecily looked Elias in the eyes, and his gaze dropping quickly seemed to be all the concession she required to her point. "It's not, you know," she went on. "I'll always remember it. Boors taught us all about speed and strength and how to endure, but my father helped sharpen our minds alongside him. Every initiate learned from him that the courage of a Guard derives from mastering and controlling your fears. It was only when you controlled fear, instead of fear controlling you, that you could be brave."

Elias looked up, and realized Cecily was smiling at him.

"We're not so different, you know. You've learned, on your own, how to turn your fear of dying into a tool. If you were really nothing but a coward, that fear would paralyze you. You wouldn't be able to think, or fight, or even escape. Terror, *real* terror, takes everything away from you but despair unless you can overcome it. But you? You learned how to use your fears to sharpen your ability to recognize and avoid danger, and how to control your fear in tight spots to get away or fight free. I spent years learning how to control my fears, so that my courage wouldn't fail me when I'm called upon. Fearing the pain of an enemy's attack is one thing, but mastering that fear with bravery? That is the foundation of the defense I perfected," she said calmly, tapping the hilt of her sword.

Elias hadn't heard someone put it like that before, and the idea that he'd somehow mastered a teaching of the Royal Guard in his old life seemed patently ludicrous, but he had trouble arguing with results. The fact of the matter was he would not have believed Cecily's capacity to defend with that blade of hers if he had not seen it firsthand. Despite being an assassin, Oliver Bones was no amateur to single combat, and he hadn't been able to strike her even once before the distraction let him get off that punch. Elias was quite aware that in a pure contest of strength and skill, without Mibotha's aid, Cecily would be more than a match for him in a fight. Maybe it was fortunate he'd been able to talk her around in the town when they first met, or he'd be long dead.

"You're an odd bunch, you know that?" he sighed, warming his hands by the fire. "Sometimes the lot of you are just like the Guard I remember, and sometimes you're…different. It makes it hard to know where I stand."

"After the last couple of days, I'd say you stand with us," Cecily said mildly, glancing at him. "If nothing else, you saved my life again."

"It's not really a habit I've ever gotten into, saving people," Elias said, looking up at her. "Why it keeps being you is beyond me. You seem more capable in all this heroic crap than I'll ever be. Maybe it's just fate having a joke."

"I don't believe in fate," Cecily replied. "Things happen or don't happen because of the decisions we make in life, not because it was destined they would. If we want something to happen, we have to work towards it, not trust in destiny. And if something happens because of our choices, we have to bear the responsibility, not fate."

"You don't believe in fate, but you also don't accept that it might have been chance that brought us to this point? No wonder you take personal responsibility so seriously," Elias remarked. Cecily nodded, not seeming to take this as a criticism.

"It's a more honest way to live. No excuses. Just the choices you and others make, and their consequences," she said. "In the end, what you have in life is what you earned, and what you leave behind are the choices you've made."

"Not everyone gets a choice in life," Elias suggested, but Cecily shook her head.

"There are some things in life you can't help, but the world spins on the choices people make. Even when it's not always your decision that changes your life, you always have a choice," she said firmly. "Nobody can take that freedom away from you, not completely."

"And here I thought all the duties you Guards have would limit your ability to appreciate freedom," Elias said, smiling a little. The comment might have nettled another guard, but Elias was a little surprised when Cecily laughed lightly.

"Hardly. Every one of us had the option to run for it when things went bad, Elias, but we all chose to stay here. Some would question the wisdom of the choice, perhaps, but it was the right choice, and we all made it freely."

The surety in her tone was oddly sobering to Elias. For just a moment, he felt a small pang of envy.

"There's something to be said for that, I suppose," he agreed, surprised to find he meant it. "I've never seen eye-to-eye with you people on a lot of things, but I've always been impressed with your conviction, even though it made my life a lot harder than it needed to be." He sighed, shaking his head as Cecily frowned at the mild accusation. "Life would've been a lot easier if I was ever certain I was making the right choice."

"You can't tell me you've never felt like you were doing the right thing," Cecily said, leaning forward. "Your life has been a very eventful one, I grant that, but surely *some* of it must have been pleasant, or you wouldn't be fighting so hard to stay alive."

Was she *teasing* him? For someone who had narrowly avoided death earlier, Cecily was astonishingly chipper. Elias was surprised to find it was somehow improving his own mood as well.

"I'll concede there might have been one or two times in the last twenty-five years I didn't fear death slightly more than I hated my life," he said dryly, shrugging and struggling to keep a straight face. "Being invited to a good dinner instead of executed when I was caught stealing in the castle, for one. That was a better day than I'd been expecting. Getting back at Lord Downell after he called me a worthless pickpocket and had some of his men beat me up, *that* I'll treasure until the day I die."

"That was your work?" Cecily asked, sounding genuinely impressed. "I was there that day. King Morys *humiliated* him in front of the entire court. I hear he crossed the ocean in shame after he was run out of the castle. What in the world did you *do*?"

"It was an interesting week. It required a great deal of subtlety, a lot of patience, and if I do say so myself, a certain level of genius to achieve. I had to crack every defense, hidden door, and safeguard in that castle to get what the king needed to expose that braying jackass in front of the court, and I wouldn't have been able to do that without some careful acrobatics, disguises, and magic."

"Your healing ability?" Cecily asked blankly, before frowning. "No, you said that only began recently. You used devices, then? I hadn't realized you were skilled in their use." Magical devices were tremendously helpful things to have, as every man, woman, and child in Yivyn knew, but the uninitiated in magic tended to avoid using them. In untrained hands, they could backfire in a great many dreadful ways, and attempts to use magic devices as weapons of war had always ended in utter catastrophe. It wasn't much of a surprise a fighting woman like Cecily wasn't familiar with their use.

"Nothing so dramatic as that. Just parlor tricks. Hand faster than the eye and all that," Elias sighed, shaking his head. "I've always had very fast hands, so it was easy to pick up the tricks. It was also a good way to hide what I was doing when the time came to demonstrate to Lord Downell that I was not a worthless pickpocket." He grinned at Cecily. "I was a *magnificent* pickpocket."

Cecily laughed again. It was a clear, pleasant sound, quite different than the tense quiet Elias was used to having in the forests. It even seemed like the seething anger had gone out of the air, or at least diminished greatly. It had been a very long time since Elias had heard something that pleasant in response to something he'd said. Cecily looked at him, seeming both interested and amused.

"Can you show me?"

"Are you asking me to pick your pockets? It would be the first time I've done that by invitation," Elias said, raising an eyebrow.

"No, no, these parlor tricks of yours. I'm curious now." Cecily said, leaning back. "We don't have much else we can do at the moment. Could you show me?"

Elias could think of one or two other things a man and a woman could do alone in the forest at night, but he was very fond of his head remaining on his shoulders, and refrained from voicing them aloud for its sake. Besides, usually when someone was asking him about something he was good at, it was at blade point with a lot of accusations close behind. Elias didn't get to show off because he *wanted* to very often.

"All right. See if your eyes are quicker than anyone else's..." Elias said, picking up a small round stone. Cecily cocked her head, smirking a little.

"Can I see if they're faster than anyone else's without you having long sleeves to hide things in?" she teased again. It being a warm night by the fire, Elias confidently conceded and set his ragged coat aside. He'd used coats for some of the tricks he'd pulled in life, but he didn't need anything more than his hands to make some magic.

"Keep your eye on the stone," he instructed Cecily, holding it between his finger and his thumb. As Cecily gave his hand her attention, Elias swept his other hand over it, snatching the stone away and holding out his closed fist as he dropped his other hand. With a dramatic flair, he opened up his fist to reveal an empty palm under the fingers. Cecily grinned, looking impressed.

"You have clever hands, Elias," she commented. "I can see why people would never play cards with you."

"No, that's because I cheated like a demon and they weren't good enough to catch me," Elias said, grinning back. "This is just a trick the hands play on the eye." He held up his other hand, and exposed the stone nestled behind his fingers, where he'd dropped it from his finger and thumb while his other "snatching" hand passed over and obscured what he was doing. Cecily's eyebrows shot up.

"I see! And here I thought you were just going to say I couldn't follow your hand disposing of it before you showed it to me."

"No. There are a number of good tricks that rely purely on speed and clever fingers, I'll admit that. But the best tricks, the tricks that really matter, are all about manipulating how people think, what they pay attention to. The cleverest trick in the book is just being able to make someone look at what you want them to look at instead of what they *should* look at. Even a slow trick will fool someone if the trickster makes sure they're not looking in the right place for it." Elias usually preferred to leave his audience wondering how in the world he'd managed to pull that trick off, but it was surprisingly pleasant to show Cecily how the trick had worked and see her appreciate the lesson it taught. Elias had learned a lot when one of the many rough, cautious men he would learn from had showed him that trick, with just the same words...

"I understand. Even someone sharp-eyed and quick-witted can't get around the trick because they're not looking in the right place for it. You're very clever, Elias," Cecily complimented him. Elias smiled a little. He'd noticed Cecily had started to refer to him by his first name today, instead of just calling him "Brook" like the others. He found he didn't mind it at all. Still...something she'd said stuck in his mind.

Bones had ruined his life with that exact knowledge. He walked into Elias's room, and then the King's hunting grounds and murdered him because nobody was looking for a dead man. He hadn't even been chased after he left the scene of the crime, because the evidence that remained had directed everyone's attention to Elias instead of the real culprit. Elias had become an outcast over a simple sleight-of-hand trick played on a larger scale.

But the shoe was on the other foot now, wasn't it? He didn't doubt Bones was out there still, alive and probably furious although hopefully quite badly injured...but as Cecily had reminded him, Bones would be completely certain Elias was dead. Elias would never figure into Bones's plans to get revenge on Amira for his humiliation…maybe he really could trick Bones this time. Mibotha's interference had moved him into the Basilisk-Eye's blind spot.

He could do a lot with that, if he was careful…but as Cecily had just reminded him, he was tricky enough to be clever.

"Well, don't leave me to hold up the evening's entertainment all by myself, now…" he commented. "There must be something you can do besides fight. Can you dance? How about you sing?"

"Take my word for it, you don't want me to sing," Cecily chuckled, shaking her head.

"Well, now you've gotten me curious!" Elias insisted, grinning at her. Cecily shook her head again, waving her arms.

"Not a chance, I say! I really can't sing a note!"

"Come, now. After all that I *really* have to hear how you sing. Nobody else will hear you, and nobody will believe me if I tell a soul, I promise."

"On your honor as a thoroughly dishonorable man?" Cecily teased, crossing her arms.

"No, just the assurance of a liar that my reputation is sure to precede me if I try to tell anyone about your singing," Elias shot back with a grin.

"You're setting yourself up for disappointment. I really cannot sing at all."

"And yet, that only makes me more interested to hear you try."

It took a little wheedling, but eventually Cecily gave up and decided to humor him. She attempted to sing part of a classical ballad, and Elias found his desire for entertainment abundantly fulfilled by how clearly it was an attempt.

Cecily had a nice laugh, and her voice was pleasant enough, but she clearly had no practice with singing. He had to cover his mouth with one hand as it became clear that his traveling companion was one of the most wholly tone-deaf individuals he had ever encountered.

Cecily finished quickly, looking embarrassed. Elias was quiet for a moment before he could comment.

"Well, I must say…you are a woman of your word," he said solemnly, before bursting out laughing at the look on her face. Cecily tried very hard to keep a straight face, putting her hands on her hips.

"You're terrible, Elias!"

"Compared to your singing voice, I'm actually feeling quite good about myself today," Elias laughed, leaning back. Cecily was unable to help herself, as soon enough she was laughing too. Elias couldn't remember the last time he'd been like this with anyone. The last five years had given him little use for laughter and plenty to be dismal about.

Elias passed the rest of the evening showing Cecily what he knew of sleight-of-hand, juggling, and a few little tricks with the fire. It was the first night in five years he'd felt completely at ease in the forest. Eventually, as the fire was dying, Cecily fell asleep, her body language suggesting a level of unconscious alertness to Elias but a peaceful smile on her face. He watched her for a little while before extinguishing the last of the flames and lying down to sleep himself.

Mibotha had said Cecily could be an important friend in their quest if he was smart. Elias had assumed that just meant that Cecily was the best means to get what they wanted out of this venture, but now he wasn't so sure. He didn't understand her sometimes, and he didn't agree with half the things she said, but Elias had never met a person with her sincerity that was not a small child or soon to be dead. No matter what Boors thought of his "excuse," there were a great many men in the world just as selfish and dishonest as Elias himself. Cecily, if she truly was exactly as she appeared, was the rarity here, not him. Maybe he shouldn't take knowing someone like that lightly.

If nothing else, Elias decided as he started to drift off, he was at least glad he was stuck with her for the time being instead of one of her compatriots. He and Cecily had absolutely nothing in common, despite what she seemed to think, but Elias would admit that of the people he'd known in the last five years of his life, she was probably the most pleasant to be around.

CHAPTER 24

The following morning, Elias and Cecily made their way through the forest, going slow still on account of their injuries but keeping out of sight as they headed for the far edge of the trees. It took nearly an entire day to make it through, but Elias couldn't help but grin when they finally left them behind. Duke Hache's territory now lay behind them, and with any luck Hache would sit there, oblivious to what had transpired on his lands, until Amira returned with an army of her own. They rested that night without any worry of soldiers tracking them, and Elias enjoyed feeling like he wasn't being hunted for once. Over the next few days, Cecily led the way. She seemed to know where she was going, and Elias was content to follow, grateful for each uneventful day that passed. At the end of the third day on the road, Cecily paused.

"It's going to be too dark to keep going soon..." she muttered, looking up. "We should find somewhere to rest for the night."

Elias nodded, not looking forward to that at all. They'd slept in the rough for the last few days, but they hadn't slept very much when you got right down to it. Camping out on the road invited bandits and throat cutters in the place of soldiers. They'd kept a wary eye out since running out of forest to hide in to avoid being jumped when the time came to rest. This was the time of day when most of the lawless men got to work. Elias knew that well enough from experience.

The problem was that trying to stay vigilant after the injuries they'd taken and the distance they'd had to travel on foot with little food or water meant Elias was about ready to drop dead and Cecily wasn't feeling much better. They couldn't keep this up, and they both knew it.

"There should be a town not far from here, if it's still standing..." Cecily went on, peering ahead. "If we hurry, we ought to be able to get there before it's too dark out."

"Approaching towns in the dark has not generally been the safest practice the last couple of years. A lot of sentries shoot first these days," Elias pointed out, remembering his encounter with the town guards before he and Cecily had met.

"I've had some experience getting in and out of towns, Elias. Don't worry about it," Cecily replied. "We'll get in, get some rooms, and make for the castle to regroup tomorrow."

"It might help if we could get some horses..."

"Yes, but I don't have the coin for a good pair of horses with me. I imagine you don't, either."

Elias decided to let the matter drop there. Pointing out that he hadn't *paid* for a horse in his life was not likely to sit well with a Royal Guard.

Fortunately for Elias's peace of mind, this town did not seem nearly as heavily fortified and guarded as the last one. While there were still signs that the town was ready to defend itself from unfriendly outsiders, most prominently its tall watchtower and guardsmen with pikes patrolling outside, it didn't look like a town that had ever been put to siege, like the one Elias had defended. You saw them sometimes, in areas the bandits couldn't get a foothold and the armies didn't cross through. Elias had always found them a good place to lie low for a while.

When you saw such a town in a dangerous territory, however, Elias had learned taking your chances with the sentries at the next town might be safer. He wasn't sure which of the two he was looking at right now, but Cecily didn't seem worried as she approached it.

"Halt!"

Instinct had Elias ready to do just the opposite and spring away before he even saw the men with spears approaching, but Cecily came to a stop calmly, and Elias reluctantly forced himself to do the same. Running at this point would only encourage them to be suspicious and give chase anyway, he supposed. There were four men, and their spears were readied in case he or Cecily made a false move. This town might not have walls, Elias realized, but it wasn't taking things easy, either. He hoped Cecily had some idea what she was doing.

"State your business!" one of the guards demanded, mustache bristling. No names involved yet, Elias thought. That was positive, at least.

"We are travelers, on our way home," Cecily replied, remaining calm. "We cannot complete our journey today, and you know as well as I do the risks of traveling after dark. We would like to rest in your town for the night and be on our way in the morning tomorrow." She slowly reached down to draw a small purse of coins out, showing it to the guards. "We can pay for food and lodging for the night, and stay only until the time to set out in the morning. Is this acceptable?"

The guards considered it among themselves for a moment or two, before the mustachioed man who had spoken earlier came to a decision.

"I doubt the two of you are bandits, but a number of thieves have tried to take advantage of our hospitality. You may stay here, but you must surrender your belongings, particularly your weapons, to us. They will be returned to you when it is time to for you to leave." That the guards and townsfolk would be watching them went without saying.

The terms made Elias nervous, despite sounding reasonable. Surrendering their belongings might give the townsfolk the temptation to take advantage of them. If Cecily handed over her sword, there wasn't much he could imagine her doing if the guards decided to keep it and told her to get lost at spearpoint.

Then again, Elias was still trying to shrug off the poison that should have killed him, and Cecily, despite giving little indication that her injuries bothered her, did not seem confident that holding onto her weapons and armor would make much difference at this point. They both needed to eat and rest more than they needed weapons at the moment.

"Fair enough," Cecily conceded, although Elias thought he detected some annoyance in her tone as well. Still, she began to disarm. Her blade was the most obvious weapon the two of them had, and Elias could see the men's tension drain considerably when she surrendered it without a fuss. Elias was examined with more suspicion, which he supposed was fair. He looked the part of a thief a good deal more than Cecily did, and he wasn't handing anything over. His dagger had been lost on the mountainside, and his bow was likely with his horse, wherever that was now. He had nothing to leave in the guards' keeping, although he made a show of going through what little he had to prove he wasn't hiding anything.

"My apologies. You can have my coat as collateral, if you'd like," he said, trying not to sound snide.

"We have all the dusters we need at the moment, mister," one of the younger guards replied, watching Elias warily. "Rags ain't hard to come by."

With some reluctance, Cecily also turned her armor over to the guards, and Elias held his breath for a moment before seeing no one gave the armor a second glance to realize its origin. He wondered if it was ignorance, like the duke's "recruitment officers," the gloom, or merely the fact that the armor was handed to them as a young woman removed it, and therefore was not the most interesting thing in the men's field of view at the moment.

Eventually, the guards seemed satisfied with this, thanked them for their cooperation and left with Cecily's armaments for the guardhouse while Elias and Cecily entered the town.

"It wasn't too long ago I'd have slept in a tree if those were the terms of getting in..." Elias remarked quietly.

"This is a consequence of the lawlessness of the land. Nobody can trust anyone else, and taking pity on a stranger in need of shelter can be fatal. This is what we're fighting against, Elias," Cecily replied, equally quiet. "But I've been through here before. The guards are a decent enough sort for these times, and they'll return what I gave them when the night passes without incident."

Elias decided to take her word for it. It wasn't like he had any better ideas for what they could do at this point.

The town seemed to ignore their passage for the most part. A few people glanced up and squinted suspiciously at them as they passed, but Elias was relieved to find that he and Cecily were apparently treated as subjects of little interest and ignored. Recognition had never been a friend to him in times like these.

"There...we can stay there for the night," Cecily spoke up, pointing out a large tavern to Elias. "They have decent rooms, and more importantly, I trust the patrons not to try anything while we're asleep. It's just a bit noisy."

"You said an inn, not a tavern," Elias muttered, gut clenching.

"What does it matter? Either one has rooms that suit our purposes for the night."

"I've had very bad luck with taverns for the last few years," Elias mumbled, trying not to get nervous. Taverns had a lot of emotional people in them, and Elias stood out in that sort of environment. Worse, taverns were always the places you'd find the goddamn bard at work, and if one of them started up that bloody song while he was there...well, it wouldn't be a pleasant night for anyone.

"It will be fine, Elias. We're not here to drink, we'll simply purchase some rooms and wait in them until morning," Cecily reassured him.

Cecily was clearly not familiar with the difference between expectations for the night and the reality of that night in the way Elias was. Looking back, one of the only phrases Elias found less comforting than "it will be fine" was "what's the worst that could happen?" Still, things had worked out better for Cecily since they'd teamed up than Elias would have had any right to expect in her position. Maybe her luck would cancel out his for the night and things really *would* be fine.

Elias didn't have much confidence in the thought, but he held onto it like a shield as he followed Cecily into the tavern. It was a smokey, dimly-lit place, which immediately set him back on edge. Places like this used to be like a second home to him, but those days were gone with his notoriety. Once more he and Cecily were briefly regarded by the patrons as they first entered, then dismissed as not of any great interest, for which Elias was quite grateful. In this kind of gloom, he wouldn't stand out at all unless someone was looking for him, and if nobody took an interest, he was pretty safe.

Cecily made her way over to the tavern's owner, a plump woman. She was surprisingly pleasant, considering how troubling the atmosphere of her establishment was to Elias. He decided to leave the discussion with her to Cecily, tuning out their conversation to look around. Maybe he was just too wary, but if something WAS wrong here, he wanted to be aware of it before it was aware of him. But nothing jumped out at him. There were men drinking and playing cards, and women both there to work and to relax...nothing out of the ordinary. Better yet, none of them paying him any mind at all.

Elias eased up slightly. One thing he had learned in his career was that sometimes a feeling was just a feeling. Still, he felt better for having seen for himself there weren't any blades being readied or signs that this tavern was inclined towards violence among the patrons. He came back to the conversation in time for Cecily to end her small-talk with the owner and buy a pair of single rooms.

Two singles, he mused, watching the money change hands. Cecily didn't have any worries at all he'd try to pull anything if left unattended for the night. It had been quite a while since someone had trusted him that much. Of course, maybe she just didn't want to share a room with him, despite their increased tolerance of each others' presence.

"There, you see?" Cecily asked, turning to him when the transaction was done. "No trouble at all. Now we can just rest for the night and be on our way tomorrow."

"That sounds good to me. I'll feel a lot better when I've slept in a bed," Elias grunted, before his stomach grumbled loudly to remind him he'd barely eaten anything all day to fuel all the activity he'd demanded of his body. Cecily heard it, despite the ambient noise, and touched her own stomach.

"Perhaps we should have a bite to eat before we rest. We won't get far if we're starving," she commented, pointing out an empty table out of the way. "Go sit, I'll see if I can pay for some food."

"I'm not sure hanging around is such a good idea..." Elias muttered.

"Neither am I, but nobody's going to pay us any mind if we blend in. Most of the people that saw us come in already forgot we're here," Cecily said. "We'll just keep a low profile and nobody will notice us."

Elias hoped that Cecily was right. Cautious as he wanted to be, he was starving. One good meal would be a blessing at a time like this. He sat at the empty table, not looking at anybody and doing nothing suspicious. To his profound relief, nobody took any notice of him. Elias had once been very confident in his ability to be a face in the crowd, but that had been years ago, in a very different life. Now he was simply relieved every time someone's eye slid over him without making the connection.

Cecily returned a while later with some water and two bowls of stew. It looked like fairly meager fare, but that was to be expected with the famine. Elias simply counted his blessings that the contents of his bowl were in any way different from the contents of his cup, and nodded gratefully to Cecily before starting to eat.

It wasn't very good, but the stew was hot and it had more ingredients in it than the tomato-tinged water he had gratefully eaten for supper some nights, so he had no cause to complain or dwell on the taste. A little more comfortable that nobody was looking at him too closely, Elias started to listen to the conversation around, tuning out irrelevant babble about gambling or work to see if there was something more interesting.

"There's talk the fighting will start up in earnest again, soon," a grizzled old man not far away was commenting to his friends. "It might not be far from here, either."

"Ah, I don't believe that for a minute. There's nothing left to make war worth it for any of them. Evangeline took all the land she meant to ages ago and she's more focused on building than expanding. Lord Dunst knows he's done for if he reminds 'em he's still around, and Steelskirts doesn't have the means to take more land even if she wants to."

"Duke Hache is moving around a lot behind those cliffs. I tell you, the bastard's not done yet."

"He can rattle his saber 'til the end of time, he's done for just the same," a woman at the table commented, waving a hand dismissively. "Vermillion Field was the end of him, he's just too thick to realize he lost years ago."

"Not like he'll roll over and die if he has a chance to bring someone down with him. No, I think Horace is right. If anyone's going to stir the pot again, it'll be Hache."

Elias glanced back to Cecily, realizing she'd been listening in, too. The Royal Guard looked rather troubled by what she'd heard.

"I knew Lady Evangeline, back in the old days," she muttered to Elias. "She was a friend of my father's...and now she's a warlord, being talked about like she's the same as Hache..."

"This disaster's done strange things to a lot of people," Elias pointed out. "Some died, some starved, some turned to banditry, some holed up and got suspicious...and a few poor bastards started *leading*."

"It's not a joke, Elias," Cecily said sharply.

"No, it's not," he agreed, raising a hand. "But it was as natural as people turning to banditry or building walls. Orderly succession is one thing, but the entire country went into chaos. Nobody was in charge anymore, so everyone tried to take charge, either to make sense of it all or so they could get some power for themselves. Good reasons and bad, selfish and selfless, we've had a lot of warlords with their own reasons for doing what they did. Maybe Evangeline was trying to do good taking control of some territory, I can't say one way or the other. But the land Amira needs to take back isn't going to be entirely lawless because there are four warlords holding a good portion of it in check for now. If not all of them resist her return, restoring Amira to the throne will be a lot easier than if the country was in complete anarchy."

"Hache will fight tooth and nail to stop her from taking power. I can't say how the others will react," Cecily muttered.

"I'll count our blessings if Hache is the only one that opposes her when she reveals herself, but the odds are about even on all of them," Elias said, leaning back in his chair. "It's going to be a long road ahead for her..."

The land will rise for its queen.

Elias paused. There was something odd about the way Mibotha had said that, but the spirit said nothing more, and its presence withdrew again. Since finding the Regalia, Mibotha seemed to be keeping its distance a lot more than when they had started. There was something suspicious in that, Elias decided, but damned if he could figure out what.

"Maybe it'd be for the best if the whole lot of them went to war," Elias heard, and he glanced over to see the table he'd been eavesdropping on had resumed their conversation. "Them and all the bandits, and Brook too, if they find the rock he crawled under. If they just made a big bloody finish of it, we'd all be better off."

"Might be no more than they deserve, but it won't make things better. The woods are near teeming with angry ghosts as it is. Restless dead, wood spirits, and other, fouler things, I wouldn't be surprised," an old man muttered, shuddering. "Foul things are starting to spawn in the forests and the rivers, and people that go there alone don't come back anymore. I've heard people say they can see Basilisk-Eye's ghost sometimes, on moonless nights."

"People think they see anything on a moonless night. I don't believe half the things they say are out there. If you ask me, the only things multiplying around here are superstitious dullards and corpses."

"Maybe not Basilisk-Eye's ghost, but he's right that there's something foul in the land. You hear about more bloody mages these days than you ever did before the famine. Wouldn't be surprised if the basilisks came back to the land while we weren't looking."

"Hah. Not bloody likely. Morys might have been shot down, but he finished the last of the hellsnakes before Brook finished him." The speaker, a burly man, took a deep swig from his mug. "Morys would've done something about these mages, too, you can bet your life on that. This sorry lot will probably try to hire them, and it'll serve them right when that bites 'em in the arse."

Shows what they know, Elias thought to himself, focusing on finishing his meal. Morys had worked out fast enough that a kingdom with basilisks would never really be at peace. He'd exterminated them accordingly; building weapons that would bring down the adults, burning their young, and smashing their eggs. The kings before him had tried to push the basilisks out of the kingdom, and a few sorry bastards had tried to make use of them. Only Morys had managed to drive the monsters to extinction.

Mages had been another matter. Elias had no proof, no mages he'd met, no court officials that showed sudden magical power in his presence, not even a cryptic reference to their presence from Morys himself. But he had known Morys, and that was all the proof Elias needed to be sure mages that could be of use had been in Morys's employ. Morys was not a man who threw away things he might need, people least of all. Elias suspected Morys had been quite well aware of what Blanche really was when he picked her to guard his daughter. He wondered idly if Blanche, capable of making a pile of bodies into ash with her power, might have found her way into Morys's employ one way or another even if she hadn't joined the Guard.

He didn't doubt that the man was right enough that the warlords would try to gather mages to themselves, any more than he doubted that they would all deny they were doing so, or that it would come back to bite them eventually.

Used in secret, looked down on, publicly unaccepted but necessary behind the scenes...that sounded like a familiar life. Elias shook the thought off quickly. Thinking mages were like normal people was where the trouble started, he imagined. Whatever else they had in common, Blanche could kill him by exhaling. They were not, and never would be, alike.

Cecily finished her own meal, saying nothing and looking bone-tired and distant. Elias could see clearly that the exhaustion she'd held off on the road was finally demanding its due, and her thoughts had not been bright ones to alleviate it. She glanced up at Elias.

"That's better than an empty stomach, at least," she murmured. "We should go upstairs and rest. We'll need our strength for tomorrow morning."

Yes, she has a point, Mibotha spoke up suddenly. Only a lot of practice kept Elias from flinching as the voice intruded on his thoughts again. *In fact, you may be well served going upstairs immediately, Elias Brook, paying no heed to anything you hear, nor coming back downstairs.*

Mibotha sounded oddly keen on Elias excusing himself quickly, and while Elias had no particular desire to stick around, he felt compelled to look around again anyway to see if he could spot why. Instinct was well and good, but he didn't like jumping to obey Mibotha for no good reason, even when the spirit echoed his own thoughts.

His contrary decision to linger and look around again was almost immediately punished when his eyes settled on a red hat with a white feather in the crowd that hadn't been there before. Elias paled as his second sweep of the tavern revealed an outfit that drew the eye like the world's most obnoxious lighthouse, and he heard the dreaded sound of fingers toying with the strings of a lute.

Oh, no. *Gods,* no. Not *that,* not *now!*

It took a herculean feat of self-restraint on Elias's part not to tear his own ears off and flee howling into the night as the lute was prepared and the tune burned into his hindbrain as a warning to start running and never stop kicked up.

"Listen, my friends, to my infamous tale! A tale of woe, of cunning, of betrayal!"

Elias had never understood why they felt compelled to open the songs up like that. All of the damn bards did it, as though they had to sound as stupid as they looked to be considered any good in their profession. He was faintly aware his teeth were grinding in a way he would probably regret if he lived to old age.

"Noble King Morys, fearing no evil / Rode out to hunt as the sun blazed high / Never imagining, as he traversed the forest / That traitors had marked this the day he would die!"

It wasn't even a *good* song, Elias reflected, not noticing his fists had clenched tight. He might have been able to live with it, somehow, if the song that had hounded him for five years, making his life worse every step of the way, had actually been a good song, but he couldn't even have that.

It was a song that never would have caught on in different times, if there hadn't been a famine followed by a lot of war. The bard who had come up with it had likely been quite drunk. Elias didn't like to imagine how else such a complete lack of talent had ever been heard far and wide. The worst part was that the music by itself was good. The composer must have come up with that part long before Morys died, but then felt the need to saddle an excellent, catchy tune with lyrics that were both rubbish musically and the social poison that had earned Elias several near-death experiences already.

He thought he might be all right with forfeiting his chance to get out of Valka if he could just make sure the man who wrote the song went there with him when it was time to go.

"Oh..." Cecily muttered, understanding Elias's expression as she heard the song start up, too. It was hard to gauge her reaction, but she was at least concerned that things were about to go bad like Elias had predicted.

"We should get upstairs," Elias gritted out, speaking mostly in hopes his teeth might not shatter if he forced some words between them. "It'll get ugly if I'm still down here when he reaches the chorus."

"For him, or for you?"

"YES."

"Right," Cecily muttered, starting to lead the way upstairs.

Unfortunately, a man stepped in their path, someone Elias hadn't taken much notice of previously. He had a look on his face that Elias recognized.

It was the song, it really was. No matter how many years went by, that tune seemed to make people remember his image on wanted posters with a clarity they couldn't achieve for the face of their firstborn son.

"I think I've seen you before, mister..."

Not drunk, Elias guessed. His speech was too clear and his gaze was too steady. He was a big man, too, and he had a lot of big friends that might not have looked up from their cards if it hadn't been for that bard. The comment had not turned a lot of heads, thanks to the loud singing, but it wouldn't have to turn many for this to get ugly.

"I've just got one of those faces," he muttered, quickly directing the face in question towards the floor. Unfortunately, this man was not lazy enough to let that pass unchallenged.

"Maybe you've got one of those names, too. Let's hear it, friend," he said in a low voice. Elias considered what might happen if he laid him out now, but the man's friends were paying attention, and the man addressing him had not left his stance open while he spoke. Elias was fairly sure he could take him if he had to, poison or no poison, but he'd been wrong before. It wouldn't be easy even if he was right, and taking on this man in a fight was only going to be the START of his problems.

"My name's Osric," he lied quickly. "Osric Weaver. I'm just a traveler, mister, and I'm tired to my bones. If it's all the same to you, I'd like to go upstairs and rest."

"Osric, huh?" It appeared the inquisitive barfly was not fooled by the bluff, even though Elias had put a lot of practice into tossing that one off as honestly as he could over the years. "You don't look like an Osric to me."

"I get that a lot, but that is my name," Elias tried, hoping that sticking to the lie might assist in forcing it through.

"Leave him be," Cecily spoke up, stepping between them before the man could reply. "He answered your question."

"Stay out of this, lady, it's none of your business," the man grunted, before jabbing a finger at the dim wall. "The posters fade, but they don't come down...*Brook.*"

Elias didn't need to look over at what the man had pointed out to know that there was a wanted poster hanging in the tavern, bearing his likeness. A poster that had likely been put up five years ago, and slowly yellowed and frayed on the wall as Elias lived five years in the cracks. Everyone in the tavern had probably glanced at it dozens of times just coming in over the last five years, and now it had finally done its work. No one was left that would actually *pay* the bounty offered on him. It was one of the reasons Elias had been able to ally, however temporarily, with other desperate men like the scavengers that had ultimately been his undoing. But Elias showing his face anywhere those posters hadn't been torn down meant there was a higher-than-usual chance someone would recognize him, and things always got ugly fast when that happened.

Elias decided if this did turn into a brawl, he was going to see if he could drag that bard into this. The evening might be worthwhile if he could beat the singer to death with his own lute, whatever else happened.

"You are mistaken, friend," Cecily said, surprisingly calm. "Still, I understand your error. Osric has had no end of grief before when people have noticed his likeness to that scoundrel. Even I mistook him for Elias Brook when I first met him. Come, let me buy you a drink, no offense taken."

She was able to lie more convincingly than Elias had given her credit for. He desperately hoped the man would go for it. He wasn't up for a fight or the more likely public beating if he didn't. Unfortunately, as so often happened, what Elias hoped for did not come to pass, and the barfly did not fall for Cecily's lie.

"I said, *stay out of this,*" the man said irritably, going to push Cecily out of his path.

Elias wasn't sure what happened next. He thought Cecily lost her footing for a moment, but in the time it took to blink the man who had been stepping towards him was flat on his face and Cecily was kneeling down to help him up.

"You're too drunk to be walking around, sir," she commented in the voice of extremely finite patience as she helped him to his feet. "Not a good state to be making assumptions or accusations. We're all feeling a little raw today, aren't we?"

"I'm fine," the barfly growled, rubbing his face as he staggered upright with Cecily's help. "Head's perfectly clear, m'foot just slipped—"

The moment Cecily took her hands away, however, the man was flat on his back, cracking his head against the floor with a groan of pain. Elias was fairly sure he'd seen Cecily's leg move very slightly, but people saw all kinds of things in poor lighting.

"Slippery as the floor is, I think it's best you get your feet off it before you hurt yourself," Cecily replied, turning to the table. "Your friend needs to be getting home, I imagine. You ought to help him."

The men at the table stared blankly back at her, and Elias could hear slow, rusty gears turning in their heads. They'd heard what their friend had said, even if the rest of the tavern hadn't over the bard's singing, but their friend had just taken two graceless and rather painful tumbles after saying it. Elias was able to tell which ones were trying to figure out what had just happened and which ones suspected they knew but were weighing the risk.

"All right, mate, the lady's got a point. Best be gettin' home before we need to be rolled there," one of the cleverer-looking men at the table commented, helping his friend up.

"That's Brook! I swear it! We can nab him!" the man protested, not as loudly due to the splitting headache he'd just acquired.

"You're seeing things, mate. You remember last year? If we half-kill every dark-haired tramp that comes by the guardsmen might start to think *we're* the ones that ought to be nabbed."

The mumbled conversation went on as they left the tavern guiding their stricken friend. As Elias and Cecily moved to the stairs more people than Elias would have liked gave them wary glances.

"I don't think they bought it," he muttered to Cecily. "We'll be seeing them again."

"If they wait until I've had a chance to lie down for a while before they work up the nerve to try something, that's fine with me," Cecily muttered, swaying a little as she led the way.

"Those were some pretty deft moves for someone in your state," he remarked, to see if Cecily would say anything.

"Not really. I was trying to lay him out cold with that first one," Cecily muttered darkly. "When my ears stop ringing and I can see straight, I can show you 'deft.'"

Deft or not, she'd gotten him a reprieve, however temporarily, from a situation that would have gone very badly for him if he'd been alone, Elias reflected. For an honorable sort, Cecily was surprisingly useful to have around.

"Mibotha, let me know if someone comes to try and get us while I'm asleep," he muttered, once he and Cecily had separated into their own rooms. It was a dark, bad-smelling, spartan affair, but it had a bed and absolutely nothing else was important at the moment.

You will know if you are about to be in peril.

Elias nodded, not bothering to change before he collapsed on the bed and let his world go black.

He'd take whatever rest he could get. He suspected he and Cecily would be leaving in a bit of a rush tomorrow.

CHAPTER 25

The knowledge of trouble not far away had often cost Elias many hours of sleep in the past, but he found rest came with no difficulty for him tonight. Both body and mind were too concerned with what he had survived already to pay much attention to what might lie directly ahead.

Sleep was usually a simple time for Elias, dreamless and quiet, but this time his mind did not rest as his body did. Elias found himself floating high above the land, taking in Yivyn from a perspective only the birds knew. From his vantage point, there were no factions or borders, merely an unhappy land, filled with a number of gaping wounds. From above, Elias could take in dozens of battlegrounds from the last five years, each carving an ugly scar into the landscape, while the drought and blight brought ruin everywhere like a pox.

To Elias, it seemed as though Yivyn was being held in a hand of unspeakable size, and he could not tell where the hand holding it up for inspection ended and the land began. He became faintly aware of emotions that were not his own, strange and yet somewhat familiar.

Anticipation and impatience were the strongest, with a worrying, desperate edge to each. Something was missing from the scene below, and all around him Elias could feel a terrible, hungry need for it to arrive. He could feel sorrow also, and a torpid confusion along with a sense of sullen resentment. There was a miasma of unhappiness all around Yivyn. Elias wasn't sure it was all coming from the people living there.

And then he felt it again, just like he had under the shrine; a massive, unspeakable anger welling up from everything.

Elias heard tiny shrieks from the landscape far below as the hand he imagined holding Yivyn up for inspection twitched, and then slowly curled into a fist of rage below him. The screams reached a crescendo below before cutting out with terrifying swiftness as the fist crushed Yivyn in its anger, long savage nails digging into the palm until blood welled up between the massive fingers. The sense of anger was not quelled by the destructive act. He could feel it swell, swallowing up all the other emotions as the blood continued to flow from the clenched, destroying fist.

Elias knew in his heart that if he turned around, he would see the bearer of the terrible wrath looking back at him. Terror and curiosity warred within him, but he found he did not dare look back.

Something about his own hands felt wrong. To distract himself from the feeling his back was turned to something unspeakably immense and very, very angry, Elias looked down at his own hands.

They were drenched with blood. As Elias's eyes widened, he felt the terrible anger shift from the broken land crushed in the fist below him to Elias himself.

With glacial but still somehow unescapable speed, the crushing fist unfurled, and bloody fingers began to reach up for Elias as the last of Yivyn was washed away in the blood seeping from the hand.

Elias's eyes slammed open, and he half lunged out of his bed before realizing there was no hand and no anger directed at him. Merely himself in a dark, empty room, soaked with sweat.

"What the hell was *that?*" he muttered to himself, running a hand over his face. It was tempting to shrug it off as just a dream, but that didn't feel right. He hadn't dreamed since he was just a kid, a trait he'd been quite glad of many times in his life. Nothing had bothered him when he slept for the entirety of his adult life before tonight.

An ugly suspicion formed that he may have observed his unwelcome guest's dream, but Elias considered this for a while before dismissing it. Mibotha could apparently be tired, based on the tone of its voice after the times it had helped him heal, but he had trouble imagining the spirit sleeping. He didn't even know if it had the capacity to do so. As far as he could tell, the spirit was nothing but a consciousness wrapped in whatever power it was using to help him. He couldn't imagine it had dreams. That it might have been having one now seemed unlikely when it had assured him he would know if someone approached. Besides, he had slept many nights with Mibotha in his head, and no nightmares had come.

He considered asking Mibotha, but he didn't trust the spirit to give him a straight answer. There was something secret and dangerous lurking under Mibotha's concern for Amira, Elias was certain, and he was reluctant to let the spirit know if it was tipping its hand to him at last.

His accord with Mibotha was reliant entirely on the spirit's own interpretation of their agreement, after all, and if Mibotha alone was capable of rescuing him from eternity in hell, Elias didn't know that anything would prevent it from altering their deal when its true agenda came into focus. He needed to have power over Mibotha when that time came and that meant he would keep his thoughts to himself.

You should be resting, Elias Brook. You'll need your strength.

"No danger coming?" Elias asked quietly. "No one moving around?"

I would have alerted you if that had been so. You should concern yourself with not being a burden on Cecily when the time comes to depart in the morning. Refusing to rest makes my part of our partnership more troublesome than it needs to be. It is not a simple thing to keep you alive, and you have not been helpful on the matter.

Reluctantly, Elias laid himself back down, closing his eyes in the dark. Mibotha had a point, he supposed. And if he was right, and they needed to leave in more of a hurry than one might hope, he wanted to be as well-rested as possible. He had no way of knowing when it would be safe to rest again after tonight.

He was not further troubled by dreams for the remaining few hours he rested, and when he next awoke, it was to a knock on the door. Since Mibotha had not informed him of anyone coming to attack him, Elias opened the door and saw it was Cecily.

"Good morning, Elias," she said, nodding politely. Elias returned the gesture, but Cecily pressed right on to business. "It's still early, but we should get out of here, quickly. After last night, I don't think we should hang around."

"I agree. You should get your weapons and armor from the guards. Meet back up with me around here," Elias suggested.

"Shouldn't we stick together? Those men might be looking for you."

"If it wasn't just a drunken fancy that they forgot in an hour, there's a good chance at least one of them took it to the guardhouse. If they did, there's a chance my wanted poster is on their mind, and they might try to arrest or execute me if I come in with you to get your things. I'll just stay out of sight while you grab what you need to, and we'll get out of here."

"...All right...but be careful, Elias. If something goes wrong while we're separated, it will be a lot harder for both of us," Cecily muttered. Elias could see the decision to split up worried her, and he would have to admit they were in trouble if Cecily was right and something *did* happen while they were separated, but he suspected walking around town after last night might draw more attention. He'd have to hide out of sight, in case people came looking for him at the tavern, but he did need to stay somewhere Cecily could find him. Cecily started to go, but then turned back to Elias.

"Actually Elias, why don't you hide out by the stable? People might expect you to stay holed up in the tavern."

The stable was relatively close to the edge of town with a decent number of places to stay unseen. Elias nodded in agreement.

"All right. We'll meet there. Don't take too long, eh?"

"Good luck, Elias. Let's hope our departure doesn't draw undue attention," Cecily sighed, heading off quickly for the guardhouse.

Elias made his way slowly and cautiously out of the tavern. A small part of him considered trying to leave through the window, but he knew dramatic gestures like that would only attract more notice in a place like this. Even if people were hanging around the tavern, Elias had experience finding the right moment to nonchalantly walk out the door he'd come in through unnoticed.

The early hour meant that the tavern was nearly deserted, but Elias still took special care that nobody was about when he proceeded out, moving casually yet stealthily as he headed for the stables. Elias relaxed a little as he neared his destination without being challenged and hoped the near-disaster from last night had been ended by Cecily's intervention, or at least delayed enough that they would be long gone by the time the town awoke.

As Elias entered the stables Mibotha sent a shock of alarm into his mind.

Hide, Elias Brook! There is a large group coming towards the stables, and quickly! it warned.

Elias didn't need to be told twice, searching around for somewhere he could conceal himself in hopes of remaining undiscovered.

The first hiding place that presented itself was a clean haystack near the entrance of the stables, and for a moment Elias considered it. Unfortunately, experience had taught Elias he was usually not the only person that considered a hiding place like that first, and his eye fell inevitably on a nearby pitchfork. He'd gotten enough of being stabbed with a pitchfork for one lifetime, he reflected with a little wince, and anyone with any brains at all was going to prod around in that haystack just to be safe.

Quickly dismissing the haystack and looking around in a hurry for somewhere else he could conceal himself, Elias next spotted another heap inside the stable. Apparently the owner had been a little lax recently in disposing of the waste. Rancid, filthy hay, bits of broken sticks, and a large number of things Elias preferred not to think about had been combined into a slumped, stinking heap. Nobody in their right mind would touch such a thing with anything but a long stick, but it was big enough for a man Elias's size to dig into, and Elias was in a hurry.

Just like old times, he thought to himself without any nostalgia at all as he went to the foul pile and started to dig into it. Find a filthy, stinking haystack, or a heap of garbage, or some other place foul enough nobody would poke around looking for you, and settle in and try not to breathe or think about what you're covered in until the mob moves on. There were days he'd needed several soaks in a freezing river just to get the stink out of his skin and clothes, but he'd gladly take that again to being caught by a mob.

In times past, Elias had tried to leave himself a peephole to observe the search for him, but he'd nearly been discovered several times for doing so. Instead, Elias concealed himself entirely and settled for listening for his oncoming enemies, still a ways off by the time he was wholly out of sight. He tried to get as comfortable as he could in his hiding place because he imagined he was going to have a few long, tense moments of sitting still in this pile of refuse before he could even make sure he wasn't observed leaving it.

Elias held his breath at first when the mob finally arrived, both to eliminate a tiny bit of noise and movement and further strengthen his hiding place and to avoid having to smell the haystack and whatever little creatures were living in it as much as possible.

For a time, there were a number of angry voices, and Elias kept very still as he heard people searching around. There was a muffled stabbing noise that let Elias know he would indeed have gotten reacquainted with the stab of a pitchfork if he'd hidden in the haystack. He kept tense, aware that all it would take was one particularly canny villager suggesting he might have hidden in another heap by the barn to make his life a lot more difficult, but to his profound relief, the sounds of the mob started to withdraw, and he could detect their disappointment. They thought he had given them the slip. Scarcely able to believe his impromptu shelter had been so successful, Elias shifted slightly, finally relaxing.

In keeping with Elias's luck, this ever so slight shift either awoke or startled a large, evil-looking rat, and Elias was able to turn and see the creature when he felt it twist around by his hand to look at him. It could have been a mouse, or something meek that would flee from whatever disturbed it, Elias reflected, but naturally Elias had sheltered in a barn with rats that looked like they could fight dogs.

Don't you *dare*, he thought as hard as he could as the evil beady little eyes sized him up. Unfortunately that had never worked for Elias with animals in the past and it didn't work this time. The rat jumped on Elias's hand and bit it with an angry little squeak. Elias was barely able to bite back a curse as pain shot up his arm, but he wasn't able to stop himself from flinching at the bite and jumping a little at the pain. As if to confirm Elias's belief that the natural order of life was things going wrong one after another, his movement within the pile was spotted.

"THERE HE IS!"

It was an all-too-familiar feeling as Elias saw the hay he was hiding under ripped away, leaving him facing all the men from the tavern last night, and quite a few new faces behind them, all glaring at him. It was a big group, some of them equipped with large blunt instruments. Elias counted his blessings that at least this group didn't have any blades that he could see.

It had been quite a while since anyone who would pay for Elias was reachable by the common folk, but the figure of blame for the war and the famine was no less reviled five years after the fact than he had been five hours after. Elias stood shakily, facing the mob, his face going slack as thoughts of avoiding what was coming gave away to analysis.

These were hard, hardy people, and it was a group of the toughest that appeared to have come. He didn't see any killers among them, not at first glance. He still wasn't sure if it was fate, luck, or human nature that the mobs that had caught him over the years hadn't killed him, but he'd been caught before by folks like this, and he suspected they would not murder him on purpose.

This did not change the fact they would quite certainly beat him to a bloody pulp and leave him to die outside town with the approval of their consciences.

"We knew we'd find you skulking around here. Trying to steal a horse and make a run for it," one of the men accused, gripping a club tightly. "But you're not sneaking off, Brook. Not without paying for what you've put us through."

You could talk your way out, sometimes. When there were only a couple of them, you could fight your way out. Sometimes you could even run away. Those three options had saved his life from the deadlier mobs he'd faced, the ones intent on lynching or worse. Elias knew running, fighting, or talking would get him killed today, and so he took a step forward, offering no threat or resistance. You didn't fight a mob like this, he'd learned from experience. You couldn't win, and it would just be worse when they did beat you down.

Don't be brave, he reminded himself. Don't turn the other cheek, or insist on standing back up. Let them smash your face into the dirt and jump up and down on you. Cry and piss yourself and beg for mercy. A brave man won't last thirty minutes against this mob. A pathetic one can crawl away with his life.

"Listen, we can—" he started, before the first fist hit him in the stomach like a brick. The blow nearly folded him in half, but he caught a powerful uppercut to the face so he was standing up when the men and women with cudgels stepped in. Elias knew better than to dodge or counter the blows, but he let himself raise his arms futilely to block as many as he could while dozens of others smashed into him. Trying to be a martyr to their rage just pissed people off, he'd discovered. Being beaten, flogged, stabbed, it could always get worse if people didn't feel like they were hurting you enough.

His attempts to surrender peacefully to the mob's beating in hope they would leave him alive were disrupted when a cudgel smashed into the back of his head, sending a shock of pain and a burst of animal fury through his entire body. Elias whirled, unable to remain passive, and smashed the heel of his palm into the attacker's face, feeling something crunch as the man went sprawling. Despite the renewed anger, Elias twisted and struggled, his plan to ride out the storm in tatters as his anger forced him to lash out again and again at his tormentors even as their clubs surrounded him and bore him down.

A well-placed kick in the fork put a stop to that. The anger was still there, but the fight went out of him in an instant as his body demanded he crumple up on the spot against the pain. A kneecap hit him between the eyes and left him seeing stars. The clubs rained down on his head, eventually driving him down low enough that the punches turned into kicks and stomps. Elias realized, with a curious detachment, that he couldn't really breathe, hear, or see. There was a lot of blood in his eyes, and as one blow after another rained down on his head, sound was reduced to a simple buzzing. He was pretty sure several of his ribs were broken, and taking a breath between the kicks to his chest and stomach was simply not happening. Instinct forced him to curl up, fold in on himself, trying to protect his head and his guts from the fury of the mob.

I hope I don't pass out, he thought with rather more calmness than he expected was proper for his position. They might kill me if I'm unconscious, intentionally or not.

He forced himself not to lose track of the pain. If that got away from him, there wasn't going to be much to keep him from slipping into darkness with nothing but the taste of his own blood informing him he still existed at the moment. It was almost rhythmic at this point, the cudgels crashing down to fill his vision with little red and green bursts as his body twitched in pain. He was fairly sure he was showing his pathetic underbelly to the mob with no trouble at all, even if he couldn't hear his own pleas for mercy and doubted they were at all coherently formed. Elias let his body fight to save itself naturally as he started to drift through the haze of confusion and pain aimlessly, waiting for the end.

It was almost nostalgic, being here, he realized. It had been a while since he'd been caught like this. He wondered if anyone was to blame, or if luck had just decided to twist the knife again. He had been terrified beyond the capacity to think the first couple times this had happened to him. How odd it was now that he felt almost bored, if only because he knew full well how much worse things would get if he didn't keep pretending to be observing his progress into a large stain on the ground like it was happening to someone else.

Just as Elias began to feel his attempts to remain conscious failing, something loud rang over the faint buzzing that had become his hearing. Elias felt like he was jolted, suddenly. The haze formed into a bloodied mess shaped like a man, squirming on the ground like a worm as if it would somehow protect him from the pain.

Then he was the writhing mess, and Elias was suddenly acutely aware that he felt like he'd been trampled by wild horses badly enough it left bruises on his soul. For whatever reason, his hearing was clear enough that the next big noise actually made sense.

"I SAID STEP AWAY FROM THAT MAN!"

I must be hallucinating, Elias decided. They beat my brains in hard enough that I can actually hear Boors shouting in my head.

An errant twitch managed to flip him over, however, and Elias saw through a blurry red haze that Boors was indeed standing before the mob, his mace out and ready for action. The mob seemed a little unsure of how to proceed. They were still brimming with anger and resentment, that was clear enough, but the sight of a musclebound giant in armor, bearing a mace was a much less attractive target than what was left of Elias Brook, unresisting at their feet.

"T-This is Elias Brook, he is!" one of the men spoke up uncertainly. "He's a wanted man, a criminal!"

"I know who that is," Boors said, taking a step forward. "Do you know who *I* am, any of you?"

"T-That's Boors the Lion!" said a thin, frightened voice. Elias's life had been saved by that tone a great many times in the past.

"Can't be, the Lion died five years ago. Ol' Steelskirts did him in! Everyone knows that!"

"I am happy to tell you rumors of my demise were only that, my friend," Boors said as he took a step forward, his face like a thunderstorm. "I am Sir Boors of the Royal Guard, and this man is under my protection. If you still wish to carry out your grudge against him, I will be your opponent."

No one in their right mind would take that challenge, and Elias was relieved to see that his attackers were clearly quite sane, if rather confused.

"But he's a traitor! A regicide, even! It's not right, Royal Guard protecting filth like that!"

"Elias Brook is many things," Boors conceded, coming over to Elias. The mob wisely drew back, quickly, as Elias finally managed to unfold himself a little. "But he is not the murderer of our King. We of the Royal Guard have discovered the true assassin, and Elias Brook has given us his aid in bringing the killer to justice. He is a true servant of Queen Amira, rightful ruler of these lands, and I will not allow one of my lady's supporters to be subjected to this treatment, whatever mistakes he has made."

That certainly got townsfolk muttering, and a few looked at Boors with something that mixed hope, fear, and disbelief.

"The princess is alive? She hasn't abandoned us?"

"The princess is now your rightful queen," Boors replied. "She will bring an end to this age of strife. Return to your homes. Await news of her coming. Prepare yourself for what lies ahead."

The mob dispersed, not from fear of Boors's mace, but looking rather dazed at the news he had given them. Elias turned painfully and looked up at Boors, wiping the blood from his eyes. He could tell just by touching his face that he was a bloody mess, and it would be much worse if Boors hadn't intervened. It was like drinking a tall mug of vinegar to realize he possibly owed the big man his life, now.

"Thank you," he managed to get out, trying very carefully to keep his mind blank to shut out the pain and the idea of being indebted to his least favorite person in the world. Boors gave him a hard glance, kneeling down beside him as he put away his mace.

"You should be dead, Elias Brook," he said bluntly. "Where is Cecily?"

"It's a pleasure to see you again, too, Boors."

"Answer me, man! Where is Cecily? Is she with you?" Boors demanded, shaking him. Elias's collarbone nearly broke as he did so, but he avoided the large temptation to black out in pain *now* as Mibotha went to work keeping his battered body together.

"She's with me! At the guardhouse!" he managed to get out. "Coming to meet me here!"

Boors's relief to hear this was palpable, and he sighed and ran a hand over his face as he sat down beside Elias to wait. Elias tried to sit up, but his ribs immediately convinced him to think better of it with a sharp twinge of pain.

"She's always been a strong girl. I couldn't believe for a second she didn't make it," Boors sighed, smiling a little to himself. He glanced at Elias, his expression becoming a little uncertain. "We were not expecting to see you again, though. The Basilisk-Eye's blade claimed everyone else it cut down on the cliffside in seconds. How the devil did you survive that?"

"It's a very long story," Elias groaned. "I'll tell you all about it when it doesn't hurt to breathe."

"Fair enough," Boors conceded. "I imagine it *is* quite a story..." Something occurred to Boors, and he grew serious again. "And the Basilisk-Eye? What became of Oliver Bones?"

"Lost sight of him. Don't think he's dead," Elias groaned, trying to focus on breathing while Mibotha worked to help him.

"Blast. I'd hoped that fall might finally be the end of that snake," Boors growled, clenching his fist. "We'll have to deal with him again, then, sooner or later. I just hope when the time comes I crush the life out of him with my own hands."

You must kill Oliver Bones.

Elias twitched. In his dizzy state, he wasn't sure if Mibotha had spoken or if he was merely remembering what it had told him. Personally, he wouldn't consider it any great loss if Bones was ripped apart by the Royal Guard instead of dying at his hands. He hated the bastard, Elias just cared that he died, not *how* he died.

"Wasn't expecting to see you," he managed to get out, trying to change the subject. "Amira...?"

"We were able to get the queen back to safety without any troubles. Blanche and I came back to find Cecily," Boors explained. He noticed Elias's somewhat incredulous expression. "Blanche refused to believe she was dead, and I agreed with her. We didn't imagine you'd have survived those wounds you took, but Cecily...we believed she made it, and we don't leave our own behind."

Cecily had said something similar, some time earlier. Elias still struggled to imagine venturing out of safety to scour bandit-infested country, or even sneak back into the place you narrowly avoided death, just to find a friend who *might* still be alive. It was pure dumb luck Boors had stumbled over him to find out where Cecily was, but looking at him, Elias could believe Boors would have kept searching until they believed, beyond a shadow of a doubt, that Cecily was gone.

"That's a lot of ground to cover," he eventually said, deciding it was the most neutral thing he could say. Boors shrugged.

"We've gotten lucky trusting in Blanche's intuition before."

I bet you have, Elias thought to himself. Blanche had said she just had one spell in her bag of tricks, but Elias always assumed people held something back when discussing what they could do. You never knew when you needed to know something everyone else didn't, after all.

"Boors!"

Elias managed to turn his head, despite a jolt of protest from his neck, to see Cecily running towards them. To his surprise, albeit not a huge amount, Blanche was already with her, and the two women were fully armed and armored again. Boors stood up, and Elias was surprised to see the big man embrace Cecily as if she was a favorite niece.

"Bless you, girl! It does me good to see you again!"

"Thankfully, Elias and I managed to get out of that river relatively unscathed," Cecily said, smiling at Boors and hugging him back. She grew serious as she saw the state Elias was in, however, kneeling down by his side.

"What happened here?"

"Mob. Happens sometimes," Elias coughed, feeling that Mibotha had managed to heal enough for him to sit up. He imagined spirit or no spirit, his face was going to be a mess for a while.

"I'm sorry. I thought you'd be safer here at the stable instead of the tavern..." Cecily murmured. Elias managed to wave a hand, trying to look more nonchalant than dead.

"I've had worse," he said, feeling a strange, idiotic need not to look like a man who had gotten ten shades of crap kicked out of him in front of the Royal Guard.

"You look like hell, although even that's an improvement on what we thought had befallen you," Blanche spoke up. Elias glanced over at her, and thought he spied something different in the way she looked at him now. Confirmation of her long-held suspicion, perhaps? Whatever she was thinking, she did not ask how he'd survived like Boors had.

"Long story," Elias groaned.

"I'll bet," Blanche sighed, turning to the stable. "The horses here aren't much good, especially not for a man in Brook's condition. You should probably ride with us, instead."

"Will we still make good enough time with two people on a horse?" Cecily asked, frowning.

"We'll make it back to the castle by tomorrow if we go now," Blanche said confidently. Elias had to admit, he could see how people would be inclined to simply follow her intuition, she sounded very sure of herself. "We'll probably make better time than we would with any horse from this stable."

"Let's clean you up and get going, then." Cecily agreed, clearly eager to be on the move again. Elias didn't feel much like moving at the moment, but he had to admit he would be happy to leave this town behind with all possible haste.

CHAPTER 26

Departure from town was quick and unimpeded by the townsfolk. People might have halted Elias's passage if he'd been alone, but standing in Boors and Blanche's way was a different story, and what Boors had told the crowd had clearly killed any thoughts of delaying the Royal Guard's departure.

Elias winced as Boors helped him up onto his massive warhorse. He wasn't in any condition to walk or ride for himself, that was true enough. His body was more or less one massive bruise at the moment and he got the feeling this was not going to be a pleasant ride for him. Cecily and Blanche mounted up together on Blanche's white charger, and the two horses set off quickly, keeping even pace despite their different builds.

Despite the immediate and painful confirmation of Elias's fears that riding was going to be an exercise in feeling every blow from his beating every step of the way, Elias was glad to be moving again. Lying in one place aching wasn't such a grand thing that he'd rather be doing that right now than moving forward. Still not wanting to seem weak in front of the Royal Guard, Elias managed to keep his grunts and groans of pain to himself, a little grateful the state of his face meant that him grimacing in pain didn't look out of the ordinary.

Trying to distract himself from how much everything hurt at the moment, Elias tried to focus on the road. He was still rather astonished how quick and well-trained the Royal Guard's horses were. He would not normally expect a horse like Boors's to make very good time on the road, especially while carrying a large, armored rider and another person, but the great beast's hooves ate up the road beneath them, and it was only accelerating. Elias had ridden a great many horses from a great many stables in his life, and he knew this was a finely bred animal.

He wondered idly if he'd ever stolen a horse from the one who bred the Royal Guard's horses. Probably not, if they'd been in Morys's employ. Elias had done a lot of stupid things in his life, but he'd never stolen from the king after Morys had first caught him. He was pretty sure he'd have remembered if he'd ever had a horse this good, even for a little while.

With the town shrinking into the distance behind them, Elias saw the sides of the road growing thickly forested. Part of him felt grateful for that; forests meant resting places with no people about most of the time, and men like Elias learned to appreciate safe havens wherever they could be found. Part of him, however, didn't like the sight of the thickly growing trees. The strange, growing anger he'd felt through Mibotha was still fresh in his mind when he looked at them, and Elias found it easy to believe the common tale that the woods that hadn't been razed in the war were haunted by angry spirits. He supposed anywhere would seem more ominous once you'd died there and found out that spirits do, in fact, exist and take interest in the sins of mortals, but the chill down his spine Elias got looking into the forest beside them was something more than that.

The woods had always been dark where they grew thick, but now Elias imagined he saw the shadows deepen to an inky blackness. It wasn't just shade from the branches growing thickly, it was like a darkness independent from the trees was lurking in the forest. You heard stories these days, much like the ones Elias had overheard in the tavern. People went into the woods alone, and never came back. Farms withered under the blight and lakes and rivers were shallow from drought, but in the forests, plants grew strong and wild, indifferent to the suffering of the rest of the land. Even Mibotha, who had been grateful to see the woods growing undisturbed in Hache's territory, had seemed oddly apprehensive about disturbing them. Mibotha was a spirit with powers over life and death. Elias couldn't help but wonder, when he looked at the darkness shrouding the woods, what something like that would be afraid of.

There was a sense of movement in the forest, but Elias wasn't sure it had anything to do with what his eyes saw. He just knew something, or some things, were moving, whispering quietly with the ambient noise of the forest to mute their words. He remembered his dream without really wanting to. The bloodied fist crushing the land in its grip filled his mind's eye, and for a moment he remembered feeling that terrible, growing rage. Tentatively, Elias tried to see if he could feel that rage again, but he was relieved when he did not feel it pressing down on his consciousness. There was something, though. Elias could feel a melancholy in the woods, a sadness that was beginning to fester into resentment.

Boors's horse stepped around a large rock in the road at around this point. It wasn't a movement Elias would have taken much notice of in normal conditions, but today the jolt abruptly reminded him he'd been beaten into a pulp today as all his bruises and bones sent out a spasm of pain at once. With a little gasp, Elias lost his balance and fell from the horse, hitting the road hard and rolling in the dust for a bit before coming to a stop in even greater discomfort than he'd been in a few minutes ago.

"Brook!" Blanche wheeled her horse around in surprise as Boors came to a quick stop. Cecily slid down from the horse quickly, coming to his side.

"I'm fine...I just—" Elias started, but Cecily didn't seem fooled.

"I was afraid of this," she said quietly, turning to Blanche. "He's in no condition to ride on today."

"Blast...I thought we'd make it twice as far today!" Blanche groaned.

"Blanche, you should ride on without me. Let everyone at the fort know that I'm fine, and Brook and I are on our way," Cecily said.

"Don't be stupid, Cecily, we're not going back without you!" Blanche sighed.

"That's right," Boors spoke up, seeming calmer as he looked down at Elias from horseback. "Brook does need more time to be ready to ride. We'll stop for today, to let him recover."

"Boors, you don't have to do that..." Cecily started.

"Don't be ridiculous, Cecily," Boors scolded. "I taught you better than that. Brook needs our help to make it back to the fortress in one piece. We don't leave our own behind."

Elias thought at first that Boors was simply referring to Cecily, but after a moment he realized that Boors was actually including him in that statement. It had already been strange enough when Cecily refused to leave him behind to make her way back to Amira, but for Blanche and Boors of all people to express the same sentiment left Elias at a complete loss for words for once in his life.

"We'd best make camp, then. The three of us can keep watch for any throat-cutters tonight," Blanche conceded, getting off of her horse.

"Three?" Elias managed to ask. For once, the look Blanche gave him did not immediately set him on edge.

"You really do look like hell, Brook. Cecily, Boors, and I will be more than enough to divide up the night watch. You focus on getting enough rest. We like you ready for action," she replied. If it had been anyone but

Blanche, Elias would have been sure she was teasing him, but since it *was* Blanche, he settled on nodding and trying to hide his bewilderment.

"Do you think anything dangerous might be hiding out in these woods, Elias?" Cecily asked, glancing at the trees. Elias could tell what he'd seen and felt and what she was viewing were two different things. Was Mibotha to blame for that? Surely it had to be, right?

"I don't…think so," he grunted, managing to sit up. "We'll be safer in there than we will be on the road, anyway."

He wasn't sure how *much* safer, but Elias was quite sure that there were people desperate enough to try attacking them if they camped out too near the road, while he had only a vague sense of something being in the woods at all. Considering Mibotha was living inside him, Elias felt it reasonable to imagine any angry spirits in the woods wouldn't bother them unless provoked somehow. He'd have preferred to ask Mibotha about that, but it was going to be difficult to consult with his companion while three Royal Guard were around. With how quiet Mibotha had been lately, he wasn't sure the spirit would even acknowledge his questions.

Still, instinct told him to go into the woods to rest, not stay on the road, and so Elias got gingerly to his feet. The Royal Guard stuck close to him, Cecily looking ready to step in if he lost his balance again, Blanche and Boors dismounting and leading their horses. Elias could tell the beasts were somewhat reluctant to enter the woods, but their fine training showed itself again, and they followed nonetheless.

Elias led the way, walking aimlessly but having the odd impression his feet knew where they were going even if his head didn't. The trees grew thickly together at first, leaving little room for four people to set up camp, but as they progressed, Elias was surprised to find that the trees spread out more. Following his feet as the space increased eventually led Elias to a clearing in the forest, a curiously pure-looking pool of water at its center and little else besides mossy rocks. Even with the greater space between the trees leading up to it, Elias realized the forest was thick and dark enough the clearing was virtually invisible until you were right on top of it. It seemed a perfect place to rest, but something made him cautious. He'd seen natural pools of water in woods before, and they had never been that crystal-clear.

Approach very slowly, and do not disturb the water. Mibotha's words came hard and quick, a command that let Elias know in no uncertain terms something bad would happen to *someone* if it was not obeyed. Elias quietly repeated what he'd just been told to his companions, before cautiously taking a step into the clearing. It felt odd to be avoiding sudden moves in a completely empty clearing, but once Mibotha had spoken, Elias was aware something was already there. That movement he had seen and not seen before was all over the clearing. His intrusion was being watched with some interest, and if Mibotha's instructions weren't followed, that interest might turn to hostility.

"It's so quiet here," Cecily muttered, stepping into the clearing. "I don't hear any birds or insects."

"…It isn't a normal place. But, I think we will be all right here for one night," Blanche concluded, looking around. Elias wondered if she saw something he didn't. "Night is falling fast. We should set up…" Blanche pointed out a large mossy rock a good distance from the pool. "Around there, I think."

Elias didn't have a problem with that. There was no way to disturb the water if they stayed near that rock. The horses didn't seem inclined to approach the pool anyway.

Boors and Blanche's saddlebags provided rations and water for the night's meal. Risking a fire in the woods or trying to drink from the pool both seemed out of the question and Elias chose going to bed a little hungry over risking disaster.

Boors volunteered for the first watch, and Elias was tired enough that sleep came easily, even in the bizarrely quiet clearing. Once again, however, he found his sleep unusually troubled.

It wasn't the fist or the rage this time. Elias instead found himself staring at a stretch of muddy badlands, stinking, damp in all the worst ways, and seemingly devoid of life. It reminded him of some of the battlefields he'd crawled through, on the worst of all his bad days. A place where the only things that could survive were those that thrived in festering corpses for a time.

As Elias watched, not sure what he was waiting for, an angry red worm the size of his finger burst out of the ground, writhing in a way Elias had never seen in a real worm. Then another burst out after it, then a dozen more, and suddenly the ground erupted with writhing red forms as though the earth had just been wounded and began to bleed, thickly and horribly. Elias felt a wave of nausea pass through him as the worms writhed in the muck. If they had voices, he felt as though they would be screaming.

They piled onto one another, blindly slithering up and over each other until they became a seething, quivering heap of red. Before Elias's eyes, the shapeless heap contracted, became more defined, until it compacted into the shape of a crouched man.

It was a lumpy, crude mockery of the human form, like it had been crafted by something that had seen a human once but didn't understand what it had seen. Somehow it was all the more hideous for its unpolished shape. It lurched to its feet, the writhing mass that formed its head twisting this way and that. Gradually, the worms poured away in places, and two dark holes opened in the misshapen creature's head like eyes.

It staggered forward, shambling drunkenly as its poorly-crafted legs scrambled to stay together. Even so, a great wave of disgust and terror passed through Elias, and he fled from the monstrous creature. It staggered on, as though it had not seen him, and Elias turned back to look as the badlands gave away to a massive green field.

The tall grass began to wither the moment the worm-creature entered it. At its touch, healthy green vegetation blackened and died. The creature walked on obliviously, and Elias watched a blight spread out from it like a ripple that destroyed everything it touched. With every step, more land withered and turned barren as the wasteland it had left behind, and the worms grew bigger and more horrible.

As it stepped from the ruins of the fields, Elias saw the man-sized monster had changed immensely. It was ten feet tall now, and a terrible hissing sound escaped from it. As it shambled closer, Elias saw the red color of the worms starting to drip off it like blood. As the red washed away, he could see more clearly the walking colony of worms had become a living mass of snakes, and the black holes in its face had become a pair of hateful yellow snake-eyes. It lurched on, its stride growing faster and steadier, and Elias saw a forest looming before it.

Previously the worm-creature had obliviously strode through the field, taking no notice of the plants dying all around it, but this time there was clearly thought and something that resembled glee in the snake-monster's movements as it lashed out with one arm to knock down the first tree in its path. The great oak screamed as though it had been human as its trunk splintered, and it rotted into nothing almost the moment it struck the ground.

Elias covered his ears against the chorus of agony that began as the monster lumbered into the forest, destroying everything in its reach, growing and growing and growing. He felt the ground give away beneath him, but he remained floating, rising up to see the monster's rampage from above.

As the last tree cried out and was silenced, it was not a mass of snakes that emerged from the ruins of the forest. Elias felt his heart stop as he recognized the impossibly muscular coils under red and green scales, the bulging yellow eyes, and most of all the faint red miasma that surrounded the creature now.

It had been a terrible giant to Elias's eyes before, but now the creature had become an unspeakable behemoth crafted from the knotted bodies of hundreds of basilisks. Its gleeful destruction had turned into a psychotic rage. Rather than move on in search of more to destroy, the monstrosity brought its "fists" down on the earth itself, and Elias heard the earth shriek and saw it tremble against the blow. The monster continued, attacking and attacking as the earth rumbled, darkened, and began to collapse around it. Elias didn't want to watch, but there was no way to look away.

With a horrible cry of triumph from its hundreds of mouths, the monster flung itself upon the earth, which splintered beneath it and began to bleed from hundreds of wounds. The basilisks hissed in chorus as the giant formed from their bodies grew still, and Elias watched as the titanic monsters began to gleefully devour one another. It didn't seem to matter how many of its brothers each basilisk tore apart, more slithered out of the cracks in the dead earth's blood to join the fray. Elias felt a strange certainty that there was no end to it. Nothing to see past this sight, everything dead but that hateful mass devouring itself, forever.

The rage Elias had felt in the land arced through him like lightning, accompanied by a surge of hatred so strong it made him feel sick. There was more fury and hate than any man could hope to comprehend directed at the destructive monstrosity before him, and it tried to burn Elias up, carry him along with it.

As he struggled not to be incinerated by the rage flowing around and through him, Elias caught just a glimpse of Amira's face before him.

Elias woke up with a gasp and a jolt, sitting bolt upright again.

Another dream. Elias wished he was the kind of person who could write these things off as "just a dream", but he wasn't so lucky. One strange dream after years of dreamless sleep was an odd occurrence. Two in a row immediately got Elias suspicious.

Were these *Mibotha's* dreams he was having? Lately the spirit had been quiet and kept its distance rather than badgering him about every little thing, but Elias was aware something in their bizarre partnership had changed since the last time Mibotha had saved his life. No, perhaps even earlier…at that shrine where they'd found the Regalia hidden away. Something had happened to him down there, and perhaps to his spirit guide as well. He wondered if Mibotha had intended for that to happen, if he was seeing all this for a reason.

He doubted it, taking a moment to think more. Mibotha had not been subtle in making points to him before. Leaving vague symbolism in his sleeping mind for him to try and interpret was not how the spirit did things. No, it seemed more likely that he was seeing things in Mibotha's thoughts it did not intend for him to be aware of, and this made Elias extremely reluctant to ask the spirit about what he'd witnessed. Something bad was going on, clearly, but Elias had never been good at asking others for help even in the best of times. Giving away something that might give him an advantage over Mibotha for what would likely be a very unhelpful answer didn't strike him as a good deal.

Vessel.

Elias turned, "hearing" a voice that bypassed his ears to land directly in his head. His gaze was drawn to the pool, where he saw...*something* floating above the water. His mind tried to force it into a shape that made sense for several minutes, but eventually gave up. All Elias was left with was the notion something as formless as Mibotha had been was addressing him, and the only adjective he could attach to it was that it was faintly blue light.

Approach. Words didn't seem to come easily to the new spirit, but it was able to put a curious amount of communication into the short, blunt words it sent to him. It held a mildly friendly hint, a large amount of curiosity and a tone of command. Elias was fairly certain this was the same thing that had been observing them earlier when they entered the clearing, but now it seemed like keeping his distance was not a good idea. He approached the light slowly, feeling it inspecting him as if looking for something.

You? Why you?

"You're probably asking the wrong person," Elias muttered. "I'd like to know more than you do."

Approach, the spirit demanded again, and Elias took a step as close as he could without disturbing the water. Again, he felt intensely scrutinized.

"What are you—"

Now is a time for you to be silent, Elias Brook, Mibotha said sharply. Elias quickly shut up, although he was vaguely aware that the air was suddenly full of thrumming that sounded nothing like language. Not just from the thing in the pool. The stones and trees began to join in, until the sound began to shake Elias down to his bones. It dawned on Elias that the entire clearing was alive in its own way. He was being watched like a hawk from a great many angles while a debate he couldn't comprehend went on around him.

Curiously, it was making him feel really good instead of terrified like he ought to be. Elias puzzled over this, before looking under his shirt to see his bruises were gone. He was healing, and a lot faster than normally. This came as a relief at first, but a thought came to Elias.

"Mibotha," he whispered.

Please don't interrupt me, Elias Brook.

"I'm sorry. It's just…let my face stay as it is for now."

What? Why?

"These bruises are as good as a mask right now. I can stay anonymous behind them a while longer, and that might be helpful."

…I see. Very well, then. It will be easier to heal it away quickly later, Mibotha said, before the thrumming resumed at a faster pace. Elias's face remained the same, but he felt stronger than he had in ages, like he could *run* all the way to Amira's castle at this point. Even his senses seemed to sharpen. Not the way they had before, but in a way that made him aware of all the little noises that still persisted in the seemingly silent clearing. Wind stirring, the most subtle movements in the pool…Elias almost heard the moss growing on the rocks.

His vision seemed clear enough for him to see something that wasn't just formless light in the clearing with him. A green, mostly shapeless but hulking creature that bore no small resemblance to the rock Elias had been sleeping by stood nearby, watching him curiously with a single, massive blue eye in an otherwise featureless body. Like everything else around him, it was thrumming quietly, at a slower pace than the thing in the pool or Mibotha in his head. Elias would normally have felt frightened, but somehow he felt perfectly in control for once. Almost like he was in a dream, Elias slowly reached out to touch the thing.

His fingers brushed against empty air, and his hand came to a stop against nothing at all, but Elias felt quite certain it was his sense of touch that was being fooled, not his eyes and ears. The blue eye regarded his hand for a moment, then turned to Elias's face for a time. The thrumming abruptly stopped dead, and for a moment there was no noise at all.

yes

Like the spirits' words, Elias heard nothing but knew what had been said. This was barely even a word, it was a grunt clinging with two fingers to meaning. But whatever the context of it had been, it was apparently the last word in the conversation. Elias felt a sense of both triumph and profound relief from Mibotha, although it faded quickly.

And in the blink of an eye, Elias was alone in what seemed like a normal clearing, feeling strong but no longer detecting any spirits at all.

"…What was that all about?" he muttered, hoping Mibotha might answer helpfully for once.

"I was hoping you would tell me."

Elias whirled around in alarm to see Blanche standing just behind him, arms crossed. The good feeling from before was immediately gone, and Elias was tempted to use his renewed vigor to bolt. Since it was a simple, mindless impulse, he crushed it down before it made him do something stupid.

"I thought you were asleep," he tried, not sure what to say.

"My shift keeping watch started…but we're not going to be attacked tonight, are we?" Blanche asked, looking around. "This place is protected by more than my sword."

"I'm not sure I follow," Elias said evasively. He would have taken a step back, but he got the impression stepping into the pool was a poor idea.

"There are spirits here," Blanche said, no doubt in her voice at all. "I can hear them…and you can too, can't you?"

Elias didn't answer, but Blanche seemed to draw affirmation from his surprised silence, just nodding to herself.

"I thought so. I think…you and I should talk now, Elias Brook," she said seriously, glancing over at the campsite where Boors and Cecily slept. "We might not have the privacy to do so in the days ahead."

"I don't know that we've got much to talk about," Elias said slowly. He couldn't tell if she was trying to get his guard down or not, and that worried him.

"I'd have expected a man with your reputation to be better at hiding their secrets…but then, it seems a lot of the things I thought I knew about you were wrong," Blanche sighed. "You and I are the same, Brook. We're both mages. You would not be standing here right now if you weren't."

"Did Cecily—" Elias started.

"Cecily didn't need to tell me anything. You took several mortal wounds but the worst you seemed to be dealing with when we found you were those bruises you'd just taken. Everyone else that sword cut died," Blanche said bluntly. "There is no natural way to have survived taking those injuries and then falling like you did. You have magic inside you, the same as I do. You're using it to heal yourself."

If Blanche could hear spirits, Elias wondered if she would hear Mibotha if it spoke up to remind him to play along with this explanation. Perhaps that was why Mibotha stayed silent, but perhaps not.

"I'll tell you what I told her, it only started just recently, and I don't know how much it will do for me. You've seen it doesn't make me impervious to injuries," he said quietly. "For the most part the damn thing's just been letting me take all the punishment people think I deserve and come back for more."

"You should be more grateful. There are a lot of people who would gladly accept a rare gift like that," Blanche muttered.

"Try living through being stabbed or poisoned to death a couple times and say that again," Elias grumbled, but Blanche impatiently grabbed him by the collar and hauled him close enough their faces nearly touched. Elias had thought Blanche's eyes were a rather fetching shade of green normally, but up close he suddenly found they reminded him more of illustrations he'd seen of giant man-eating cats that lived in the jungles far across the sea. Her other hand was raised, and that heatless white fire danced along her fingertips. Elias got the feeling his facial bruises would be the least of his problems if she slapped him now.

"Our kind gets one trick, Brook, and only one. That power defines us, whether we wanted it or not. Complain about it to Cecily or Boors or anyone else if you want, but *not to me*," she hissed. Elias raised his hands, hoping to avert Blanche's wrath.

"All right! All right! I won't!" he said quickly. Blanche held him a moment longer, and then released him, her palm still burning. Elias thanked whatever lucky stars might still exist, but couldn't help but continue the conversation rather than keep quiet in hopes Blanche left it at that.

"The power defines you? What does that even mean?"

"I've never seen it manifest as late as it has with you...but you can't heal anyone else with that power, can you?" Blanche barely needed to wait for Elias to nod to confirm her reasoning. "Do you think it's a coincidence that your magic is the power to *survive*? With the life you've lived?"

Elias let that one pass. He knew it was no coincidence he had this power, but not in the way Blanche thought. Blanche looked down at her own hand.

"No one can choose how it manifests. We're not like the wizards, drawing magic from outside sources and shaping it into a device. The power comes from inside, in the form it chooses, and it never changes.

You can shape a device's power to please you. With us, the power shapes us to please itself. Nobody can get away from that."

"Then why are you here, protecting people, instead of burning the planet to ash?" Elias countered. "That talk all sounds very nice, but I'm not so convinced."

"It defines you. Controlling you…that's a different matter," Blanche said, giving Elias a difficult-to-read look. "I am here because this is my place, Brook. Behind Amira, with Cecily and the others…that is where I belong. I need a purpose to shape my power. To stay human."

"What?" Some of what Blanche was saying reminded him of Boors' words to him not so long ago, but there was something different at work here. Elias couldn't help but investigate. If he never understood Blanche, he would be afraid of her for the rest of his life, and he would have no power to defend himself if the worst came to pass and they opposed one another. Blanche smiled mirthlessly.

"I am Amira's sword," she said, eyes bright with an intense conviction. "A sword is forged and wielded for a purpose, destroying its wielder's enemies and protecting the things they love. It can be sheathed when it's not needed…stop hurting people until there's no choice but to draw it out again. That is who I am. That is what I have to be to exist with other people." Blanche held up her hands, and Elias felt fear creep back into him as her arms were consumed in those eerie white flames again. "If I can't be the sword, then I am *this*. An unnatural fire. I can't warm things with this power, and it's only luck that lets me illuminate dark places with it. I can't make things using my flames. They just destroy everything they touch indiscriminately until there's nothing left to burn."

"If there are people that would consider my gift something to be grateful for, I know a fair few that would kill for a weapon that potent to be a part of them," Elias pointed out, mostly in the hopes Blanche would put out the flames while considering his point. To his astonishment, Blanche ran her burning hand over her face to no effect. The flames didn't seem to do anything while they remained in contact with her, even though Elias had seen a single gout of that white fire annihilate a pile of bodies with no evidence they'd ever existed.

"Those people would be ignorant of the reality. Try watching it run rampant, even just once, and say that anyone would want it again," she said quietly. "It's like being a match in a world made of kindling. You have to control it, never let it touch something you care about. Never let it get away from you or someone could *die*."

A dozen horrible images filled Elias's brain as Blanche said this, but she doused her flames and turned away, shaking her head.

"Why am I...? I don't know what I hoped to do, telling you this. We're not the same, not at all..."

"I could have told you that," Elias muttered, scratching his head. "But being nothing like me is doing pretty well for yourself, generally speaking."

"It was stupid. It's just been such a long time since I'd seen anyone else who..." Blanche stopped, shaking her head again. "Forget it. It's not worth discussing. But I wanted to thank you, before we went any further."

"Thank me? What, for the Regalia?" Elias asked, feeling rather wrong-footed. Blanche was always so inscrutable, downright scary...it was unnerving seeing her acting like a normal person towards him, even a little awkward.

"What you did for my lady was noble, and brought her hope. That was well-done, but I thank you for that only as the Captain who stands by her side," Blanche said, turning back to him. She looked almost vulnerable for a moment. "I wanted to thank you for Cecily."

"Cecily?" Elias repeated, bewildered.

"That fall would have killed her, and your actions denied Bones a chance to find a way to kill her. You did everything you could to make sure she made it home safely, and I owe you a great debt for that. Thank you. Thank you for helping her," Blanche said quietly, bowing to Elias.

"...You're welcome," Elias managed awkwardly. Blanche had looked for a moment like she might cry. Even if it had just been a moment, Elias was left less sure what to think or expect of her than when they'd started talking.

He was really starting to hate private conversations with the Royal Guard. Everything about them seemed a lot easier to understand before he knew them. Boors, Cecily, and now Blanche...how was it he kept walking away from these private talks feeling like he knew more and understood less about them?

"You're not really like soldiers at all, are you?" he asked. The question seemed to surprise Blanche, who just stared at him in confusion. "I've been around armies, seen the tactics...every general tries to minimize losses, but I've never seen an organization like yours take each of its losses so...personally. The lot of you accomplished some fairly remarkable things in the past few days, but the way you've mourned your dead, or risked coming all the way back here, away from your duty, just to try and find Cecily if she was alive..."

"We're not as naive as you might think, Brook," Blanche said quietly. "Each and every one of the Royal Guard took their oaths knowing the day might come when they would have to lay down their lives or sacrifice whatever was necessary to protect their sovereign from danger. It is not an oath for the faint of heart, and as the Captain, I have shouldered the responsibility of knowing there may be times I need to sacrifice my friends for my lady's sake. But..." Blanche looked away from Elias, her eyes coming to rest on Cecily's sleeping form.

"Necessity does not negate tragedy. *Nothing* can make the loss hurt less, no matter how much glory, necessity, or duty was involved. Every one of us that falls decreases our family by one, forever."

"Family, huh..." Elias muttered, following her gaze. Cecily's father had died to save Blanche as well, hadn't he? He could see how that might have impacted Blanche's outlook on sacrifices being made.

It must be nice, in a way, to trust someone who started out as a stranger like a family member, but that was just another way Elias did not see eye-to-eye with the Royal Guard. He'd trusted his parents to look out for him and each other because they were a family, but everyone he'd met since was a different story. They didn't have obligations to him beyond what could be forged through trade and influence, and Elias thought it was important to keep in mind how fragile those sorts of obligations could be.

"That's right. We weren't all noble sons and daughters in the Guard," Blanche said. "Some of us, like Boors and I...it was where we could belong."

"Wait, Boors?" Elias cut in. "He was the queen's bodyguard when Morys was courting her. I remember people wondering if it was part of the queen's dowry to have "The Lion" sworn into the Royal Guard in the bargain." He'd remembered seeing Boors at a distance at court. A giant, well-armored, famous enough to have that nickname before he even became a knight in Yivyn's service when his homeland joined the country. What did a knight's knight like Boors have to do with belonging anywhere?

"You don't know much about where he came from, do you, Brook?" Blanche asked, seeming to see his thoughts and not approving.

"I know he was from Eclon, back when it was a territory of its own instead of a province of Yivyn," Elias said, shrugging. "Never been there, myself, I just heard it was a fairly prosperous place." Knowing Morys, that alone might have made the king curious enough to look into creating ties with it. Although Elias gave credit where it was due, Morys would not have taken a bride from Eclon unless he'd found and fallen in love with a woman with a good head for statecraft, as it had been with Amira's mother. Most people agreed Morys courted her for her intelligence more than her money or her beauty, but Elias had always privately suspected it was helpful that she had both of those in abundance as well.

"They had their own language for a long time. Hardly anyone uses it anymore since it joined Yivyn, and it never caught on here," Blanche sighed. "He told me, a very long time ago. People here called him The Lion because the nobles knew *Lehr* meant "Lion." But Boors's second name was *Lehrbrek*. Lion-Breaker. That's the closest thing he ever had to a family name, and no one outside the Guard even bothered to learn it. I was amazed it never seemed to bother him."

"So, he wasn't born a knight, he won it?" Elias guessed. If he styled himself, it didn't surprise Elias much Boors would pick a name like "lion-breaker" to fill in an empty surname.

"No. He wasn't a knight at all until he knelt before Morys," Blanche said quietly. "*Lehrbrek* was the second name the queen gave him to acknowledge he was a human being." She looked over at the rock Boors had fallen asleep sitting against, seeming watchful even in repose. "Boors wasn't born a knight, and he didn't win it. Morys gave him the title to honor his services to the queen. Boors is lucky none of the nobility cared about Eclon any more than you do, Brook. If they'd investigated, I don't know how Morys would have dealt with them finding out he elevated an ex-slave to knighthood."

"*Boors?*"

"Eclon required a greater workforce than its population could provide to be so prosperous. It wasn't that uncommon for captured enemies from territorial conflicts to be slaves. Boors was the son of two of them," Blanche said. "He was raised, if you could call it that, by the overseers. He would probably have lived and died as a manual laborer whose name didn't matter to anyone if he hadn't saved the queen's life one day. Can you imagine that? The reward he got for killing a lion by himself to save a stranger's life was to be given the rights most of us are *born* with, and the privilege to put his life in danger again and again in the service of others."

Elias swallowed, trying to sort this out in his mind. Yivyn had not, on the whole, ever had a strong tradition of slavery, and Morys had turned away easy money participating in the trade himself, but he'd known on some level it wasn't uncommon in territories outside of Yivyn to enslave rather than kill defeated enemies. Elias had been treated like the dirt beneath people's feet sometimes, but he knew he still rated higher than a slave did. If it had been commonly known Boors was a freedman, Elias could only imagine the outrage of the landed knights that a nobody from nowhere, a man who had been property during the years they were being educated and groomed for court, had been raised to the same status as them. It was a pretty safe bet Boors would have faced endless difficulties, maybe even assassins, for such an insult.

"He never resented them. Not his old overseer, not the people of Eclon…he didn't blame anyone for anything. He was glad to have the chance to serve the person who set him free. He didn't know what else to do with himself, he told me," Blanche murmured. "He was grateful his path brought him to Yivyn. Because he had us. A family."

"Why are you telling me this?" Elias asked, feeling uncomfortable. This was like talking to Cecily all over again. Elias was used to people telling him things in the expectation he would feel obligated to share things with them in return, but it wasn't like that with the Guard. First Cecily, and now Blanche…they just told him things for no reason he could see, not expecting him to repay the favor in some way. He still didn't understand what they hoped to accomplish by dumping that information on him out of the blue, but he was past the point of being too worried about putting his foot in his mouth to just ask. Blanche regarded Elias without answering for a long moment, before shrugging.

"I overheard your argument with Boors when we started on this journey. Everyone did. But I've had time to think about what was said… and I think both of you had better points than you realized. We don't really know anything about you, besides what little we've learned riding together these last few days. But Boors was right, too. You don't know anything about us, either. That might have been all right when we were enemies, but…" Blanche sighed, shaking her head. "You're with us, now. You aren't a Guard, but you're one of us all the same. And for that to work, we need to understand you, and you need to understand us."

Elias tried to respond several times, but nothing came to him as a response to that. Blanche waited for him to say something for a short time. When the silence grew long, however, she just shrugged, seeming to understand his difficulty and turning to go.

"Get some sleep, Brook. We'll all need our rest for what's ahead."

Blanche walked off to resume her watch, leaving Elias alone again.

"What the hell…" he muttered to himself, trudging back to the rock and lying down where he'd been resting before. Despite closing his eyes, sleep did not come quickly.

Why were they treating him like this? Just because they had proof he was innocent after wanting him dead for five years? He could understand that being grounds for a few well-deserved apologies, but that wasn't what was happening. They were acting like he was their *friend* now, and Elias didn't know what he was supposed to do with that. Nothing had changed for him recently except Mibotha's intrusion into his life. He wouldn't have done any of this on his own, not if he had any choice in all of this. It felt... wrong that people's treatment of him would turn like this, just because he'd been forced to risk his neck for them to save his soul.

They wouldn't think so well of him if they knew it was all a lie, he concluded. If Mibotha's involvement in all of this ever got out, and he had the feeling it was going to one way or another, all those words would just be words again and things would be how they were before. Maybe worse, if whatever Mibotha's intentions for Amira were proved to be dangerous to the young queen. He was walking a very narrow edge here, trying to keep his balance...but he'd fall for sure if he tried to turn around. There wasn't any choice at all but to go forward.

Elias felt almost angry as he curled up to go to sleep. The Royal Guard was a family, apparently. Sure. Stranger things had happened. Maybe it was the sort of group slaves and mages and people with nobody left could trust in each other and pretend everything would be all right as long as they kept the faith.

Him being one of them, though? No. It was just wishful thinking and misguided, wholly unmerited sympathy that led to that line of thinking. He didn't understand them and they didn't understand him, and despite what Blanche said, that wasn't going to change. They were too different to ever see eye-to-eye. For one thing, the Royal Guard, against all observable evidence, were optimists. He'd seen that in their endurance of life's trials in the belief something might change if they never gave up. They weren't the sort of people he'd once taken them for, perhaps, but he was sure he understood their determined faith in the ultimate fairness of the universe.

Whatever else might change about him, Elias would always be a pragmatist. How things ought to be wasn't how things were, are, or would be. There was no defense against that but to be a realist, and looking at reality, Elias knew he didn't belong anywhere. He never would.

CHAPTER 27

Despite his troubled thoughts going to sleep, Elias was not tormented any further by dreams that night, and he awoke feeling more refreshed than he had in a long time. He was a little disgruntled to find out that all three of the Royal Guard were already awake, making their preparations to leave. Elias got up quickly. Even though he knew perfectly well they meant him no harm, Elias had never been at ease waking up to find someone had been moving about while he wasn't alert…especially not after Oliver Bones had paid him that fateful visit.

"Ah, you're awake. Are you feeling any better, Elias?" Cecily asked, glancing up from a conversation she'd been having with Blanche by Blanche's horse. Elias nodded slowly, dusting off his ratty jacket of any debris it had picked up sleeping on the ground.

"A lot better, actually," he remarked. It reminded him of when he'd first left the woods with Mibotha newly attached to him, actually. He was more than just healed, he felt like he'd been filled up and allowed to overflow just a little. Cecily nodded, seeming glad to hear it.

"It looks like your face still needs some time to heal up…but I thought you might feel a lot better after some time to rest," she said. "I slept better than I have in ages here. I feel like I could take on a whole battalion like this."

"It'd be nice if the feeling lasted until the fighting actually starts," Blanche sighed, shaking her head. "But I don't think that's too likely. At least we can get in a long day of travel today since Brook is feeling better."

Elias shot Blanche a look, but she appeared entirely uninterested in him, just focusing on preparations with her horse. There was no sign the conversation from last night was on her mind at all.

"Do you think we'll make it to rejoin the others today?" Elias asked.

"I'm not sure, but I think we've got a good chance of it. We didn't get as far as I wanted to yesterday, but I have a good feeling about the time we'll make today," Blanche replied, shrugging a little. "Is there anything you need to do before we go, Brook?"

Elias considered suggesting breakfast, but it would just be more of the trail rations from the saddlebags. He was used to going without meals, and he didn't want to be the one who suggested eating if the others seemed prepared to go without. He doubted they'd eaten while he was asleep, and Elias was unwilling to let himself look weaker in front of the Guard.

"No. I'm ready to get going," he said, shaking his head.

"Good. Let's get out of here, then."

The forest seemed a fair bit brighter as Boors and Blanche led their mounts out of the clearing and back to the road, Elias and Cecily following behind. Elias paused at the edge of the clearing, and looked back at it.

He saw nothing in the clearing, but he felt it watch him leave just the same. He wasn't sure he'd ever really know what exactly had happened here last night before Blanche came to talk to him, but he knew something important for him and for Mibotha had transpired here. He just wished he'd understood more of it, even if knowing might make things more difficult.

Elias didn't look back again until they were nearly back to the road. When he did, his backwards glance showed only trees filtering dim forest light. The clearing was lost to sight, as if it had never existed. After all the other things that had happened to Elias in his journey, who was to say it hadn't?

Elias shook his head to try and clear it as he got up on Boors's warhorse while Cecily and Blanche mounted up together. He couldn't afford to speculate too much on the spiritual aspect of his life, he decided, important as spirits might be to his destiny. He'd be making guesses from what little information he could understand, probably come to all the wrong conclusions. It would distract him from the affairs of the physical world he was already embroiled in, which were quite taxing enough without anything else on top. The one spirit he needed to have pegged was the one in the back of his head, holding the threat of eternal damnation over him if he failed. He'd sort out where other spirits factored into this once he had a handle on the situation with Mibotha, and he felt only a little closer to that than when he'd started. Still, Elias suspected as they advanced towards their goals, that sliver of progress would continue to grow until he had a real opportunity to gain understanding of the spirit. He was already sure enough of two things. For one, their partnership was a means to an end for Mibotha, one that involved Amira somehow. For another, he was certain now that Mibotha's decision to make its move through him was linked somehow to these bodiless feelings of anger and resentment he was becoming aware of through their connection, and probably linked to the disturbing dreams he'd been having about the land coming to ruin. It wasn't much to go on, but there was an inkling of Mibotha's true designs in there somewhere. He could work with that, if he was patient. He just had to make sure he didn't take it too fast, and risk Mibotha taking a more extreme stance, or too slow and be caught off-guard when Mibotha's hour came. For the time being, he'd bide his time and focus on making Amira's return to power happen. None of this mattered if he still was sent to Valka at the end of it, after all.

"What's the plan from here?" he asked, breaking the quiet the group had been riding in. "Amira is the queen by law now that she has the Regalia, but that won't let her disperse armies, and her claim is no more valid than any warlord's as things stand."

"As much as I hate to say it, Brook, you're right about that," Blanche sighed. "Queen Amira would be happy if this whole business could have been resolved just by her claiming her birthright before us, but that's far too optimistic an outlook. Some might suspect her to be a fake after this much time has passed, and even without that, there is no getting around the fact she cannot take her place as queen and quell the chaos if she cannot enforce the laws that give her the right to rule. Revealing herself means Queen Amira will have to be prepared to deal with every would-be usurper as she draws Yivyn back together. She'll be doing it with the entire Royal Guard behind her, but…getting to the Regalia was the easy part in all this, unfortunately."

It was funny how after every time he'd cheated death in the last couple of weeks someone reminded him it was only going to get worse in the immediate future, Elias thought to himself. There *had* to be a point where things stopped getting harder, but he privately suspected that point was when he died for good. Even then, with his luck doing the impossible and then dying might *also* be "the easy part."

"Even in the old days the Royal Guard was a force that defended the castle and its occupants. Correct me if I'm wrong, but that's not much of an army, especially after five years in hiding," he pointed out.

"You figure correctly. There are only a little over a hundred of us left, although we at least have the advantage that our ranks are the only ones that have not been worn down by the warring. Many of the warlords have depleted forces by this point, and many of their finest soldiers and equipment haven't survived," Boors spoke up. "The numbers involved still favor our enemies, but it's possible to use tactics to make up for it, especially if any of the warlords bend the knee rather than fight Amira's return."

"It's a possibility, I suppose, but if we can't make that happen, an alliance between the warlords could ruin any hope of turning this around," Elias sighed. "We're just lucky they all hate each other."

"It's a thorny problem, and no mistake, but it's not one we came all this way to give up at," Blanche said, eyes narrowing as she stared down the road. "There is a way to do this, and we WILL find it. Everyone is coming together, we will be planning our tactics once we're all back at the fortress." Blanche glanced over at Brook thoughtfully. "Your presence there might be quite welcome, Brook…"

"There's a first time for everything, I suppose," Elias muttered, rolling his eyes. "But I'm no tactician."

"Maybe not, but you are clever, and good with subtle work. It's going to take more than courage to see us through this trial. Before all this is done, I suspect Queen Amira will have need of your cunning," Blanche replied.

Like father, like daughter, Elias thought to himself. Still, the notion his input might give him a ghost of a chance of doing things *his* way rather than theirs was an encouraging one. Morys had only asked for his advice in very narrow, specific instances. He must have really impressed Amira if she was willing to let him advise her alongside whatever military geniuses she might have had tucked away for a rainy day all these years.

It would probably behoove him to have a slight inkling how to make Amira's task possible before they got there, he realized. He was going to look very silly indeed if Amira finally doing him the honor of asking for his counsel was met with nothing more than the obvious analysis of their slim chances. Royalty wanted ideas and results, not a summary of the facts, in his experience. And while the facts suggested that Amira would need to be exceptionally lucky to pull this off even with the greatest soldiers and tactics in the world, she needed solutions that would let her do it. He needed a way to make this happen more than any of them. Amira, Cecily, and the others at least had a chance of going somewhere nice when they died if he told them to live out their lives hidden safely away from the conflict.

Mibotha's rumblings had given Elias the sneaking suspicion that Amira's ascendency would be supported by more than just swords and shields, but while calling on Mibotha's aid had worked out remarkably well for Elias so far, he didn't think he could trust in the spirits to see this through. If it were that simple, Mibotha probably wouldn't be using him in the first place. Besides, he wasn't sure Mibotha's plans for Amira lined up with Amira's plans for Amira, and if there was a conflict, Elias did not want to be caught between them.

No, he wasn't going to contribute swords and battle plans, or a prayer the spirits would take up Amira's cause and even the odds somehow. Elias had been the underdog, staying only a fraction of a step ahead of death and disaster nearly his entire life. Terrible odds and unrealistic expectations dictating the possibility of surviving another day were Elias's world, and as Amira had said herself, it was his world she and the Royal Guard had entered when they left their castle walls.

If they were going to make it in his world, Elias had to lend them the things that had seen him this far. Skill, subtlety, no small amount of cunning, and most importantly, fear. He'd never heard of a war being won by cowardice in history, but history had always been tragically biased in favor of the brave.

CHAPTER 28

The steeds of the Royal Guard proved their worth to Elias once again. Without all his injuries to distract him, he was able to better appreciate how their hooves seemed to devour the road ahead at an astonishing pace. He couldn't tell if they were making good time or not, since the roads they were following were unfamiliar to him, but given their speed Elias had a hard time believing they weren't progressing towards their goal.

"We're not heading back to where we were before, are we?" he commented to Boors, hoping for an affirmation of his own idea of where they were headed. Boors shook his head.

"No. The fortress you joined us at has been vacated and hidden again since we left. It will be a secret we can call on if we need it in the future. Everyone will be converging at the second hidden fortress, us included."

"Striking from seemingly out of nowhere…makes sense," Elias said, more to himself. Those castles could let Amira hide in plain sight while she had a war to win. He'd have heard about it if even one of them had been discovered in the last five years, he was certain of it, and Yivyn was a big place. King Symond's one good idea might end up doing more than saving his grandchildren's lives, it might actually be an advantage that helped Amira retake her throne. "Are we close?"

"We're making better time than I expected. We should be there by early evening," Boors remarked, glancing ahead. "Hopefully there's no more surprises before we arrive."

"I'm all right with no more surprises for the rest of my life, but we can't have everything," Elias muttered.

With his luck, Elias would have expected bandits, or some sort of patrol of soldiers, or just a monster that no one had ever seen before springing fully-formed from the earth to slow their progress, but once again it seemed the three combined Royal Guard had better luck than he did. Their journey was fast-paced and uneventful. Elias didn't feel much like talking during the ride, so he mostly let his mind wander as they rode.

Part of his mind considered Amira's odds, and if there were any tricks he'd learned over his career that might make the overwhelmingly difficult task before them more doable, but it wasn't the primary focus of his attention at the moment. He couldn't make bricks without clay, and without any sort of accurate picture of what Amira had to work with, his advice would be vague and possibly inaccurate to the realities of her situation. He contented himself with little seeds of plans, things he could choose to discard or plant when he had more information to work with.

For the most part, Elias let the passing landscape fill his mind up. Yivyn was a big place, and while Elias had travelled further than many born into his circumstances, even being a fugitive had never taken him so far that he came close to filling in the map. He'd never been in this area before. It looked like it might have been an agricultural center in the past. It was a lot flatter than he was used to, with far fewer hills or forests, or even swamps, although he was grateful for that particular absence. For the most part, it seemed to be fields, some of which Elias could pick out as farms that had first become barren and then turned wild again after the people were gone. Weeds and tall grass were everywhere, giving the area a subdued, unkempt vitality.

What interested him most was the olive groves they passed. Elias had missed olives the least of all the crops that disappeared in the drought, but he had been at court long enough to know they had been quite popular there in the old days. The farmer who had owned this grove had likely made a very tidy sum off of them, but whoever that farmer was, he was gone just like the rest.

"I'm surprised there aren't people here," he muttered. "This had to have been good farmland, but now it doesn't look like anyone's been here for years."

"People avoided these fields for a long time. Nothing grew here for years after King Morys died," Boors sighed. "It's only recently things have started to change out here. There's been a little more rain, and the blight is relenting. Nature's taking these places back from the dust, but there's still so many places that are little more than badlands. If things go wrong, if the drought worsens on top of the fight to reunite the land, Yivyn will be a kingdom of dust."

"Or a kingdom of trees, when the rains come back," Elias muttered, thinking about the feeling he had gotten from the forest they'd passed through. That strange sense of despondence from the trees, and a subtle but growing resentment beneath it. Holding that feeling in his mind as he looked at the unusual shapes of the olive trees, starting to grow strong again, Elias couldn't tell if they looked more like they were dancing or writhing in pain.

"Who can say that might not be what the gods feel we deserve, if we can't fix things?" Blanche muttered, staring grimly down the road. "If we wipe each other out, a kingdom of trees might at least rule this land more benevolently."

"Don't think like that, Blanche!" Cecily scolded. "We can restore the peace, and help Yivyn recover from all of this. We just need to end the war and work together with Queen Amira to heal the land's wounds." Blanche sighed, shaking her head and looking over her shoulder. After the other night, Elias wasn't as surprised to see the often-inscrutable woman had a small, fond smile on her face.

Blanche was like a different person when Cecily was with her, Elias had noticed. Less guarded and calculating, more warm and sincere. Elias had seen a cool intelligence and a worrying ferocity in Blanche when she was alone, but with Cecily, she seemed normal, pleasant even. Even talking about Cecily had been the only time Elias had seen Blanche look truly vulnerable, more unsure of herself than when she'd crowned Amira in front of them. Elias wondered if Cecily even realized the effect she had on Blanche, or if she saw her friend through very different eyes than everyone else did. Her brighter way of looking at the world didn't seem to change the world, from what he could see…but oddly enough, her brighter way of looking at Blanche seemed to change the other woman completely.

It was a curious power Cecily had, he thought to himself, but it was certainly something formidable. It made Amira care deeply about her safety. It had brought two of the most important members of the Royal Guard far away from their duty on the unlikely chance she was alive. It had even drawn him into all of this too deeply to walk away now, even if it wasn't his soul on the line.

"That's why I like riding with you, Cecily. You always make everything sound so easy," Blanche said, turning slightly in the saddle and ruffling her friend's hair affectionately.

"Maybe not easy, but certainly doable," Cecily replied, grinning. "We've gotten this far, haven't we? Anything's possible."

"Some things exist outside the realm of possibility," Elias spoke up. "Everyone at the fortress being happy to see me alive, for example, that's just plain impossible."

"It's not impossible!" Cecily insisted, although after taking a moment to think on it further, she frowned and sighed. "J-Just...*very unlikely*, that's all." Elias burst out laughing at that, and to his surprise, Boors and Blanche did as well. It was the first time he'd ever heard Blanche laugh. Cecily shook her head, trying to keep a straight face, and pressed on. "You never know, the spirits might give you a hand at some point..."

"Spirits making my life easier. That *would* be an interesting change of pace," Elias sighed. With how quiet Mibotha had been lately, it was hard to resist the temptation to jab at it to see if it was even listening.

You're hilarious. Just remember you said that next time you get a pitchfork in your guts.

Mibotha's grumpy interjection was almost comforting, in a way. Elias hadn't been inclined to ask the spirit why it was being so quiet since they'd gotten the Regalia for fear of Mibotha feeling the need to lecture him some more. But Elias was personally happy to hear the spirit talking. If it stayed quiet too long Elias had trouble avoiding the suspicion it was up to something. Goading Mibotha into staying involved in what was going on might let him keep a better eye on its thoughts.

"We're getting close. It won't be long, now," Boors remarked. Elias turned, peering ahead to see if he could pick out their destination from here. Obviously Symond's hidden castles wouldn't be much use if they were easy to spot. But unless he'd built underground, Elias couldn't imagine a large structure would be concealable in a flat area such as this. There were no natural features, like a hill, to build it into. Nothing seemed to jump out at him.

"King Symond hid these things very well, didn't he?" he muttered. "I didn't notice the last castle until we were right in front of it, but there's nowhere to hide one out here. Are we close enough to see it from where we are?"

"In a way. Does *nothing* ahead jump out at you, Brook?" Boors asked, glancing at the horizon. Elias had no intention of missing something after a hint like that, so he peered ahead suspiciously again, willing something to jump to his attention. More fields lay before them, still mostly unattended. Elias suspected sooner or later there was going to be a lot of jostling to reclaim this area when things quieted down. Further on, there was a river, and then the flat land dropped away into a deep gorge—

"That's impossible," he breathed, staring ahead at the distant valley.

"So quickly? You do have sharp eyes," Boors remarked, looking impressed as he turned his attention to the gorge as well. "We hope that the enemy will draw the same conclusion as you on the matter."

"He hid it in the *valley*? That doesn't make any sense!" Elias protested. "Hollowing out some hills to disguise one castle, maybe, but the work involved in a process like this...how could King Symond possibly have kept it secret?"

"I'm afraid I'm not privy to that information. These castles were all built some time before I even came to Yivyn," Boors said, shrugging nonchalantly. "This one isn't merely well-hidden, it's extremely difficult to attack or even infiltrate if you aren't being shown the secret ways in. It's the perfect place for Queen Amira to hide while she plans."

Elias nodded slowly, still a little dazed by the realization of where they were headed but seeing some of the sense in that. If he had the right idea of the castle's composition, it was nearly impossible to surround it, and the only target it would present to the enemy if discovered was the front wall. With some proper preparations, it would be far more difficult to besiege than the castle lurking invisibly in the hills.

"If you have questions, Brook, I imagine you might be able to find some answers when we're safely inside," Blanche spoke up. "We're almost there. We shouldn't linger out here."

The sun was starting to set at this point, but it did give the valley extremely impressive lighting as they approached it. The stones that would be a plain, dusty brown in normal lighting became a fierce red-gold in the fading light. Even without the knowledge there was a castle hidden cleverly behind those stones, Elias had to admit it was a very majestic sight. He glanced over at Blanche.

"It's quite a place, but...how do we get in, exactly?" he remarked, looking at the ravine separating them from their destination.

"First things first, we cross the bridge," Blanche said, shrugging as she pointed out a sturdy wooden rope-bridge to Elias. "There's no way into the castle on this side, but there are a few ways in once we cross."

Elias just nodded, peering at the well-lit canyon walls as the two horses began to make their journey across the bridge. Surprisingly, it had been built sturdily enough that it barely swayed under the weight of the horses. Considering the depth of the canyon, Elias felt quite grateful there was no apparent risk of the bridge collapsing, but it occurred to him that if the Royal Guard cut this bridge while an enemy was trying to use it, they could kill any poor bastard trying to get across the canyon with a few simple cuts and make even getting at the castle from anywhere but the canyon floor nearly impossible. Without some way to get in from above or use the entrances Blanche intended to, the enemy would have little hope of making a siege or storming the castle. The only flaw Elias could see in it was that sending troops forth from this location would likely be almost as difficult as getting them into it in the first place.

Eventually, the two horses were across the bridge, and rode on for a short time until Blanche came to a stop near a massive rock, which looked like it hadn't moved an inch in centuries. Elias recognized the small silver bell she drew out of her cloak as identical to the one Cecily had used to open the gate in the hillside castle, but the short pattern Blanche rang out with it was different. The ground gave a brief, low rumble in response to the pattern, and Elias saw a rune flare blue on the ground before a passage opened at their feet, leading downwards. Elias couldn't help but be reminded of the entrance to the hiding place of the Regalia, but he noticed the methods for accessing the shrine had been very different from the ones used to access the castles. Deciding that might be important, he tucked the little thought away for later. Blanche and Cecily dismounted, and Boors swung down from his horse as well.

"Welcome to Deephome, Brook…" Blanche said, starting to lead her horse down the path with her. Elias was impressed the animal went into the narrow-looking passageway, and even seemed to fit comfortably in it. Boors went next, leaving Cecily and Elias to bring up the rear.

It hadn't been so very long ago that Elias had been granted entry to another secret castle, he recalled as he followed Cecily down. But there he'd been bound hand and foot and dragged across the stones like a carcass. Here, he was coming in with the Royal Guard, *mostly* of his own free will. Even better, nobody in this castle was likely to try and kill him as soon as they saw him.

He hoped.

CHAPTER 29

Deephome Castle's location had left Elias expecting a dank, rugged place, but he was surprised to find it pleasantly well-lit when the passage ended. Familiar runes cast a great deal of light, keeping the gloom at bay even without the sunlight. More than that, this place felt finely crafted rather than hewn. He would need to find out more about how it had come to be, if there was time…

"Captain Blanche! Sir Boors!" Elias looked up to see several younger Royal Guard saluting Blanche and Boors. Blanche returned the gesture before handing over her horse's reins to one of them.

"At ease. How have things proceeded in our absence?"

"Nothing of significance to report, Captain. The queen continues to make preparations for a war council. In all honesty, we weren't expecting you back so soon," the Guard replied. He brightened as Cecily came into view, completely ignoring Elias. "Dame Cecily! It's good to see you are well!"

"Thank you, Corin," Cecily said, smiling a little. "It's good to be back."

"We should present ourselves to Queen Amira. Corin, where is Her Majesty now?" Blanche asked.

"In her study, Captain. She asked specifically that you and Sir Boors come to her upon your return."

"Well done, Corin. Please, take our horses to the stables. They need their rest for what's ahead," Blanche sighed, before turning to the others as their horses were led away. "To the study, then. Queen Amira will want to know we found you safely."

Elias was struck as they walked together that the layout of Deephome was very similar to that of Morys's own castle, the same wide, spacious corridors, turns in very familiar places. It wasn't exact, and the light coming from runes made a difference, as did the different coloring of the stone, but Elias realized it was based heavily on the now-abandoned castle Amira had grown up in.

In a sense, the one he had grown up in as well. Maybe that was why he felt both familiarity with his surroundings and a sense of being out of place. It wasn't a new sensation in his life. He wondered if Amira felt at home in halls that mirrored the ones she'd run about in as a child, or if this place reminded her of times long gone. He wouldn't blame her if Deephome brought her no comfort at all.

Blanche clearly knew where she was going, and it didn't take much time at all for her to lead them to a spacious room, rounded like many of the larger rooms in the castles Elias had been in. This one had even more light, from some carefully-placed panels in the ceiling to let in the sun during the day. Mostly, though, it held shelves and shelves of books, charts, maps, and other materials, all orbiting a huge, well-stocked writing desk. Elias recalled a very similar one as Morys's preferred workplace. He wondered idly if this desk was a replica or the very same one Morys had given him so many orders from.

Amira sat at it now, looking much smaller against the enormous, impressive furniture. The uncertain young woman clad in armor was gone, but Elias was surprised to find the grim, regal young beauty that had first been prepared to judge him for his part in her father's death had not returned. The dark green dress Amira wore was finely made, but its style was far more casual than the impressive white gown she had worn when Elias first saw her, and the girl's long red hair was braided out of the way rather than allowed to hang loose. One would not imagine the studious young woman at the oversized desk was the rightful queen of Yivyn, perhaps just days away from marching to war to reclaim her birthright. When she looked up in surprise at the sudden entry, the delight that lit up her face and propelled her into Cecily's arms was certainly not the guarded regality one might expect.

"I knew you were alive!" she said without preamble, smiling up at Cecily. "Thank goodness you've made it back safely!"

"Elias and I had a few rough days, but we've come away in better condition than most who've crossed the Basilisk-Eye," Cecily remarked, seeming a little embarrassed by Amira's informal but sincere greeting. "We worked together to get to safety, and Blanche and Boors soon found us to help us make it the rest of the way. We would not have had much hope of making it back so quickly if it hadn't been for your decision to believe in us and send them to search, milady."

"You are your father's daughter, Cecily. I knew it would take more than that villain and a fall to stop you," Amira said, releasing Cecily. Elias saw the realization she had just acted as a young woman seeing a good friend alive instead of a sovereign greeting her returned bodyguard cross her face, but Amira didn't so much as blush, just struggled briefly to turn her grin into the more familiar small smile. She turned to Elias, and she didn't seem nearly so surprised to see him alive as Elias might have expected in the circumstances, although she studied his features.

"You are injured, Elias," she observed, appearing to decide stating the obvious was more polite than asking "what happened to your face?" "Are you in need of medical aid? We have healers here in the castle…"

"Just a few mementos from the last town we stopped in, Queen Amira. They will heal fine with time, and certainly aren't worth wasting your healers' time," Elias replied nonchalantly.

Amira considered this for a moment before nodding. Then, to his surprise, she bowed her head to him respectfully.

"When we met again after five years apart, Elias, I sincerely wished I would never have to see you again. But in these last few days, you have done me no small service. Your guidance was instrumental to the reclamation of the Regalia, and my birthright. That one act is the seed from which my entire future now begins to grow, and I thank you for it. But more than that, you have fought alongside my Guard, helping them protect me and each other at risk to yourself. You have helped a dear companion of mine find her way home, and you have come all this way to rejoin us even though our arrangement had been completed. You would have been within your rights to go your own way, but here you are." Amira studied him for a moment, as if considering something before she went on. "Thank you, Elias Brook."

There was no option for him to go his own way, and there might not be for the rest of Elias's lifetime…but there was no way or reason for Amira to know that, and so Elias did not let the thought linger on his mind. Even if it had, it would have needed to compete with his surprise Amira was thanking him at all. He'd merely done what he'd promised in order avoid getting his head chopped off, as far as they knew, and he'd naturally have stuck with Blanche and Boors after Boors stopped that mob from turning him into a smear on the ground.

More than that…Morys had *never* said anything like that to him. Elias might have stuck much more closely to things a sane person would attempt and accomplish in the old days, but he would certainly have remembered a day Morys thanked him like that.

He realized the stunned silence had gone on several times longer than he'd meant it to, and he coughed awkwardly, dropping his gaze to the floor.

"You're welcome, your Majesty. I was considering going my own way, but I figured I didn't have anything better to do, and since Boors kept my face from looking worse than it is..." he remarked, forcing a shrug. "Sticking with you has worked out better for me than anything else."

Amira seemed to find something interesting about that, but Elias didn't get a chance to study her expression too intently before it was gone.

"Yes, I suppose that does make sense," she remarked absentmindedly, before seeming to focus again. "Anyhow, I am glad to have you with us, Elias. Your help was vital to us getting this far, and I feel we may have need of it again before this is over."

"I'll do what I can," Elias conceded. "Just don't ask me to be leading any charges."

"No, I suspect that would be a terrible waste of your considerable talents," Amira agreed, growing more serious. "But there will be a number of factors beyond just strength in battle that will come into play here, and I would be glad of your aid on that front."

Elias felt some relief hearing that. It had been more or less what he expected, but he'd feared he might be forced into more violent heroics by circumstances or by Mibotha. He would still be in danger, but Elias felt a lot better than he once might have about facing *his* kind of dangerous work again after seeing a battlefield up close and personal a few too many times.

Now we have finally reached a point where your talents can truly serve the good of this land. Our true mission has just begun, Elias Brook, Mibotha said, seeming cheerful at the thought.

Elias had considered this entire thing so far his true mission, but he wasn't about to talk to Mibotha in front of Amira. To tell the truth, he was starting to get used to being informed regularly that they were now approaching the REAL work in his journey. At this point, he'd be surprised if Mibotha didn't say that there was still the hard part just ahead if they actually pulled this off and reunited the land.

"Well, if you need some cleverness amidst all this heroism, I am your man," he remarked, crossing his arms.

"I'm glad to hear it, Elias," Amira replied, before looking the four of them over. "You all had a long ride here. Please, go rest for a while. There will be a meeting in the war room in two hours' time to discuss our plans, and I would like all four of you to be there."

All four of them nodded. Elias was both glad that he could say he had a formal invitation from the queen when he showed up at the meeting and glad he would have a chance to lie down on a *good* bed for a while first, if Deephome was anything like the other castles he'd been in.

"Very good. To your chambers, then. I had rooms prepared for each of you," Amira said. "Rest well. You have earned it."

Amira returned to her work as the group left her study. Elias saw her searching for something on the desk, but didn't linger to see what it was. Blanche turned to him as they stepped out into the hallway.

"I'll come by everyone's rooms in two hours to lead us to the war room. You can sleep if you would like to, Brook. You look like you could use it."

Elias did not particularly relish the idea of being awakened by Blanche, but it might be good to try sleeping now if those awful dreams were kept from bleeding through into his mind. A few hours dreamless sleep would do him good.

Blanche led them through the twisting corridors with a surety that made Elias follow without question, and headed up a flight of stairs. Elias recognized them as similar to one set of stairs he'd never had a reason to take in the old days at court, and so he stuck close behind Blanche, Cecily and Boors trailing a little further behind. Seeing the distance, Elias decided to make use of an opportunity and drew closer to Blanche.

"Amira didn't seem very surprised to see me alive," he remarked in a low voice.

"My lady had great faith in your capacity to cheat death from the start. Combined with my own suspicions about you, she had good reason to believe that fall had not been the end of you any more than it was of Cecily," Blanche replied calmly.

"You told her about me, then?"

"Did you think I just idly chatted to Cecily about it? I don't have any secrets from my lady, and she values me telling her what I think," Blanche said bluntly. "Since I suspected some extraordinary powers at work in you, I made sure my lady knew of what I suspected. You of all people should know how important it can be to know one thing no one else does."

Elias would have to concede if pressed that Blanche's assessment was completely true. Knowledge was power, and a little secret piece of power only you and a few select others could access was a very useful, and sometimes very dangerous, thing. Still, it was a reminder that Amira's court did not seem as friendly to secrets as Morys's had been. Perhaps understandable, since Elias suspected all the secrets and under-the-table work were the primary reason Morys was able to be assassinated at all, but it might give Elias less room to maneuver than he would like in the future. He'd have to be careful not to confide anything in Blanche unless he wanted Amira to know it too, and that probably went for Cecily as well.

Blanche didn't seem to have anything more to say on the matter, just leading Elias and the others into a hallway with a great many evenly-spaced doors on either side. A servant greeted them, apparently with instructions from Amira.

"Your room is here...sir..." he said to Elias, gesturing to one not far from the stairs. Elias wondered if that moment of hesitation had been because he was obviously not like the three Royal Guard he had come here with, or because the servant had been told who he was. He supposed it didn't matter.

Elias opened his door, watching Boors walk into his own chambers and Cecily and Blanche walking down the hall together, the servant trailing after them. With a sigh, Elias closed the door behind him.

The chambers were more spartan than he'd expected, but then this castle had likely not been intended for luxury. It had a dresser, a table, a change of clothes blessedly lacking in fist-sized holes, and a very comfortable-looking bed, which was about all Elias needed from it.

Not bothering to remove anything but his boots, Elias flopped onto the bed, feeling bone-tired all at once as he closed his eyes and let himself rest.

CHAPTER 30

The dreamless sleep Elias desired eluded him. Some awareness niggled at him that this was all happening within his dreaming mind, but despite that he could not unchain himself from the dream.

This time, he saw two figures wrestling on the ground before him, both in the shape of humans, but with the wrong details.

One of them was a figure carved in the shape of an androgynous human sculpture, its skin appearing to be rough bark and a singular eye, like a ring of molten gold in the midst of a green pool, burned in the center of its face. Long, strong arms tried to catch and strangle its adversary, but time and time again the thin but powerful fingers missed their mark.

Its opponent was shaped as a human, but Elias felt only revulsion watching it. It was crouched like an animal and covered in reptilian scales. It was blind, its face almost completely featureless but for a misshapen, lipless mouth brimming with uneven fangs bared at its enemy. The creature was covered in a malodorous, dark slime, and every attempt its opponent made to catch it in an iron grip failed as it slipped away, dripping the foul ooze and cackling. Its own hands, more birdlike talons than anything else, swiped clumsily at the wooden cyclops's chest, gouging lightly but to little lasting effect.

As Elias watched, however, the scaly abomination let out a hiss, suddenly plunging its claws into the ground. The earth blackened and bubbled at its touch, and a viscous red substance began to bubble up from it as though the ground itself had been wounded by the blow. The bark-skinned creature gave a wordless cry of dismay, staggering back as if struck as its opponent gouged into the ground again and again. Elias noted it seemed to have trouble keeping its footing in the red muck at its feet.

The blind creature's renewed assault came quickly and mercilessly. One long leg swept out and knocked its enemy's feet out from under it. As it fell, the scaly creature pounced, hitting its adversary hard and beginning to bite and claw at it viciously as they tumbled to the ground. The cyclops fought back savagely, even as it bellowed in pain both from the monster's attacks and the red muck seeping into its wounds, but Elias saw that its chance to retaliate was bleeding away swiftly. In a horrible moment, the scaled creature's hideous head shot forward, and its misshapen teeth closed on the single unprotected part of its prone enemy, the eye. The bellow of agony intensified, as did the savage struggling of the pinned creature, but Elias knew that the cyclops could no longer win this fight.

Raw, sickening hate surged through the very ground beneath Elias's feet, and then up and through him into the air like inverted lightning. Elias felt the familiar, terrible anger, but this time it was within him instead of outside. He wanted to kill the scaled monstrosity more than he had ever wanted to kill anything in his life. He became aware of a knife, gripped surely in his hands.

You must kill Oliver Bones.

Mibotha's voice echoed in his head, and Elias was once more unsure and unable to care if it was a message or a memory. This time, it wasn't alone.

Must kill. Vessel. Kill it. The imperious tone of the spirit from the pool joined Mibotha's more coherent statement in his mind. All around him, Elias started to hear the thrumming from the clearing that night, this time more rhythmic than the one he'd heard. More like a chant.

kill

Elias felt more than heard the word of the rock spirit, but it filled him up completely for a moment. Unable to control himself amidst the thrumming commands of the spirits and the anger flowing from them into him, Elias charged at the scaly monstrosity.

His heart skipped a beat even so as it turned blindly to face him, snarling in surprise before it pounced on him.

It was impossibly heavy and strong for its scrawny frame and human size. It was like being hit with a battering ram that could hate. There was no option to not be borne to the ground by the blow, merely the option to go down struggling with the slippery thing even as it tried to get a grip on him. Elias stabbed and hacked wildly, feeling like his body was no longer under his control. He wounded it, maybe dozens of times, but he felt the claws hacking at his skin, which resisted far less than bark, felt the teeth ripping chunks of him away.

Elias spun madly through the dream, no longer able to tell himself apart from his adversary or the voices screaming as they fought like animals. Blood and ichor were everywhere, but he wasn't sure who any of it belonged to. It was hard to think through the haze of rage and desperation that assaulted him from the inside and the outside, so little of it his own.

The dream only came to an end when the rage flowing through Elias gave away to despair, and he suddenly became aware of himself in the tattered shreds of his body as the spirits cried out in dismay.

The blind monster gave an oddly familiar cry of savage triumph, and the last thing Elias saw was its teeth close on his throat.

He sprung awake with a cry, heart hammering in his chest as he shook, covered in sweat.

"What *is* this, Mibotha?" he hissed, too frightened to hold back from asking any longer.

What is what? What did you see? Mibotha asked, sounding puzzled.

It wasn't in Mibotha's nature to play dumb. If it was bewildered by his reaction, it genuinely did not realize what Elias was seeing when he dreamed.

"I…" Elias ran a hand through his hair, trying to consider where to even begin. After a moment, he sighed, lying back.

"No. It was nothing. Forget about it," he muttered. He wasn't sure anymore if he was more worried that Mibotha wouldn't give him a straight answer if he asked about the dreams, or that Mibotha *would*.

"Brook?" Elias was surprised to hear Blanche outside the door as she knocked. His cry hadn't been that loud, he thought, but then he realized he must have been asleep for two hours.

"I'm coming," he called, deciding to put the dream out of his head for a little while. He had learned that Mibotha was not intentionally showing him all this, and indeed was not aware he was seeing it at all, but that was all he'd learned and he was honestly afraid what he would discover if he found out more.

First things first. He was going to focus on advising Amira and planning out their next actions. It would give him something to distract from the disturbing dreams, and maybe making some progress with restoring Amira would make progress towards ending the nightmares.

Elias didn't exactly look like a respectable person to ask for advice on affairs of state or war, but he didn't have anything to change into and he wasn't about to try and find clothes that suited him that belonged to someone else. He just pulled on his boots and opened the door to join Blanche, already accompanied by Cecily. Boors similarly was coming out of his room a little further down to join them. Cecily glanced at Elias's face, frowning.

"You look terrible, Elias. Are you feeling all right?"

"Rough sleep, that's all. I'm fine," Elias grunted, rubbing his bruised face despite the twinge of pain it caused.

"If you're sure…" Cecily muttered dubiously.

"Everything I've got will look worse than it is while my face is like this. Let's just get to the war room," Elias said, trying to hurry things along. He wasn't in much of a mood to wait around, and the distraction of focusing on what he'd need to do soon would be quite welcome at this point. Blanche nodded, leading the group back down the stairs. The hallways were less familiar now, and so Elias paid close attention to Blanche's path; it might prove useful to have some idea where these rooms were without Blanche guiding him.

The war room was behind a pair of impressively large mahogany doors, which Blanche opened slowly enough for Elias to confirm there was already a meeting in progress within, or at least a conversation.

As it turned out, there were four people at the large table in the war room with Amira; an old woman Elias didn't recognize, a heavily bearded, barrel-chested man Elias vaguely recalled from his days at court but had entirely forgotten the name of, a young woman with straight black hair that did not look entirely at home in these surroundings, and…

Oh, joy of joys. After all the horrible, bloody fighting, General Brycen was somehow still alive.

Elias remembered him of old. Captain Thurgood's commanding officer, supposedly one of Morys's leading military minds, and an absolute braying jackass every waking moment there wasn't something for him to fight. Elias had hated him the moment he'd set eyes on him, and getting to know the man over time had not helped at all. Brycen was a man of aggressively average height. A tall man like Elias could look down at him easily, something Brycen had always seemed to take as a personal insult. He'd cultivated muscles as a way to compensate, Elias supposed, but the man had always looked ridiculous to him with his very broad shoulders and slightly-too-short legs. His mustache was an obsessively cared-for feature of his face, but no amount of pride and love would turn the dark brown bristles jutting out of his upper lip charming, nor make his eyebrows look less like a pair of giant, fuzzy, excitable caterpillars. His nose was slightly too big for his face, while those suspicious beady eyes were too small. All in all, one had only to look at Brycen to think him an oaf. Observing his behavior would soon give lie to that assumption, of course. An oaf still had a sort of bumbling charm. Brycen just had a loud voice and a short temper.

Elias had not seen eye to eye with Raulin Thurgood on most things when they were both sober, but he didn't need to get drunk with Thurgood for them to share a distaste for the general's presence. Elias was simply astounded that a war that had claimed so many of the best and brightest had somehow left the likes of Brycen and Duke Hache untouched. If the gods had a sense of humor, Elias suspected it was not a very good one.

He imagined there would have been an awful lot of yelling and saber-rattling if Brycen had recognized him when he glanced over the newcomers to the room, but as he'd intended, the bruises on his face made a good mask and prevented Brycen from recognizing him. The general just observed them all in a flash, nodding vaguely at them as Amira looked up from the map.

"Thank you for coming so promptly, my friends. I believe everyone is here now...let's begin," she said, taking a seat. Everyone else quickly took their places at the table, Boors sitting the closest to Amira while Elias decided to sit further away from the others. Amira cleared her throat, beginning to speak.

"With the Regalia back in my possession, my family's treasures have been restored, and I am recognized as queen by the gods," she said, going back to looking at a map on the table rather than her audience. Elias could detect a hint of nervousness in the practiced words. "But reclaiming the Regalia was only the first step in a much larger project. I am the queen by right, but that will mean nothing until rule of law is restored to Yivyn. I would like to achieve this with no further bloodshed, but I fear that it will be a supremely difficult act to reunite the land without battle at this point. The warlords holding this land, Duke Hache in particular, are unlikely to surrender their gains from the last five years of war, even for a chance at peace," Amira sighed. "The hidden castles my grandfather built have kept us safe, but the time for hiding is rapidly coming to a close. One way or another, it is time to take action."

She glanced at Brycen, and Elias tried not to groan when he realized she was giving the general leave to start talking without restrictions; never a good move, in Elias's experience. Brycen felt the need to stand up, clearing his throat loudly.

"A masterful summary, Your Majesty," he began, leaning over the map and glancing at the gathered audience. "As has been established, our mission to restore Yivyn to its original glory is blocked in all directions by usurpers who will not bend the knee without a fight. At the moment, the enemy's numbers make this a daunting prospect, but I believe I have hit upon tactics that will let us use the element of surprise to turn the tables!"

Using surprise had always been a welcome approach for Elias, but he was familiar enough with the speaker that the notion did not fill him with hope for the proposed strategy.

"Now, then, our forces are small, but strong and well-trained. Reclaiming the Regalia, despite enemy interference, proved they are capable of fighting a significantly larger force and triumphing with minimal loss."

Elias saw Amira frown slightly at that, but the young queen said nothing and Brycen took no notice.

"Therefore, I propose we use the element of surprise to put our small but potent force where it will have the greatest impact, right here, in Lord Dunst's territory!" Brycen declared, tapping his index finger on the smallest territory of Yivyn depicted on the map. "Lord Dunst has never recovered from the depletion of his armies and lands two years ago, and has kept out of sight and out of mind to avoid drawing the eye of other warlords that might finish him off. He and his men have no stomach for further battle. I believe a single strong show of force will break his will to resist, and he will surrender without any great difficulty. This will be our foothold! The falling pebbles that start an avalanche!"

Oh, *good*, he was getting dramatic already.

"Unless, of course, a single strong show of force doesn't work," Elias remarked, breaking Brycen's flow and getting an extremely dirty look for it. For a moment he thought Brycen recognized him. He'd have expected it, after hearing his voice, but the general appeared too eager to dismiss Elias to really think about who he was at the moment.

"Lord Dunst has little to gain and everything to lose now, with things being how they are. I suspect he will surrender to the first force that moves against him rather than see his army routed once and for all and be at his enemy's mercy afterwards. The others have ignored this weakness, but we can exploit it and use it as a springboard to even the odds of the true battle!"

Elias considered if he should hold his tongue to avoid turning this meeting into an argument, but he looked around to gauge the room. He noticed that while Amira seemed to have that curiously blank expression she could put on like a mask, Boors, Blanche, and Cecily all had rather grim expressions. They weren't the fools he'd once taken them to be. Elias could tell all three of them were turning over this dangerous, foolhardy stratagem in their heads, but while he was fairly sure they didn't like the sound of it, loyalty would compel them to go along with Brycen if his was the only voice offering a plan today. Elias also risked a glance at the two at the table he didn't know, and quickly discounted the notion that Brycen's plan would be defended there if he spoke. The old woman looked resigned as she listened, while the young lady sitting by her side…Elias paused, considering her a moment longer. She wasn't even looking at the map, her hands were clenched in her lap, and she was staring down at them with a sullen, frustrated expression quite different from the nervousness he'd seen in her earlier.

There was room for him to speak his mind, he decided. This council was being held in check at the moment by its direct approach to problem-solving and loyalty quieting the voice of dissent. Brycen's plan didn't appeal greatly, but if it seemed the only way to give Amira her birthright, the men and women at this table would see it done, even at a high cost. But they'd listen if he offered an alternative, and Elias had no desire to stay quiet in a situation like this.

"Revealing ourselves in a small, easily-surrounded area as the first step towards victory?" Elias raised an eyebrow. "Please, do go on, I *really* want to hear this now."

Brycen momentarily glanced at Amira. The queen's face stayed neutral, but Brycen looked a little flustered as he pressed on, and Elias could spot the gears turning, ever so slowly, in the back of his mind as he gave Elias another glance.

"Lord Dunst's province is small, but the point is that we can gather strength there, enough to fight against more troubling foes. With a proper display of force, Lord Dunst ought to surrender with both our army and his almost completely untouched. From there we can cut a deal to render his soldiers subordinate to our own. Our forces will more than double in one fell swoop!" he explained. "Then, with the region under our control, we can further bolster our strength by recruiting from the peasants in Lord Dunst's territory—"

"That won't work," Elias said bluntly, leaning forward. "Even if everything else up until then goes perfectly, this strategy won't work, and it will start right there."

"And that is your expert military opinion, is it?" Brycen asked angrily. "I am *trying* to lay out our plan of attack, sirrah. If you would cease contradicting me for five minutes—"

"I'll agree to that if you can stop being wrong that long," Elias replied, crossing his arms as everyone at the table gave him an astonished stare. "Your plan is going to get everyone here killed. Dunst isn't as strong in the field as the others, but he's an excellent tactician, and he'd finally be up against a force that doesn't massively outnumber his. Even with the weakest army, he won't crumple the second we draw our swords. There will be a battle, likely more than one before he starts to lose his footing. We won't get his whole army or his support, and all of the others will have time to prepare while we fight him. Hache might even be ready to make an all-out attack on our rear before we've finished fighting Dunst. But even if none of that happened, if Dunst really did just roll over for us when we walked up, your idea of trying to conscript the people to fight our battles is going to take all the wind out of our sails."

"There isn't another option. We need the soldiers to defeat the enemy!" Brycen shouted, banging the table with his fist. "These are the facts! There is no disputing them!" he turned to Amira, looking quite angry now. "Your Majesty, who *is* this dullard, and why did you invite him to a council of war?"

"I believe you have already met, General," Amira replied evenly.

"Although I'll forgive you for not recognizing me. You have an awfully big nose to be looking down to remember faces that well," Elias said snidely. Perhaps it was his tone, or just the niggling memory finally connecting, but he saw recognition, anger, and hate flare in Brycen's eyes.

"*You!*"

"Was he not informed how the Regalia were reclaimed, Your Majesty?" Elias said, allowing himself to look a little hurt as he glanced over at Amira. Amira shook her head.

"No, Elias, General Brycen is aware of the situation. We have already had a lengthy conversation about it," she sighed, as Brycen fumed.

"Your Majesty, Brook may have proved…less culpable than my men's findings initially indicated," he said, trying to keep his voice smooth even though it looked like even *thinking* Elias's name and "not guilty" together physically hurt him, "but I don't think I need to remind you that this man is an admitted liar and a thief, and it was his unguarded tongue and cowardice that cost your father his life. Whatever use he managed to make of himself, one good deed does not absolve him of a lifetime of wickedness. I do not feel we should hold this meeting with him here."

"I fear General Brycen may have a point, Your Majesty," Elias agreed, rolling his eyes. "I do not think this council needs an unscrupulous, unreliable coward when you have brave men like our esteemed General back from hiding under rocks for five years."

"Why, you—!" Brycen would almost certainly have drawn his sword if ladies weren't present. Elias would freely give the man that the weapon wasn't just for show, but Brycen liked to rattle his saber more than draw it in "gentler company." Elias honestly felt more threatened by the old woman and the girl he didn't know than Brycen. He'd had scrapes with men with short reach and shorter tempers before, and he looked back on most of them fondly.

"Sir Boors, if General Brycen and Elias Brook continue this squabble another word, you have my permission to knock their heads together and throw them out of this chamber," Amira said sharply, glaring at both of them. Boors nodded, seeming like he was trying not to laugh. Elias got the impression that while he was still not one of Boors's favorite people, he ranked a good deal higher than the General. Even so, Boors might enjoy enforcing Amira's will if Elias couldn't refrain from jabbing at him.

He might have risked Valka if Mibotha had told him the road to redemption required him to sit through an entire meeting being polite to General Brycen, but it was too late for regrets now. Brycen settled back down, looking embarrassed.

"I apologize for my outburst, Your Majesty. It will not happen again."

"I also apologize for General Brycen's outburst. I tend to have that effect on people, for some reason," Elias said. The sound of Brycen's teeth grinding was a sweet melody to him, but Amira's disapproving look made him flinch a little.

"I invited you here against the advice of several of my retainers, Elias. Please show me my belief in you was justified, and remain civil while we discuss this matter," she said quietly, her tone not leaving much room for argument. Elias wouldn't be able to needle Brycen any further without seriously angering Amira, he suspected, but there was always more time to knock the pompous old fool down a peg later.

Please don't jeopardize everything I've brought you back to life and kept you healthy for over these last few weeks over a petty grudge, Elias Brook.

Elias suppressed a sigh, fidgeting slightly in his seat to get comfortable again. It appeared he had no option but to take the high road on this occasion. Truly, this *was* a journey that would change him as a person.

"I will do my utmost, Your Majesty. I'm sorry I needed to be told twice," he sighed, hoping Amira didn't ask him to apologize to General Brycen as well.

Amira, fortunately, appeared aware she was not a miracle worker and decided instead just to back to business.

"Thank you for your words, General Brycen. But I wish to hear more than one opinion before I can judge what the best course of action truly is," she said, trying to be diplomatic before she turned her attention to Elias. "I would hear what you have to say on this matter, Elias. Please, if you have any insight you think might help..."

Despite the fact that he'd been told Amira might have need of his services in winning back her land, Elias still found he was not entirely ready when the moment finally came. This sort of thing had never been a part of Elias's life. He'd never sat at the long tables, contributing his voice among others. Morys tended to talk with him privately in more out-of-the way places, and had never in Elias's memory asked for his advice in front of his guards and officers.

Still, to let this moment sink in too long would create the impression he didn't know what to say. He knew perfectly well after talking like that to Brycen, he needed to be able to avoid looking like he was pulling something out of thin air after he was scolded for criticizing Brycen's plan. He needed to talk quickly, and it needed to be good.

Fortunately, Elias imagined outlining a better plan than Brycen's was a task he would trust to most of the horses he'd ridden, and he was a fair bit more eloquent and clever than any of them. It had been odd to hear Amira ask him his opinion, but he at least had one ready for her.

"The people are your best weapon in this, Ami—Your Majesty," he began, looking serious. "But not the way Brycen advises. Not if you just use them as soldiers. The people are sick and tired of the fighting. They welcome the idea of someone like you coming to put a stop to it all, but conscript them and you'll lose them forever. You'll be no different than all the rest to them, just another warlord."

"Ridiculous! Queen Amira has something none of the usurpers do, a legitimate claim!" Brycen interjected, pounding on the table again. "It's their *duty* to rise up against the ones that tried to take the land for themselves, damn it, and we can't make her queen in fact as well as law without them doing so!"

"Are you sure about that?" Elias asked, leaning back. "I've been out there, Brycen, among those people. I saw what it was like when they heard her name for the first time in years, heard that she hadn't abandoned them. She's not the queen to them right now." Elias's train of thought was cut off by an explosion of objections. Brycen slammed his fists on the table, and Elias could see even the Royal Guard looked stunned and outraged by what he'd said. Still, it was nice to see that they gave him a moment of quiet when he held up his hands to continue. "No, listen to me. She is *not* just the queen to these people. She is so much more than that now. She's a symbol of hope they're clinging to, and if we have any sense, we'll use that. People expect the queen to bring an *end* to all of this, not make them fight on her behalf to do so. As far as everyone out there is concerned, there's been enough bloodshed already. All we'll do is hurt our cause if we try to make people that are sick of war fight for us."

"How do you propose they're any help to us, then?" Brycen demanded, seeming eager to catch Elias off-guard. He was disappointed.

"The soldiers across Yivyn are depleted. There are strong standing armies in every territory, yes, but they've all been whittled down to a fraction of the strength they had at their leaders' peaks. If you compare the number of soldiers each of our enemies have to the number of common people, tired of all the battles in their lands…I think you'll find we have all of our enemies combined outnumbered if we can make those common people our allies."

Brycen seemed baffled by this, but Elias took some hope from the sudden interest Amira was unable to hide at his words. He quickly pressed on, deciding not to give Brycen a chance to interrupt him now that he was starting to get to the point.

"Queen Amira and her brother both vanished from the view of the people almost immediately after King Morys died and the chaos started. In their view, the good times came to an end for this country when Morys died and his heirs disappeared. It's not hard for people to make a connection that things might go back to how they were if Morys's heir returns to power. Even as just a faint hope, that is a powerful tool for us," he started to explain. "People have tried to look after themselves and found what safety they could under the warlords because there wasn't anything to rally for. Hache, Dunst, Evangeline, Steelskirts…they all have the same amount of legitimacy as far as lordship over Yivyn goes. The people would just take sides with the one protecting them the best, but introducing the queen to this balance of power changes *everything*. If we're careful, the simple fact she's leading us is a more powerful weapon than anything our army can ever field."

"I had not taken you for a romantic, Brook, although I had a fairly accurate grasp of your tactical ineptitude," Brycen said snidely. "You have yet to say how this affection of the common man, as long as we ask nothing of them, is going to stop armies of our enemies."

"Because no one in their right mind will be the one to attack the queen in a climate like this. Fighting each other, they're warlords, just equals with some people preferring one and some preferring the other. With no leader, who's to say they're wrong for taking charge in these dark times? But attacking the heir of Morys when she returns? That's not just another war for the people to suffer through, that's *treason*. Anyone that makes the first move against her might well have a full peasant revolt on their hands and probably lose most of their army to desertion. None of them can survive that kind of catastrophe befalling them. Hache might risk it, but the others? They won't dare move against us if doing so will make them a traitor, attacking the queen everyone has such hopes for."

A quick glance around the table showed Elias he'd gained some ground. Boors looked genuinely impressed, while the old lady and young woman were both thinking. Even Brycen didn't have an immediate objection, although he did not look like he liked what he was hearing.

"You may have a point, Elias. But the hidden castles are all inside territories at least loosely controlled by warlords. How do you propose we reveal ourselves to the world without one of our enemies trying to silence us before news spreads in their territories?" Amira asked.

"I've been thinking about that. There's one way that seems like it'd work," Elias said carefully. He could almost imagine people holding their breath before he spat it out. "We shouldn't go on the offensive. Our forces ought to retake the Castle before we do anything else."

There were a number of castles in Yivyn, but it would have been moronic to anyone at the table to ask which one he was talking about. In the last five years of war, and a hundred years before that, there had only been one *the* Castle, Morys's castle. It was unsurprising, then, that shocked silence exploded into everyone trying to speak at once, until Amira brought her hand down on the table to restore silence. After a moment, Brycen finally composed himself enough to speak.

"Enrilth? You want us to try *reclaiming the capital* first?" he asked incredulously.

Elias would normally have found Brycen's dismay very amusing, but he'd questioned the notion himself, even if he was committed to it now. He'd been born and raised in Enrilth, first growing up in the shadow of Enrilth Keep and then living in it himself. He'd had to leave, and leave in quite a hurry, at the end of his time there, before things got really bad, but he'd heard what happened to it when Morys was gone.

The famine had hit there the hardest, and war was close on its heels. When Amira and her brother disappeared and the Regalia were unaccounted for, everyone's eyes turned towards the capital city and Morys's seat of power at its center, the center of all Yivyn, in the older days.

One invasion into what had once been the safest place in the country had been the end of any chance of peace. Four more followed, and then no less than seven armies had fought to the death to try and take control. Enrilth was a graveyard the size of any three farming provinces, and its population was far greater if you knew where to dig. Elias had never set foot in that place again after he'd fled with a bounty on his head. Even when he turned to scavenging, there were some things you didn't touch.

No one held Enrilth now, because nobody in their right mind wanted it anymore. Even Duke Hache wasn't *quite* mad enough to try to take it a third time. It was still the center of Yivyn. A gaping hole in the map the warlords carved their territories around but did not enter. Anyone who had lived there was long dead or fled. The sheer amount of bloodshed in the attempt to take it meant Elias was inclined to believe that all the rumors were true; Enrilth was devoid of life, but cursed. If Elias was to go looking for evil spirits, he'd try the castle Amira grew up in before the woods.

It was abandoned, barren, probably haunted, and unwanted. It was also the last possible place anyone would expect them to be.

"No one has taken any interest in Enrilth in years. The warlords don't even consider it when they make plans anymore," he argued. "No one will be watching what goes on there. Nobody will try to impede our progress through the area. They probably won't even notice Enrilth Keep is occupied again without us spreading the word ourselves."

"Leave it to Elias Brook to suggest attacking an *empty castle* as his grand stratagem," Brycen said snidely. "And how, pray tell, will that help us at all?"

"Do you think it will be lost on people what it means when Queen Amira is revealed alive and well in her father's seat of power, calling for an end to civil war?" Elias countered. "That will seem like a sign from on high to them, her doing the impossible to restore the rule of law to Yivyn. Since the warlords ignore Enrilth entirely these days, we can be settled into the strongest fortress in Yivyn before they even know there's a possibility to attack us. Moving supplies to the castle, setting up the defenses again…any attack in the warlord's territories gives them opportunities and excuses to do battle with us in a way we're not equipped to handle. Making our way to Enrilth, in secret? We have all the opportunities we need to set ourselves up before moving on to our next step, and it lets us dictate the terms any enemies stubborn enough to fight us would need to meet us on."

He could see it in his mind's eye. The forgotten wasteland Enrilth had become would be hard traveling, but they would not be chased through it, or likely even noticed until they were ready to be noticed. It wouldn't be an easy journey, but on the other hand, they could take all the time they wanted to make it a manageable one. Any foe, particularly one like Hache, would be left facing an ugly situation. Even risking a revolt and attacking Amira at that point meant marching his weary, superstitious army through the forests they hated, over the mountains they tried to avoid, across territory filled with bandits and enemies, and finally directly into a haunted place where Hache's army had met not one, but three devastating defeats in the past. All that with the promise of needing to besiege a powerful fortress miles away from any safe source of supplies at the end of it. Elias almost imagined even Hache would think better of it, but it was really a coin toss if his wife would spot the obvious for him or not. And if Hache didn't move, Elias was reasonably confident of a lasting impasse while everyone tried to figure out how things stood now. That was time for the influence of popular opinion to make rebellion against Amira unfeasible, he hoped, and from there, Amira had all the cards.

"I've always known you were craven, Brook, but this is simply too much! If you're wrong about all of this, your plan will be leading all of us into a trap! We'll be surrounded, easily!" Brycen growled.

"By soldiers who already fear evil spirits enough they won't enter the forests on their own land? By armies that will need to trek through a wide expanse of land they can't live off of just to get a chance to attack us after we've moved our supplies into the Keep? Enrilth is the strongest fortress in Yivyn. Even the first invasion couldn't conquer the castle. It fell during the second only because the defenders abandoned it, and even then it took some time for the invaders to enter the castle. They weren't able to settle in enough to hold it. For us, if we've had enough time to settle in there, it's a different matter entirely. Only soldiers that would walk into Valka for their leaders will even consider besieging Enrilth Keep again."

"It's a considerable journey to the Keep, much of it through that expanse of land you just mentioned. And we'd need to bring supplies, slow ourselves down just so we don't starve there! What if we're attacked on the way, with no defenses?" Brycen demanded.

"How likely do you think that is? Even bandits won't hide out in Enrilth anymore. Once we're in that territory, no one will be looking for us, let alone chasing us into it," Elias replied, as evenly as he could. "If we can display sufficient stealth and subtlety to reach Enrilth's borders unnoticed, there will *be* no attacks on the way."

"Your Majesty, I beg of you, don't listen to this tripe!" Brycen groaned, turning to Amira. "Don't consider how the *enemy* will react to a plan like this, consider your own people! The men and women out there will gladly die in battle for you, but throwing their lives away in that graveyard for a man like Brook, just to avoid battle? This is lunacy!"

"Is this just some kind of *game* to you, Brycen, or are you truly just that stupid?" Elias snarled, standing up. "You're outnumbered, outflanked, and have no way of raising our strength to an acceptable level without throwing away one of our best advantages. Being brave and aggressive is just going to get us attacked on all sides and killed, but if you think outside the box for *once* in your life, we might live through this!"

"Don't try to muddy the issue, Brook, I can see right through you," Brycen hissed, and Elias saw real hate glittering in the man's eyes. "This is just like how it used to be. You always slithered out of trouble and brought down better men with tricks and lies. Never risking *your* life, of course, you always left that to someone else! What's the next phase in your grand plan, Brook, using this impasse you seem to be working towards so you can open a few doors in the night and let assassins do your dirty work?"

"You're the one trying to muddy things here," Elias growled, unable to obey Amira's command and stay civil in the face of this. "What I did in the service of King Morys isn't relevant to this plan. I'm trying to keep our queen alive while she reunites her kingdom. All you seem to have in mind are inventive ways to make sure she dies gallantly. Is that how you plan to honor Morys's legacy?"

"I plan to see my queen retake what is rightfully hers when the land rises for her!" Brycen practically screamed, face turning a deep crimson as his eyes bulged. "Not be led into a trap and abandoned by you, Brook! It's *your* fault we're here! It's your damn schemes and lies and cowardice that caused all this! Well, now your time is over! It's going to be courage and fortitude that bring us out of this dark age and restore the law, not another of your slimy, craven plots! This country has enough filth on it from your hands as it is! Isn't it bad enough that the king was betrayed to his death by it, and the land ravaged over it?"

"For once, Brycen, *shut up*," Elias snapped, glaring at the general. He'd almost forgotten with time just how *much* he'd hated the pompous bastard. "You're in here now, talking about courage and fortitude, leading Queen Amira to victory. *Where the hell were you before? Where were you* five years ago, when Eckard tried to stop the fighting and got killed in the night for his trouble? Where were *you* three years ago, when Hartmut and his followers went down fighting at the Vermillion Field? Hell, where were *you* two weeks ago, when I was helping Amira reclaim her birthright? Because it seems to me it's only now that someone else has done all the work that you come slithering out from under your rock to mess it up like you always have!" Elias realized he was shouting now, but couldn't seem to stop himself. "I'm as craven as they come, Brycen, but at least I have the decency to *admit it!*"

"How *dare*—" Brycen's sword finally leapt out of its scabbard, gleaming in the light from the runes illuminating the room as the people at the table all leapt to their feet. "I'll kill you, right here! To your face, with my own hands, Brook! More than you ever had the courage for!"

Elias didn't hear any empty threat in that cry, and was about to move to defend himself when Cecily's sword flicked through the air, glittering like a fish turning quickly in the water. Brycen's rage turned into surprise as Cecily disarmed him with a single movement, and he suddenly found himself looking her in the face. Elias was surprised to see the cold anger there.

"That was too far, General Brycen," she said, her voice so calm it was worse than if she'd been growling or shouting. "The arguing was bad enough from a man of your position, but no one, high rank or low, bares steel in my lady's presence. *Especially not at a friend of mine.*" Brycen took a step back, struggling for words, but Cecily's expression kept him silent. "If you wish to use your sword in this room, I will be your opponent."

Brycen spluttered, caught between extremes of rage, shock, and fear, but eventually he spluttered some excuse along with a halfhearted expression of his outrage and stormed out of the room. The old lady followed after a moment of shocked silence, and the younger woman made several apologies to Amira before swiftly excusing herself.

When they were gone, Cecily sheathed her sword and sighed.

"I am sorry, my lady. That was ill-done," she said, immediately apologetic as she turned to Amira. Elias personally would not say stepping in to defend him had been ill-done, even if he'd been fairly sure he could have beaten Brycen. Even if he had, though, it would only make things worse for him, and they might be quite bad already.

Amira sighed, putting a hand over her face.

"Don't blame yourself, Cecily. The mistake was mine, for holding the council like this. You have my thanks for ensuring it was only shouting that came about from that error."

"My lady, you can't blame your—"

"I am feeling very tired, all of a sudden," Amira muttered, slumped in her chair. "Please, I would not waste your time keeping you here further. I…just need to think."

The Royal Guard appeared to take that as a very politely worded command to leave, and they all bowed before obeying it as such. Elias started to follow them out, feeling a little troubled that he'd played a part in Amira's soured mood.

"Not you, Elias," her voice followed him, stopping him in his tracks. "We need to talk."

CHAPTER 31

Elias had suspected he might not get off so easily for throwing Amira's war council into disarray, although he couldn't say he had many regrets about what he had said and done just now. If he had been quiet, Brycen's terrible plan might be the only one that was presented, and Amira might well have walked towards her doom. Still, he was not looking forward to the notion of facing the young queen's displeasure as he turned to face her. With her guards and all other observers gone, Amira lowered the hand from her face to look intently at Elias.

"Keep the door closed, Elias. I would like for us to speak privately, and this may be the best opportunity I have in the immediate future to do so…even if it came about in less-than-ideal circumstances," she sighed.

"For what it's worth, I'm sorry the war council had to come to an ugly scene like that, but I don't regret what I said to Brycen," Elias said, trying to sound firm as he walked back to his seat.

"General Brycen is not the man I would have picked for this position, but Lord Hartmut, as you pointed out yourself, is dead. Lady Estrella is not a military leader, and I would not ask her to try and learn strategy at her age. Major Theodora has some capability, but she's young and inexperienced. Brycen would perceive it as a grave insult if I turned to her for advice, and she has done no wrong to me that I would be cruel enough to ask her to gainsay her superior in front of the council. I am using what I have available to me, Elias, and it would be unspeakably selfish in my position to ask for more. Brycen is not a man you will ever think fondly of, and I understand that. But he is here, and whatever his faults may be, he has endured these last five years on my account. I owe him my gratitude for that." Amira gave Elias a small smile. "Perhaps he could have done more than he has, but he isn't the only one that has come forward in this late hour to help me, is he?"

Elias grimaced. She had him there, true enough.

"I see your point. Even so, you are the leader here, not him. You owe everyone your judgement more than you owe them your favor. I *know* you didn't think that plan was a good idea. I had to say something, or no one would have shut him up," he sighed.

"I had hoped the discussion would remain civil, and that perhaps others would not feel reluctant to contribute their thoughts, but I did invite you out of more than gratitude for helping me find the Regalia again," Amira admitted, shaking her head. "As you said, I owe my people my judgement, and in my judgement I need to hear more than one voice before I decide what is best. General Brycen is not an inept man. My father had very little patience for the incompetent. But he thinks in straight lines, and he is used to having more to work with than he does now. I had imagined adding your voice to the discussion, someone who doesn't think in such straight lines, would help a plan emerge from the resulting discussion." Amira's face fell, and she sighed. "Unfortunately, I underestimated the chance that discussion would become nothing but shouting. I should not have thrown everything together so carelessly."

"That was my fault and his, not yours," Elias said quickly. It was strange to be apologizing to someone over something he said, but...he couldn't help but feel of late that Amira deserved at least that much from him, and probably a fair bit more beside. "It seems I can't seem to get away from any discussion I'm involved in returning to a matter of character sooner or later, and I've always been on poor footing there. I doubt people will consider my plan now."

"They will if I tell them to," Amira said quietly, surprising Elias. Her gloom seemed to fade as she regarded him over the table. "I had hoped you would come to this council with an idea no one else would offer me, something that would make all of this seem possible at last. You didn't disappoint me, Elias. You exceeded my expectations."

The smile Amira gave him was no bigger than a normal smile on the face of a girl her age, and even here it was slightly guarded, but Elias found it hard not to think of it as a grin compared to Amira's usual expressions.

"You think the plan will work?" Elias said hopefully, leaning forward a little. This was important. Even the greatest of all possible plans would be under fairly intense scrutiny if it came from him. If Amira endorsed the plan, her retainers would use all of their power to make it happen, giving no thought to the fact Elias had come up with it in the first place.

"Your reasoning was sound, and at this point I feel a movement no one would see coming is our greatest chance to make the five years we have hidden ourselves away matter. But beyond that…" Amira touched her chest, closing her eyes. For a moment, it seemed difficult for her to speak. "My mind could justify it. My heart *knew* this was the path I would choose to walk when I heard you say it. I think I would have known setting out for Enrilth was the right thing to do even if you hadn't explained it as well." Amira opened her eyes, looking seriously at Elias. He got the strong impression she was trying not to laugh or cry, possibly both at once. "Of all the people I called on for advice, you were the one who told me it was time for me to come home."

All at once, Elias understood that it hadn't been his tactics that had impressed Amira so. Even as a queen, it was unlikely she admired the trickery that had seen Elias through so much of his life the way he did. But she had wanted an alternative to leading her brave, tiny, and in all likelihood doomed army into battle, and Elias had given her a way to lead all of her loyal servants out of danger. More than that, he had given her a plan to return to the halls where she had been born. Enrilth Keep wasn't just the strongest position in Yivyn for them to take and hold, it was where Amira and her brother had been raised, the home of the Royal Guard.

For a long portion of his life, Elias had wanted to think of it as *his* home.

"Ami—Your Majesty…" he started, but Amira held up a hand.

"We can concern ourselves with titles later, Elias. Until this plan of yours works, I'm not truly a queen," she said quietly.

"There are several hundred people outside that door that would suggest otherwise," Elias pointed out, a little surprised to hear Amira talking like this.

"And I am more grateful to them for that than you can imagine, Elias," Amira whispered. "I can never begin to repay the kind of debt I owe them. Most of them swore oaths to my father, not to me, and of words no more serious or binding than those spoken by the ones that turned against me. But they saved me, served me, suffered for me…"

Amira's voice remained almost perfectly level, but Elias realized she was starting to cry freely without her voice trembling at all.

"When Father died, I was supposed to become the queen, but I became nothing," she said, staring at empty space instead of Elias. "My father *was* the king, but Oliver Bones took him away. None of his power, or his wisdom, or any of his other virtues passed to me along with the right to wear the crown, and people came to take that right from me in a moment after he was gone." Amira shivered slightly, and Elias wondered if she had ever breathed a word of this to anyone before. Surely she would have confided in her Guard before him...?

"The king is a sliver of divinity in the mortal world as long as no one strikes at him. But when someone shoots the king with an arrow, he dies like any other man, and the illusion of divinity is broken. When they struck at my family, it shattered. Suddenly my father was no longer the untouchable king, just a dead man in the forest. Everyone finally saw me as I was. A weak, foolish little orphaned girl who knew nothing about the world," Amira said bitterly. "But some of them still saved me, even though I wasn't important. Blanche has a power in her I can never match, and Cecily has courage I will never have...either of them was worthier in all things than I was, but they nearly lost their lives protecting me anyway. Cecily's father lost his life because of it. For me and my brother, a pair of sheltered children who couldn't survive a day outside castle walls alone, they've done all this for *five years,* with little hope their deeds would ever be rewarded. Because...they think I matter. And that's why I have to succeed. That's why I have to become the greatest queen I can be. Even if I wasn't the child of royalty, even putting aside all the rights I should have by law...I need to be a great queen because the people outside that door have suffered and died believing I could be one. If any of them discovered the truth? That...I'm just a weak girl making this up as I go?" Amira hugged herself, trembling. "I can't *do* that to them. I can't let any of them see me like this, not even once."

Elias stared at Amira, completely lost for words for once. He had known, from the very moment he'd seen her after five years on his own, that this trial had drawn the joy and vitality out of Amira like water from a well, destroying the cheerful child she'd been, but to this extent? Elias realized he was deeply disturbed to hear Amira call herself nothing. That wasn't a thought he could imagine a rightful queen having. That wasn't meant for people like her, people others admired and fought for. That was for people like him to think.

"I heard so many people decry you for being a liar, when all this started," Amira said, looking at him. The silence seemed to make her uncomfortable, and since she'd said this much the rest came spilling out to fill it. "But I've felt like one for so long myself. I'm...*pretending* I know what I'm doing, that I'm as sure as all of them are that I will be brave and just and wise if I get a chance to make everything better. I'm...I'm *scared,* Elias. I'm scared of how I feel out in the world, without walls around me to keep everything out. I'm terrified of letting everyone down after they've done this much for me. I'm even scared of my own people. What you said to Brycen, Elias…he wasn't where anyone could see him, but he was contributing what he could to protecting me. When I reveal myself, claim I am the lawful queen of Yivyn and call for an end to the fighting…" Amira clenched her fists. "Won't they ask me what you asked? What do I say to them if the people's question when they know I've returned is "where were you?" They have fought, and suffered, and died for five years because I wasn't there. Where was I when they were starving, or praying for an end to the wars? I was hiding while my people fought, suffered and died."

Elias wanted to tell her thinking like that was completely wrong. Brycen had been a grown man, fighting his chosen profession, but he'd stayed out of this for five years until he stepped forward now with a plan that would undo what little Amira had gained with his help. Amira had been a child, scared, in mourning, and trying to grow up too fast while her world fell apart around her. No one could blame her for not being able to act before now, could they?

Elias believed he could feel Mibotha's distress, seeing the queen it was working to raise up to restore the land crying as she told them these things. It was grieved, but also agitated…even scared. Mibotha was frightened by what it heard from her, he was sure of it. Elias did not share that fear. Part of it was that he was not afraid to see Amira as she was, rather than what she pretended to be, or even how she saw herself falling short of everyone's expectations. The other part, the much more significant one, was that there simply wasn't room to be afraid. Seeing Amira like this filled Elias with a guilt like he'd never felt before. Not when he heard Morys was dead, not when he saw the wars starting… there had always been something else. Fear, rage, resentment, survival, there had always been something that let him hide from it at a moment's notice. Here and now, however, he was as defenseless as Amira, and one thought filled him up until it spilled out all at once.

"I did this to you."

"W-What?" Amira looked up at Elias, seeming more surprised that he'd spoken than by what he'd said. Elias sank low in his chair, and any attempt to be nonchalant or calm faded. For once, he felt every bit as wretched as people had often imagined he ought to be over all that had happened.

"This shouldn't have been your life," he choked out, face ashen. "All this loss, all this fear, all this pressure…you didn't deserve any of this. But it's my fault this happened to you."

"Oliver Bones shot my father, not you," Amira said quietly. "I know that now, and you've always known it…" Was she just trying to comfort him, or had she truly let him off the hook that easily? Either way, Elias suspected she would not have responded so kindly if he had not sidestepped questions he didn't want to consider the answers to earlier.

"Oliver Bones killed your father. He probably did it for Duke Hache's pay. But he never would have pulled it off if it wasn't for me," he whispered, forcing himself to finally admit to it.

"He threatened you."

"He did. And I told him everything he asked me for to save my life," Elias went on. "You know that already. But you wondered, didn't you? I had a room in Enrilth, out of the way but still part of the castle. I did most of my work behind the scenes. People didn't pay me that much mind before everything went wrong. I never volunteered anything, but I know you must have wanted to ask how he got to me. How he knew to use *me*."

"You weren't an assassin. You weren't his partner!" Amira said, and Elias was astonished how certain she sounded considering the insinuations she'd heard when the group had confronted the Basilisk-Eye in person. "I *know* you weren't."

"I wasn't. But I was your father's link to the underworld, and those links go both ways," Elias said quietly. "I did things for your father. Things he couldn't have associated with his name. Often things that were against the law. I was careful, and I always tried to be subtle, but I wasn't perfect. My best wasn't good enough. Oliver Bones and I moved in the same circles down there, but I didn't know that. I thought he was dead. I didn't know he'd started that rumor himself. I wasn't thinking about him at all in those days, but he took an interest in *me*. I never worked with Oliver Bones…but when a man named Atticus helped me with my work for your father, I didn't think anything was wrong. I was connected with a lot of rough people from that world in those days." Elias put a hand over his face. "I kept thinking about it, afterwards. That I couldn't possibly have known. But it doesn't matter. I was the connection between the castle and the underworld. I was the tool the Basilisk-Eye needed to get access to your father. If I'd seen through him earlier, or been more careful, or had the courage to die that night…gods, if I'd just had the courage to go after him once I knew he was after Morys…" Elias looked at Amira.

"None of this would have happened. This wouldn't be your life. But it is, because of me."

Amira was quiet for a long time. Elias wondered if she had started to hate him again in that long pause, and had to admit he wouldn't blame her if she did. Eventually, however, Amira stood up, walking over to him.

"You've carried that knowledge every day for the last five years, haven't you?" she asked quietly. Elias found himself shaking his head.

"No. Some of it's always been there, gnawing at the back of my mind, but I had thousands of ways to never think about it, keep it from weighing down on me. I never needed to feel sorry for anyone else in the last five years. It was enough work feeling sorry for myself," he muttered. "I never had to carry it like this before I saw you again. Before I was reminded what I did to your life trying to save mine."

"...Yes, Elias. You were involved in my father's assassination. But I know you, now, much better than I ever did in the old days," Amira said, looking Elias in the eyes. "Listen to me, Elias. You were Bones's link to my father, but Oliver Bones is one of the greatest assassins that has ever lived. If it had not been you, he would have found another way. You did not kill my father. Duke Hache and Oliver Bones did." Amira looked down, biting her lip. "You ran from it...but in the circumstances, staying where you were might have gotten you killed under false charges. But you've come back, helped us try to turn things around...and you've taken responsibility for what you've done. You're a better man than I gave you credit for when we met again, Elias, and I think you're a better man than you believe yourself to be."

Elias stared at Amira in shock, once more completely unable to respond to the sentiment, even with gratitude. Amira seemed to press on.

"When you came to me for the first time after five years, dragged in by the Guard, I thought you'd only come all this way to try and save your own skin. But...I think I *do* understand you now, Elias. We've both made mistakes and been unable to help as much as we should have while Yivyn suffered around us...but thanks to you coming back to face what happened, we both have a chance to make amends now. We can save Yivyn together."

Elias considered telling Amira she'd been perfectly right to think he was just trying to save himself when they'd joined forces. Hell, he would never have taken the first step in this journey if Mibotha had not forced him to with the threat of sending him to Valka if he didn't, and he'd complained and felt sorry for himself every miserable step of the way.

And yet, somewhere in the midst of all this, still complaining, still feeling like he wasn't a real part of this unlikely partnership with the Royal Guard, he had found it harder to ignore the notion that it wasn't just Mibotha that wanted him to redeem himself. After hearing what Amira had said…he *did* want to make things right.

"What do you say, Elias? Shall we put an end to this together?" Amira asked, offering her hand to Elias.

Elias supposed he ought to have done something more dramatic, like drop to his knees and give Amira his most heartfelt thanks for believing in him after all that had happened, but if he had responded like that, perhaps he would not have been Elias Brook. As a result, he managed a smile closer to his usual one and nodded, accepting Amira's hand and standing up.

"I'm with you, Amira," he agreed, before forcing a shrug. "After all, it's not like anyone will ever let me forget it if I fail."

Amira laughed, shaking her head.

"No…I don't think anyone will forget for either of us if we fail. But we will not. I believe in your plan…and I believe in my people. Ultimately *they* will be the ones that end this war and strife, not us. But we need to give them the hope it can be ended, first."

"If we can take back Enrilth and let the word spread, it will work," Elias assured Amira, sounding a little more confident than he felt. Still, he'd gotten this far, and his instincts told him he was right. He just needed to trust in himself and hope whatever luck had come with Mibotha into his life would hold enough that he could actually pull all this off.

"I believe you. We'll have to begin making plans for the journey." Amira glanced at the door. "I had best get going, then…I'll need to convince others before we can even start. Try to stay out of trouble, Elias…"

It was a mild scolding, letting him know Amira hadn't forgotten about the argument earlier, but Amira smiled at him again before she left the room, leaving Elias alone in the chamber. Well, almost alone.

This was…not what I expected of you, Elias Brook.

"Do you disapprove?" Elias asked, taking advantage of finally having no one to listen in. "I remember you saying this is all for nothing if Amira is killed, and the other plan will certainly accomplish that and very little else."

No, I don't disapprove. This is a much better plan than anything I had been expecting. We were beginning to prepare for things to get much worse.

"We?"

Not all of this conflict is visible to you, Elias Brook. Cherish your ignorance on the matter, Mibotha said bluntly. *I will simply say that we were prepared if Amira had to give battle to reclaim her birthright, but it was a solution I had keenly wished to avoid. I...I am grateful you have given her another way, Elias Brook. You have helped more than you could realize by speaking your mind.* Mibotha's voice seemed a little kinder than usual, which surprised Elias, but he could also tell the spirit was pleased with itself, too. *Joining forces with you was a gamble that has worked out far better than I ever expected, Elias Brook. I am glad I took the chance you would be the one we needed.*

"And I'm glad I didn't bleed out in a forest alone and go to Valka, so I guess we both got something we wanted," Elias remarked dryly. "So the spirits are with us on the plan to retake Enrilth?"

We can use your plan. I will be able to help you, Mibotha said.

"That's a relief...I was starting to worry about what I'd do if there really were angry ghosts all the way to Enrilth Keep..." Elias muttered.

Oh, there are. We will have to contend with them if your plan is going to work.

That brought Elias up short for a moment, but he just sighed.

"Of *course* there are."

He thought he'd made a lot of progress today, but he realized he'd forgotten the more things changed, the more they stayed the same.

He'd come up with a plan to save the country. Now came the harder part of pulling it off with unforeseen dangers dogging him every step of the way and the promise of more hard work at the end. What else was new?

CHAPTER 32

Elias had no great desire to go back to his room and try to rest. Even with Mibotha pleased, he suspected he might continue to have nightmares when he slept until something big changed. He had a plan that might let them save Yivyn, but he hadn't accomplished any of it yet, and he was pretty sure the thought wasn't what counted in matters like these.

There was the matter of Oliver Bones, too. Elias was as certain as ever that he had not seen the last of the Basilisk-Eye, although with any luck, Bones was not expecting to see him again. The assassin was vital to some part of all this, he knew it. These nightmares had started to remind him of Mibotha's odd command. Oliver Bones had to be killed, and Elias was growing increasingly certain he had to be the one to do it. If nothing else, Amira would never be safe while Bones was alive. After their last confrontation, Elias was sure that Bones would never stop coming after her, and the time Amira would be able to hide from him was drawing to a close.

Which meant an important step in Elias's uncertain plan was to try and figure out how in the hell he was going to prevent the master assassin from eluding the guards and going right for the kill against Amira once they reached Enrilth and made it clear the queen had returned. Elias wanted to imagine that the Haunted Wasteland would give Bones a great deal of trouble trying to sneak up on the castle, but he felt sure that if anyone could and would cross it alone and unnoticed to reach their target, it was Bones. His attack would come, and come swiftly, with or without Hache's troops backing him up. If he managed to do what he did best this time, everything Elias had accomplished so far would mean absolutely nothing. Even putting the prince on the throne instead, if he somehow escaped Bones's vengeance, wouldn't work. People needed a *sign* for the sort of belief Elias's plan hinged on. The beloved Princess Amira, returned to be queen and end the war, *that* was a sign. If she was killed moments after revealing herself to the world, however, there would be no such mysticism behind Elendri's ascension, and the plan would fall apart. They would be trapped in Enrilth, and warlords would attack them until they all died. Mibotha had made it clear enough that Amira was the key. For his plan to work, he needed a foolproof way to see the Basilisk-Eye coming before he could get into position to strike.

No, wait…maybe sight didn't have to come into it. Not for him.

"Mibotha?" he muttered.

Yes, Elias Brook?

"You've been able to widen your awareness before to keep me alert to enemies approaching. How far off would you be able to know Oliver Bones was coming?"

Focusing on just his presence? I could pick him out from miles away.

Far enough to keep him from getting anywhere close to bow range… some of it would still come down to Elias's own cunning, but he was confident this at least gave him a chance.

"Good. I want you to focus constantly for his presence. We need to know when he gets within a mile or two of Amira, and I want to know his location as exactly as I can as he gets closer."

I believe I can help you with that, Mibotha agreed. *Unfortunately, I cannot guarantee accuracy beyond his proximity. Some of that you'll have to figure out for yourself.*

"My main concern is just knowing when he's close enough to risk using his bow…" Elias muttered. They'd gotten lucky last time that Bones had chosen to fire a couple shots and then show himself. That wouldn't happen twice, and if Elias didn't get the drop on Bones this time, a lot of people were going to die before the assassin even presented a target.

Do you have a plan to fight him? You made a good attempt at killing him on the cliffs, but in a battle between the two of you, the advantage is still firmly his.

Elias noticed Mibotha didn't seem to doubt for an instant his belief that Bones was alive and well. Unfortunately, the spirit's question had echoed a niggling doubt of his own. He'd gotten in a lucky shot on Bones when they fought but the assassin defeated him quite easily that day. By all rights, he should not have even lived long enough to drag him down to the river, let alone walk away afterwards. If he didn't turn the tables, and do so dramatically, Bones would kill him again easily when they met.

"I've been hoping I'll figure something out," he muttered. "With any luck at all, he won't see me coming, especially not with my face like this. But I need to be able to take him out before he can overpower me or kill someone else."

You are a clever man, Elias Brook. If you have endured this much, you will discover a way to defeat Oliver Bones, Mibotha declared, and Elias was rather surprised by the sincerity of its vote of confidence. He just hoped it wasn't misplaced this time.

Elias was left alone with his thoughts for some hours, aware of activity around him in the hidden castle, but not approached by anyone or disrupted from his own thoughts. In his mind, he ran through ways he might stop the Basilisk-Eye by himself, if things came to that. Many of the prospects had gloomy outcomes.

Hand-to-hand? Remembering Bones's speed in their last fight, Elias wondered if he'd even manage to replicate the one lucky shot he got in last time before Bones overcame him. That sword against Elias's dagger was an even worse scenario, and one he might well not get up from if Bones tried to take his head off this time. Elias was quite proud of his skill with a bow, but Bones was the one man in all of Yivyn he did not dare compete against in that regard.

He had to take him by surprise. That was all he could imagine working. Oliver Bones was a foe Elias had no chance against in a fair fight, and even in the kind of fight Elias preferred, Bones was still the better fighter by a wide margin. No matter how fast or how smart Elias was, he was certain Bones would be faster, more vicious, and a whole lot stronger. But none of that mattered if Elias could stab him in the back or slit his throat before Bones could realize his peril. The trick was how to sneak up on someone like Bones, especially before Bones could get in position to assassinate Amira.

As he pondered the matter, many gloomy scenarios flashing through his mind, Elias's solitude was finally broken by Cecily approaching him.

"Elias!"

"Hm?" Elias snapped out of an unpleasant imagining of what might happen if he missed his mark against Bones, turning to Cecily quickly. "Oh, hello, Cecily."

"Have you heard? The order has been given!" Cecily said, looking both excited and a bit out of breath. "Queen Amira has made your plan our strategy for retaking the kingdom! We're going to Enrilth!"

"It was approved that quickly?" Elias was honestly surprised to hear it. Morys had rarely reached major decisions like this so quickly, with all his advisors about. Amira must have exerted her absolute authority as queen. "What about Brycen?"

"The General was willing to argue that point to the death against you, but despite his best efforts, he had no choice but to concede. My lady was quite adamant," Cecily said, grinning. "It was quite a surprise to the soldiers, but preparations are already being made to depart! By morning, we'll be on our way back to Enrilth!"

"You seem eager to be off, for someone who just got here," Elias joked, taking Cecily's good mood as a positive sign even though he'd come to realize it was a fairly normal thing for Cecily. It was infectious, even he felt more optimistic about their chances while she was around.

"I only wanted to be here to reunite with everyone and figure out what we were going to do next," Cecily said, laughing a little. "But I'd been imagining a battle, or some sort of strike against Duke Hache. I never imagined we could actually go *home* instead…"

Her reaction didn't surprise Elias, but it was another good sign. Cecily probably spoke for the entire Royal Guard here, and Elias could see how Amira's will had been so quickly embraced. This wasn't Elias Brook's plan to sneak away from the conflict anymore. It was Queen Amira's plan to return to her home, and bring the Royal Guard back where they belonged. Despite the undesirable journey just to get to Enrilth from here, Elias was now quite sure the journey would be undertaken with high morale from the Guard.

"There's been enough war in the last five years. One more won't solve the problem. Retaking the seat of power and bringing the queen home is going to do more than taking the fight to the enemy would, I'm sure of it."

"I believe you," Cecily agreed. "The whole Guard is with you on this, Elias. We're protectors, not soldiers. Going back where we belong, and making the capital habitable again…that is what we've always hoped to do, and if it could end the war and avert more bloodshed, that is the best path we can take."

"I don't know about there being no bloodshed, but it would be on better terms than if we go and seek it out," Elias sighed. Cecily nodded, seeming to catch his point.

"Hache."

"Yes. We can't rule out him taking the gamble on attacking us, or sending Bones to try and kill us before things get too difficult for him to succeed. Hache knows there's no going back for him, and Amira returning to power could be the end of him for good this time. He will act against us, and we'll need to counter it."

"You're probably right, but I don't envy Hache's soldiers the task ahead of them if he tries to come and attack us once we're in Enrilth Keep," Cecily pointed out. "If that is to be the trial we have to overcome to show our lady will not be brushed aside, we can do it."

"That's the hope, anyway. If we're lucky, Hache won't be able to manage that, but…" Elias trailed off, hesitant to share his concern about Bones coming with or without Hache's support to finish what he started. Cecily seemed to understand without him needing to spell it out.

"If the Basilisk-Eye does come, we will defeat him once and for all this time," she said confidently. "We have come too far and done too much to let him stop us now."

Elias had to wonder just how times like these had produced someone as effortlessly optimistic as her, but perhaps that was simply how Cecily had managed through everything that had befallen her. Still, he had to admit, though it had irritated him at first, he couldn't deny he admired Cecily's boundless confidence, the way she looked at their situation. It hadn't escaped his notice that her hopeful outlook drew people to her in a way he would never have anticipated. Amira admired Cecily's courage, valued her company, Boors looked after her as a part of his own family… and it had not been lost on Elias that Cecily's outlook had a transformative effect. He'd seen it in Blanche, observed the way all the danger and chilly intelligence in her gaze melted away to something warmer when Cecily was with her, and now he was starting to feel it himself. He was different when she was around, less suspicious or cold or self-pitying. Her view of him was better than the reality, and he found himself unwilling to let her down.

Amira was the symbol of hope the land needed, but Elias realized it was Cecily that they were all drawing that hope from. Amira, Blanche, and now him. Cecily made him want to hope, not just that they could actually succeed, but that he could be better than he was. It was truly a remarkable power she possessed.

Elias saw Cecily blink curiously, and he realized he'd been quiet, and staring, just a bit too long. He cleared his throat awkwardly.

"I hope for everyone's sake you're right," he sighed. "If we don't put him in the ground, Amira will never be safe."

"With the protection of the castle and the skill of the Royal Guard, it will take more than Oliver Bones to stop us." This time, Elias heard steel behind the confident words. This wasn't bravado to Cecily at all. She sincerely and fully believed that coming for Amira again would be the last mistake Oliver Bones ever made. Elias wished his own assurance in the success of their plan was so strong. Cecily seemed to lighten up quickly, not allowing the shadow of Bones's return to spoil her good mood.

"Come on, Elias. There's one last meal being held here before we start the long march home. The Guard want to drink with you before we head out, for luck," she laughed, grinning at Elias.

The Royal Guard wanting to have a drink with him, for luck? One month ago, Elias would have accepted this without argument as proof he had gone insane and lost all contact with reality.

"As long as I'm not buying, sure," he laughed, following her.

The final meal in the hidden fortress was an experience like nothing Elias had ever had before. There had been royal feasts during his time, plenty of food and drinking and music, but Elias had always enjoyed these events on the edges, staying out of everyone's way and drawing no attention to himself. These events were for the enjoyment of others, the knights and lords and their friends and family. It wasn't for him, he was just a guest, and one given roughly the same consideration as the tapestries he tended to enjoy his meal next to.

This time, he sat among the Royal Guard, feeling like a completely unexpected surprise guest and the man of the hour all at once. Others had not been pleased to see him as he'd entered, but the Guard who had been with him accepted him easily, and those who hadn't trusted in their friends. The Royal Guard that had not joined with him on the expedition to reclaim the Regalia were all still sorting things out, from what Elias could tell. Two weeks ago, he had been one of their worst enemies, but Elias could see that the things he had done were starting to sink in. He'd been cleared of treason, helped Amira reclaim her Regalia, saved one of their own, and now he had come up with the plan that was bringing them home.

Elias had expected very little from his alliance with the Guard. He'd been certain one day Cecily would turn on him, he would come to blows with Boors, or Blanche would kill him. But here they were, drinking together without so much as a sharp word. They had actually accepted him. It was a tremendous shock to Elias when Blanche leaned across the table to lightly tap her tankard against his.

"I never thought I'd say this, Brook, but I'm glad we have you with us," she said, not raising her voice but somehow perfectly audible to Elias over the din. "You've made all of this possible. Thank you."

Blanche smiled at Elias, and Elias noticed there was no calculation, no possible inscrutable dangers hidden in her expression this time. It was...just a smile. The simple sincerity of the whole business was something new and strange to Elias, but there was no misconstruing it. Blanche, the one he understood least of all the Royal Guard, felt just like Cecily did about returning home, and she had the same gratitude to him for it all the others had expressed. He didn't get the feeling she wanted something more from him anymore. Maybe, completely by accident, he had already given it to her. He found himself curiously bereft of smart remarks, and had to settle for tapping his tankard against Blanche's and raising it with a little smile.

"…You're welcome."

It was a strange night for Elias, and it brought a strange thought with it. Maybe he had been mistaken, that night in the grove. Maybe his certainty he would never belong anywhere was wrong. Maybe with these people, being acknowledged, even thanked…maybe this was his place. With them.

It was something he would lose almost as soon as he'd gained it if his plan failed, he knew. One more reason he had to succeed. One more thing he couldn't let Oliver Bones take from him.

Even depleting the hidden fortress's alcohol reserves wasn't enough for Elias to feel more than lightly inebriated when the night was over. It appeared to have been enough to get Cecily quite drunk, however, and Elias heard her continuing to laugh and sing old songs as Blanche helped her off to her room. Boors left on his own, giving Elias a respectful nod as he departed. Elias was surprised to find he cared. Seeing the hall emptying quickly of people who welcomed his presence, Elias decided to make himself scarce, heading back to his own room.

He felt good. Better than he had in a long time, and not just from the beer. For a moment, all his world-weariness felt far away, and he allowed himself to *know* he could pull this off rather than hoping for it desperately.

Whatever the reason, his deeds, his thoughts, or the drink, Elias slept soundly that night.

CHAPTER 33

Deephome's occupants emptied out of the castle before the sun rose the following day, beginning their journey under the cover of darkness. Amira's remaining soldiers, her retainers, her officers, a little more than two hundred Royal Guard, and one Elias Brook formed up around the supply train that was going to stand between them and starvation in the Haunted Wasteland surrounding Enrilth.

Elias wasn't that worried about having to defend the supply train, but…Deephome was hidden along the borderline where Lord Dunst's small territory brushed against Evangeline's much larger swathe of land. It was unlikely either of them was watching this area very closely, but it was still a day's journey to reach the Haunted Wasteland and then three more days to reach Enrilth and the castle itself. Today was the day they would be in the most danger from bandits, soldiers, and other such threats. Elias wasn't worrying about tomorrow right now, especially since he had only a vague idea what it would involve.

It would be very stupid bandits that attacked Amira's entire military force, of course, but Elias was concerned what might happen if anyone noticing them brought down soldiers on their heads. They had to protect their supplies, and get them through the Haunted Wasteland. If they couldn't pull that off, and bring everything to Enrilth Keep more or less intact, holding the castle in the middle of the desolation that surrounded it would be a much more daunting task. They had to ensure today's journey did not see any disruption to the supply train reaching their destination. Tomorrow's concern would be Elias hoping quite fervently that Mibotha had enough clout in the spirit world to help him keep whatever angry ghosts lived there from ruining everything.

"Have you ever been back to Enrilth, Brook?" Blanche asked, breaking Elias's train of thought as she brought her horse up next to his. "During the years you were out here on your own?"

"No, I haven't. I ran when it was still the jewel of Yivyn, and I never dared to go near it again," he sighed. "Especially not when I heard what was happening. First it was too dangerous to approach, then…it felt wrong to disturb it, even if the land wasn't haunted. Too much had happened."

Blanche nodded, and Elias found she had a surprisingly understanding expression on her face.

"We're the same. We didn't all flee at once, but the Guard had to go into hiding quickly as it became clear we couldn't hold back the storm that was coming down on us. We haven't dared go back there since," she muttered. "For years we abhorred the Haunted Wasteland and you the most out of everything in Yivyn. More than the warlords, more than anything." Blanche sighed, shaking her head. "The man we thought had killed the king was somewhere beyond our reach, a living testament to our failure…and that horrible scar in the middle of the kingdom, perpetually reminding us how completely we had failed our king. This is the first time since I fled it with Queen Amira that I'll have seen Enrilth."

Despite Blanche's earlier excitement about returning home, Elias felt some sort of tension from her today there had not been last night, and wondered if she was looking forward to settling back into the castle but not the homecoming itself. He could sympathize, he supposed. He wasn't looking forward to riding across miles of unforgiving territory dotted with unmarked graves and angry spirits either, but Blanche's unease felt like it lay elsewhere. Elias decided not to ask. He still wasn't sure he wanted to know more about Blanche. He could detect something ugly there, and was not inclined to go digging for it.

"Where are Cecily and Boors? I was expecting them to be right with you," he said, trying to change the subject. Blanche shook her head.

"Cecily will be joining us soon enough, but Queen Amira has need of her at the moment," Blanche said. "Boors will be staying by the queen's side, to protect her and Prince Elindri."

"The prince…" Elias sighed. He didn't know Elindri as well as Amira. The boy had only been five when Elias had fled the castle in quite a rush, and the prince had taken no part in any of the quest to restore his sister to power so far for his own safety.

"Ten years old, and very hard-headed…" Blanche said, shaking her head. "My lady wanted to try and make an arrangement to keep him somewhere out of sight and out of danger in case anything happened to her, but he was very adamant. His father would have been impressed by his arguments last night. As long as he stays near Queen Amira and Boors, he should be quite safe."

"He and Amira argued?" Elias asked, before flinching slightly when Blanche gave him a reproving look for just using the queen's name.

"They don't argue very often, but it has been increasing of late. Queen Amira does not want her brother bearing the burdens she began to struggle with at his age, but every year he becomes more determined to take some responsibility himself. He will grow into a fine man, if we make it through this," Blanche muttered.

"We will make it. We've gotten this far, haven't we?" Elias pointed out. Both of them seemed to know right away that that was Cecily talking, not him, but it seemed to lift both their spirits to hear it said.

"We have. After all this time, we can finally hope this might be the end of it," Blanche agreed.

"I don't know about the end of it..." Elias said, thinking about all the times he'd risked his neck only to be told it had been the easy part of this journey. "But it will be the step that changes everything, for sure."

"This is the breaking point. If things don't improve from here, they never will, and that kingdom of dust or trees we spoke of will come to pass," Blanche sighed. "As Cecily would say, failing now is not an option."

"My feeling is we don't want to live to see what happens next if we fail here," Elias said, mostly to himself as the dreams he'd been having flashed through his mind unbidden. Blanche gave him a curious look, but when Elias did not elaborate, she surprisingly let it drop.

"It will be strange, being back in the castle. There hasn't been a soul inside it for years," Blanche sighed. "Those fortifications were built to last, but making it the way it was will take years of hard work and a turn in the weather, even if this ends without fighting."

"If that's the worst thing we have to worry about, I'll thank the gods ten times a day," Elias sighed. It would be strange, trying to end the war while hiding out in the ruins of the most important place in his life, but it beat any alternatives he could think of. He just hoped Blanche was right about there not being a soul inside the walls when they got there.

The mood brightened considerably as Cecily joined them, not looking like she had considered even the possibility of failure.

"The supply train is moving more smoothly than we anticipated. We should have an easy trip to the border from here," she said cheerfully, bringing her horse in to ride along with the others as the group began to move a little faster.

"With this many armed guards, no bandits would risk attacking us. They're not well-organized enough to challenge us head-to-head, and most of them are bandits in the first place because they wanted an easier way to get food than joining an army," Blanche said. "I don't foresee any major complications today…I'm worried about when we cross the border."

She didn't elaborate, and didn't need to. Even Cecily didn't seem to be looking forward to the journey across the Haunted Wasteland, and she did not have it on good authority, as Elias did, that there were going to be a lot of angry spirits lurking between them and their destination. Even if the spirits didn't bother them directly, no force's morale would be high going through that desolate place. Its only good point would be that you'd have to be quite mad to send troops after anyone in there.

"Well, then, we'll just need to get through the Wasteland as quickly as we can to reach the castle!" Cecily said, refusing to let anything diminish her excitement. "Getting through all that will be nothing after the expedition to get the Regalia back."

"There won't be any soldiers breathing down our necks, at least," Elias muttered. Even Bones shouldn't be a concern until word about where Amira had resurfaced spread. Hopefully whatever damnable luck had allowed him to nearly corner them in Hache's territory would not help him this time.

Even if it did, if Bones struck out from Hache's territory today, it would take too much time to overtake them *here*, let alone in the Wasteland itself. Elias was sure that Bones would not be able to catch up from where he should be at the moment. They would have the castle by the time he was on them. Hopefully that would make a difference.

Even the knowledge that it was extremely unlikely they were to be attacked today didn't do much to set Elias at ease as they travelled under the slowly rising sun. Some of the worst times in Elias's life had come when he believed himself safe from harm, and this journey had him jumping from the frying pan into a successively bigger series of fires. As such, he was on guard much of the day for some unforeseen disaster to befall them as they traveled.

For once, though, Elias's bracing for the worst proved unnecessary. Nothing bad befell them as the day wore on, and they grew increasingly close to the border without seeing a single soul. Elias's wariness gradually decreased, and eventually he surveyed their surroundings merely to take them in rather than searching for danger.

Despite the years of war, the countryside looked surprisingly peaceful here. It was nothing but an illusion, he knew. People were afraid to travel here alone and beyond that were miles and miles of desolate, barren land. But one could be forgiven for thinking the wide plains they crossed now, a gentle breeze stirring tall grass, was a land at peace, growing strong. For once, Elias didn't feel threatened. There was danger featuring prominently in his immediate future, but it didn't feature prominently in his present, which was a new experience for him.

He felt at ease, maybe for the first time in more than five years. Strange as the thought was, Elias realized that here, in the company of people who had been his enemies, marching to an uncertain future with the promise he would need to fight one of the deadliest men in the world soon, was still the happiest he'd ever been in his life. Perhaps it was more a comment on how he'd spent his life than where he was right now, but there was no shaking the feeling. After all the complaining and misfortune and distrust, somehow he felt good here.

While the day's reprieve from danger and chaos was very fulfilling for Elias, it was only a day, and it seemed to come and go with alarming swiftness. Compared to the less pleasant stretches of travel that had shaped Elias's life, it seemed like the journey to the border took no time at all.

Elias felt some of his serenity bleed away as the group came to a stop at the edge of the Haunted Wasteland. The grasslands and their relative safety now lay behind them, but ahead lay a vast stretch of hard, barren ground, deep ditches, and snarled patches of scrubland as far as the eye could see. Their destination wasn't even visible from their current vantage point, merely terrain that looked like it would become a desert before it grew anything green again. Elias hid his annoyance as he saw Brycen come up beside him, giving him a hard look.

"And your plan is for us to march through *that*?" he muttered, glaring at Elias and then the wastes stretching away before them. Elias knew that Brycen would not directly disobey Amira, not even on this, but he had long since learned that Brycen staying quiet was simply not something you should ever expect from life.

"It will work," he said calmly, both to Brycen and himself. He was surprised that it was Amira who made the first move in the group, her horse trotting forward cautiously. The animal clearly did not want to go into the Wasteland, but the well-trained beast overcame its misgivings.

Seeing Amira confidently cross over the border, everyone else began to follow.

"This is lunacy," Brycen growled, turning his horse so he wouldn't have to ride next to Elias. "Gods help us all if you're not as clever as you think, Brook."

Elias didn't bother to respond, and just kept riding. The Wasteland didn't really seem like a part of Yivyn to him, certainly not the part where he was born and raised. He'd remembered this region's rivers and forests from when he was young, some of the best hunting grounds in the country. Now, there wasn't a tree or any sign of water for miles, just torn-up ground, sickly yellow grass, and low-growing brambles.

"It honestly looks more like it was cursed than just ruined in all the fighting," Elias muttered. Blanche nodded when she heard him, still looking deeply troubled as she surveyed the landscape.

In a manner of speaking, it was, Mibotha said darkly in the back of Elias's mind. Elias turned some curious attention to the spirit, but Mibotha refused to elaborate. All Elias could feel from Mibotha as they proceeded was a deep, festering rage as it observed the ruined landscape through his eyes.

"I'd heard how bad things got back here, but I didn't want to believe it was true," Cecily said quietly, shivering a little in her saddle. Elias noticed everyone, himself included, seemed unwilling to raise their voices here. Maybe it was the unnatural stillness of the air, or the sheer quiet the place carried without their presence. Elias couldn't hear any birds, or insects, or any of the little noises that had made even still places like the spirits' grove seem alive.

This wasn't land like any they'd crossed before. This was a massive corpse they were traversing, and the sky contributed to the gloom with grey, hopeless clouds blocking out the sun.

"I'm starting to think reuniting the land isn't the only impossible task we're facing here. Is it even possible to make this place livable again?" Elias asked, feeling daunted by the notion of ever fixing all this.

It will happen for Amira.

Mibotha sounded like it was spitting each word. Elias had seen it mad, but not in this strange combination of fury and desperation. For the first time since Amira's unorthodox coronation, Elias was again afraid of the spirit sharing his body.

The land will rise for its queen, Mibotha said, and Elias realized the spirit was saying it more to itself than it was to him. He had the sneaking suspicion that the phrase meant something different to Mibotha than it did to him. He wished he could talk to the spirit without risking the entire group overhearing his half of the conversation, but he would need to be further away from everyone than he was prepared to go in a place like this to have that kind of privacy. He decided it would be best if he just let Mibotha stew on whatever dark thoughts it was keeping to itself. With luck, that would be the only angry spirit he had to contend with for the time being.

And then he saw them.

Some of them were in the dry, thorny thickets that clung stubbornly to the dusty ground. Some of them crouched by ditches or scars of land that had once been streams. Some of them milled about aimlessly by rocks.

They weren't like the invisible but powerful presence Elias had felt with spirits before. These were visible, but somehow much fainter than the shapeless powers he'd met. They were blurred, smudgy imitations of human shape, like a weak, crude charcoal drawing of a man. No two were exactly the same shape, or the same color, or the same opacity, but they all resembled something that had been crafted in the form of a man.

They didn't have features, not really. Their heads were just shadowy lumps with no face to speak of. But the one feature they all had in common were the dull orange eyes glowing in their heads, focused on the living disrupting their land. Faint as it was, Elias could feel resentment all around them, and realized it wasn't just Mibotha he was beginning to feel rage from.

He cast a worried glance at Blanche, and saw she had paled, too, but the rest of the group seemed completely oblivious to their peril.

The Haunted Wasteland was as aptly named as Mibotha had warned him, it seemed. And Elias was going to need to figure out what to do about the angry ghosts that inhabited it a lot sooner than he'd planned.

CHAPTER 34

Don't panic, Elias thought to himself. You knew this part was coming, even if you were hoping you were wrong.

Trying not to make any sudden moves as dozens of dull orange eyes stared balefully at the living intruding on the dead land, Elias slowly led his horse to walk besides Blanche.

"Any ideas?" he whispered, keeping an eye on the spirits. They were just milling around for now, but he didn't know what these things were capable of, and that worried him. At this point, he didn't care if Blanche or Mibotha was the one who answered.

"I-I don't know," Blanche muttered, keeping her voice down to avoid spooking the others and trying to control her expression. "I've never actually *seen* them before. They've always been invisible."

Hm. She hadn't seen the rock spirit in the grove? Or maybe she'd just come upon him too late to notice it. Interesting, but not helping their situation at all.

"I haven't seen anything like them before," he said, watching the slowly gathering spirits warily. "I don't know if they can hurt us or not."

They cannot hurt the living nearly as much as they would like to. They are only the shadows of wasted lives, Mibotha muttered. *But they still have enough power to be dangerous. They will still try to kill you, if they can. Stay calm.*

Easier said than done. The unmistakable shadows drifted about the group. Some seemed unwilling or unable to move more than a few inches from where they had started, and Elias was glad to see them fall behind, but others kept up with them, even though their movements crudely mimicked a painful, difficult walk.

rrrr...ooo...

It became very obvious to Elias as he watched that the ghosts seemed to pay more attention to him and to Blanche than they did to the company obliviously riding alongside them. He felt a chill run down his spine as some of the spirits shuffled painfully towards him. Maybe it was just his imagination, but the eyes on one seemed brighter as a whisper-soft noise halfway between groan and growl escaped it.

…rrrr…ooo…rrrrrrooookkk…

Elias considered praying to any god that was listening that it wasn't trying to say what he thought it was trying to say, but he had never been that lucky before and he doubted he was about to start now.

rrrrrrooooooook…rook…roooookrook…BROOOOOOOOOOOOOOK! The almost pitiful, eerie groaning transformed into a howl of rage as one phantom's dull orange eyes turned bright red. Before Elias could do anything, the spirit swiped at his leg, its vapor-like arm wielded more like a cudgel than any claw or fist Elias had seen. A biting pain went through Elias's entire leg, and he grunted, suppressing a cry of pain as it went numb at the blow. His horse reared, frightened but not able to tell where the source of its distress was, and Elias was nearly thrown from the saddle. He wondered if he would live if he was thrown to the ground with these things around.

Gods damn it, that *hurt*! There didn't appear to be any blood or injury on his leg, but he now knew these creatures could harm him and intended to do just that.

"Elias? What happened?" Blanche asked, seeing the spirits closing in around them. No one else had noticed anything strange yet, but Blanche could at least see the spirits, even if she hadn't felt the blow he took.

"Nothing…" Elias said, trying to think very fast. If he let on there were angry spirits all around them, this was going to get ugly. People would panic, the train would fall apart, and he suspected the evil spirits wouldn't care who ran and who stayed if they started to attack everyone.

If they just attacked him, though, he was going to have a hard time seeing them through this without exposing that anyway.

The ghostly arm hit him in the stomach this time, and Elias doubled over in the saddle, feeling the bottom drop out of his stomach as cold spread through his core. Mibotha had not adequately warned him just how much the touch of these things could hurt him. Elias was now very certain that the things attacking him had the capacity to kill.

The spirit's next blow hit his horse instead of him, and this time the animal shrieked in panic, hurling Elias to the ground and running.

Blanche wheeled in alarm as Elias was hurled to the ground, the spirits closing in.

"Brook!"

The dull orange eyes suddenly turned into a sea of red sparks in the dark forms gathered around Elias, and he felt his heart stop as the dull resentment and rumbling anger gave away to a savage, terrifying *glee* in the creatures around him. This time it was three arms that smashed down upon him, sending racking pains through his entire body, and this time Elias couldn't stop himself from screaming in pain, sending a ripple of alarm through the train. Elias lashed out desperately at his attackers, but it was like trying to fight smoke. His blows passed uselessly through his attackers, and he thought he heard one chuckle darkly before plunging both its hands into his chest, cutting off his next breath. More pressed in, and Elias saw his future smothered in the darkness of their forms.

"He's writhing! What's happening?"

"Evil spirits…by the gods, it's true!" he heard someone shout, but he could no longer see anything through the forms of the spirits.

"Everyone, calm down!" Blanche's voice rang over the growing furor. "Cecily, go get his horse!"

Keeping Cecily from getting involved in a fight she couldn't see, Blanche could think on her feet Elias had to admit, although he didn't know what they were going to do now. He struggled to try and drive away the spirits, but nothing he did seemed to effect his attackers in the least. His blows passed through them harmlessly, while his body went numb except for the blinding pain and terrible cold each time they struck him. This wasn't a mob beating he would survive. He didn't even know if there was anything for Mibotha to heal this time.

"Brook, hold on!" Blanche's voice rang out sharply again, and for a moment the darkness full of red eyes was disrupted as Blanche's hand plunged through the mass of angry ghosts to try and drag Elias to safety. Elias held on for dear life, hearing increasing sounds of panic beyond the spirits as the men observed him being rescued from something none of them could see.

He tried to cry out a warning to Blanche as she pulled him loose, but it came too late, and a spirit struck at Blanche. She spasmed in pain, collapsing next to him and struggling to catch her breath, but Elias noticed the spirit seemed hurt by touching her, jerking back rather than pressing its attack. Unfortunately, this just brought back the rage that had first started the attacks. Elias felt certain this was about to turn into a bloodless but still very lethal catastrophe.

GET BACK!

The angry spirits quailed in surprise as Mibotha's voice blasted out of Elias, feeling like it had screamed from the center of his chest at a volume Elias had never experienced before. He was astonished that even Blanche didn't seem to notice the terrifying roar. For him, it was almost deafening.

The spirits hovered uncertainly, eyes returning to the dull orange from before. Elias didn't doubt that they still meant him harm, but he could feel anger laced with trepidation as Mibotha's ferocity covered Elias and Blanche like a shield. Elias wondered what would happen if it came to a fight between the spirits. Mibotha was invisible, but its powers were undeniable. Despite the pain they'd inflicted on him, the visible ghosts felt somehow insubstantial and weak by comparison. Even so, there were a lot of them, and only one Mibotha.

"Elias! Blanche! Are you all right?"

Elias turned his attention in surprise to find Amira looming over him and Blanche on horseback, looking down at them. At first he struggled for a way to brush this off without worrying the young queen, but then he realized the spirits' eyes had turned to her when she appeared. What was more, it dawned on Elias as he followed her gaze that *Amira could see them.*

Despite still looking a little pale, Blanche seemed to see that everyone was on the verge of panic, and Elias was surprised to hear her lie as she stood.

"Brook's horse was just spooked, milady," Blanche said, helping Elias to his feet. "This place has been frightening the animals since we entered. I don't think they like it here any more than we do."

"I see. That is unfortunate," Amira said, staring down the angry spirits with a serious expression. Maybe it was just Elias's imagination, but they seemed to be shrinking away from her. "Are you all right, Elias?"

"I'm fine. My leg hurts a bit from the landing, but that's it," Elias said as nonchalantly as he could, rubbing his injury from the ghost. Amira nodded.

"That's good." Amira turned to face everyone else, and Elias realized that her coming over to him had drawn a lot of attention from the living as well as the dead. At least it appeared to have quelled the panic before it could go too far...

"I know this is hard on all of you," she said, raising her voice. "We're a long way from our old positions of safety, and there is a long, unfriendly road ahead of us. But do not forget why we're out here. We are going home, back where we belong. We are going to put an end to this fighting once and for all. Do not lose faith!" Amira turned back to Elias and his ghostly attackers, looking serious. "Everything will be all right. We will *make* this right."

To Elias's enormous surprise, several of the angry ghosts seemed to fade away at Amira's words, their passing less dramatic than some dust being lost in the wind. With a noise like a sigh, nearly all of the spirits vanished, and the one who had attacked Elias seemed to diminish, losing its angry air and slipping silently back to where it had been hovering without purpose before striking at Elias.

He couldn't help but stare at her, knowing well enough he could not demand an explanation here in front of everyone but too surprised to pretend it had been nothing. Still, he saw Amira's eyes silently begging him not to say anything about it, and he eventually just nodded as Cecily returned with his horse.

"You're right, Your Majesty. Although I think I speak for all of us when I say Enrilth will be a welcome sight after we've put this place behind us," he said, trying to keep his tone light as he slipped up onto his horse.

"Just be careful you don't get bucked again, Brook. Someone might trip over you next time," Blanche said, turning her plain relief the ghosts had dispersed into a little teasing as she remounted.

"Yes, yes…thank you for grabbing my horse, Cecily," he sighed, remounting quickly and nodding gratefully to Cecily.

"No trouble at all, Elias," Cecily replied, but he was fairly certain he saw something between confusion, suspicion, and doubt on her face. She suspected that Elias was hiding something from that peculiar incident, but she appeared to be restraining herself from asking.

It occurred to Elias that there were probably going to be a lot of questions that needed to be answered when saving Yivyn was not everyone's first priority.

It had set off some muttering when Elias had been thrown from his horse, but the others seemed to settle down, and even relax a little more, once Amira had said her piece and returned to the head of the train. Elias rode quietly, still seeing the Wasteland dotted with spirits, but they seemed to be observing from a distance for the moment. Was it Amira that prevented them from approaching, or merely their own unwillingness to move? Either way, he got the feeling that small group dispersing had just been the start of the danger these things posed. He was going to need to work out how to stop them from derailing his plan before any of his other enemies got a chance to.

"She could see them," he whispered under his breath when he saw there was enough distance between him and the others to speak very quietly. "You didn't tell me she was a mage."

She's not.

"...What?"

No matter how Elias asked, Mibotha did not speak again. Elias didn't like its silence.

CHAPTER 35

For something Elias had been so certain would work, the expedition through the Haunted Wasteland was not off to a grand start. He had, for the most part, recovered from whatever damage the angry ghosts had done to him, as had Blanche, but he was left feeling twitchy and ill-at-ease from the encounter, and he wasn't the only one.

The others were all on edge after what had happened, not sure if what had happened to Elias was nothing to worry about or a sure sign that their endeavor was doomed. Elias didn't want to imagine the reaction if anyone besides Amira, Blanche, and himself could see the indistinct spirits all around them. He'd been ready for it to be dry and desolate every step of the way to Enrilth, but the constant feeling of those dull orange eyes watching them, never knowing if one of them would turn to red and start swinging? He hadn't been ready for that. Their expedition was surrounded from the first step, and they were lucky that the spirits seemed unwilling to attack again after Amira had dispersed the first group. He got the feeling that it wasn't going to last, particularly since Mibotha's renewed quiet suggested the spirit was either troubled or very active at the moment.

Mibotha had kept the group from getting tired to ride through the woods out of Hache's territory not so long ago. He hoped whatever it was doing now might be similarly helpful.

"We just need to hold out a few days," he whispered to himself, trying to keep his spirits up. "Once we reach the castle, it will be fine."

Well, as fine as things could be when you knew Oliver Bones appearing to try and kill everyone at the time of his choosing was something you were going to have to deal with sooner rather than later, but it was still a welcome prospect compared to grappling with things that appeared to be made of pain and malice. He could at least *hit* Bones.

Still, their journey through the Haunted Wasteland continued, muted and fearful, but no one would turn back after they'd come this far. Elias had to admit, he respected the loyalty that kept every man and woman that followed Amira marching on. Any army would have had deserters by now.

Because the scrubland was so monotonous, it did not escape Elias's notice when their surroundings began to change. The new scenery gave him precious little comfort.

Out of the desolation of the worn down wilderness and into ruins swallowed up in the Wasteland. Elias could feel the morale of the expedition sink even further as the gutted remains of what had probably been a farming village five years ago came into view. There wasn't much left but splintered skeletons of buildings. Even bones seemed to have been lost to the dust years earlier. Places like this were said to be all over the Wasteland. From what he'd heard, towns and villages that had meant no one any harm had not been spared when the territory around Enrilth was razed in the fighting.

He would have expected there to be far more angry spirits in the village, but he was surprised to find that only one or two of the black creatures dwelt within it, staying close to ruined dwellings and making no effort to move from them. He noticed something new inside the town, however. They weren't like the charcoal smudges the angry ghosts resembled, rather more like faint outlines of human forms with nothing to fill them in, drifting aimlessly in the dust. Some of them were far smaller than Elias liked to think about.

"The sun will be gone soon," Cecily remarked, breaking the relative silence they'd been riding in as she looked at the sky. "Maybe we should rest here."

"Let's keep going," Blanche said quietly, and Elias was surprised to hear how small and tight her voice sounded. Blanche sat rigidly on her horse, looking into the distance like she was trying not to see anything before her. Elias didn't think he'd seen her that pale before, even when the evil spirits were right on top of them. "We can still cover more distance."

"Not enough to matter, I'd say," Elias sighed, looking at the tired expressions of the other guards and soldiers. "We wouldn't get far enough to justify setting up camp in the night. I'd rather be settled in before it gets dark out here." This place was creepy enough in the day, and he had no idea if the spirits were any more or less dangerous at night.

"Elias is right, Blanche. We're not likely to find anywhere we'd rather stay the night than right here in this horrible place. We might as well set up while we still have some light," Cecily insisted.

Blanche bit her lip almost hard enough to draw blood, but just nodded curtly, saying nothing more. Elias did not see much of her during the set-up of camp for the night, but when he did he noticed she did not share the others' relief to be settling down after the harrowing first day through the Wasteland.

"What's wrong with Blanche? She's...different," he remarked to Cecily, helping her set up a fire. Cecily cast a worried look at her best friend, and Elias could see clearly the question had been eating at her more keenly than at him this whole time.

"She gets like this sometimes. Ever since we were children. Getting her to open up when she does is hard. I'm probably the best in the world at it, and I still fail most of the time," she muttered. "It will pass, but she won't say anything about it now or later unless she wants to." Her attention turned to Elias, and he was startled by how serious she looked. "Just let her be, Elias. If she needs someone's help, she'll let us know. You'll just make her mad if you go to her without her inviting you in."

"Duly noted," Elias grunted, casting another curious look at Blanche before dropping his gaze quickly when she looked at him. He had to admit, it wasn't just curiosity that made him wonder what was wrong with Blanche. He was actually concerned for her, even though he would freely admit her sudden intensity was making her scary again.

Intimidating and mysterious as Blanche might be, though, she had tried to save his life without a second thought that day, and Elias realized he couldn't forget that any more than he could forget that Boors had stopped that mob from beating him to death. Like it or not, he owed her.

"I think part of it's this place," Cecily suggested, glancing around warily. "It's so desolate and still out here, but there's something in the atmosphere of this place. I think we're all facing our demons out here."

"Some of us more than others," Elias muttered, glancing at the spirit watching them from inside the skeleton of a house.

Still, Blanche's behavior and the odd sense that he owed it to her to help kept him awake more than any concern over the spirits attacking them in the night as the camp settled down to sleep. The two darker spirits he could see seemed content to remain where homes had once stood, as though defending them. Perhaps they were, although Elias kept an eye on them all the same. Because he was awake, he was the one who saw Blanche, wearing no sword or armor, leave the encampment alone. In different circumstances, it would have been a difficult decision, but tonight there wasn't any way Elias could resist following her, slipping away from his makeshift bedding as silently as he could after her. He wasn't sure if his stealth was necessary. Blanche was walking as if she was in a trance, paying little heed to her surroundings. Still, Elias suspected Blanche might be capable of killing him by accident if he got careless and startled her while she was like this, and so he followed her very carefully.

Her path carried her worryingly far away from the encampment. Elias did not much like the idea of spirits catching them out here this late at night, but now he was really stuck with her. He couldn't leave her alone out here, and he was certainly not going to come this far from the camp and then head back alone. If nothing else, the spirits seemed to have some difficulty attacking Blanche they had not had with him. Between that and Mibotha, the two of them were safer if they stuck together out here.

Blanche's path eventually carried her to what appeared to be the stump of a broken tower. She came to a stop at its base, staring at the weather-beaten stones with a lost expression. Elias moved a little closer, frowning. He couldn't tell what kind of building this had been before, but this tower was rather out of place in a rural area like this.

"You can stop skulking around. I know you're there." Elias jumped in alarm when Blanche spoke up, but she didn't turn around to look at him. "I wanted to be alone, you know."

"Being alone out here, surrounded by evil spirits that want to kill us? I'm sorry, I don't think that's something you should want right now," Elias remarked, trying to hide his nervousness. "Why the hell are you this far from camp, anyway?"

"I had to see if it was still here," Blanche muttered, touching the stones of the tower. "I didn't want to come anywhere near this place again, but...I couldn't help it..." she looked over her shoulder at Elias, seeing dawning comprehension on his face. "This is where I grew up, Brook."

"In a tower?" Elias asked, stepping closer. He got the feeling Blanche was only talking to him because he was the only one there, and she was carrying something heavy inside her that needed to be set down. She didn't need any prompting to go on, and Elias got the feeling he was just there to listen as words started to tumble out of her.

"I was born a stone's throw away from this tower. Maybe in the place we're resting now, maybe one of the other wrecks forgotten in this gods-forsaken place. I don't remember where it was anymore," she muttered. "I had four brothers and sisters...one older, and the rest younger. I was just supposed to help out on the farm, like my brother..."

Elias flinched as Blanche's hands ignited, and she stared down into the flames.

"I was seven when it happened the first time. My father's plow horse...something startled him that day, and he went wild. Nearly kicked my head in. I remember being terrified, scrambling around on the ground while he was flailing around...and then I put up my hands to try and shield myself..." Blanche shuddered, closing her eyes.

"They heard me crying for help, and came running just in time to see me set him on fire. I'll never forget it...the way it smelled...the way he *screamed*...he was dead before anyone understood what was happening. He burned to ashes right in front of me, and nearly took the whole stable with him.

"After that...my parents didn't know what to do with me. I think they believed me when I said I hadn't meant to hurt him, but it didn't change that I immolated a horse three times my size with my hands. My siblings thought I was a monster. They wouldn't go anywhere near me. It started to get worse. I started to burn whenever I got angry, and I couldn't control what happened when I did. No one in my family knew what to do about it, me least of all. So they gave me up." Blanche turned to the tower behind her, staring at the crumbling stones bitterly. "A wizard, out here in the countryside, making devices. He knew how to work with magic. Maybe he was the only one for miles and miles that did. I don't know what they said to him when they brought me here, but he agreed to take me off their hands. Then they left, and I never saw them again."

"And the wizard?" Elias asked. He'd met one or two of them before, the engineers of magical devices, but he'd never really asked one of them what *their* opinion on mages was. He had trouble imagining that a wizard would be able to resist having a chance to learn more about humans that didn't need devices or outside sources to manipulate magical power. Blanche's flames intensified, consuming her arms entirely, and Elias stepped back in alarm. Blanche's expression reminded him of a jungle cat that wanted to maul someone again.

"He was an evil old bastard, the man who lived in this tower," she replied. "I was one of a couple children he took in. Mages, like me, that nobody else knew what to do with. He wanted to figure out how we *worked*. Half the time, he was eaten up with curiosity about what we could do, testing all the time to try and learn our limits, and how it worked. The rest of the time, he was furious. Despite everything he could do with his knowledge, the magic he used wasn't a part of him like it was with us. He felt threatened by our existence, and he took it out on us. When we did something wrong, he hurt us. When his blood was up, he hurt us. When an experiment failed, he hurt us. He said we were abominations…worthless mistakes of nature. After a while, I started to believe him." Blanche hung her head, the flames starting to die out. "I was stronger than he was, even then, but I was too frightened to stand up and fight back, or run away…where would I go? Who would take in something like me if a man who understood magic better than I ever would despised me for what I could do? I just endured it, everything he did to us. I think a part of me hoped that if I just held on…eventually he'd understand what was *wrong* with me. He could fix me. Make me like everyone else. I wouldn't have to live with *this!*" Blanche's arms flared blindingly white before extinguishing themselves as she punched the tower's base in frustration, dislodging several stones. Elias could see Blanche's fists bleeding even in the gloom, but Blanche didn't seem to notice. There was a long silence for a moment as Elias struggled for anything to say that didn't sound laughably insincere or trite, but eventually she turned back to him, starting to lift up her shirt.

There were times in the past when Elias would have, and indeed had, paid good money to see a girl that looked like Blanche without her shirt on, but he flinched in surprise at the gesture. First because no matter how attractive she was, Blanche scared him, and then when he saw what was concealed underneath.

Elias had picked up a massive collection of scars over his career, particularly of late, but Blanche could rival him in that department. Her stomach and sides bore scars of dozens of cuts, some small incisions, some vast gashes, and some stab wounds As Blanche turned to show him her back, Elias saw the familiar marks of old, thorough whippings crisscrossing her back. Elias winced as he realized there was an enormous burn scar in the small of Blanche's back below where she'd been whipped. He felt an immense relief when Blanche finally hid the injuries again, although he was afraid he would not be able to get the image of Blanche's bare back out of his mind nearly as soon as he would like to.

"I didn't know then why it was me he came after the most, out of all of us. Now, I think it was because I scared him, even then. He found it maddening, how my flames could be so harmless while I held them but destroy everything they touched when I let them go. He tried to see how I dealt with normal fire once, and I was the one he cut into looking for something that shouldn't be there, some source I was drawing it from. He probably would have killed me eventually if Morys hadn't found out about him."

"Morys?" Maybe Blanche was about to confirm what Elias had suspected, Morys had indeed taken mages under his wing. Elias also knew both morality and pragmatism would have forced Morys to stop this wizard of Blanche's the moment he was aware of what was going on.

"The Royal Guard came for him one day. Boors broke down the door when he wouldn't let them in. They were there to arrest him at first, but Boors saw one of the others before he caught up to him..." Blanche looked Elias in the eye, and he had trouble describing her expression.

"Every single Guard that came to rescue us that day testified that he fell out the window at the top of the tower attempting to escape from Boors. Broke every bone in his body," she whispered. "Afterwards, they took us out of our rooms. I still remember that they all seemed as frightened as we were...all except Boors. When I wouldn't leave my room, he picked me up...and he told me everything was going to be all right."

Elias took it all in silently. Blanche shrugged as she continued.

"I don't know what became of the other children. King Morys assured me they would be taken care of, after what they'd been through, and I believed him, then and now. I could have gone with them, but I asked to start training to join the Guard instead."

"Because they saved you."

Blanche nodded, and her expression softened immensely.

"There was a debt I didn't think I could ever repay there, but I had to try. I must have seemed insane to anyone watching me. A humorless, underfed husk of a girl trying to train alongside the flower of Yivyn's youth. I was small, I was weak, and I was unstable. Looking back, it's a miracle they didn't turn me away, but no one would gainsay Boors, and he said I could stay. Most of the other trainees didn't think I belonged there. But I had nowhere else to go, and I wanted to stay with them, more than I ever wanted anything before. More than I wanted to be normal. So I adjusted. I became stronger. I became smarter. I started to grow again, and stopped being afraid. I had to belong here. That was all that mattered to me anymore."

"It worked. Look at you now," Elias remarked, feeling an odd compulsion to try and cheer Blanche up. She was less scary when she was in a good mood. "You're the Captain. The queen's right hand. Even Boors answers to you now."

"Little of that was on my own merit," Blanche muttered, looking down. "People weren't sure I could be trusted while I was in training. No matter how hard I worked, I was still a mage. Still...unnatural. No one thought someone like that was ready for the responsibilities the high-ranking Guard dealt with. No one except Boors, who had seen how far I had come in that time…and Cecily." Blanche made a noise that was somewhere between a laugh and a sob, shaking her head.

"I hated her at first, you know. I couldn't stand her. I was better than her at nearly everything, after all the training I'd done. I was faster than she was, stronger, smarter, tougher, willing to work harder and longer than her or anyone else. But everyone loved her, and I scared people. Everyone expected greatness from her, while everyone worried my drive was unseemly. I had to rebuild myself completely to earn a place with the Guard, and all Cecily had to do was be born." Blanche ran a hand through her hair, her gaze seeming a million miles away. "I became obsessed with her for a while. I had to beat her at everything, show that I was better than she was over and over and over again. And I did…everywhere but the sword. I trained like a madwoman, but I could never catch up to her. I beat myself half to death against her defenses. Then I started winning anyway. Because she *let* me when she saw what I was doing to myself. I was furious when she did that…and I hurt her for it. Everyone thought I was a brute, coming after her that fiercely. No matter how much I excelled, no one would ever acknowledge me…except her."

"*Blanche was already beyond me when we first met. We were the same age, but she seemed…**perfect**, while all I had was skill with a sword. It was the only thing I could excel at enough to call her a peer, but even with that, our pasts separated us. I was just a silly girl at the time…I couldn't begin to understand her, even though I was trying my hardest,*" Elias remembered Cecily saying.

"I thought she was mocking me, at first, when she wanted to be my friend, or she just hoped I'd stop coming after her and go easy on her," Blanche murmured. "When I realized she wasn't being cruel or after something, I thought it was just because she felt sorry for me, and I hated her more for it. I underestimated her. *Everyone* underestimates her. I was a bitter, driven bitch, eaten up with resentment, fear, and pride. Everyone looked at me and saw an accident waiting to happen. Everyone *knew* one day I'd lose control, and it would be a disaster. She thought I was amazing, even when I beat her down to try and prove myself. She was the only one, myself included, that realized how lonely I was, and reached out. When I finally realized what an idiot I'd been, when I was ready to take her hand…I…I still think of what might have happened to me if she hadn't come into my life. What I might have become. It isn't a person the king would trust to be near his daughter, or someone that the Royal Guard would turn to in a time of crisis."

Elias almost wanted to ask Blanche to stop talking, but he couldn't, not after they had come this far. Still, it was strangely disturbing hearing

Blanche's thoughts traveling such familiar roads. He'd never understood Blanche at all before. It was *impossible* that she was the one most like him out of all the Royal Guard, wasn't it? Blanche met and held his gaze, and Elias realized she was crying.

"I'm not worthy of all of this. Amira would have been too frightened of me to let me be so close to her if she'd known any better, but Cecily insisted I be her partner guarding the princess. My life isn't so important that Cecily's father should have died to protect it, but he was the one that gave himself up for all of us instead of me. I'm not such a great leader that I should have been Captain of the Guard, but when the Captain was dead, Cecily got the others to support Amira appointing me. Amira... sometimes I think she wants to be like me, never realizing how little I would be on my own. I've been her sword these last five years, but it was Cecily that chose not to become Captain, that gave me this purpose in her place. Everything good in me comes from her. She was the one that thought I was great...and I can't help but try to be the woman she thinks I am. Sometimes I forget that I'm not..." Blanche reached up and covered her face with a hand, her shoulders shaking. "But out here...I remember who I was...who I am...everything I failed to do..."

"Blanche—"

"No," Blanche cut him off, trembling. "Don't say anything. Why did... why did I tell you all—i-it doesn't matter. I'm begging you, forget tonight...don't let Cecily know you ever saw me like this..."

"He doesn't need to."

Blanche and Elias both looked up in surprise as Cecily stepped into sight, a serious expression on her face. Blanche seemed both shocked and humiliated, taking a step back.

"Cecily..."

Cecily closed the distance between them in three strides, and for a second Elias thought she was going to slap Blanche across the face. Instead, Cecily pulled her best friend close and embraced her.

"You idiot," she said quietly. "You always make me worry about you when all you have to do is open your mouth."

"How long were you listening?" Blanche asked weakly.

"Long enough," Cecily sighed. "I thought you knew to come to me when you felt like this, Blanche."

"Can't help it. I can't change who I am," Blanche said, trying not to meet Cecily's eyes. She didn't have much choice when Cecily raised her face, looking serious.

"Do you remember what they told all the Guard trainees?" she scolded, and for some reason she glanced at Elias as Blanche nodded meekly. "Who you were is not who you are…"

"…And who you are is not who you will become," Blanche whispered. Cecily nodded, smiling at her friend.

"That's right. The two of us know life's one great certainty. If you would just remember it, there wouldn't be so many doubts in you in the first place," she chided.

Blanche gave Cecily a wavering smile, before wrapping her arms around her and starting to sob quietly. Cecily held her friend patiently, but her gaze travelled to Elias, and her eyes sent him a message as clearly as if she had spoken it aloud.

Thank you.

Blanche recovered her composure soon enough, although she was quiet and subdued as she headed back to the camp with Elias and Cecily. As Elias walked, a pace or two behind them, something of what had been exchanged this night would not leave his head.

Who you were is not who you are, and who you are is not who you will become.

Even after Cecily and Blanche went to their own beds for the night, Elias lay awake for hours, staring up at the sky as that one phrase ran through his mind over and over.

CHAPTER 36

The next two days were some of the most miserable travel Elias could remember. Blanche had returned to her normal self, if a bit subdued, but everyone's mood fared poorly as the trek across the Haunted Wasteland continued. Little arguments abounded, broken up by long periods of tense, worried silence from the entire supply train. No one was eager to press on, but staying still seemed equally worrying.

Two more attacks by the evil spirits did little to improve the mood of the group. With Mibotha's help, Elias managed to drive them away from killing a soldier who had wandered ahead to scout, while Amira dispersed the bigger attack as the group went through a dead village full of angry ghosts. Most of the train, vaguely aware of their peril but unable to see it all around them, were now constantly on edge, jumping at shadows and snapping at one another. Elias knew they were going to hate him even more than they once had if this plan of his didn't work, but they were all dead if it failed anyway. None of that mattered, he reminded himself, because it *would* work. He was staking his life on this, after all, and if there was anything he'd gotten good at over the years, it was staying alive in bizarre and improbable ways.

Still, even he was beginning to wonder if he'd have suggested this if he'd known what they would be in for, when the cry finally went up.

"Enrilth! We've made it!"

"The capital lies ahead!"

It was almost comical how quickly the news brought spirit back to the entire group, but Elias could see how being told the slog through a seemingly endless wasteland filled with murderous angry ghosts was almost over would make anyone energetic. Even the sight of the devastated castle town wasn't enough to offset the newfound determination that drove them forward at a much quicker pace.

It seemed to him that simply being told the harrowing journey was at an end had brought about a change in their attitude. This entire miserable journey, they had been reminded of their failure, confronted with the desolation that had come in the wake of it, and tormented, quite literally, by the ghosts of the past. But now, with their destination in sight, something had changed. *This happened because we failed* had become *We will not fail this time. We will fix this.*

The Haunted Wasteland had been a testament to their failure to keep Enrilth and the kingdom surrounding it safe. But old and long-neglected as it was, Enrilth Keep was home, and a promise that after enduring five years, they had finally earned their second chance to save Yivyn.

"We really made it…" Blanche said, staring at the still-distant form of the castle as she rode alongside Elias.

"Of course we did. As if a mere Haunted Wasteland would be enough to keep us from coming home!" Cecily laughed, in even higher spirits than usual. There was no disguising the longing in her eyes as she followed Blanche's gaze to the castle. "It's finally time to stop hiding and show ourselves to the world! Queen Amira can finally sit where she should have been these last five years!"

"Let's make sure we've got fortifications and supplies settled in first, before we get to that," Elias said quickly. It would be a couple of days before the word really started to spread, but he wanted to be dug in quite well before that happened. Probability suggested they would need to fight whatever Hache could throw at them, Bones among them, the moment they were revealed.

I hope you enjoy the trip, you bastard, he thought to himself with a touch of smug satisfaction. Let's see how the ghosts take it when *you* try to march across three days of wasteland.

"At least getting the castle ready to defend us from any attacks should be simple enough. Supplies are the only thing I'm worried about. The supplies we've brought won't last us forever," Blanche muttered.

"They can last us long enough to figure something out," Elias said, although this had been on his mind as well. They had managed to get a lot of provisions this far, but would Enrilth be able to support the Royal Guard again while in this state?

Let me worry about that, Elias Brook.

Elias tried not to jump in surprise as Mibotha spoke up in the back of his mind. He felt a large amount of grim satisfaction coming from the spirit, while it appeared to feel his curiosity without him saying anything.

You've done well to bring things this far. You have Amira crowned and about to resume her father's seat, in a position where striking at her will be extremely difficult. You focus on making sure no one comes after her. Leave the land to me.

Mibotha said nothing further after that, but Elias could tell that the spirit was quite active again. He wasn't sure what it was up to, but he was surprised to find he trusted in it to help out with his problem, even if he didn't know how he was going to explain it when whatever Mibotha did to help did show up.

Hm…wait, if it was going to help out with the land not being able to support them…good gods, did Mibotha actually have the kind of power to grow *food* out here? That hardly seemed possible, but if it could do that…

…It would seem that a dead land came back to life the moment Amira sat down in her rightful throne. If they could even spread a *rumor* of that, people would think the gods themselves reached down to put Amira back on the throne instead of a spirit, her loyal retainers, and a very determined thief. Even people with everything to lose from Amira taking her country back might bow down before that. If Mibotha made it appear Amira's ascendency would end the drought for good…would even Bones be crazy enough to strike at her then?

Yes, he would, Elias decided quickly. That was why he had to stop Bones and any support Hache gave him from succeeding. With them out of the way, everything else would fall into place, ideally with no more wars or conquests needed. Things might go back to how they used to be. Elias glanced at the men and women around him. No, perhaps if they were given a chance to put right what went wrong five years ago, things might be *better* than they used to be.

The castle town lay in ruins, but Enrilth Keep had held up better than Elias had any right to expect it would have. After hearing about all of the fighting, Elias had half expected a tottering ruin, ready to collapse at any moment. But Morys's ancestors had not been men like King Symond. When they had considered their legacy, they had built a castle with the intent that it would last forever and defeat any attack. Enrilth Keep had upheld its purpose remarkably, only falling when its strength crumbled from within. The fortifications all appeared to be mostly intact. While the castle wasn't as majestic as it had been after several years of neglect, it still looked like a stronghold Elias could trust in to keep out any enemies that were willing to brave the Wasteland to attack them. The walls and towers stood straight, just as tall and intimidating as he'd remembered them. While there were signs of the damage the sieges had done, it seemed like not a single one of Enrilth Keep's attackers had managed to breach the walls. What damage there was would probably be fairly simple to repair with time, and while Elias wasn't a master castle-builder, it looked to him like the walls would be more than strong enough to hold off even a powerful attack.

One immediately obvious difference between his memory and the current reality, however, was the front gate. Elias remembered tall, oaken doors and an iron portcullis ready to be dropped down at a moment's notice, an impressive entrance for guests and a stern warning to outsiders when closed. Now, the front gate was merely a gaping hole in the solid walls, the doors ripped from their hinges and nowhere to be seen and the portcullis a twisted ruin rusting on the ground.

"The gate…"

"The walls were too hard to breach, and even climbing over them was incredibly dangerous no matter how entrenched the besieging force was. It turned out the keep's only real weakness in a siege was that its gate couldn't be as strong as its walls…" Blanche remarked. "Restoring the gate is going to be our primary concern for the castle's fortifications, getting started."

"How are we planning on doing that, anyway?" Elias asked. "It's not like there's going to be much wood of any real quality for quite some distance." If he'd known how the castle's gate had fared, he might have taken that into account when he proposed running here. As it was, a castle with a wide open front door wasn't much good as a stronghold. "I didn't think about the gate."

"Fortunately, Queen Amira did," Blanche remarked, gesturing to the supply carts. "Our supply carts are for more than transporting what we'll be living on for the next few weeks. They are the materials we'll use to rebuild the gate. We'll still need to reconnect Enrilth with the rest of Yivyn for the castle to be sustainable, but we should be able to get the castle in working order on our own for a little while, at least."

"Good, now we just have to hope this all goes exactly like I planned." Elias said, glancing over at Blanche and Cecily. "Just to warn you, that has never happened thus far in my life, so I'd prepare for the worst if I were you."

"There's a first time for everything, Elias," Cecily chuckled, and Elias knew perfectly well by now that she really meant that. Surprisingly, Blanche nodded along with her, seeming in much higher spirits than before.

"You've gotten us this far, Brook, and I can't thank you enough for that. It was thanks to your skills that we're here at all," she said gratefully. "But this is our home, and restoring and defending it is what we do. You've gotten us this far, now it's our turn to take the lead."

We really can do this, Elias thought to himself in amazement. I'd be completely done for on my own, and they wouldn't have much hope without me, but between us, we've somehow managed to pull all this off. I got them around the battles that would have ended their return before it began, and now they're in position to do what they were always meant to do.

As Elias watched Amira's court joyously reclaiming the castle, he felt a pride in himself like he'd never known before. Was this what it felt like to help others? Elias could imagine a man getting addicted to that feeling. Maybe that explained much of what he didn't understand about the heroes that had come and gone before him.

Still, amidst the triumphant atmosphere was one grim thought: *this is still the easy part.*

Amira and her Guard could finally save the land, but his part wasn't through. For all of this to work, Elias knew in his heart he still had to fulfill Mibotha's last command.

He'd gotten them to Enrilth. Now he had to kill Oliver Bones.

CHAPTER 37

As the Royal Guard got to work settling into the castle and working on the gates, Elias wandered off on his own to explore. The dusty hallways were much as he remembered them, although he noticed most of the tapestries that had decorated them were long gone and few of the fixtures he remembered stood in one piece anymore. The outside of the castle was as strong as ever, but the inside showed more signs that the castle had been sacked.

It was a little disquieting, seeing it like this after five years. He'd fled before anything bad had happened, hearing about Enrilth's fate but unable to really visualize what had become of it. Now, his memories of the seat of Morys's power clashed with the reality around him, and he had to suppress a shudder as he wandered alone.

He hadn't expected any sort of animal to be desperate enough to try and make these dry stones their home after all this time, and he wasn't disappointed in that regard. Still, the Haunted Wasteland hadn't been uninhabited just because nothing *lived* there, and Elias searched the old castle for any sign of lingering spirits. He was a little surprised his search didn't seem to be turning anything up.

"It's so empty..." he muttered. "I would have expected angry ghosts to linger here, of all places."

This is not a place for them. No spirit lingers here now except myself, Mibotha said, sounding quite certain. Elias paused, looking around to make sure no one was around to listen.

"You seem very sure of that, Mibotha. You've seemed very sure of everything that has to do with the royal family, I've noticed," he said, leaning against a wall.

You know I am not given to doubt or falsehood. Is it so strange that I am sure of myself when I speak? Mibotha replied, and Elias honestly couldn't tell if it was being evasive or not.

"I mean you seem to know a lot about this castle, the Regalia, everything. You know something about Morys and Amira you're not telling me, and it's getting rather late for that, don't you think?"

You have other concerns, Elias Brook.

"I know I do, but not right at this moment," Elias countered. "I think we have more than enough time before Bones gets here to discuss this."

Why do you care?

Elias was brought up short by the bluntness of the response, but he could feel Mibotha scrutinizing him with something closer to interest than hostility.

What concern is it of yours what I know and what is important to me? Do you seek some sort of advantage in understanding my business, Elias Brook?

That should have been a harsh accusation, and one that should have stung all the more for being quite accurate, but it was too calm, and strangely Elias didn't feel defensive at it.

"The whole time we've been together, I've been trying to figure out how to get you off my back without going to Valka," he conceded. "But this isn't just about you and me anymore. I don't know how much any of this was about me to begin with, as far as you were concerned, but Amira's a different story. All of this has been about *her* in some way, and I want you to tell me why. I know she can see spirits, but you've kept hidden from her even though I can feel how focused you are on seeing her take the throne. Is she some kind of weapon to you? A vessel?"

My last hope.

The strange, nonsensical answer brought Elias up short.

"What?"

Morys was a weapon in a war he wasn't aware of. We helped him, without his knowledge, and he helped us. It killed him, in the end, Mibotha said quietly, seeming to have trouble bringing itself to elaborate. Elias kept quiet, trying to coax an explanation forth.

You've mentioned basilisks before. You know of them as creatures of magecraft.

"I was around during the last great hunt," Elias muttered, shivering.

The truth is more complicated than you realize. The basilisks were not born into this world naturally, that is true, but the human who gained the magic to spawn the first of that monstrous brood was guided to do so.

"Guided...?" Elias began to see the shape of what Mibotha was trying to tell him. "An evil spirit was responsible?"

Not all of my kin love this world as it is, and their numbers and their malice have only grown with time, Mibotha growled. *They have a different vision, for this world, and for our own realm. The disagreement simmered for centuries before it turned to violence. We aren't creatures of flesh and bone, like you. We do not make war in a form I can properly explain to you, but you understand well enough the nature of a struggle for dominance. We were winning, at first. We took it as a sign we were bringing our wayward brothers back to the proper order of things, but then they changed the rules. They moved the battle from our realm into yours, in the bodies of great magical serpents.*

A part of Elias wanted to think that didn't make sense, but somehow he found no difficulty in believing Mibotha, remembering the basilisks. Their sheer size, their power, the flickers of wicked cunning that sometimes let them turn the tables on their hunters, and most of all, that venom. Poison so strong the presence of a basilisk killed plants and scorched the earth where they passed. So deadly their breath could nearly dissolve their prey where it stood. The poison had been the proof that basilisks operated by the rules of sorcery, not nature. That was why Morys embarked on his campaign to drive the basilisks into extinction, and then scour every trace of their remains from the world.

"They came into the world as basilisks, so you used Morys to fight back." It was a statement, not a question.

Taking mortal form, dragging your world into our fight, was not a tactic that had occurred to us when this began. Even once they changed the battleground, we were reluctant to manifest ourselves as so many of them had. Your world would simply have been consumed by warring monsters if we did so. We fought the foe less directly, by guiding humans. One of my kin gave the blacksmith the inspiration for the devices he built for Morys to hunt the basilisks. I helped Morys hunt them, and helped purge the ground of their taint when they lay dead. We tried to keep the full extent of what was happening from Morys, but we underestimated the enemy. In our unwillingness to act directly, as they did, we had become reliant on Morys to fight the enemy here. So they killed him before resuming their attack on us.

"Bones."

And the drought, and the blight, and a number of the other ill turns the world has taken in the last five years, Mibotha said sadly. *We are **losing** this fight, Elias Brook, and if we don't turn back the tide, it will only get worse.*

Understanding suddenly clicked into place for Elias. This focus of Mibotha's, its need…it wasn't just about Yivyn's fate. He could practically see the answer written in the air before he spoke.

"We're both responsible, aren't we?" he said, unable to put any real force behind it despite the size of the revelation. "You're as guilty in all of this as I am. You used Morys as a weapon, and Bones killed him for it by using *me.* The wars, the famine…all the lives ruined, it was part of *your* fight. All of this is on your head as much as mine."

The ensuing silence made Elias certain he was right almost immediately, but even so it felt like a short eternity before Mibotha spoke.

No, Elias Brook. It would be easy to say we are equally to blame for what has happened, but that is not true. Elias opened his mouth to protest, but Mibotha pressed on. *I used Morys, and then I failed to protect him from the consequences of my actions. Your responsibility for his fate, and Yivyn's, is nothing compared to mine.*

Elias recognized Mibotha's tone, and realized why he felt no vindictive glee in his realization. This was *it,* the big secret that was supposed to give him an advantage over Mibotha. If he'd learned this earlier, he would have used it against the spirit as early and as mercilessly as he could. At another time, he'd lay into Mibotha for the hypocrisy of rubbing his past in his face while ignoring its own culpability…but he knew that tone of voice from his own confession to Amira days earlier.

How many nights for five years had he tried to focus on who else was to blame besides him for Morys's death? He had told himself time and time again that what he had done that night was nothing compared to the incompetence of Morys's guards, or that Bones would have found another way without him. He had stayed sane for years by clinging to the belief that it wasn't his fault Morys died. It had helped keep him going, to push all that responsibility onto others, and he knew the part of him that wanted to wash its hands and lay the entire bloody business at Mibotha's feet was still following the instincts of the man he'd been. But he did not take the freely offered chance to take revenge for Mibotha's moralizing and blame.

He should hate Mibotha more than he had when they were just getting started, but Elias realized for the first time he understood perfectly how his unwanted partner felt. He realized he actually felt sorry for it.

"This isn't just about defeating your enemies and saving Yivyn, is it?" he went on. "You used Morys for that, but doing so got him killed, and it might end up getting Amira killed, too. Part of this is about making things right with her, isn't it?"

You have the truth of it, Elias Brook, Mibotha admitted. *I do not have the power to turn back time and undo my mistakes, any more than you do. I am obligated to fight the enemy in any way I can, regardless of innocence or guilt on my part. But...what I allowed to happen to Morys was wrong. I used him as a weapon, and then failed to protect him when my actions put his life in danger. My arrogance and my blindness to danger are the cause of all of this. You would not have needed to weigh Morys's life against your own if I had only...*

"We're both to blame," Elias cut it off. Mibotha seemed astonished to hear this, but Elias was even more astonished to know he meant it. "Bones played us both. He flew under your notice so he could kill Morys for your enemies without you realizing what was going on until it was too late, and he used me to do it. Maybe if you'd been sharper, he wouldn't have gotten to me. Maybe if I'd been braver, he wouldn't have gotten to Morys. But we can't change the past, like you said. All we can do is try to do better in the present. You need to redeem yourself here just as much as I do, and we're not going to do that lamenting what might have been."

You are right, Elias Brook. Thank you, Mibotha admitted, seeming awkward but sincere in its thanks. Elias nodded, but felt the need to press on while he and Mibotha were being honest with one another.

"We've gotten Amira here, and if my plan works we should be able to take a big step towards making her the queen in fact as well as name. But what happens after that, Mibotha? She's not her father. She's not a weapon."

No. That was never my intention, Mibotha said sharply. *Amira is not a weapon we can use against the enemy. She is the only hope we have of healing the land.*

"What?"

You are the one I trust to defeat the enemy's agent. If you can deal that blow to them, destroy the agent they use on this world as they struck down Morys, we can turn the tide against them. After so many of them took mortal form only to be killed by humans, losing their last weapon in this world will break their grip on it, lock them out from interfering long enough for us to defeat them once and for all. But that alone won't restore the land. The people have been changed by our fighting, ordinary folk left to suffer and die on our account. Their ghosts linger, unable to move on. The land has grown dark and twisted under the enemy's power, and the spirits of the forests and rivers have grown wild and full of rage. Yivyn will still be torn apart by war when ours is finished, and it will never recover from the damage that has been done unless Amira is able to reunite her people and soothe the sorrow and rage that will soon consume this land. She is not my weapon, Elias Brook. She is the only hope I have that Yivyn will live on.

"Your last hope, you said."

She is the only chance I have left to save this land and atone for my mistake, Mibotha said. *Between you and I, there is enough power to defeat Oliver Bones, and my brethren have sufficient strength to defeat the enemy for good if that is done. But we can't heal this land, not without her. If Amira dies, Elias Brook, all of this was for nothing.*

"And she'll die for sure unless someone kills Bones," Elias sighed. "He'll never stop coming after her."

Precisely. Which is where you come in.

"Why me, Mibotha?" Elias asked, unable to hold it back any longer. "I'm hardly the strongest person or best fighter. Any one of the Royal Guard is better than I am. One to one, Cecily or Boors could probably beat Bones in a straight fight, but I can't. Why does it have to be me?"

I did not lie when I explained our alliance at the beginning of this, Elias Brook. I did not seek you out for my plan, and yet you were brought before me, Mibotha said, sounding unusually thoughtful. *My kind put little stock in coincidence, and it seemed to be the hand of fate that offered you to me. It seemed impossible mere chance would bring me into contact with the man blamed, perhaps unjustly, for my failure to protect Morys from the enemy. You struck me as an appropriate agent for my plan, and an expendable one should it go awry. I recognized qualities in you that might let you succeed where more honorable men failed. But I must admit…I did not truly understand you, or the depth of your quality. I expected very little of you at the outset of all this, and merely hoped you would make it far enough for me to reach Amira's court and try to work towards Yivyn's salvation there. If you did better than that, and even managed to redeem yourself in the process, it would have simply been an additional benefit.*

Elias sighed. He'd gotten used to going through life knowing he wasn't that important in the grand scheme of things early on. In fact, his importance as a scapegoat for the assassination and the war had been an interesting if unwelcome change of pace for him. Still, it did sting a bit to know that his life had been saved because Mibotha needed a ride and he seemed like a better prospect than waiting for someone else to wander by.

You impressed me, Elias Brook, despite your best efforts to the contrary. The expedition to find the Regalia showed me you were far more than I had taken you for. I was...angry someone with your talents was saddled with your personality. But as time has gone by...

"Hold on, are you about to admit you were wrong about me? I want to get someone to record this for posterity," Elias cut in, unable to resist a grin of smug vindication.

*Obviously you are very, very far from perfect, but I will reluctantly concede you are not the **worst** human being I have ever known,* Mibotha said, its thoughtful tone turning grumpy at the interruption. Elias found himself wishing Mibotha had a face, he'd have liked to see its expressions for this conversation.

"I can work with that," he sighed, nodding.

You are a man who is capable of great things when he sets his mind to it, Elias Brook. For most of your life, you have held yourself back for one reason or another. But our time together has given you a chance to stand tall for once in your life, and be the man you were always capable of being, Mibotha said, getting serious. *You are not the great warrior your new comrades are, but neither are you the hapless coward you were content to think of yourself as. You are resourceful, determined, and most of all, you know how people think. Of all the people here in this castle, you are the one Oliver Bones thinks he knows the best, and the one I suspect he knows the least of all. I believe it **was** the act of a higher power that you and I were joined in this way, Elias Brook. I do not claim to understand the ways of destiny, but together we can defeat Oliver Bones, and redeem ourselves by bringing an end to this dark age. Why you, you asked me? Because...I believe in you, Elias Brook. That is all there is to it.*

Elias was rather surprised by the sentiment, and noticed Mibotha sounded both sincere and almost embarrassed when it said it.

"Well, either we save everything together or I'll be the first man who's doomed two worlds at once. No pressure, eh?" he tried to joke. 'Thank you' sounded somehow too trite a response.

You won't fail.

"I have to admit, the vote of confidence from you is rather refreshing," Elias said, smiling in spite of himself.

*It's a simple statement of the facts. You have not failed so far, and you will not fail now. **I'm** with you, after all.*

It really *would* be useful if Mibotha had a face, Elias thought as he sighed and shook his head. It would make it a hell of a lot easier to tell when it was trying to get a rise out of him or just...being Mibotha.

Elias soon finished his cursory inspection of the castle, content there were no evil spirits lurking about. He headed for the castle's study, suspecting he might find Amira there. His instincts proved to be completely correct, and he arrived to see Amira giving instructions to her attentive retainers.

"—And the return journey through the Wasteland is still too perilous to be worth the risk. For the time being, we will stay here and fortify the castle during the time it takes for the birds to reach their destinations. We will have to trust in word beginning to spread that way."

"As you wish, my lady, but sending a small band back through the Wasteland may still be necessary if the message is to spread far enough."

"That may be, but we will determine that at another time," Amira said calmly, turning her attention to the group as a whole. "You have your instructions. Keep me informed of any new developments."

"Of course, Your Majesty," the group answered as one, before dispersing. Few seemed to take much notice of Elias as they left quickly, looking busy, but Amira turned to him the moment they were all out, smiling a little.

"Ah, Elias. I was wondering where you'd gone off to."

"I'm not much good at fortifications...or heavy lifting, for that matter," Elias said lightly. "So I had a look around the castle, just making sure it wasn't...occupied."

"That was a good thought, considering the journey here," Amira sighed. "I hope your search came up empty?"

"The ghosts out there appear to have stayed away from the castle," Elias said, nodding. He looked at Amira seriously, trying to figure out how to put the question he had to ask. "I have to admit, I...wasn't expecting you to be aware of them."

"I would think it fair to say you've done a number of things I wasn't expecting as well, Elias," Amira said, raising her eyebrow.

So the various things Elias had done with Mibotha's aid hadn't escaped her as well. If Mibotha did not want its assistance known to Amira, this was going to be an awkward conversation.

"Has Blanche passed on her thoughts about my abilities to you?" he asked, deciding to stick with the simplest route for the time being. Amira nodded slowly.

"She did not intend to spread around her suspicions you were a mage, to avoid putting everyone more on edge than they already were, but she did share them with Cecily and myself. Was she correct, then? You are a mage?"

For a moment, Elias strongly considered abandoning all lies and just telling Amira what was going on. Considering how important she was in all of this, maybe she deserved to know the truth before they went any further.

He stopped himself at the last moment, however, thinking about how his story would sound, and how it would affect Amira. She was already struggling under the pressure heaped on her to save the kingdom and her people. She had no idea she was the key piece in a war between spirits. He still didn't have that good a grasp himself on how far this matter went, and it occurred to him that the last thing Amira needed at the moment was to know it wasn't simply Hache's coin that made her a target for Oliver Bones.

"As far as I can tell, yes, although it only manifested a few days before we met," he said, feeling a little awkward lying to her face but promising himself he would make amends for it later. "My wounds heal much faster than normal, and there are some...other things as well. It let me see the spirits in the Wasteland..." Elias looked at Amira seriously, both legitimately curious and wanting to shift the conversation. "You could see them as well. They reacted to your words." It was a statement, but Elias did his best to make sure there was only a question hidden in it, not an accusation. Even so, Amira looked troubled, and Elias noticed her look around for any eavesdroppers before she answered.

"I've always been able to do that. I don't know how, or why, but..." she admitted, her voice dropping low. "I could see...strange little things when I was a little girl. Sometimes they looked like rocks, or strange animals... most of them didn't look like anything at all. Elendri couldn't do it, and nobody else saw what I did. They thought I was playing pretend," Amira shrugged helplessly. "As time went by, I learned not to talk about it. It just worried people, and the only one with any idea what I was talking about was Blanche. I'd never seen so *many* before this expedition..." she looked at him, serious as the grave. "They...were in *pain*, Elias. All of them were crying out so terribly it frightened me. I'd never seen spirits like them. There was so much pain and anger."

That made sense, Elias thought. Amira was rarely outside of the castle before Morys's death, and afterwards she was sequestered in one fortress after another, kept hidden for her own safety. Based on his experiences, the spirits that had any visible form were mostly found in forests and wild places, where Amira would never have gone in her young life. Elias suspected the angry ghosts they had encountered haunting the Wasteland were a different sort of thing entirely from the forest-dwelling entities he'd briefly encountered.

"I think those were the spirits of people. Ones that were killed in the fighting around Enrilth," he suggested. The thought was troubling. The warfare there had been some of the worst, but he remembered other battlefields. Had spirits like that been milling about, invisible to him while he'd stolen from their fallen bodies? What would the Vermillion Fields have looked like to Amira's eyes?

"I think you're right. I only hope that restoring Yivyn will bring them rest," Amira murmured, eyes dropping to the floor.

She means that, Elias thought to himself. Those things scared the hell out of me, but she pities them. She was trying to soothe them when she came to help me rather than fight them. What's more, it *worked*.

"I think it will," Elias said, feeling a little positive feeling from Mibotha almost like a nod. "Until then, we'll just have to leave them be, I think."

"It seems there's not much else we can do but hope," Amira sighed.

"Never had much hope, especially not in the last five years, but..." Elias said with a little shrug. "There's nothing for it, we've gotten things rolling, and all there is to do is see it through."

...Oh, no.

Elias blinked, a little surprised to hear the sheer dismay in Mibotha's voice.

I can feel him on the edge of my awareness, Elias Brook. Oliver Bones is in the Haunted Wasteland. He is making his way here, and at terrible speed!

"Bones?!" Elias gasped out loud, causing Amira to stand up in alarm.

"Elias? What is it?"

"I can...I can *feel* him out there! He's headed this way now!" Elias gasped. Surprisingly he *could* feel the distant presence of his enemy through his link with Mibotha...a cold, slimy feeling almost like some foul wind washed over him. In his mind's eye, he saw a cloaked form moving with terrifying speed across the Wasteland. He couldn't tell if it was his imagination or Bones himself he was seeing.

"That is impossible!" Amira protested, deadly pale. "He should be miles away! Word of our presence here hasn't even reached Hache's territories yet, and the journey to the Wasteland is longer from where he started!"

"I know. This doesn't make any sense...but if you trust me on anything, Amira, you will trust me on this. He knows we're here, and he is coming to kill you," Elias said, hands shaking. He thought he had days, maybe weeks to get ready for Bones to make his move, but this? There was no coincidence in this. Even a spy couldn't have arranged for Bones to catch up to them so fast. Elias could only conclude Bones had used the same unknown method he'd nearly trapped them with in Hache's territory.

He is not alone, although the others are having trouble matching his pace. They will be here by sundown tomorrow.

"There are men with him. They'll be here by dark tomorrow. We have to get the Royal Guard ready to fight and that gate ready to repel them!" Elias said desperately.

"How are you doing this, Elias?" Amira asked, clearly frightened by the change in Elias's manner as much as the news.

"I can't explain how, but you have to trust me," Elias insisted, shaking. "*He's coming*, Amira. We have to be ready to stop him."

It was impressive, almost frightening, how quickly the scared young woman fell away and the Queen of Yivyn stood before him.

"You are right, Elias," she agreed, walking to the door of her study. "I did not come all this way to die here!"

Two of the Royal Guard were at her side immediately as she opened up the door.

"My lady!"

"Spread the word throughout the castle. Hache has used some sorcery to track our progress, and is trying to silence us before we can restore the castle," Amira said, her voice reflecting no doubt at all in Elias's words. "Get everyone ready! I want the Royal Guard ready to fight and the castle in a position to withstand attack! We have no time to delay!"

If the Royal Guard were at all confused how Amira was certain of this, they did not show it. They had their orders, and jumped to them immediately. Amira turned back to Elias. For the target of an assassination, she seemed more confident than Elias had ever seen her... and more angry.

"They're coming for me here. In my *home*," she said quietly. "I have dreamed of these walls every night for five years, Elias, and they want to kill me inside them. I will not live in fear anymore. Not *here*." She made a fist, and Elias found Amira looked more powerful. Even though her size and frame remained unchanged, her presence seemed to tower over her physical body. "They will hope to find us unaware and frightened when they come for us. If they understood us at all, they would never have dared fight us here." she turned, walking out of the room. "Get ready, Elias. One way or another, I mean to end this here."

She's right, Elias Brook. It has to end here. Mibotha said quietly. Elias nodded, feeling something of Amira's confidence flow into him despite the situation. He should be on the verge of panic, but just being in Amira's presence as she decided to stand her ground had left him feeling strong and serene.

"I must kill Oliver Bones," he murmured.

You are a man who has done the impossible more than once to stay alive, Elias Brook. All I have left to ask of you is to do it one more time.

Just one more task. One last obstacle between him and redemption. If he killed Bones, all his debts were paid.

"One more time," he repeated to himself, looking out the window and *feeling* Bones drawing closer. "Just one more time."

CHAPTER 38

Most people Elias knew that heard they were going to be attacked shortly when they had previously believed they would be safe for some time would show a great deal of consternation, even panic. Even in an experienced group like Amira's remaining servants, Elias would have considered it understandable if they had been scared and in disarray as word got around. But Amira's vassals were remarkably stoic in the face of this threat, and Elias was deeply impressed how their situation only seemed to stiffen their determination to be ready for the oncoming attack. There wasn't any sign of alarm, or even desperation, just a sense of purpose and resolve as everyone worked to ready Enrilth Keep for battle. Elias, who had to spend the entire day with Bones's nerve-wracking presence weighing on him as though the assassin was standing right behind him, envied them. He certainly wished he had a measure of their serenity as the day of bracing for the storm marched inexorably towards the night of its arrival.

Perhaps all that time expecting the worst should they ever be discovered was helpful, Elias thought to himself. They've known great danger every day for five years. It's so familiar that it can't shake them anymore.

"How much of the gates can be restored before nightfall?" Boors was asking one of the soldiers, looking serious.

"We were expecting to have a couple weeks for that task, not a day... we can set up a barricade in that time, but we can't make and fortify a real gate. They'll still be able to enter the castle if they can scale whatever we throw together in that time."

"I see. It's likely that the hammer will fall here, then," Boors muttered, glancing at the gate. "We'll try to make the entrance as narrow as possible.

I'll hold the bridge with a few Royal Guard, while the rest of you focus on making sure no one gets into the castle around us…"

"Y-Yes, sir!" the soldier said, seeming to take considerable relief in hearing Boors would be holding the bridge against the enemy. "How many do you think we'll be facing, sir?"

"A force larger than ours could not have made this kind of time, not even if they started moving when we did. For once, my young friend, I suspect the numbers are not against us," Boors said, making a fist. Elias would concede that was a cheerful thought. Gods knew he would want to have any army with Boors in it massively outnumbered before making an attack. Still, it would be best to make sure that they didn't put all their eggs in one basket.

"We're not just preventing them from walking through the front door, I'd hope," he said, stepping closer. Boors turned to Elias, actually seeming pleased to see him.

"Ah, Brook! Not to worry, your warning has given us time to set up further defenses around the perimeter of the castle. If they think they'll find a less obvious path in unguarded, they will soon realize their mistake," he replied, smiling humorlessly. "A small force can defend this castle, but it takes a mighty army to attack it. Our battles have rarely been on even terms these last five years, but this time the advantage isn't with the enemy."

"Maybe not…but Oliver Bones is. Defenses or no, we can't afford to make any mistakes tonight," Elias said worriedly. "Be careful, Boors. Whatever attacks we have to repel might just be distractions for Bones to do his work, and he could be anywhere when night falls."

"You're right. I merely hope that fate places him in my mace's path tonight," Boors said grimly. "Every man and woman here will fight to their last breath defending the queen, Brook. No matter what happens tonight, Bones *will not* accomplish his mission."

"On that, we agree," Elias said, shaking his head. "If you can crush that bastard's head with your mace, he won't slither away this time." Unfortunately, Elias strongly suspected after all Mibotha had told him that he'd have to fight the deadliest man he knew to the death personally, but it was nice to imagine a world where the salvation or damnation of Yivyn didn't depend on him.

"You should meet with Cecily at the armory, Brook. You could use some more protection than that old coat," Boors remarked. Elias glanced down at his threadbare attire and nodded.

"You've got a point. I'm not sure this coat could protect me from a stiff breeze," he conceded with a chuckle as Boors laughed, nodding. Elias had never been at home in heavy armor like Boors clearly was, but the idea of having some protection from the wounds he was likely to suffer tonight was very appealing. Even knowing he could heal a great number of them away, anything he could do to make tonight hurt less was welcome. He left Boors to continue leading the gate's defense and Boors had the situation pretty well in hand. Army tactics had never been Elias's forte any more than fortifications. He preferred to make plans that let him avoid fights entirely or win before anyone knew he was there. As long as nobody asked Brycen what to do, he thought to himself, they should be fine.

Cecily was with Blanche in the armory when he entered, adjusting her armor while Blanche sharpened her sword. Both looked up sharply as he came in, but they quickly relaxed after seeing it was him.

"Elias! There you are," Cecily said pleasantly. "I was about to go looking for you."

"You were?" Elias asked, a little surprised but not at all displeased to hear it.

"If it's true, and we're up against Oliver Bones, we figured you need to be better equipped than that for tonight," Blanche said drily, giving him a look. Elias could tell Blanche was a lot more interested in *how* Elias knew Oliver Bones was coming than the others. On one hand, that was good, it indicated one of the people Elias most wanted on his side during the fight was confident enough she was still thinking about the information rather than simply reacting to it. On the other hand, Elias was aware he wasn't going to be tricking Blanche of all people into thinking this was just a part of his "magic" if she started asking pointed questions.

"I really hope I'm wrong, but I usually don't get what I want," Elias sighed, feigning nonchalance as best he could.

"We'll be a little better-prepared to take him down this time, at least. He'll have trouble using that damn bow of his when he's on the outside of the castle," Blanche muttered.

"He's a good climber. I hope he doesn't manage to get somewhere high without being noticed and start taking shots," Elias sighed.

"We've taken measures against that…and even a man like Oliver Bones would find these walls nearly impossible to scale bare-handed. They're more treacherous than they look," Cecily replied.

"Good. He's not likely to fall and break his neck, knowing our luck. But if he has to be on the ground where people can see him when he joins the fight it could save a lot of lives."

"Here, Elias. We set these aside for you," Cecily said, handing him some armor. "I know you aren't a great believer in heavy armor, but this light…"

Compared to the gleaming plate Boors did battle in, what he'd been given was hardly armor at all. Even compared to Cecily's very light array, it was a step back. All the same, Elias found himself brought up short at what Cecily gave to him.

Armored gauntlets and greaves, in the same style as Cecily's, along with a very sturdy-looking leather coat. A quick inspection by Elias revealed light metal plates hidden in it. What had given him pause, however, was the coloring of the metal. He recognized the silvery-blue sheen, but he had never touched it before, never worn anything of that material even in disguise or jest. He looked at Cecily.

"These are for Royal Guard," he said, trying to make it sound lighter than he felt. Suddenly it felt wrong to accept any of it. "They might slow me down too much." He offered her the bundle she'd given him, but she pressed it back to him, gently but firmly.

"You have served the royal family the same as we have. Since we joined forces with you, we've come to understand that. You've fought alongside us, helped us all this way. You are one of us, Elias, and you have every right to wear that armor," she said quietly.

Elias looked over at Blanche, but she just nodded in agreement, giving an almost imperceptible shrug as if scolding him for thinking she would disagree with Cecily when Cecily looked this serious.

"Thank you," he managed awkwardly, nodding to Cecily. Cecily just smiled at him.

The gesture of acceptance was not one Elias would forget any time soon, but it was also quite a practical one. It wasn't just a special symbol of fellowship they'd given him, it was also good armor. Only an idiot would go into a battle without the best protection he could gather, and Elias suspected whatever speed he lost wearing it would more than be compensated for by having much less healing to do after the fighting was finished. He'd had enough of nearly dying for a while, even if he suspected the universe had plenty more in store for him.

A pair of long, well-balanced daggers caught Elias's eye, and he picked them up, testing the weight. These were of a better make than the dagger he'd carried around before he'd gotten stabbed, or the ones he'd picked up while in Hache's territory. Light enough to throw accurately but longer than most daggers he'd seen.

"I can make good use of these," he remarked.

"I'd imagine so," Blanche agreed. "You should grab a bow, too. If we can see Bones and whoever's with him from the walls, maybe you can get a shot in at him."

Elias nodded, although it was not lost on him that Oliver Bones probably had a longer bowshot than he did. Taking a shot at him meant being inside his range. Elias sincerely hoped the Basilisk-Eye wouldn't have much chance to use his arrows tonight.

Elias felt a fair bit better-prepared for the task ahead once he'd donned his new equipment and picked up a bow and quiver. Blanche nodded, sheathing her sword as she stood up.

"That's a better look for you, Brook. A little less scruffy," she chuckled. "You look ready to go into battle for once."

"Appearances can be deceiving," Elias replied automatically, but the truth was he did feel something closer to anticipation than fear this time. This was going to be the most important night of his life, he was aware, he had begun to hope whatever mixture of skill, luck, and Mibotha's aid had seen him through everything that had come before would carry him through now.

"Let's hope not. The sun will set soon, we don't have long before the attack comes," Blanche said, getting serious. "We should take our positions. Brook, you're going to be on the castle walls, above the front gate. You're a good shot, and I want Boors to have as much support as we can give him throwing back anyone that attacks the gate."

And then, unbidden, Elias saw a familiar stretch of wall in his mind's eye. A secret door opened in the stone, unnoticed by the defenders guarding the walls, and a cloaked form slipped out of the darkness behind it...

"No," Elias answered, before realizing how blunt that had sounded when Cecily and Blanche both looked at him in surprise.

"What do you mean, no?" Blanche demanded, recovering quickly and looking serious.

"Helping Boors drive off any attacks at the front gate is all well and good, but I've never known Bones to go in through the front door when he knows there's a back door he can use," Elias said partially to himself, putting the bow and quiver down.

"A secret entrance?" Blanche guessed right away. "We've covered that. We sealed up the one Cecily and I used to get Amira to safety, and we've found another..."

"You probably know the layout of this castle a lot better than Bones does," Elias conceded, "But he knows one way in you don't. Let me show you."

Blanche and Cecily both followed Elias quickly, and Elias was relieved to find that his memory served him well. The blank expanse of wall between two rusted suits of armor had not been guarded.

"This is a secret passageway?" Blanche muttered.

"I suspect this was one secret Morys held a little too close. This was my secret way in and out. I bet there were others only Morys knew about," Elias explained. "Bones got close to me in disguise to try and learn this place's weaknesses. I'm pretty sure he spied me using this passage, and that's how he was able to get in here and come after me that night."

"If he had a way in, why didn't he just go after the king then?" Blanche asked, looking surprised.

"Caution, maybe, or harder to pin it on me. Morys was never more heavily guarded than when he was asleep. No one would believe I could get through to him and there would've been witnesses. Out hunting it was easy enough to pick him off without being seen and vanish," Elias muttered. "He knows this entrance, and I'll bet he thinks its secret died with me when we fought at the cliff. He's not coming through the front door. This is where he'll emerge when the fighting starts."

"He'll completely avoid all our defenses," Blanche conceded, looking alarmed. "We need to get a team in place on this door, so we're ready for him when he comes out."

"I'm going into the tunnel," Elias said almost to himself, making Blanche and Cecily jump in surprise.

"What? *Why?*"

"I can try and take him by surprise down there," Elias said, turning around. "He won't be expecting me after our last fight. In an open area, I don't have a chance against him. But I know how to fight in tight spaces, and I fight dirty. I might catch him off guard down in that tunnel, and kill him. If not, you can unleash hell on anything that comes through this door that isn't me."

Beyond the almost prophetic insistence constantly pounding through his mind that he had to kill Oliver Bones, he knew it was insanely dangerous to meet the man alone in that tunnel rather than fight him with a group. And yet…

"This is my risk to take before it's anyone out here's," he said, unnerved to realize he meant that. "I've got a much better chance of walking away from that fight than anyone else. It might save everyone you put out here, end it before a single Guard is sacrificed." It was a low blow, striking directly at Blanche, but he *knew* he had to do this part alone.

"That's…that's *stupid!*" Cecily insisted. "You don't need to do this all by yourself! We're sure to stop him if we work as a team! You don't have to prove anything to us by fighting him alone!"

"I'm not doing it for you," Elias said quietly, silencing Cecily. He gave the two a half-hearted smile. "I'm a selfish man. I always will be. I'm doing this for *me*."

Cecily opened her mouth to try and talk him out of it, but Blanche seemed to understand, holding up a hand.

"I don't think we can change his mind, Cecily," she said, looking at Elias reflectively. As when they'd first met, Elias could see Blanche weighing him up, but somehow it was not as unnerving as it had once been. There was still calculation in Blanche's gaze, and it was no easier to determine her thoughts than it was before, but it felt like much of the coldness had bled out of it. Eventually she reached out and put a hand on his shoulder.

"I'll entrust this to you…Elias."

Elias moved to open the passageway and glanced back at the two. He wondered if this was the last he would see of either of them. There was a moment of hesitation in which a lot of things floated unsaid between the three of them. Elias closed it off before any could make it into words, giving Blanche and Cecily a brief nod before stepping through the secret door and sealing it behind him.

His friends had their own battles to fight. Swords, glory, and courage in defense of their home. That was where they belonged.

This was where his path had taken him. This was where all the decisions he'd been asked to make to save his soul had led him. Struggling in the darkness with the Basilisk-Eye to determine who would see the next sunrise.

He is coming, Mibotha whispered as Elias's eyes adjusted to the gloom. *He is nearly here.*

"I know," Elias whispered back, staring at the darkness ahead. "Let's finish this, Mibotha."

Elias Brook

His heart was pounding, but his hands were steady. He was sweating bullets, but his breath came slow and calm. Knowing what lurked in the shadows before him, Elias slipped into the darkness to meet it.

CHAPTER 39

The tunnel was longer than Elias remembered. Someone who didn't see in the dark as well as he did would likely have found it very difficult to navigate, but he was able to make his way almost purely on memory.

How good was Bones's night vision, he wondered? A man like him would surely be able to see in the dark, but was he *that* good? Would he dare bring a light source into this passageway? Elias considered it and then discarded the notion. He'd be able to see Bones very clearly in this gloom if the assassin had any light with him, even from a long way off. Bones wasn't likely to take that kind of risk, even if he thought no one else knew about this place. He *liked* the dark.

About halfway through the tunnel, Elias found what he was looking for, a well-hidden little alcove he swiftly ducked into, hiding himself as effectively as he could in the darkness. He was in luck. If Bones used this entrance to get into the castle at all, he hadn't gotten here in time to stop Elias from reaching the perfect place to launch his attack. He could get the drop on Bones from several angles, depending on his timing…it could be the difference between life and death down here.

Life and death…

His mouth was dry, he realized. He was barely breathing, pressed up against the wall so hard it hurt. Even the faintest exhale seemed like it would echo deafeningly in the dark, silent passageway. Trying not to let the determination he'd carried into the passage waver, Elias held his breath and waited for his opportunity.

And waited.

And waited.

Each breath seemed impossibly loud as Elias snatched one little huff of air after another, not daring to breathe normally. His hands had been steady when he'd walked away from Blanche and Cecily, but they were starting to shake. Everything was shaking. Pressed against the wall like his life depended on it, nearly invisible in the gloom, Elias trembled like a leaf in the wind. He could barely comprehend the silence of his hiding place over how loud his breath sounded to him, or the thunderous noise of his heart pounding far too fast.

The anticipation was killing him, and the anticipation had nothing on what was going to happen next. Elias was tempted to think waiting for Bones was worse than actually fighting him, but he knew that was a lie. Even so, just the knowledge of the assassin's approach was a strange, quiet torture. The determination and confidence he had felt after talking to Amira seemed to drain away as a cold, sinking dread seeped into his body. He could feel Bones's presence already, like snakes crawling across his skin, stealing away all his borrowed courage.

He was caught, like a rat in a trap, and that knowledge was made so much worse by realizing he'd walked into it freely. Facing Bones by himself, somewhere he could ambush him and have an advantage over the Basilisk-Eye for once, had seemed the height of cleverness in carrying out Mibotha's absurd command at the time. Down here, Elias wasn't sure anymore. Familiarity had never endeared this passage to him, but it had never been like this. Before it was dreary, but now the air seemed heavy with doom. He wasn't the only thing holding its breath in anticipation of the bloodshed soon to come, this whole place felt like a tomb.

His tomb.

Every second seemed to pass like an eternity. Surely his heart would have to calm down or explode if this kept up much longer? If he hadn't faced Bones once before, Elias would have started praying for him to show up, just to free him from the anticipation…

You must kill Oliver Bones.

Five words had driven him down here by himself, but pressed up against the wall, Elias wished he had protested more strongly. Mibotha *believed* in him. Great. What was he supposed to do with that? Elias was focusing everything he had on not panicking and fleeing down the tunnel, and he wasn't even in any danger yet.

Why did this have to be *him*? He was a nobody! Just a sneak-thief too lucky to die and too unlucky to stay out of trouble! He stole things, hid from trouble, got things done in the dark! He didn't slay evil to save the day! There was an entire army of people that did that for a living at the end of the hallway. Why in the world had he thought it was a good idea not to just leave this to them?

I can't do this, he thought to himself. There's no way I can do this. I'm going to *die* down here!

The hell with that! He needed to change the plan. He could run ahead of Bones, get Cecily and Blanche to open the door for him, and take Bones down with the Guard watching his back. It took Elias a moment to realize his legs wouldn't obey him. The notion of Bones catching up to him in the dark as his courage failed him and he fled overwhelmed him, and he stayed pressed desperately against the wall, his mind racing.

What was I *thinking*? he demanded internally. His big talk about fighting Bones alone had crumbled completely. Whatever confidence he'd built up in the light of day hadn't followed him into the tunnel. Here, in the dark, he remembered how things really were.

He was a coward. He always had been, and he always would be, and he was afraid of Oliver Bones. Fear was supposed to keep him alive, not get him killed. But Elias knew this terror he felt wasn't like the fear that had given him strength in the past. If he tried to use it to stay alive, it would weigh him down and Bones would cut him to pieces.

Then it will all fall apart, he thought to himself, shaking like a leaf and struggling to control his breathing and steady his hands. *I'm going to die,* and then everything I've done, all I suffered, was for *nothing*! One mistake tonight, and it all comes crashing down around me. It won't matter how hard I fought to get this far. I'll fail, and my deal with Mibotha will be over. It asked too much of me! They all had!

And then, as his mind reeled at the fragility of his efforts, a thought came to him.

I could let him walk by, and then escape through the tunnel when he's gone. He'd never know I was here.

A part of him rebelled against the idea out of hand, but Elias looked out at the dark hallway. The idea had merit…

He could slip past Bones in this darkness. He could take his chance and run for it before anyone wondered where he'd gone. Bones wasn't looking for him, and the others had bigger things to worry about. Cecily and Blanche could kill Bones, couldn't they? Why *not* leave this to them? Cecily and Blanche were stronger than he was. They could kill Oliver Bones thanks to the trap he'd helped them set. He would have upheld his part of the bargain without throwing his life away. He'd come up with a cover to explain how Bones got past him, but that would be easy. He'd just describe what *would* have happened if he risked his neck for no good reason, and they would accept that. Mibotha didn't care *how* Bones died, it just needed him dead. The spirit couldn't complain if Elias gave it the results it desired. And if the worst happened…if Bones killed them all… then there was nothing he could do to stop that anyway. Whether he fought or not, it would be the end of Amira and Mibotha, and there would be no one to punish him for running away instead of dying with them. He'd be free.

He wasn't a hero. He was just a clever coward, and the time had come to look to his own survival. He'd done all he could, all anyone could reasonably ask of him and more. He wasn't going to die for them, not like this. If Bones fell today, it didn't *matter* who killed him. Mibotha would get what it wanted and have to let him go. If they were doomed, then they were doomed with or without his help, and Amira and Mibotha wouldn't be able to punish him for what he chose to do right now.

It wouldn't be much of a life, running out into the Wasteland, but it was a life. He had told Cecily it didn't matter if he lived for nothing, just so long as he kept on living. Cecily thought one day he would understand how the Guard could sacrifice their lives for others. Cecily thought he was a better man than he really was. Cecily…

Footsteps finally broke the silence ever so slightly in the darkened hall, and Elias found his heart rate slowed as they delivered him from the terror of anticipation. The presence of death just around the corner sharpened his panicking mind. He knew who mattered most to him.

There in the dark, where nobody could see or hear him, Elias made his decision.

CHAPTER 40

The sun was beginning to set when the attackers first came into view. They'd been approaching quietly, like bandits at first, but when it became clear the castle was manned and alert, impossible to approach in secret, they began to form up for combat directly. As Boors had expected, it was not a mighty army that was drawing near. The force was no bigger than their own, if that. Enough men to attack a castle, especially when it was unguarded by tired folk in the middle of the night, but not a massive, well-supplied army ready to besiege it.

They weren't wearing the vermillion uniforms of Hache's soldiers, but there was no doubt whose lands they had come all this way from. They were armored, but to what extent was difficult to determine under the dark cloaks they had come wearing. They hung about at the edge of bow range, as if hoping they could stare down the defenders.

"They know we've spotted them. What are they doing?" one of the Guard muttered, shifting uncomfortably.

"They're in no rush, now," Boors answered, standing firm at his position on the bridge. "They were expecting to catch us unawares as it got dark, but now things have changed. They're taking their time to figure out what they can do now."

It didn't look like the attackers had any sort of a supply train. They had likely only been equipped well enough to make it across the Wasteland as quickly as possible. Only about half of them were mounted, but Boors knew it was possible to get a great distance on a horse in a hurry if you had no care for the beast's survival. It was likely they had all been mounted at the start. Boors wondered if they had given any thought to their return journey, or if they had all been sent here with no intention of their returning alive. They couldn't withdraw; to flee now was to starve in the wastes. They had come out here as assassins, but thanks to Elias's warning they had no option but to charge right at their enemy's position of strength. The thought gave Boors some comfort, but not much. If Oliver Bones was behind all this, it was quite probable the killers making plans before them had come as a distraction. If they managed to break through and kill Amira, it was merely a happy accident for the Basilisk-Eye, of that he was certain.

But they were here to kill, and distraction or no, Boors knew he could not let a single one of them pass him into the castle. Boors put down the visor of his helmet and stepped forward slightly, tightening his grip on his mace with one hand and bringing up the broad, heavy shield he'd taken up for this battle with the other.

"This is the only warning we will give you," he called. "Leave now, and you will not be pursued. If you seek to enter here, you will have no mercy from us."

The enemy did not respond to the call, or even acknowledge they had heard it at all. They wouldn't be as easily shaken or quick to panic as the men they'd fought in Hache's territory. Boors hadn't expected it to go any other way, but he had felt obliged to offer warning before the bloodshed began. The ripple of movement that started it was almost invisibly small in the gathering gloom, but Boors had been a fighter for a very long time, and his bones told him to brace himself more than his eyes as the others followed his example.

There wasn't any rallying cry or command from the enemy. Those that still had their horses charged as one, the troops on foot surging in behind them. With surprise off the table, they seemed to realize their best route into the castle was to bring their full might against the ruined gate and force their way past the barricades and Guard. The defenders had predicted as much, and while they didn't dare use caltrops in territory they meant to keep safe for a long time, the attackers still had to ride headlong into a storm of arrows from the archers Blanche had stationed on the walls. Horses screamed as the merciless shafts rained down on them, killing some, laming others, and bearing a great many riders to the ground, never to rise again as their comrades charged over them. As one rider made it through the arrows to reach the drawbridge, the Guard behind Boors stepped forward and thrust their pikes upwards together. One finished off the wounded horse, while the other dispatched his rider.

The men on foot had been making an uneven rush for the gateway, keeping their shields up against the merciless fire from the archers, but it was becoming clear the attacking force could only choose between flowing into the long, dry trench that had once been a moat where archers and pikemen could strike down at them or trying to fit their entire army onto the drawbridge and push past its defenders.

Desperation to get out of the killing ground the archers had created leant speed to the attackers' advance, but Boors strode forward as the first of them approached the drawbridge and swung his mace with all his strength.

He was close enough to see the dismay ripple through the man's fellows as his feet left the ground and his body was flung through the air before landing in a crumpled heap. He had warned them, even knowing it was useless, but there was no mercy now as Boors raised his mace and bellowed in challenge.

"I AM BOORS THE LION!" he roared. "THIS BRIDGE BELONGS TO ME, AND NOT A SOUL WILL CROSS IT WHILE I DRAW BREATH!"

There was real fear in the attackers now, but Boors had long since learned to respect the strength of desperation, and he was not surprised when the enemy surged forward to meet his challenge. Offering a quiet prayer to any god that was listening that his mace would not fail him today, Boors stood his ground. As his fellow Guard on the bridge stepped forward to meet the attackers the battle was joined in earnest. Dozens of blades slashed at Boors, deflecting off his armor or his shield but feeling like he was being beaten with hammers. The pain of each blow was old and familiar, and Boors embraced it like an old friend as he waded into the bloody work before him, crushing men like flies left and right. The bridge and gate were his responsibility, and he would defend them to the death. He merely hoped that Oliver Bones was here, and drawing close to a bloody end among these other murderers under his mace.

"It's begun," Cecily muttered, looking up as she heard the sounds of battle outside. "Boors and the others must be fighting now."

"It was where we predicted the hammer would fall hardest, diversion or not," Blanche muttered, but she paused when she saw Cecily's expression. Awkwardly, she put a hand on her friend's shoulder. "He'll be fine, Cecily. On that bridge, with the others backing him up, you and I both know Boors will never lose."

"You're right," Cecily sighed, although she looked relieved to hear Blanche say it. "I just hope our other line of defense doesn't lose, either."

"If Bones comes at us this way, we have an entire squad here ready for him…and if anyone can fight him one on one in that tunnel, Brook's skills certainly make him the best option. I'm sure he's thought this through, and he'll know to escape to us if Bones is too much for him," Blanche tried, although she didn't sound nearly so sure of this. "We have that snake caught in a trap this time. If he tries to use this door to get to the queen, we have him right where we want him."

"What is all this? Why are you all back here?"

Blanche turned in surprise to see General Brycen and Amira standing behind them, Amira looking puzzled to see a unit of her guard protecting what appeared to be a wall while Brycen looked outraged.

"The enemy is at the gates, Captain Blanche! Making their strongest attempt to overwhelm Sir Boors and storm the castle! Why are so many of your men here instead of supporting the gate's defenses?"

"General, I have reason to believe the men striking at the front gate are a diversion to draw our attention and keep us blind to another entrance," Blanche said calmly, pointing at the wall. "Particularly this one."

Brycen caught on surprisingly quickly, and his eyebrows shot up.

"A secret passageway? How in blazes did we miss one? They've all been sealed up for years!"

"We didn't know about this one. It's one the king had Elias use, and he remembered it when we were discussing where to put him on the defense," Cecily explained quickly. "He believes Oliver Bones knows about this passageway, and he's likely to try sneaking in here while we're busy fighting against the soldiers he brought with him."

"Wait, BROOK was the one who brought this up?" Brycen said sharply, fists clenching. "Where is he now?"

"While we were setting up to confront Bones if he comes out this door, Brook went in to try and ambush him. He knows that tunnel better than anyone else, sir, he's our best chance at nipping this assassination attempt in the bud without Bones ever setting foot in the castle," Blanche explained, raising a hand. It did nothing to calm Brycen.

"You *idiots!* You let him into a secret passage *alone* on the eve of a battle!" he demanded.

"We wouldn't have known there was going to *be* a battle if Elias hadn't warned us," Cecily said sharply, realizing what Brycen was getting at. "The plan was sound."

"You fools! You're treating him like he's a Guard, a man of honor! This was probably his plan all along!" Brycen shouted, his face darkening. "Didn't you find it at all strange that after he managed to cook up this ludicrous scheme to strand us out here, an attack came immediately on our heels? Brook somehow knowing an enemy was coming long before anyone could have picked them out stinks to high heaven, as does the enemy's timing despite our secrecy! This was a *plot*, you trusting fools, and you opened a door for him to walk right out and get away with it!"

"That's completely ridiculous!" Cecily insisted, before looking to Blanche for support. She was surprised to find that her certainty was not shared by the others, and even Blanche looked troubled by the accusation. She pressed on in spite of it. "Elias gains nothing from aiding in a plot to assassinate the queen! And if he'd wanted her dead, he had plenty of opportunities to attempt it before now!"

"He's a bloody thief, did you truly underestimate the depths of his greed and his cowardice?" Brycen growled. "He has everything to gain from stranding us here and helping our enemies silence us if he's been in the employ of one of the traitors this whole time! Any warlord could easily have bought him with money and promises of bettering his lot! Maybe all of them did! He had neither the wit nor the courage to raise a hand against the queen himself, but mark my words, he has been plotting and waiting for his chance to betray us all this entire time!"

"An elaborate scheme, seeing as he nearly laid down his life to see it through," Cecily countered. "Despite his past, Elias has proved worthy of trust since he's joined forces with us! You do him wrong to accuse him like this."

"I don't think I do! This whole business has been too damned convenient," Brycen growled. "He shows up out of nowhere after five years, claiming he's seen the error of his ways? Where was he before, this penitent sinner? What proof do we have anything he told you was true? None! And then he knows where the Regalia are, and leads you on a merry path into enemy territory to reclaim them! He led you right into Hache's lands, and tried to bring his armies and his assassins down on the queen's head while pretending to help you to earn your trust. Don't you *see* it? He and the Basilisk-Eye have been in this together from the very start! It's all been towards this end, to draw the queen out of hiding and kill her here! And because you idiots held the back door open for him while he slipped away, he'll get away with it, just like he got away with betraying the King—"

"Enough."

Amira didn't even raise her voice, but the hallway went silent in an instant. Brycen turned to her, looking worried he'd angered her, while Cecily noted the Guard seemed very uncertain and ill at ease after what they'd just heard.

"My lady—" Brycen started.

"Your thoughts are appreciated, as always, General, but I believe in Elias Brook," Amira said quietly, her voice hard and flat. "If he has truly gone into that tunnel alone to defend me from the Basilisk-Eye, we dishonor his courage by doubting him. If he has betrayed us, then it is past the point where suspicion would have done us any good. His warning gave us the advantage tonight, and I choose to believe in him. If he thinks this is where Oliver Bones will come to seek my life, we will trust his advice, and we will hold this place until that door opens."

"Yes, Your Majesty," Blanche said, bowing. The others murmured, but mimicked the gesture. Blanche turned, drawing her sword.

"If that door opens, we will only have a moment to determine who is on the other side. If it isn't Brook, no matter who else it is, strike to kill," she ordered quietly as the other Guard readied their weapons.

A moment passed, then two, and the tension in the corridor grew as the sounds of battle went on outside. Were they wasting their time here, Blanche wondered? Even if Brycen didn't have it right, what if Elias's hunch had been wrong? It seemed to her that Brook and Bones had been playing some sort of cat-and-mouse game with senses she didn't understand. Bones had predicted their movements when he had no way to do so, and Elias had reacted before he could know they were in danger. How *were* they doing it? Was it simple treachery, as Brycen put it, or was there another secret Brook had kept from them before going into that tunnel? The man seemed to have no end of them, even as she thought she was starting to make progress getting the measure of him. Even if Brook had the best of intentions, if Bones outmaneuvered him this one time, Amira's life might be the price they paid–

And then she tensed, as the door swung open and someone stepped out. Her stomach dropped as she realized it was not Elias that had come to them through the tunnel.

His sword drawn, and his green cloak more snarled and worn than it had been that day on the cliffs, Oliver Bones turned to face the momentarily frozen Guard, seeming amused. Five men followed behind him, short swords drawn and posture tense. The Basilisk-Eye shook his head slowly, regarding the Guard arrayed against him and his lackeys without any sign of distress.

"All this, for me?"

The mocking question was barely in the air before Blanche and Cecily's swords passed through the spot Bones had been in an instant earlier. The lithe green form was like a blur as it struck back at Blanche, but Cecily's sword narrowly intercepted it. Blanche turned rapidly, and felt the familiar heat spread through her veins as she released a wave of white fire at her attacker.

That should have been the end of it, but Oliver Bones practically blurred in every direction as he evaded the gout of flame. One of his men was not so lucky, and cried out in alarm as the flames consumed him. Desperately, Blanche jumped back and poured more flame out, trying to box the assassins in and burn them, but Bones was unscathed even as his fellow killers were caught up in the conflagration. The Guard shouted and pressed in, but the Basilisk-Eye wove hypnotically around the clustered attacks, an ugly little laugh boiling up from his throat.

"One of Morys's mages!" he hissed, the sheer hostility of the words stinging like a blow. There was something between fury and a savage *glee* in the man's horrible, rasping voice as he glared at Blanche. "I thought I got all of you, but he hid you in the Guard…clever. Clever!"

Even the sound of Bones's voice seemed to have only become more loathsome since their last encounter, but Blanche felt like there was something *different* about the vile assassin this time. He'd been amused when he saw them last time. Now he was almost manic, reacting to a trap that would have killed a slower man with a deranged glee. His eyes had been dull and cold and put Blanche in mind of the color of phlegm before, but now they were bright, hungry, and seemed to burn in the sunken eye-sockets behind the metal mask.

None of that seemed important to Blanche, however, as the full weight of his words sunk in.

Beatrix. Jocelyn. Bernard. Guy. Hugh. She'd never found out what happened to any of them, after she'd gone her own way to join the Guard. She'd always hoped they had gone to live peaceful lives, somewhere away from all this. That maybe the war had passed them by, knowing they'd suffered enough already.

Hearing the Basilisk-Eye now, Blanche knew those hopes were nothing but wishful thinking. They were dead, all of the children she had grown up with in that horrible tower. Elias might well be dead somewhere in the tunnel. Everyone she knew of that had been born like her was gone. By *his* hand.

She was vaguely aware Cecily screamed some sort of warning to the other Guard. Everyone rushing away as the heat spread from her veins to fill her entire body. Oliver Bones seemed to fill the entire universe for Blanche, and a word slipped out through her clenched teeth.

"BURN."

She savored the brief expression of surprise in Bones's unnatural eyes as the hallway all around him exploded. Blanche didn't need her hands to guide this, she just unchained the power and let it rage. It was a familiar, sweet sensation, letting it run wild after a lifetime of chaining it up, holding it back. Blanche knew she had the power to tear the world in two in her hands, and for one brief moment, she reveled in it as she turned it on the monster who had come to take everything from her.

There was silence as the inferno subsided, leaving sections of wall and floor burned away into nothing. Blanche could feel the stares beating down on her even as she struggled to regain control of her breath. Terror and exultation warred inside of her. Blanche could not deny the ecstasy that ran through her, letting her power flow rampantly in an explosion of pure, powerful emotion, but that strange joy had always frightened her as well. She had reveled in unleashing her magic, despite the destruction it caused. She could not blame those who looked upon her with fear, and she turned to face them, looking exhausted as she struggled to regain control of herself.

"That's the end of him," she sighed, preparing to give new orders when she noticed the Guard saw something move behind her and whirled around.

"Not quite."

Blanche stared in astonishment as Oliver Bones stood up in the wreckage she'd immolated. Flames clung to his cloak, his body, his mask, rendering him a man-shaped white torch, but there he stood when not even ashes should have survived. Blanche brought her arm up in panic, calling on the power again, but Bones was on her in an instant, gripping her arm in an impossibly strong grasp.

"I see why she saved you to use against me," he rasped, eyes staring out from under the burning mask and hood, bloodshot but otherwise unharmed. "You're strong. *But I'm stronger.*"

Blanche's flames had never harmed her, but the fist beneath them crumpled her armor as it smashed into her stomach like a battering ram. All the breath went out of Blanche's body, and she was hurled backwards to crumple into a ball as the burning assassin turned his attention to Amira.

"Setting a welcome like this for me...you're *very* well-informed, your highness!" he shouted to Amira through the press of bodies trying to pin him down and kill him. "What a nasty child you are, *spoiling the surprise!*"

The Guard, despite what they had seen, were not slow in coming to their captain's aid, and charged Oliver Bones as one. But their opponent was inexorable, charging right back and cutting a quick path through their ranks. Without warning, he was behind the Guard, and bearing down on Brycen and Amira. As the Guard scrambled to surround him again, the long blade flicked out and took Brycen in the throat, and then there was nothing between Amira and the Basilisk-Eye.

Brook failed, Blanche realized in despair as time seemed to slow to a crawl. We've all failed.

Oliver Bones had reached Amira.

CHAPTER 41

Everything burned. Inside and out, he was aflame, and the heat did not relent. He wanted to scream, but he couldn't take a breath. Whatever air there was left was a choking fume feeding the flames.

Everything hurt too much for coherent thought for what felt like an eternity, but the first two words to punch through the wordless haze of pain only made things worse.

"I failed."

Just two words, but they gave enough clarity to the situation that everything else came back into order. Elias drifted weightlessly through a universe of burning agony, the words drilling deep into his consciousness. It was over. He'd failed his task. And now he was going to spend an eternity in Valka.

The one time I try to do the right thing instead of run when I had the chance, and I end up dead and in Valka anyway, he reflected, closing his eyes and gritting his teeth against the formless pain bearing down on him from everywhere. *Just my luck.*

He hadn't expected Valka to be like this, though. From what he'd heard in the temples, it was a barren expanse of boiling heat, no water, and razor sharp rocks drawn out into a never-ending path of cliffs and pits. Elias had expected to spend the rest of eternity walking that path if he failed, but all there was here was the agonizing heat and a sense of weightlessness...

Stir yourself, Elias Brook!

That hadn't been something Elias was expecting. He'd been sure that once the eternal torment started, Mibotha was going to have other things to worry about while his soul wandered Valka, but the spirit's voice was calling him.

327

You must get up, Elias Brook! You cannot let it end here!

"What's the use, Mibotha?" Elias managed to croak, finding a sliver of breath as the burning pain subsided slightly. "I couldn't do it. I'm here because I failed."

It's not over yet! Not like this! Sincere as it was, Elias could also tell that Mibotha's desperation was growing by the second. Whatever the fallout of his defeat had been, it must be pretty dire to have the spirit in a state like this. *You MUST get up, Elias Brook! You must kill Oliver Bones, before it's too late!*

"I can't," Elias said weakly. It took all the strength in him just to say that much. "I can't kill him. You saw."

In the dark, where no one could see or hear him, Elias made his decision.

This close, he could tell it was more than one person about to pass him in the tunnel. Barely breathing, stilling his shaking hands, Elias became a part of the dark wall as each passed in turn, waiting, gauging the footsteps until he was sure the last of them was walking by. Only then did he spring into action, popping out of the gloom like he'd been conjured there by magic and plunging one of his daggers deep into the man's neck before anyone realized he was there.

He'd been hoping it would be a quick and silent kill, but the man managed to make a choking cry as he was slain before he jerked and fell to the floor, and Elias realized his target had been misplaced. Oliver Bones hadn't been at the back of the group, like he'd been expecting. He'd stayed at the center!

Elias had learned long ago never to walk in front, but Bones had proved too clever to fall for the reverse, either. In the middle of the pack, he was far enough away from anything that hit the poor bastards walking in front, and had cover against anyone that tried to take the group from behind.

Like he had just now, which left Elias alone and facing down Bones and a small squad of his lackeys. His unfortunate victim's death-cry had alerted the others enough that short swords were out, and Elias realized however difficult his imagined solo battle with Oliver Bones in this tunnel might have been, it would have been easy compared to fighting Oliver Bones and nine other men.

"One Guard in the tunnels? How...interesting," Bones hissed, his form now unmistakable among the killers starting to advance on Elias. *"Take him alive. He might know something useful."*

Four of the nine converged on Elias, apparently not expecting much trouble subduing him with their short swords against his two daggers. They were quick, he acknowledged that, but not **nearly** quick enough.

Elias's blades were moving before his assailants' feet, raking a red line through the first man's eyes and another through his nearest fellow's throat. One screamed and flailed as Elias kicked him back onto the third man, while the other fell to the ground without a word, making the fourth step over him to stab out at Elias.

They didn't spend much time worrying about their fallen, these men, and Elias didn't either. He felt the blade slide off an armored plate in his new coat as he evaded it, but his knife sunk into the man's wrist just below the palm and traced a long, ragged line up to his elbow. The man could well die from a wound like that, but not nearly quick enough for his purposes. The second blade punched up just behind the man's chin as he dropped his sword, leaving Elias with a handy shield to maneuver into place as the fourth man untangled himself from his blinded ally and tried to cut him down. Elias dislodged his blades as the still-warm corpse absorbed his opponent's attack for him, pivoting around the dead man and plunging both knives into his last attacker's back. The man's body armor protected him from the worst of the attack, and Elias had to duck under a surprisingly quick slash at where his head had been earlier, but Elias was quicker, and his next stab went through his attacker's exposed eye and bore the man to the ground, where he would never rise again.

The first injured man was still wailing, trying to get his bearings and recover his sword. He neither saw nor heard Elias before his throat was cut and he fell to join the other three on the ground. Making an effort not to look winded, Elias stood up and tried to stare down Oliver Bones. The Basilisk-Eye seemed genuinely impressed, if not that worried. Not so for the five men behind him, however. Elias knew fear when he saw it, and he saw the trepidation about being the next to attack him he'd hoped for. Maybe he'd miscalculated. If he could use one of them as a shield, he might be able to catch Bones off-guard and kill him like this.

The Basilisk-Eye seemed aware of the situation as well, as he glanced at the five men now behind him.

"Go down the passage. Flush out any others and secure the door for my arrival," he said simply, as though one guard killing half the men he'd brought with him was not a matter of any great significance to him. "I'll take care of this."

The thugs did not need to be told twice, and Elias braced himself. He'd wanted to fight Oliver Bones himself, and in its infinite spite, the universe had for the very first time given him exactly what he wanted.

He barely saw Bones move before the first fist slammed into his face, sending him stumbling over the men he'd just killed. It was like being hit in the head with a thunderbolt, and the two punches that followed hot on its heels set off red and green explosions behind Elias's eyes as his head snapped back. If his face had not been bruised beyond recognition already when he'd stepped out to face them, it certainly would be now.

He's not even going for his sword, Elias thought to himself. He's just going to beat me half to death with his bare hands for information.

"I'm in a hurry, so I'll offer you a deal," Bones said, advancing on Elias. Elias thought he saw an opening and went to capitalize on it, but a kick almost too fast to follow laid him out. "Answer my questions, I'll kill you quick. Drag this out, death will be a relief." Elias started to get up, but Bones grabbed him by the throat and hauled him up to slam him against the wall, once, twice, three times. When he was pinned, he couldn't even see straight anymore.

"So? What will it be? Quick, or painful?" Bones hissed, tightening his grip.

Elias managed to catch Bones in the side with a kick, enough to get the hand off his throat, but Bones was on him again in an instant, and another punch nearly cracked the stone wall with the impact against his body.

"Painful it is," Bones hissed.

Elias struck hard and fast, trying to regain some of his momentum, but it was becoming increasingly clear Bones had him outmatched. Elias desperately scrambled through every trick he had; going for the eyes, the throat, dropping low to try and take his opponent's legs out from under him. Bones countered them all with a contempt bred from familiarity, and one bone-breaking blow after another hammered Elias down. His head was swimming, his vision was nearly shot, he could barely hear a thing, and his nose did not feel like it was anywhere close to where he liked it on his face. Bones kept on coming, driving Elias back. Eventually he grabbed him by the throat again, this time starting to squeeze. Elias didn't doubt that Bones could close his fist around his throat if he really wanted to after observing the freakish strength in the man's arms.

"You should talk, while you can still speak," he said, as though they were having a casual conversation. "You can't even imagine how badly I can hurt you before you die."

Elias's reply was barely even a gasp. His bloody lips moved slightly, and a little noise came out, but it appeared to have been what Bones was waiting for, and he was pulled closer.

"Louder."

*And that had been what **Elias** had been waiting for.*

"You didn't watch my hands," he repeated, clear enough to be heard as he stabbed his dagger with all that was left of his strength just beneath his hated enemy's ribs.

*Bones made a small choking sound, half surprise, half pain, and the grip on Elias's throat slackened. As the master assassin crumpled at his feet, Elias was only kept from whooping in triumph by his crushed throat and the knowledge those five killers remaining would make mincemeat of him in his current state if they came running. But it didn't matter. He'd done it. **He'd killed Oliver Bones!***

"Got you, you son of a bitch," he wheezed, collapsing against a nearby wall. He felt almost weightless with relief. He'd won. He was probably blind in one eye and half-deaf from the beating he'd taken, but Bones was the one on the ground with a knife in his heart and he was still here. The Royal Guard could take care of the rest, and tomorrow–

Bones twitched, and Elias's heart stopped.

I got him, he told himself, remembering how sometimes a body seemed to move a little after life had departed. I definitely killed him with that stab. I only would have survived a wound like that because of Mibotha, and it would have taken him time to heal me.

*Don't get up. I **know** I got you. Don't get up. Don't get up. Don't you dare get up.*

Before Elias's disbelieving eyes, Oliver Bones stood back up, pulling the dagger out of his chest and turning to Elias.

*"Is that the best you've got?" he hissed, and the dead eyes inside his mask seemed to **burn**. As Elias stared up at his adversary in disbelief, he saw something change in Bones's gaze, a feeling rather like lifting the lid off a basket of cobras and seeing the **writhing** underneath. Mibotha's immense, wordless dismay filled his head immediately, confirming Elias's worst fears.*

Bones wasn't just a tool for the evil spirits Mibotha was fighting against. He was their vessel, just like Elias. If he didn't stop him here, Blanche, Cecily and the others were going to have to fight a nearly immortal Oliver Bones on top of everything else!

Mibotha frantically started trying to repair Elias's body enough to give him the strength to rise again, but Elias was still a mess while Bones seemed to have easily shrugged off having his heart perforated already, and he drew his sword. Elias didn't dare move as the thin, deadly blade was laid against the side of his nose, the very finest point an errant twitch away from jabbing into his tear duct. If the blade moved in any direction at all besides backwards, or a tear connected that blade to his eye, Elias suspected he would be in a great deal of pain, if not for very long.

"You are dead, friend. That's already decided. But how I kill you depends on what you do now," Bones hissed. "You're good, for a Guard. Much better than I was expecting. I want to know if you're the only surprise Amira left guarding her back door, and where your friends are expecting me to come after the little queen. If you tell me, I'll shove this blade through your eye. You'll die too fast to comprehend how much it hurts." Bones's eyes narrowed dangerously. "If you don't tell me, I'll nick your heart with this blade like you nicked mine with yours. Only...my blade is poisonous. It took me a lifetime of study to perfect this kind, and I've been saving it for tonight." There was a flinty, impatient anger in Bones's voice, but on some level, he was enjoying this, Elias could tell. "It will take you a couple minutes to die after I stick you, but your heart will more or less dissolve and turn your blood into acid before you do. My...friends have an abiding interest in pain, you see. They love seeing people die from this. They tell me those few minutes of dying are like an eternity on the inside."

Mibotha had not been able to expunge the poisons from last time very effectively, Elias recalled, and this was a poison Bones saved for special occasions. They didn't have days to lie up healing it off. He didn't even know if Mibotha could bring him back if his heart wasn't there anymore.

"What's it going to be?" Bones asked. "Die in agony to protect a little girl a few minutes longer, or help me and go to your reward quickly?"

Elias managed a wordless snarl, despite his heartbeat quickening in anticipation of its immediate demise. Bones sighed, shaking his head.

"Defiant to the end. Typical Guard," he grunted, moving the blade away from Elias's eye. "I suppose it's my fault for trying. You are too stupid to know when you're beaten and too loyal to run, so I didn't offer...but I thought you might at least have the sense to die cleanly. Honor won't make your end any better," Bones sighed, shaking his head. "Die the good death. So small-minded. It's a shame I killed Brook last time. He could have made this more fun for me...but I guess it doesn't really matter. He'd have done the smart thing and run when he knew I was coming."

"Go to hell, Bones."

A little flower of pain bloomed in Elias's chest as the thin blade slipped between his ribs to pierce his heart. Already, he could feel a heat in the wound that shouldn't be there.

"You first," Bones said drily, withdrawing his sword and starting to walk down the hall.

Elias tried to take a breath, but his lungs wouldn't move anymore. A spasm of blinding pain wracked his body, and he collapsed into a heap on the floor. He'd failed. He hadn't been able to slow Oliver Bones at all, let alone kill him.

The thought tormented Elias's mind until the pain began in earnest. Then…everything burned, and there was nothing left to think about but the pain.

Elias gritted his teeth, trying to shake away the memory, but there was no relief from the pain of his failure or the eternity of burning agony it had consigned him to.

"I failed, Mibotha. I can't kill him. I don't know if anyone can," he croaked, barely able to speak through the pain.

You can. You MUST! If you fail, we have come all this way for nothing, Elias Brook! Mibotha practically screamed. *He is like you! You and you alone know how to kill him for good! If you do not get up, Elias Brook, Amira and everyone she brought here with her will DIE!*

"It's already too late for that!" Elias cried out in a ragged voice, curling into a ball in a futile attempt to block out some of the pain. "I'm in Valka! I *failed*! There's nothing more I can do!"

You are not in Valka, Elias Brook. You are trapped in your body, and your body is trying its hardest to die, Mibotha said desperately. Elias was astonished to hear the strain of exhaustion in its voice. He was the one with a poisoned heart, but Mibotha sounded more like it was dying than he did! *I have been doing everything I can to stop you from slipping into the afterlife for good this time, but I can't save you anymore. If you do not have the will to stand up and fight, you will succumb! This pain will be your reality, FOREVER! I need you to FIGHT, Elias! Don't stop clinging to your life now! Not now, when we're so close!*

"How can we win, Mibotha?" Elias asked desperately. "He's stronger than me, faster, more vicious! We're wounded, exhausted, and outmatched, and he's just getting started! With whatever's riding in his body tonight, he can probably do anything we can but better!" He twisted as another spasm of pain burned through him, desperately wishing for Mibotha to show him some way out of this. *"How can we possibly win?"*

You have two things he does not, Mibotha said, its voice tired and almost pleading. *You have a reason to dream of tomorrow and keep on living. Bones is nothing now, an avatar of poison and death. He does not have your will to live on, only a need to destroy. And you are Elias Brook. The man who does the impossible, no matter what's required, to see tomorrow's dawn! I...*Mibotha's voice faltered, and grew faint for a moment, *I no longer have the strength to restore your body, or to fight on without you. If you give up here, we are both finished, Elias Brook. I can't do anything to protect Amira and the others without you.*

Once upon a time, Elias Brook had found himself in the gap between life and death, being given an ultimatum by the spirit. Mibotha had been his master, able to hold the prospect of eternal damnation over his head and guide his actions in exchange for keeping him alive. But there were no ultimatums or demands, and no threats, merely the facts of what would come to pass if it ended here. Elias found he actually felt more sorry for Mibotha than he did for himself, if only slightly.

Please, Elias Brook. I need you to help me finish this, Mibotha said faintly. *We can save Amira. Save Yivyn. TOGETHER.*

No ultimatum. Just a plea, after forcing Elias to do some of the most stupid, dangerous...and important things he'd ever done in his life. He could turn it down, Elias realized, but then what? Just another failure after all that? Wandering Valka with Bones laughing at him, knowing he'd done all that ridiculous penance for *nothing*?

The hell with *that*, he thought, feeling himself surge upwards into a sitting position as the world slipped back into blurry shape around him.

"One more time," he breathed, and opened his eyes to find himself back in the tunnel.

He was in unimaginable pain, but at the moment gratitude to still be among the upright and breathing was proving a very small but effective balm. He staggered to his feet, picking up his dagger in a shaking hand and starting to stumble down the tunnel.

"One more time," he repeated, like a prayer.

One more task, and all our debts are paid. We are the only ones who can do this, Elias Brook. You and I must kill Oliver Bones together.

Bleeding everywhere, body a mess, no strength in his arms at all, and a nightmarish poison trying to boil him alive with every step he took as Mibotha toiled to keep his spirit in his body, Elias reflected. All in all, not the circumstances he'd have hoped for for his final confrontation with a freakishly strong, nearly immortal master killer possessed by evil spirits, but then, Elias had never done his best work in the circumstances he'd hoped for.

On the bright side, when Bones tore him apart this time, Elias was fairly certain wandering Valka forever would seem almost pleasant.

CHAPTER 42

Despite the devastating blow she'd taken, Blanche surged to her feet, although the world felt like it was moving in slow motion. She knew she could never reach Amira in time to stop Bones from cutting her down, and she didn't dare release her flames with them that close. Despite that, she charged, feeling like she was moving underwater, in the desperate, vain hope she could somehow reach the burning assassin before he completed his task.

She was too slow, too slow by far, but to her astonishment, there was no fatal slash. Amira's eyes met the Basilisk-Eye's crazed gaze, and the burning assassin…hesitated. Amira stood her ground, seeming to see something Blanche could not in the burning madman who had come to strike her down.

"Stop this," she said quietly, holding Bones's eyes as the sword failed to swing at her. The entire world seemed to stand still, the Guard too terrified to move and break whatever spell was keeping the queen safe from the poison sword. Despite his maniacal shift in attitude and the fiendish energy Bones had smashed through the Guard with, the assassin now seemed transfixed, struggling with himself to even move. Amira started to raise her hand, and it seemed to Blanche that for just a moment, the flames enshrouding Bones blew back as if recoiling from her touch. "I can see you," Amira went on, speaking as though she were in a trance. "All of you. You don't have to do this…"

Bones twitched as if Amira's voice was hurting him, and for just a moment, Blanche got the strangest feeling that he would actually put down his sword. It only lasted a moment. Without warning, the "spell" holding Bones in place broke, and he let out an angry howl.

"*I **want** to do this, you little fool!*" Bones's arm shot out with lightning speed, but it wasn't the killing stroke that Blanche had dreaded. It was a powerful backhand that sent Amira flying. Amira was flung to the ground some distance from her assailant, an enormous bruise already forming on one side of her face but otherwise unharmed when she should be dead.

Blanche was almost too surprised to bring up her sword in time to stop Bones from skewering her as she ran to Amira's aid. Bones turned to face her, eyes shining insanely within the inferno that should have been consuming his head. The metal mask he was wearing now looked like a warped ash carving more than steel. If Blanche's flames gave off heat, she was sure it would be molten, but she knew it should not be *anything*. Bones and everything around him should have been reduced to ash, but he seemed to radiate strength, his eyes boring into her even as he burned.

"Don't worry. I'm going to kill her last," he rasped, pressing his attack. The blows came fast and brutal, and Blanche's sword was batted to the ground and her pauldron narrowly saved her from taking a fatal cut. "When she's seen all of you die failing to protect her. When her spirit is broken. *When I can take my time doing it.*"

Blanche managed to duck another fatal slash, and desperately released another intense gout of flame into Bones at point-blank range in the hope this time he would fall. The assassin gave an inhuman screech of agony and staggered back, but the mad eyes fixed on her didn't dim, if anything, they grew brighter as Bones let out something between a scream and a laugh. Blanche went for her sword desperately, rolling out of the way as Bones's sword sliced close enough to shave a few hairs from her bangs. Even its proximity made a little burning line across Blanche's brow as she came up, sword in hand.

"What *are* you?" she demanded, feinting to the left before trying to retake the offensive. Bones's movement was agonized and lacking in grace, but its speed was supernatural, and her blade only found empty air.

"Nothing worth explaining to a dead woman," Bones hissed, trying to finish her off. Blanche could see his sword coming, but it was too fast a movement for her to have any hope of blocking it.

There was a resounding clang as Cecily's sword intercepted the kill stroke for the second time that night, and Blanche turned in surprise to see Cecily, sweat beading on her face with the effort, push Bones's blade back, making the assassin stumble a pace before recovering. The rest of the Guard moved to surround Bones again, spears and swords at the ready.

"It doesn't matter what you are," Cecily agreed, helping Blanche to her feet and stepping forward. "Whatever you are, we're putting an end to you tonight."

Bones laughed in her face, the sound deep, dry, and horrible. Blanche's flames twisted as if caught in a foul wind as he reached up with his free hand and gripped his shoulder.

"No. This was decided years ago," he hissed, staring Cecily down with his mad but intensely focused gaze. "You've held onto a dream for five years. It's time to wake up. *I am your reality.*" he gripped his cloak and shoulder, and suddenly ripped the blazing garment from his body. Blanche and the others watched in stunned horror as cloth, armor, and flesh alike tore away from his body as if they were parchment. So much of what he had been sloughed off that Blanche was certain nothing should have remained when it was done, just crumbling bones. But the Basilisk-Eye stood even as the grisly remains fell to the floor and burned away to nothing.

Blanche had seen too many dead and mutilated bodies in one lifetime to ever sleep as soundly as she wished, but the *thing* standing before her was all the worse for still being alive in that state. Raw tendons, twisted into shapes that seemed unnatural on the bones they were bound to, steamed for a moment in the air. Oliver Bones seemed to be nothing beneath his cloak and armor but warped sinews and little spots of blackened skin or disgustingly glistening bone. Blanche didn't need to be an anatomist to clearly perceive the *wrongness* in the twisted apparition's form. Its hideous appearance attacked the eyes, but there was something invisible and obscene clinging to every inch of it that chilled Blanche to her very core. A sense that had nothing to do with her sight made her aware of a strange writhing movement in Bones, the raw muscles looking to her like masses of red worms and snakes crawling over the assassin's bones. The horrible thing exhaled, and the steam that the tortured muscles had emitted darkened, and condensed. Blanche wasn't sure and didn't care if new skin was forming over the nauseating spectacle before them, but something did cover Bones anew. A strange dark miasma clung to the wretched creature like it was part of his flesh, one moment pure black, then with hints of a dizzying, toxic-looking array of reds, greens, and purples visible in the darkness. It swaddled Bones from head to toe as both skin and clothing, but even as the gruesome exposure ended, the horrible writhing did not go away. Blanche imagined she could see great serpents slithering, coiling, and uncoiling in the strange, dark vapor. A strange noise, like a constant, malicious whispering of many voices, emanated from the vapor as Bones stood tall, seeming like a black smudge on the air, more shadow than man now. Blanche's heart sank as she realized the assassin resembled the evil spirits of the Haunted Wasteland, only more substantial. Indeed, dull orange and red lights flickered and disappeared like brief glimpses of distant stars in his body, but the same horrible eyes leered out of the formless void that had become the Basilisk-Eye's face. Bones let out a satisfied sigh as the grisly transformation was completed, and Blanche became aware of a faint thrumming from the shadowy mass he had morphed into. The eyes focused again. There was not even the slightest trace of sanity in them, but they burned with terrible purpose.

"Now, then," the thing that had been Bones rasped, the whispers twisting to echo its words, *"Shall we end this?"*

The nauseating spectacle of Bones's transformation and the nightmarish creature that leered at them now had frozen the Royal Guard's initiative entirely. They might have stayed still, stupefied with revulsion and terror until their enemy killed them at his leisure, had Cecily not answered his challenge.

"FOR THE QUEEN!" she roared, charging at the monstrosity. Her cry broke the spell, and Blanche and the others charged with her.

For all the bravery of their charge, it was like fighting fog, or the dark of the night. Bones seemed to be everywhere at once, laughing at them as he flung his would-be attackers about like leaves or slashed at them with his deadly sword. With every movement, Guard were swatted away to strike the walls and ceiling with terrible force, or else scythed down by that terrible sword, never to rise again. Blanche feared the fiend would rout them then and there if it was not for Cecily's interference. Even against this new and terrible adversary, Cecily fought like a woman possessed, her sword seeming to be everywhere as she parried, deflected, or countered as many killing blows as she could manage. While the creature's relentless assault staggered her a step with every parry she made, Blanche marveled at her friend's speed and focus as she matched the inexorable monster they fought stroke for stroke. Neither of them was able to press the attack and land a hit, but Cecily used herself as a shield for the others to try and catch the elusive creature off-guard. Even with all its terrible strength, the thing that had been the Basilisk-Eye could not overcome Cecily's sheer skill with the blade, and the battle turned into a frantic, turbulent stalemate as they dueled. But the monster fought with no sign its exertion was taxing it, while Cecily was pushing herself already. If they did not finish the fight soon, its strength against her skill would be a small matter compared to the gap in their endurance.

It was in the midst of this chaos that Blanche saw her opening, and without hesitation, she took it. Breathing raggedly from the exhaustion of blocking one punishing blow after another, Cecily managed to force the poison sword into one of the walls. For a fraction of a second, it stuck there, and the creature had to turn its attention to freeing its blade. In that fraction, Cecily shifted almost imperceptibly, and Blanche stepped through the spot she had been defending, white flames springing into being all along her sword as she stabbed deep into the dark, swirling form before her and was rewarded with a bellow of rage and pain.

The creature's counterattack was swift and merciless. It roared, and Blanche felt like she'd been struck head-on by a charging bull, hurling her away as her sword clattered from her hands as she went flying down the hallway. Cecily and the other surviving Guard, too, were hurled away, landing heavily on the ground as the monster freed its blade and turned to Blanche, its entire form quivering with rage.

"This is the end of it," it hissed, raising the sword up to finish Blanche off. Blanche tried desperately to marshal the strength to roll out of the way, but she found she couldn't move at all after the last blow had sent her flying.

Before it could deliver the final blow, however, a dagger flew into the creature's chest, lodging there where its heart should have been. The monster stopped and turned, half in surprise, half in outrage at the new interruption, to see a bloodied figure leaning against the secret doorway.

Blanche knew there was no one it could be but Brook, but you would not know that to look at him. The thief's already-bruised face was beaten into a mask of livid bruises and cuts. He was soaked with blood and looked dead on his feet. Despite this, he managed a shaky, half-hearted smile.

"I sure hope so," he replied, meeting the stunned gaze of the monster. "I don't know how much more of this I can put up with."

CHAPTER 43

Taking that first step down the passageway with a body that should've been dead and a mind in a haze of pain was one of the hardest things Elias had ever done in his life.

As was the second step. And the third. In fact, Elias conceded to himself as he dragged his carcass across a wall to keep upright, leaving more faintly sizzling blood behind than he liked to think about, every bit of this ordeal was an act of tremendous heroism he would never get the proper credit for. Amira owed him a medal for every step down this gods-forsaken, much too long hallway.

"I'm not going to lie, Mibotha, I've lost a lot of fights feeling better than this," he groaned, immediately regretting his decision to speak as his throat protested.

This is a terrible poison. I haven't seen one this strong or this virulent since the last basilisk died. Maybe Oliver Bones managed to find a way to adapt their venom for his own purposes. Weakening it enough to slather his sword only seems to have made the death less than instantaneous. Mibotha murmured, its voice increasingly faint. *If you possibly can, Elias Brook, you must avoid that blade. I...I don't know if I can heal this.*

"Thank you, Mibotha. As always, your words are a comfort in my dark times," Elias groaned, dragging himself along further and trying to work feeling back into his fingers to use his daggers when the time came.

Still...if Mibotha wasn't sure it could heal the wound Elias had already taken, a solution finally presented itself to him. That blade might be too poisonous for Mibotha to heal, but Elias would bet that poison Bones had been saving for tonight would hurt him just as badly. If Elias could just get him with that sword and then tell someone whose heart *wasn't* trying to dissolve to cut his damn head off...

That was a pretty big *if*, and there was a lot more hallway between him and it than Elias would have liked.

Courage, vessel.

Elias was surprised when the haze of pain cleared slightly, and his long-gone balance reasserted itself. He managed to stand upright, realizing it wasn't Mibotha who had spoken. Strength forced itself back into his cramping limbs, and Elias became aware he could see clearly again, and detect a familiar thrumming from the very stones around him.

Take heart. Not alone.

triumph

The rock spirit, and the one from the water…Elias still felt like a dead body on strings, but he managed to force himself to run as the thrumming began to fill him as well. It felt like his bones were humming in time with the stones, but it was a strangely pleasant feeling, particularly compared to what it was keeping at bay. He realized he could feel Mibotha thrumming within him as well, and he didn't need to understand the language of the spirits to feel his partner's gratitude for the reinforcement.

They will lend us all the power they can, Elias Brook. The rest is up to us.

"It's getting a little crowded in here…" Elias coughed, picking up his pace.

We are still vastly outnumbered by the spirits possessing the Basilisk-Eye.

"Well, if I was going to wait for the numbers to be on my side before I did something, I'd have died in a gutter years ago," Elias grunted. You got used to overwhelmingly negative odds after a while.

One more time, he reminded himself, holding it in his mind like a prayer. Just one more time, and then I'm through.

The prayer did not help much as he opened the secret door to find a scene of carnage before him. This section of the castle looked like someone had stacked up barrels of Demon Dust in the hall and set them all off at once. A section of the wall and floor had been burned away, bodies littered the ground, some dead, others wounded and slumped against the walls. Elias felt a surge of panic as he saw Amira lying some distance away, but to his profound relief, she shifted, trying to get up.

In the midst of all this stood something Elias had never seen before, part human and partially a dark haze like a stain on the air. Elias knew there was nothing else it could be but Bones, but the monster before him bore little resemblance to the assassin he'd been expecting to fight at the end of it all.

That is not merely Oliver Bones. Not anymore, Mibotha said grimly, disgust etched in each word. *That is the legions of our enemy condensed into one body.*

And strangely enough, Elias could see it himself. Every inch of the thing that had been Bones writhed and whispered. While the terrifying creature moved with the purpose of one guiding mind, Elias could see dozens, maybe hundreds, of malevolent spirits urging that one mind onward.

The thought that he had to fight *that* when the old Oliver Bones had been too much for him and this one had defeated a unit of Royal Guard was shoved aside when Elias realized that the creature was advancing on a stricken Blanche, readying itself to finish her off before she could rise.

"*This is the end of it,*" Bones hissed, and Elias could hear the legion of voices echoing his words as he went for his killing strike.

Despite all that he'd been through tonight, Elias found it was the easiest thing in the world to hurl one of his daggers from the doorway right into Bones's chest, striking the Basilisk-Eye in the same place he'd fatally wounded him before. He knew he was in trouble as the creature turned in outrage and surprise to stare at him, but he couldn't help but smirk a little. He suspected it wouldn't be recognizable if his face looked half as bad as it felt.

"I sure hope so," he replied, meeting the stunned gaze of the monster. "I don't know how much more of this I can put up with."

"*You!*" Bones's eyes widened as he saw the wound he'd given Elias still hadn't closed, and yet he stood before him now. "*How—!*"

Elias could feel rather than see the panic in the legion of spirits inhabiting Bones, but strangely very little of it was directed at him. Bones was aghast that he was alive, but Elias could feel the attention of all the spirits swing towards Amira in their alarm, and Bones snapped his head around to look at her.

"*No...*" he breathed, and only an anticipatory flying tackle by Elias to knock the possessed assassin down stopped him from charging at Amira as she struggled to her feet. There had been no misinterpreting that motion. Whatever arrogance or sadism had been keeping Bones from trying to kill Amira until he was done with them, it was gone now. Elias got the feeling the panicked creature he'd just tackled was more dangerous than the one that had littered the floor with Blanche and the Guard.

This was only confirmed when the creature barely had to flex its arm to drive him off of it and into the nearest wall with a force that made him feel like he'd cracked most of his bones.

The room was practically spinning as Elias managed to right himself, but fortunately in the time Bones had taken to get moving again, Cecily had managed to find her feet, and stood between Amira and the assassin as Blanche scrambled up to help her.

"Milady, *RUN!*" she shouted. Elias panicked momentarily when he saw Amira hesitate, but fortunately the girl was smart enough to know that she was not aiding anyone by remaining in this dangerous position while they tried desperately to defend her. Amira fled down the hallway as Cecily tried to hold Bones back.

"No you don't!" Bones snarled, pulling the dagger out of his chest with his free hand and hurling it after her, but the blade only grazed Amira's side, deflecting off of her armor without stopping her. Elias thanked whatever gods might be listening that Amira had had the sense to wear the best armor she could find for the duration of this attack, but seeing her disappear around the corner let him join Blanche in focusing on Bones and rushing to Cecily's aid.

Trying to bury a knife in Bones had not been an easy prospect at the best of times, even when Elias had thought it would do more than slow him down. In this position, Elias didn't know what hope he had besides some desperate attempt to hold Bones down long enough for someone to remove his head. He tried not to think about his chances of actually accomplishing that as things stood. He suspected if they somehow lived through tonight, nothing Elias had to face afterwards would ever seem unreasonable again. Blanche managed to catch his eye as Cecily focused on Bones's sword. All three of them knew that blade was death to them, and so far the only one who had any luck with following it was Cecily. That still left the two of them against one preoccupied enemy.

Together, then.

White flames began to flicker along Elias's dagger and Blanche's sword. Teaming up with her like this was one of the last things Elias would have expected at the outset of his journey, but it beat the hell out of trying to bring down the monstrosity they were fighting against with nothing but his knife, his wits, and some spiritual aid.

Cecily took a step back, and managed to bind the next lightning-fast slash that came at her with her sword and force it against the ground. It would only hold for a few seconds. Elias could already see the terrible muscles straining under the vapor enshrouding Bones, but it was an opening.

As one, he and Blanche charged in, slicing at Bones's exposed flanks. Elias was rewarded with a pained growl as his dagger found its mark, but Bones released the grip of his sword with one hand, and his free arm shot out like a snake to grab Blanche's wrist. Much like Blanche's breastplate, her armored gauntlet warped and crumpled under the power of his grip. Blanche cried out in pain as Bones twisted his grip, bringing her to her knees and forcing his sword up from Cecily's bind.

"You're just prolonging the inevitable, mage. Your kind's time is over!" he snarled, twisting again. Elias could hear Blanche's arm break as the motion nearly ripped it free of her shoulder.

Cecily plowed into Bones, hacking desperately at every inch of him she could reach, but Bones laughed and kicked her hard in the stomach to send her sprawling. Elias used the knife embedded in Bones's side as a foothold to jump up and grapple the sword-arm with his entire body, but Elias had ridden horses less wild and powerful. It was all he could do to stop Bones from forcing Blanche onto the blade. Bones gave a snarl of frustration and then snapped his arm like a whip, dislodging Elias.

"Struggle all you want. You don't have the power to change anything!"

Blanche opened her eyes, blurry with pain, and glared up at Bones as he shook Elias off.

"You talk too much, Bones," she spat.

For the second time that night, Blanche's flames exploded out, enveloping the hallway, her body, and Bones alike. Elias needed to shield his eyes against the brilliant white light they emitted, but there was no blocking out Bones's scream of rage and pain. Elias could see the dark form, briefly stripped of its vapory cloak by the clinging flames, release Blanche and stagger back several paces, trying to get out of the flames. Blanche, her equipment smoldering but unharmed aside from her mangled arm, rose up with the last of her strength and drove her sword one-handed through Bones's knee and into the ground, pinning him down like an insect. This was their chance. Maybe their only one.

"Cecily!" Elias shouted, helping to haul the guard to her feet. "We need to cut off his head!"

Cecily nodded, hefting her sword grimly and charging at the stricken assassin before he could free himself. She'd been driven to the edge of exhaustion, had the wind knocked out of her again and again, and nearly died to dozens of near-miss parries in the last few minutes alone, but her killing stroke was astounding.

So was the speed with which Bones raised up his arm to intercept it. The flames consuming him went out as the darkness surrounded him in force again, and he looked up at Cecily. His eyes no longer looked like anything human. They were two red supernovas burning in his sunken eye sockets, and the rage in them seemed like more than one human body could hold.

"ENOUGH."

Elias knew what was going to happen before it did, but his mind refused to believe it even as he watched it happening. He was vaguely aware he was in motion, willing every muscle in his body to its limit, but he was slow, far too slow. He felt like he was encased in molten glass, able to see what was happening before him but helpless to reach it, to stop it.

The legion of evil spirits within him releasing spiteful cries at the Guard who had stood in their way so many times that evening, Oliver Bones ran Cecily through with one lightning-fast, savage stab. The fatally poisonous blade pierced her armor like it wasn't there, slashed through her heart, and came out the other side soaked in her blood. Dark miasma from Bones's hand surged along the blade into the wound, like snakes slithering to a meal. Elias's heart froze, horror spreading through him.

Bones straightened up, and with a contemptuous motion, kicked Cecily off of his blade and into Elias. She seemed to weigh nothing at all as he caught her, but her skin had gone more pale than Elias could ever imagine, and her veins were dark and frightening to look at as the corruption consumed them. Her eyes were bloodshot, blurred with pain and exhaustion, as they found Elias's face. She seemed…almost confused, for a moment, and then apologetic. Even now, she did not look scared. Her lips moved. She tried to say something as the poison burned a hole in her heart.

It never got out. In the moment it took for Elias to catch her and meet her eyes, Cecily was gone.

CHAPTER 44

Time seemed to stand still in the hallway as Cecily's last breath dispersed into the air.

Elias remembered when he'd found out his parents were dead. It had been a year or two before the end of Morys's reign when the news had come to him. It hadn't been old age or violence that carried them off, they had simply gotten sick while he was away, and they were gone when he returned.

It had been like getting stabbed with the wound never healing. The only people in the world that had ever really cared about him, the only people he'd ever trusted and belonged with, gone forever. It had been a trial some days just to stand and walk straight afterwards, to even get out of bed, but the world had kept going, and so had he. He was alone in the world, and couldn't trust anyone anymore, but there was no time to stop and lament while there was work to be done staying alive himself. Maybe it had been his distance from the event, maybe it had just been that he had been a self-absorbed son of a bitch in those days, but life had gone on without his family, and Elias had gone on living.

This was similar. He had lost the only person he trusted completely, and he would be dead, too, if he did not keep moving. And yet it was completely different. As he watched Cecily's eyes dim, her last gasp strangled by poison right in front of him, Elias knew the world had ended. Life couldn't go on from this, and neither would he. It was over. He had died again and again since his journey had started. Each new death had hurt more than the last. But this somehow hurt him, crushed his strength and his capacity for thought into nothingness, more than every wound that had come before it combined.

He was vaguely aware of Mibotha's desperate cries for him to fight on, but they echoed meaninglessly in his mind. He was frozen, numb, barely able to react as Bones freed his leg and stood, mad eyes gleaming with savage triumph as Cecily died.

Most sounds seemed distant, vague, unimportant, but Elias could hear Blanche's despairing scream as she saw Cecily. He saw one of the most powerful women he'd ever known scrambling along the ground, unbalanced and blinded by tears as she tried to reach Cecily, screaming denial at what her eyes told her.

Elias had heard Blanche cry out before, when Bones had nearly torn her arm off with his bare hands, and there was no doubting that this scream held far more pain. There wasn't any more courage or calculation or fury in Blanche. She struggled to Elias's side in such despair the enemy no longer existed in her world, looking more like a lost child than the captain of the Royal Guard.

Elias was aware he should have been screaming along with her, echoing that pain and despair with his own, but he couldn't. Losing his family had *hurt*, in a way even dying hadn't. With this, numbness seemed to consume him utterly as Cecily slipped out of his arms. He and Blanche stood dumbly over her body even as Bones walked towards them, in no hurry to finish them now as he saw all the fight go out of his enemies.

He's going to kill both of us, Elias realized, the thought sounding more like an impartial third party's than his own. Then he'll kill everyone else, and kill Amira. Yivyn, maybe the world, will be destroyed.

He knew that, now, and yet he couldn't *care*. Cecily was gone. That one fact seemed to consume everything, even the knowledge that he was about to die and let Bones and the evil spirits within him win. All he could wrap his head around was how *wrong* it was. He remembered every step of this gods-forsaken journey with her. He saved her life, and she helped him find the Guard. They worked together to find the Regalia. He saved her from the river and Bones, and she'd helped him find his way back to Amira. She'd given him hope things could be better, something he'd never expected to have in his life. She'd helped him feel at *home* for the first time in years.

She'd believed in him, despite everything he'd done, and he'd gone to fight the Basilisk-Eye alone because of it. He'd given up his chance to run away and hope he'd figure something out because of her. He'd come back from the most painful death he could imagine because she'd counted on him.

And now she was dead. Because he hadn't been strong enough to stop Bones when he had the chance.

It wasn't right. It wasn't *fair*. He'd come back to fight and probably die stopping Bones, not for *this!*

The despair consuming him found the last emotion left in Elias, but even as it pressed down on it, something even despair couldn't consume flared back to life in Elias's chest.

Rage.

"NO."

Blanche looked up in surprise, and Bones paused, seeming to sense something amiss. Elias's fists clenched so tightly his palms started to bleed, and Mibotha's words were drowned out under the roaring fury filling him up. For once in his life, Elias refused to crumble to the universe's latest injustice against him. He had endured a lifetime in the shadows, giving his all to causes no one even remembered. He had been blamed for crimes he didn't commit, vilified by people no better than himself, murdered at random in an argument over dead men's belongings, and judged, judged, judged by everyone he had met. And now one of the only people that had ever really been on his side was gone, with the few others that had ever given him a chance soon to follow. *Because he hadn't been good enough?*

"NO!" he roared again, barely able to see straight in his rage. "NOT LIKE THIS! *NOT FOR ME!*"

Bones overcame his surprise at the enraged shouting quickly, seeing there was nothing more to it than a ragged, broken man unable to accept one of many deaths. His blade arced towards Elias, ready to bring their battle to an end and do what he'd come here to do.

Elias opened his mouth again, and this time the sound that came out had nothing to do with human language, or noises his throat was able to produce. It wasn't a word, or even a scream. It was a sound like someone had smashed a hammer against the fabric of the universe, sending out a shockwave of rage and loss through the world. The stones of the castle thrummed in sympathy with it. The air seemed to warp and twist in obedience to it. Blanche's dwindling flames seemed to rise up in respect for it. Bones skidded back as though he'd been shoved by an invisible giant as the ground rumbled beneath their feet, but Elias did not see it.

Elias stepped beyond his body, and saw the world fall away beneath him. He saw himself, briefly, a tiny speck standing alone against the mightiest army that had ever been. He saw the world at his feet, and became aware of a great invisible one beyond it. The size and power of the forces beyond his body would make even the most arrogant man comprehend his utter insignificance in comparison.

Elias roared denial to the heavens and earth, and the infinity around him twisted in response to his wordless demand.

His consciousness flew higher than it ever had with Mibotha's aid, and Elias saw Yivyn in its entirety. Great, glowing lines ran along the ground like human veins, invisible to the naked eye, and even amidst the war and famine, the land shone with life.

Spirits. Hundreds, maybe thousands of them, spirits of stone and tree, cavern and lake, wind and sky. Hidden away from warring spirits and mortals alike, their anger and their resentment festering as the world writhed in pain but doing nothing. He had been afraid of their anger before, when he still felt fear, and now he realized Mibotha and its enemies alike feared that anger stirred into action when the war became too much to endure.

None of that mattered to Elias now. He saw the power, far away and refusing to help, and knew that it *should* be stirred into action, but they would not come when called on to fight. So he did not call them. Elias lashed out with his mind, and realized the anger of the spirits was nothing measured against his own. They cried out in protest as his will dragged them from their caves and trees, but their voices were drowned out in the furious roar of his demand. Elias saw the ley lines of Yivyn twist as if in pain as he tore the spirits from their hiding places, and then warp into a spiral centered at his body's feet. He saw the spirits pulled, in their hundreds and their thousands, along the lines, helpless to deny him the power he demanded. He saw them reach him, a great mass of light gathering where he stood.

Elias opened his eyes, and felt the very blood in his veins thrumming with power, a bright light of many colors breaking through his skin. A maelstrom of power filled him up from head to toe, spirits beyond counting thrumming in time with his heart beating. Wounds evaporated from his flesh like they had never been there. His blurred senses sharpened and expanded beyond anything he'd imagined. The power Mibotha feared would tear Yivyn and the world asunder had been awakened, and it was *his*. For a moment, Elias felt sure he could reach up and pluck down the sun from the sky. His body was restored, better than it had ever been or ever would be again, and unlimited power flowed into and through him. He focused all this power into his rage and at Bones.

Elias met the gaze of Oliver Bones and the legion of evil spirits gathered within him, and saw they were afraid.

"You?" he whispered, recognizing Elias for the first time but stepping back in disbelief. *"No, that's impossible! You CAN'T be—!"*

Elias's first blow launched Bones across the hallway, smashing him into the wall at the end hard enough the stone cracked. Elias picked up his second dagger as Bones recovered quickly and charged back at him. He'd found Bones almost too fast to follow before, but now it seemed as though the assassin was moving through water.

It was the easiest thing in the world to slide under the assassin's blade and cut his legs out from under him. The Basilisk-Eye howled and fell to his knees, but Elias lunged at him, stabbing into him again and again and again. Bones healed rapidly, forcing himself to his feet and trying to defend with his sword, but Elias drove him back relentlessly. Bones defended with all his speed and cunning, but he was outmatched. Time and time again, Elias found the gaps in his defenses, stabbing, slashing, feinting, and driving Bones before him.

His defenses falling apart before the furious assault, Bones dropped his guard and made a desperate attempt at a decapitating blow, but Elias slipped under it, and within Bones's guard.

A hero might have cried out the names of the ones he'd lost as he struck down his enemy, but Elias lashed out in silence as his body thrummed with power, a fury beyond any words guiding him. His hands blurred as his daggers tore the Basilisk-Eye apart, stabbing and slicing through his legs, his sides, his heart, with blinding speed and power. Elias practically climbed his stunned adversary, cutting all support out from under him and forcing him down with a flurry of merciless strikes. Finally, he plunged both his daggers into Bones's shoulders and forced the possessed assassin to his knees with a force that shook the floor. Bones collapsed, his body unable to heal from the sheer number of wounds Elias had dealt to him, his vaporous cloak ragged and writhing in pain around his mangled form. He could hear them, thousands of vile spirits, screaming in fear and denial.

"Elias!"

Elias turned to see Amira dashing back to them. Through his new eyes, he could see the queen was surrounded by a radiant aura. The long, white sword she was carrying had a strange, dangerous glow that extended beyond its edge.

"The Sword of Absolution," Amira had said to him once, a lifetime ago. *"It breaks all enchantments and sweeps away the regret and the grudges of those it slays. Their attachments to this world are severed along with their life, and their spirit does not linger to haunt the living."*

Amira had not known for certain if the legend of the Sword's power was true, but she had seen the multitude of raging evil spirits within Bones before she had fled. Elias realized only now that she had not run to hide. Amira would never have done that. She had gone to get them a weapon she hoped could kill Bones. Without a word, Amira threw the sword to Elias, and he caught it out of the air easily. Bones, or perhaps the spirits inside him, let out a great cry of dismay, and lashed out desperately with his sword, but Elias parried the strike with such force it disarmed Bones.

As the long, deadly sword flew from his grasp, Bones looked up. For a moment, his eyes were human again, but it didn't make the sight of them any less abhorrent to Elias. The assassin seemed more dazed or confused than scared, like he couldn't comprehend what had just happened to him.

"That's…not right…" he gasped, the power flowing out of his voice. "You *can't* be doing this! You're *nobody*!"

Elias hefted his sword, staring down at Bones with no mercy at all.

"That's right."

Bones made a horrible sound as the blade effortlessly sheared his head from his shoulders, his body twitching horribly before collapsing. Elias watched as his head fell away, hitting the floor with a dull thump and rolling a few feet before coming to a stop. As the dark vapor enshrouding it dispersed, nothing was left underneath but a gaping white skull.

Elias looked at Bones's sword, surprised to see the blade corroding where it lay. As Bones's head came to a stop, it practically dissolved. Whether it was the poison he'd used finally destroying the blade or a supernatural force, Elias neither knew nor cared.

The grotesque form of what had once been Bones's body spasmed horribly after its head was severed, and the darkness cloaking it writhed as if trying to escape or strike back at Elias. The movements were already weak, and as Elias turned, they grew still. The darkness dispersed like a mist being blown away in the wind, and the formerly human body beneath it blew to pieces like scattered flecks of ash. When the body dispersed completely, nothing but a forlorn, anonymous skull and the ruined remains of a poison sword lying a few feet away remained to prove that Oliver Bones had ever been.

Elias could feel the spirits still thrumming with power within him, seeking direction as he turned to Blanche and Amira. For them, there was no celebration in this triumph. Whatever satisfaction Elias might have taken in Bones's defeat was ash in his mouth now. He saw Amira's face pale as she realized Cecily lay among the slain. Blanche was cradling Cecily's body with her one good arm, the other hanging uselessly by her side. To see Blanche's face streaked with blood and tears did not disturb Elias nearly so much as her eyes. It wasn't just that the ferocity and cunning that had once made Blanche's eyes so frightening had bled away, it was the dead emptiness that had replaced them. Elias's grief had hurt more than anything he could imagine when Cecily had died, and he could see from Amira's face as she fell to her knees that she felt as he did. But Blanche…Elias knew just from looking at her that Bones killing Cecily had slain Blanche, too. She was the only Guard still breathing in the hallway, but she was as dead as the rest of them. Amira went to Blanche, trying to comfort her despite her own sorrow, but Blanche stared at nothing, completely lost in her despair.

The temptation to let his power and rage dissipate, to let the ungodly exhaustion it was holding at bay overtake him as he grieved alongside them, was enormous, but Elias clung to his fury at this injustice. He didn't need the power to pluck down the sun from the sky. He didn't need the power to make the foundations of the earth crumble and twist to his whims. He just needed the power to fix one last mistake. To make things right one more time. Amira looked up desperately from the unresponsive Blanche as Elias reached them, but Elias could only focus on Cecily's lifeless form.

What felt like the strength and vitality of an entire planet surged through Elias as he sank to his knees and put his hands over the wound in Cecily's chest. He took a deep breath, trying to gather it all together, small enough that he could manipulate it. The sheer effort of it made sweat drip down his face as his bones felt like they would be shaken to pieces, but eventually Elias took all of the power he had borrowed in hand.

With one exhalation, he began trying to force it out of him and into Cecily's lifeless body.

What are you doing, Elias Brook?! Mibotha's voice came sharp and fast, full of surprise and a very real worry. Elias could feel the wordless confusion of the multitude of other spirits within him, but he kept going, trying to make his will known as he kept trying to channel their power.

"Heal her," Elias breathed, voice ragged but filled with command. "I don't care what it takes. All of you, *HEAL HER!*"

You don't understand. This isn't the same as how I saved you, Elias Brook! If you lose all of this power at once…!

Elias realized, with some surprise of his own, that Mibotha wasn't worried about itself or the spirits he was forcing to restore Cecily to life. It was worried about *him*.

Channelling all of us healed your body, Elias Brook, but if you sever your connection to our power like this, your body will not survive the shock. This will KILL YOU. Mibotha warned. Elias sighed, and closed his eyes.

"Will it save her?"

…It will.

"I don't care, then. Do it," Elias whispered, and he felt Mibotha fill him one last time. At the end of their long journey together, he felt the spirit's sorrow as keenly as his own, and they spoke as one.

"Goodbye."

Then Mibotha was gone. Elias heard Amira shout his name as the world fell away.

He'd only grasped it for a moment, but Elias had not been able to comprehend the sheer scale of the power he'd called on while he had it. It was only as he gave it up that he realized how much there was. It felt as though an ocean of living, thrumming *power* poured out of his hands and into Cecily, breaking out of his body like a dam bursting and leaving exhaustion and weakness like Elias had never known in its place. Elias didn't fight back against the loss, he simply focused on directing every last bit of the power he'd sacrificed into healing Cecily.

He'd expected darkness to take him as the last of it flowed out of him, but light filled Elias's vision, wiping out all details of the world. With a serenity like nothing he'd felt in life, Elias closed his eyes and let himself be swept away.

CHAPTER 45

Elias hadn't known what to expect after he'd let himself be swept away in the light, but he'd been ready to face it no matter what it was. It seemed a bit anticlimactic, then, when he found himself floating through a bright, misty world, his body weightless and insubstantial as his surroundings.

This did not appear to be any sort of heaven, unless the gods were much more boring than their priests suggested, nor did it appear to be Valka, which was admittedly a very positive factor in his reaction to finding himself here. It didn't even look much like the vaster spirit world he'd briefly comprehended while enlisting supernatural aid in saving the day. So where *was* he?

His surroundings reminded him of the place between life and death where Mibotha had spoken with him before, but that seemed unlikely to Elias. Mibotha had not been ambiguous about what would happen when he gave up all of his power to save Cecily. He'd made his choice, and he was dead for good now. Surprisingly, the knowledge that his life was over didn't stir any regrets in him. He just wished he knew if his sacrifice had worked.

"That was a miracle, what you did."

Elias whirled around, alarmed to hear Blanche's voice. What on earth would she be doing here? She was one of the only people he'd been sure wasn't dead before he died!

At this point, Elias became aware of something in the mists below him, and looked down to see his body on a bed. He looked better than he had in five years, if you didn't count the distinctly non-vital stillness about him. Blanche was sitting beside the bed, looking battered but far, far better than he'd last seen her aside from her arm in a sling.

"Queen Amira and I dragged both of you to the physician afterwards. He says it's like Cecily was never injured at all. She DIED, right in front of us, but she's right as rain now. You did that, Elias. You killed the bastard that did her in, and you brought her back to us." Blanche lowered her head, and Elias could see she was crying.

"I'll never be able to thank you enough for that. For all you've done for us. But I want to try, Elias. I don't know if it's possible to square a debt like the one I owe you, but if you come back one more time...if you just open your eyes...I'll do everything I can to do just that."

The mists swirled slightly, and Boors stood by the bed next. The man looked like he'd wrestled several well-armed bears to look at him, but also that he'd given the bears the worst of it.

"I'd hoped I could shield everyone from this, you know," he said gruffly, looking down at the floor rather than at Elias. *"I prayed before the battle, for fate to put the Basilisk-Eye in my path. To let me strike him down, avenge the king and all of my friends that died because of him. If I could just do that, I thought, everyone else would be safe. We would turn back the rest of this tide and carry the day once that snake was dead and broken at my feet. But he got around me, again, and too many good people died because of it."* Boors looked at Elias's unmoving body. *"But we'd have lost a great many more if you hadn't been there, Brook. Maybe we would have lost everything."* Boors reached out and patted Elias's body on the shoulder once. Elias touched his own shoulder, but didn't feel anything. *"So don't lie up too long, and don't slip off without saying goodbye, eh? It would be poor form to leave us toasting victory without you."*

The mists swirled again, and this time it was Cecily by the bedside. Elias felt a massive wave of relief wash through him. As Blanche had said, she looked as though she hadn't been in a fight at all. Her demeanor was more subdued than normal, but Elias could see clearly enough even his lifeless form didn't seem to be enough to take away that hopeful look she had.

"Blanche told me about what happened, after I woke up," she said, running a hand through her hair. *"I don't know what you did, Elias, but Blanche said it was a miracle. If even half of what she remembers is true they'll write much better songs about you than the old ones for years to come. I promise I won't try to sing them,"* she laughed, as if she were just sharing a joke with a sick friend rather than paying her respects to a corpse.

If they ever find the damn bard that wrote the first one, Elias thought to himself, they should force him to make some lyrics worth remembering this time. And he would need to make a tune so catchy nobody would remember the first one anymore.

"You saved my life, Elias. That's the third time you've done that now, and this time you saved Blanche and Amira as well," Cecily went on. *"People have always muttered about you, and maybe some of them always will. But I want you to know that everyone here knows the truth. Despite what you'd have people think, you're one of the bravest, most determined, and resourceful men I know. That's why I'm sure that you're going to pull through this, Elias. You've always found a way before, and I know you will now."*

Elias rather wished he was the sort of man that could be brought back to life by a couple kind words from people he liked. Somehow dying when they were talking to him like this seemed almost rude.

He'd assumed that was the end of it, but he was surprised when the mists swirled one last time, leaving him watching his body with Amira by his bedside, sitting alone. The young queen had removed her armor, and the elegant golden dress she wore in its place reminded Elias that Amira was blooming into a remarkably beautiful young woman as well as a queen. She was holding something in her lap. A book, Elias realized, leather-bound and well taken care of from the looks of it.

"Maybe I should have told you about them earlier," she was saying, running her fingers along the cover. *"I don't know what you would have made of them, but perhaps they would have made you feel better."* she held up the book, seeming lost for words for a few minutes.

"Before you helped me find the Regalia, and before you brought me back here, these were all I had of him," she said, her voice shaking a little. *"It isn't much of an inheritance, a couple old journals from my father, but I cherished them all. I read them over and over for years...it was the closest I could get to ever hearing his voice again. It was like being close to him, just for a little while...now I'm the queen, and living in the place I grew up again. Mother and Father are all around me here, because you brought me home."* Amira wiped her eyes for a moment, opening the book as if she didn't need to look at it to find her place.

"I learned a lot about my father, reading his journals. A lot of it was tactical, or political...information he thought I should have when I was older, lessons he wrote down in case he never had time to teach them. But I learned about his feelings, too. Things he was afraid of, things that made him sad, the accomplishments that made him truly proud. He wasn't a very sentimental man, my father, but he was a good one. One of his only regrets was you."

Elias had not been expecting that, and it stung a little more because of it. He'd known when he started working for Morys that he'd been joining up to a dangerous venture with little gratitude in it for him, but at least *some* gratitude was owed for the services he'd rendered, wasn't it? Had Morys simply been ashamed that he needed to ask for the things he'd ordered Elias to do?

"I know what you did for him, and what he did for you. He created a place for you, in the shadows of the court. You were visible, but overlooked, known and not known. That was what he needed you to be, and so he kept you there, a part and not a part of our world. I don't think he realized, at first, what that did to you. What it's done to you this whole time. He watched you grow from a clever boy into a hard, cunning man, Elias, and he knew you were what he'd made of you, no matter where others laid the blame. He talked about you a great deal in this journal, about how you might be of great use to me if I knew how to use you…but he regretted, even before he was in danger from the Basilisk-Eye, how he'd treated you. He wrote to me…to be better to you than he had been. He saw as much as anyone else your cowardice, your cunning, your desire for recognition…but he saw there was good in you that few of his retainers would ever imagine. That if he had treated you differently, he was sure you would have been one of the most loyal men in all of Yivyn."

Amira closed the journal, and then reached out to touch Elias's hand.

"I can't make the past go away, Elias. None of us can, and we both have reason enough to wish we could. You can go seek your apologies from my father, if you wish. After all you've done for me, I have no right to demand you stay. But if you come back to us…I promise, on my honor as queen, my home is your home. There will always be a place for you here."

Amira swallowed and took a deep breath after the words spilled out, and then gave Elias a sad little smile and left him to rest alone.

"I wish I'd been alive for most of those conversations," Elias sighed, turning away from the image of his unmoving body. The reality that it was all over for him was starting to sink in, and he blinked back tears. He didn't have any need for a steadying breath anymore, but he went through the motions anyway. "So, this is it, huh?"

In a manner of speaking.

Elias recognized Mibotha's voice just as he recognized the vague, formless light that joined him in the mist. To his surprise, it didn't seem content to stay shapeless, as it once had. As it joined him, Elias briefly beheld a blind child, a majestic eagle, a beautiful woman, a proud, feral-looking man, and a massive, awe-inspiring beast that bore little resemblance to anything Elias had ever seen in his life...eventually, however, Mibotha condensed into the form of an old, wise-looking human, appearing neither male nor female to Elias's eyes. For once, Mibotha had a face Elias could see, and it smiled kindly at him.

"Mibotha? You're..." Elias searched for words that accurately summed up the feeling of watching it take that many forms in a moment. "...more solid than I remember," he finished lamely, finding none.

I have little use for forms much of the time. They are primarily a cumbersome sort of clothing for me, Mibotha sighed. *But...I felt a certain desire to wear a shape when I came to meet you here.*

"Would it be crass of me to ask why you picked that one?" Elias asked. The woman had not been wearing much in the way of clothes, from what he'd briefly observed, although fortunately the elderly shape Mibotha had assumed was. Mibotha just gave him a look, and Elias held up his hands in apology, stifling a chuckle. If you couldn't joke before you went to your eternal reward, when could you? He grew a little more serious as he went on. "Where are we, Mibotha? Is this the afterlife? It doesn't...look like anything I'd been expecting." Elias had never been a very pious man, but he remembered well enough the endless painful path Valka promised and the Golden Land where the good dwelt in happiness for eternity. Even purgatory wasn't supposed to look like this. Mibotha seemed to understand his puzzlement about where his actions had landed him in the end, although it didn't answer directly.

You managed to redeem yourself and atone for both our failures, along with averting the greatest cataclysm that would ever befall the mortal world. Trust me, Elias Brook, there is nothing left for you to prove to anyone. Mibotha bowed before Elias, who had to admit the respectful gesture from it felt very strange after all they'd been through. *Thank you, Elias Brook. Your world and mine are safe now, because of you.*

"So your war is over?" Elias asked, glancing at the spot in the mists he'd seen his vision. "Amira and Cecily and the others...nothing is going to come after them now that Bones is dead?"

The enemy gambled everything on destroying Amira before she could counteract the chaos they'd unleashed. Without her, they were certain they could use Bones as their avatar to complete Yivyn's destruction and cut us off from the mortal world entirely while they gained power to finish our war at their leisure, Mibotha explained. *Their interference made Oliver Bones all but immortal, far too powerful for any mere mortal to overcome. The risk of him being slain seemed nonexistent...until you managed to draw all of that power into yourself. With Bones dead and the spirits empowering him severed from the mortal world, their power is shattered. You and Amira together have managed to banish them permanently from the mortal world, and there will be no recovery for them in ours. The time of basilisks and monsters is over in your world, Elias. What Amira will have to face moving forward is the evil ordinary humans are capable of, and that I know she can overcome.*

"That's a relief," Elias sighed. He looked down at his hand, frowning a little. He still remembered, briefly, the feeling of becoming like a god… shouting orders in his anger at the world and the spirits in it, and being obeyed. Feeling the lines of power that made up the world shift to converge under his feet. He looked up at Mibotha.

"How did I do that, Mibotha? I sure as hell wasn't trying to, I was just…" He trailed off, unable to find the right words.

I don't know, Mibotha admitted, shrugging helplessly. *By everything I know of the intersection between mortal and spirit, it is completely impossible for you to do what you did. Perhaps it is fortunate that no one could have predicted you could do such a thing. It was something the enemy couldn't plan for or defend themselves from.* Mibotha looked at Elias. *I cannot give you any explanation for how you did it, Elias. It might have been some extension of our bond. No man has ever stepped as far through the boundaries of death and returned as you, and none have done so as often as you did in our time together. Dying and rising may have changed you into a different sort of being than the one you were when you came to me. Or perhaps it was a quality you always possessed, buried until our meddling brought it out in you. It could even have been a force greater than humans or spirits interceding on your behalf in response to your need. We will never truly know. All I know is that all spirits, good and evil, believed there was only one human in all the world who could drive back the darkness and heal the land, and Oliver Bones planned to slay her before she matured enough to do it.*

"Amira."

Her gift is nearly insignificant at this point compared to the importance of her capacity to bring peace back to this kingdom. But when she is grown, I suspect she will be very powerful indeed, Mibotha said gravely. *I know you felt the power and anger that dwells in the forests of your world. Many spirits, lesser in power and ambition to those that warred but far greater in number, watched but did not interfere in our conflict. Their intervention would have ended the war decisively for whoever they aided, but they had the power to destroy both of us and humanity if nothing soothed their rage before they acted. With time, Amira might have grown strong enough to calm their anger, even stir them to action on her behalf, as you did when you commanded them to aid you. But if she died, it is likely the nature spirits taking action against the enemy would have been an apocalypse for humanity. Her powers were never a consideration for me, only her role…but the enemy feared both. If they assassinated her, Yivyn would collapse into chaos and we would have little capacity to stop them from ravaging it. Then they would not need to live in fear of Amira growing into her potential and becoming a force capable of destroying them outright. Putting all their power behind Bones to slay her while she was still young and vulnerable was worth the risk to them. I don't believe they would have dared attempt it if they had realized you could achieve through force of will, even just for a moment, the collective power of* **all** *spirits.*

"And in the old days everyone would have been cross with me for stealing it. How things change," Elias said, trying to make light of the situation. It was really too much, all this talk of queens, gods, destiny, and spirits. He'd just been trying to stay alive, like always, he certainly hadn't meant to become temporarily omnipotent. It was quite a relief, in many ways, to know his involvement with all of that was over. Mibotha nodded, turning towards an increase in the ambient light. Somehow, just as the spirit's human form looked neither male nor female, its expression managed to be both happy and sad.

If anyone is proof that a man can change, it is you, Elias Brook. I may have bullied you into starting your journey, and circumstances may have forced you to keep going at times, but…ultimately, I can take no credit for how you've changed, beyond the happy coincidence that my plan set your feet on the path you followed to this end. What you did for Amira and the others is miraculous, and will live on in Yivyn's memory for years and years to come. I don't know how many will understand the remarkable thing you did for yourself along the way. You are a very different man than the one I gave my ultimatum to at the beginning of all this, Elias Brook. You have changed your fate in a way few ever will…and you have earned this.

Elias watched as the light before him coalesce into a magnificent white staircase, leading up into a brightness like the sun. The pathway to heaven could hardly be more obvious, and its appearance made Elias feel a little weak. That was it, then. No more dying and popping up to get back to work. No more being told the absurdly difficult thing he'd managed to accomplish was the easy part, and another, still more unreasonably difficult task lay before him. No more fighting for his life or wondering how his quest for redemption was much different than being tormented for his sins. This was the reward he'd worked for but never dared to believe he deserved, all this time. He looked to Mibotha for confirmation, and saw the elderly head nod. Still, he hesitated.

"When you first joined me here, you said this was it 'in a manner of speaking,'" he recalled. "Did you mean that you just wanted to talk to me before I went to the Golden Land?"

No, Elias Brook. I meant "in a manner of speaking" because this is it for the two of us, Mibotha said simply. *Whatever you decide to do now, you will not come to this place again. This will be our last meeting.*

"Whatever I decide?" Elias's eyes widened slightly as the significance of the bedside conversations he could hear finally hit him. "I'm not dead, am I?"

Your life-force was snuffed out by the power you wielded to kill Bones and sacrificed to save Cecily, Mibotha said. *Your spirit has left your body, and you are here, at the threshold between heaven and earth. You are dead, Elias Brook. You chose to die so Cecily would live. But your spirit may be the most stubbornly determined one I have ever encountered. It has not let go of its connection to your body. I cannot force you to do that, and I have no desire to. The only one that can break that connection is you, if you walk forward into the light.*

"...And...if I don't?" Elias asked, not sure why he was pursuing this line of thought while paradise waited before him but unable to help himself. Mibotha just smiled a little.

If you go forward, then the story of your life ends here. You will die a hero, venerated by humans and spirits alike as the truth of your tale spreads. You will go to your eternal reward in the afterlife, and there will be no further hardship or suffering for you, not even after the end of all things. Mibotha nodded behind Elias, and he saw a place where the mists thickened and swirled strangely. *If you go back, I cannot say what will become of you. You will awaken in the bed you saw, but I will not be with you. You will live the remainder of your life, with whatever triumphs and failures you find in the world. You will be judged for all of it when it comes to an end. There will be no guarantees, many responsibilities, and likely much hardship if you return to the mortal world. If you die after this, there will be no healing, no decisions to make, and no recovery. Your life will be yours, and it will once again be the only one you have, for good or ill.* Mibotha inclined its head. *One way or another, this is the last time we will see each other.*

Elias and Mibotha stared at one another for a long moment, neither of them saying anything. Elias could tell just from looking at the spirit's face that they both knew what he was going to do, and he held out his hand.

"You know, you have easily been the most aggravating person, human or spirit, that I've ever met. Many of the worst experiences I've had in my life have come about while we were together," he said, unable to keep from smiling. "And yet, I find I'm actually happy I met you. Strange as it is, I'm going to miss you, Mibotha."

I took you for a selfish, lazy, and needlessly pessimistic coward when we met, Mibotha replied evenly, but it was grinning. *And while I was completely right to do so, it has been a very enlightening...and very humbling experience to see how much more there is to you. It has been an honor to know you, Elias Brook. I wish you the best of luck.*

The two shook hands in the quiet light of the world in between, and briefly held it with the gravity of two people who knew their journey together was now finally and irrevocably at an end. When the moment ended, Elias released Mibotha's hand, and turned and started walking into the swirling mists. Mibotha watched him go, its human form starting to dissolve into the light around it.

Farewell, my friend.

CHAPTER 46

And then Elias awoke.

He'd half-expected his body to leap awake and sit up the moment his spirit was once again inhabiting it, but it was more like a little twitch as his eyes slammed open and his breath caught in surprise. His body clearly hadn't been expecting him back, and when Elias tried to sit up, he found he could barely move enough to do it. There was no strength in him at all, and his limbs were completely stiff. He was starving, too, he realized. How long had he been on the threshold?

"Elias!"

Elias turned as he sat up in the bed, seeing Blanche and Cecily come into the room. Blanche looked momentarily stunned to see him up, but Cecily grinned and ran over to hug him.

"You've come back to us! I knew you would!"

He had woken up to considerably worse situations, Elias reflected, taking the opportunity that was presented and slipping his arms weakly around Cecily's shoulders for a little while before they broke apart.

"I'm glad to see you, too," he said, his voice feeling a little weak before he coughed. "You both look a lot better than last I saw you. How long have I been here?"

"You've been laid up in that bed for two weeks. Honestly, if I hadn't seen you shrug off some of the things you had, I'd have expected you to starve to death," Blanche remarked, coming over to join them. Either she was making less of an effort to be inscrutable or Elias was better at reading her, but he could tell she was pleased to see him up but controlling it more. "Everyone's had a hundred questions about what happened that night, myself included. I was *there*, and I still don't know what I saw except that it was a miracle."

"I *did* it, and I'm not sure I can explain much of it," Elias sighed, trying to massage some feeling back into his arms. Blanche looked at him for a moment longer, then nodded, seeming to accept that.

"Well, I guess the explanation doesn't matter much. You won the day, and that's what's important," she said.

"I've been in this bed for two *weeks*?" Elias asked, groaning as he tried to stand up and finding this took a lot more strength and balance than his body had right now. His muscles were slow to respond to the return of his soul, apparently, although his stomach had wasted no time reminding him it had not eaten a proper meal for far too long.

"You were barely breathing. If you weren't still warm after days, we'd probably have buried you, but there was hope you'd pull through," Blanche remarked, glancing at Cecily.

"You won't have much strength for a while, Elias. You've been abed too long. For now, just rest and recover," Cecily urged. "We'll go tell the queen you are awake."

"I don't suppose you could tell the chef as well?" Elias asked hopefully. "I certainly *feel* like I haven't eaten in weeks."

Blanche smiled. It was a more pleasant sight than Elias remembered.

"We can arrange that," she replied.

It was Amira, in the end, who came with a bowl of stew to his bedside. Elias had very little strength, but found he had quite enough to devour the simple stew as though it were the most delicious thing he had ever tasted. It was gone so quickly there was plenty of time for him to sit and talk with Amira afterwards. Amira seemed to know that whatever questions she had for Elias about what he'd done that night had no answers he could share, and she didn't ask.

Losses in the castle's defense had been blessedly light thanks to his warning, she told him. Many of the Guard who had stood with Blanche against Bones had sadly laid down their lives trying to stop him, but the other defenders had been able to make good use of the advantage of defending the castle and Boors holding the bridge to wipe out Hache's other assassins without great losses.

"It wasn't just my life you saved that night, Elias," she said seriously, hands folded in her lap as she sat by his bedside. "If they had caught us by surprise, it might have been far, far worse. You saved all of us. How can I possibly repay you?"

Elias shifted slightly, sighing.

"Let's not worry about that right now. I did owe you already," he pointed out gently. "I'd rather call things even here."

He'd thought a lot about what was owed him for the disproportionate level of suffering he'd endured to atone for his sins, but now that it was all over, he found there was very little he actually wanted from the girl in front of him. The feeling might go away later, Elias was aware. But for now just being alive made him content. He wanted to enjoy that while it lasted.

He was rather surprised when Amira leaned forward and hugged him tightly. At the moment, there was more strength in her arms than there was in his own.

"Thank you for coming back to us, Elias," Amira whispered, closing her eyes as she held onto him. Elias was shocked for a moment, but slowly his features softened into a smile and he wrapped his arms around Amira weakly.

"Thank you for wanting me back, Amira," he whispered back.

It took about another week, but strength gradually returned to Elias's body. He still felt quite drained from his ordeal, but his muscles seemed to realize there was a great deal to live for yet, and he finally regained the strength to stand up and leave his bed.

It was a strange world that awaited him when he left the room behind. The castle he'd spent so much of his life in was still being restored after its years of abuse and neglect, but Elias had never felt so comfortable within the walls before. The Royal Guard had all been eager to echo their queen's thanks and celebrate the man who had made all this possible once he was among them again. Elias had his hand shaken and been enthusiastically slapped on the shoulder so many times on his first day walking about again that he suspected he might need Blanche's sling when she was done with it. Being greeted like some kind of hero, especially by the Royal Guard, was an experience Elias was not sure he'd ever get used to, but he would be lying if he said he did not enjoy it.

Even stranger in the world was the view beyond the castle. The day Elias finally left his room, it rained. The sight of it was so astonishing that Elias stood by a window, losing track of time as he watched the rain pour down in sheets. The lands beyond Enrilth Keep were barely visible through the torrential downpour, but it seemed to Elias they were nowhere near as dry and desolate as they had been when they'd arrived.

Elias lost track of time just watching the storm, trying to remember the last time Yivyn had had more than a weak drizzle, enough to keep the people from starving entirely.

"Everything's coming back to life, it seems."

Elias was snapped out of his trance to see Boors join him at the window, looking reflectively out at the rain.

"Hm?"

"Ever since that night it has been different. The drought just… vanished," Boors remarked, watching the rain fall thoughtfully. "It has rained more in the last three weeks than it has in the last three years. Things are staring to grow as if they'd been waiting for this day. Even the Haunted Wasteland is starting to respond. All our talk of a kingdom of dust or trees, it feels like all we had to do to stop it was to triumph here."

Elias wondered if he ought to tell Boors how close to the mark his musings actually were, but decided against it. For the time being, he just felt he ought to let Mibotha's secrets lie.

"Blanche described it as a miracle, what happened that night, but it seems to me like every day since then has been a miracle," Boors went on. "The rains have come back. The land is starting to come back to life. Even you've recovered as the land has regained its strength. Yivyn has been dying for years, but now it seems to burst with new life. Maybe it's right for the people to take it as a sign."

"Word is coming in from beyond the Wasteland?" Elias asked, glancing over curiously. Boors nodded.

"It took a little time, but contact is being established. Your instincts were right. The queen being revealed to the world just before the drought finally ended has the land in an uproar. Everyone's taken it as a sign Queen Amira's return has finally pleased the gods," Boors said.

"Hache couldn't have been happy to hear that," Elias chuckled, relieved to hear some good news about his plan.

"No, and he liked hearing Amira lay his treasons bare before the world even less. Hache was never a popular ruler, but this was the breaking point for his lands. His people rose up against him, and his soldiers deserted. Hache and his wife have fled Yivyn, from what we've heard. With any luck, that will be the last we hear of them."

"Good riddance," Elias said bluntly. That was a relief. He'd been afraid they might have to go fight the crazy bastard even after this last attempt failed. He sighed contently. "Well, the queen back on the throne, miracles, people grateful to have her back, it almost seems like everything's solved itself while I was asleep."

"Not at all," Boors groaned, shaking his head. "We won the battle, and that seems to have ended the war. But now the fighting and adventure are done with, and we're left with Enrilth and the shattered territories around it. Envoys from the remaining warlords will be arriving soon, and I suspect not a single one of them will be rejoining us immediately. They've all been in charge too long for that," Boors sighed, crossing his arms and giving Elias a pained look. He was happy with what they'd accomplished, Elias could tell, but he wasn't looking forward to what came next one bit. "You helped wrap up the war very nicely for us, Elias, but you woke up in time for *politics*."

"Ah," Elias said glumly, "So killing Bones was still the easy part." Boors let out a booming laugh, and Elias struggled to keep a straight face. He'd passed up on paradise for this, he realized. What on earth had these people *done* to him?

"There should be little real danger reuniting the land now, at least compared to before," Boors sighed. "But it will take a great deal of work, and cunning. I fear I won't be able to aid the queen as much as I would like in the days to come, but I think she will want your advice."

"I'm not really much of a politician," Elias pointed out. "I annoy people."

"I suspect the queen will want a number of very stiff-necked people annoyed before long," Boors said placidly. "But you're clever, and you know how people think. Those talents have helped us. With luck, they'll help us finish what we started as well."

"I seem to recall a knight, when all this started," Elias remarked, glancing over at Boors. "who thought I was a great fool, and not worthy of trust. That if I was a clever man, I would not have been where I was when we met."

"I know that knight," Boors said, his face not changing a bit. "He saw a man before him that thought only of his own survival, that seemed to know nothing of service or sacrifice. An unpleasant man the knight resented having to work with, even as the man resented his presence in return." Boors turned to Elias, looking serious. "You knew a knight that thought you an unreliable fool. I knew a man who cared about nothing but himself. But I did not, I think, meet Elias Brook until some time later. I am sorry to know that…and glad that I met you."

Boors's hand moved again, but this time Elias did not flinch at all. He wasn't surprised when Boors held out his hand to him.

"Thank you, Elias Brook. For everything you've done for us. Thank you for showing a stubborn man who you really are."

Elias was surprised how easy it was to bring himself to shake Boors's hand, almost as surprised as he was when he still had a hand after placing it in Boors's grip. He and Boors were not friends, he didn't think, but the animosity he'd once held for the man had faded. It was a strange feeling, to shake hands in mutual respect with a Guard, but Elias decided that some of the strange things he was encountering since his recovery were things he hoped would become familiar.

———————

As Boors had commented, Elias's strength seemed to return faster as vitality infused the land around Enrilth again. Soon enough, he felt well enough to be roped into some of the many rebuilding projects in progress around the castle with only minor complaint. Elias no longer felt spiritual power in his body, not even the mildly invigorating freshness his partnership with Mibotha had first given him. However, his journey had given Elias a newfound respect for the strength he'd always had, even if it regrettably involved him with honest manual labor, a thing he'd avoided since he was seven.

It started to dawn on him that he never saw Blanche involved in the projects, however, despite Boors and Cecily diving into them as enthusiastically as the rest of the guard. Perhaps that was what prompted Elias to seek her out after weaseling out of helping Boors repair the castle gate before the envoys would arrive.

He found her wandering one of the hallways alone, arm still in its sling. She glanced up when he called to her, pausing to let him catch up.

"Oh, Elias. I thought you'd be working right now." There was a mild reprimand in there, but Elias sidestepped it without guilt.

"Boors seems to have things well in hand," he replied, shrugging slightly. He grew more serious as he looked at the sling. "How is your arm doing?" Blanche's expression soured as she looked down.

"I was lucky, the doctor said. If Bones had put in a little more effort, he'd have ripped it out entirely. I'd probably have died," she said quietly. "It will mend, but not quickly, and not completely. It probably won't ever be quite the same again, certainly not with a sword." Blanche smiled, but it wasn't a happy expression. "We can't all heal as well as you, Elias."

Elias opened his mouth to say that he would have leant it to her if he could have, but the words got lost as his attention focused on Blanche's twisted shoulder and broken bones. He wasn't in any pain, but it was as though he could feel Blanche's injuries, see their shape...

This is wrong, something in the back of his mind told him. This can be fixed.

"Hold still a minute, Blanche," he heard himself say. Blanche looked puzzled, but did as he asked. Elias's mind wasn't quite sure what he was doing, but the rest of his body seemed to have it figured out. He could feel Blanche's injuries, and somehow knew that if he gently laid his hands *here* and *here*—

Blanche gasped, not in pain but in surprise as Elias's hands glowed. Elias's awareness of her wounds, the strange disruptive feeling their pain gave him, gradually shrank and faded away into nothing. When he took his hands away, Blanche looked at her arm. Very slowly and carefully, scarcely believing the evidence of her senses, she lifted it it out of the sling and held it straight before making a fist. When it became clear she was not hallucinating, and her arm was indeed restored, she looked at Elias in astonishment.

"How did you do that?"

Elias wished he had a helpful answer. Once the knowledge of what he had to do wore off, he was left just as shocked as Blanche to see he'd actually healed her arm.

"I-I don't know!" he admitted, looking at his hands. "I just looked at your injury, and then...my body just sort of moved on its own!"

"Magecraft..." Blanche whispered, looking at her restored arm and then back to him. "You can use it to heal others. Not just yourself!"

"So it seems," Elias said helplessly, aware that shouldn't be possible. He'd never been a mage! Mibotha was just healing him from the inside, that wouldn't have given him the ability—

Blanche's ancestors likely interacted more closely with my kind than their fellow humans did. A mage is not some aberration upon the face of the world. They are humans whose blood carries a boon from the spirits. Nothing more, and nothing less.

Mibotha's words came back unbidden, and clarity struck Elias like a hammer blow. Blanche's powers had probably been a boon from the spirits she'd indirectly inherited. *He'd* briefly held every spirit in the mortal world inside his body, and commanded them to let him heal Cecily back from death. Was it any surprise holding that much power from the spirits might have transformed him more than he'd thought? He realized Blanche was staring at him, and he raised his hands defensively.

"I promise, I couldn't do that before," he said quickly. "I could never do anything like this until just now." To his surprise, Blanche smiled a little, shaking her head.

"It's all right. You just surprised me. Thank you, Elias," she said quietly, removing her sling entirely. She looked at Elias's hands thoughtfully. "I would tell Amira about that, if I were you. I think it's something she ought to know about."

"I guess, but…" Elias frowned, seeming more troubled than Blanche now. "You're the experienced mage, Blanche. What just happened?"

"You remember what I told you? I've always assumed a mage's power defines them. Maybe that's not completely accurate," Blanche said simply, looking Elias in the eyes. "Tell me something, Elias, since you fought Bones, is there something that matters more to you now than the ability to survive?"

Elias was surprised by the question, but his mind flashed to the final moments he remembered from that night. Cecily dying right in front of him, and how watching her die while he was helpless to do anything but watch had hurt more than any of the deaths he'd endured. The explosive rage against the injustice of the loss keeping him from sinking into insensible grief and then, that moment of complete serenity, knowing nothing mattered but being able to save her life, even though it would kill him. Elias nodded mutely, and Blanche did not seem at all surprised.

"As above, so below, some say," she said quietly. "Who knows, Elias, if you can change, maybe we all can."

Elias didn't have any chance to find out what she meant by that, as Blanche turned quickly and walked away. He did not follow her.

The encounter with Blanche, and his newfound power to heal, kept Elias from sleep, and it was a warm, dry night compared to the many rainy days that had come before. He found himself wandering the castle, moving aimlessly out to the ramparts to look up at the sky.

It was beginning to sink in, he realized, that his quest was over. There were no further pleas or demands from the spirits. From the looks of it, there would be no more wars to fight, for the first time in the last five years. Oliver Bones and the evil spirits were gone, never to return. He'd done everything he'd set out to do since his first death in the forest. And yet, life went on. His quest was over, but his life wasn't. There would always be something more he needed to do, another change in his future, one more hard part until the day he died. For the first time, Elias fully appreciated that nothing ever really ended. There was just a place the teller stopped talking. So it would go with him, until the day he died one last time, and life went on without him. The thought didn't trouble him as much as it once might have.

"Can't sleep?"

Elias looked over his shoulder to see Cecily behind him. He nodded slowly, and Cecily walked over to join him on the ramparts.

"It's hard for everyone, you know. It's been a month now, but it still doesn't feel completely real that we're actually *here* after five years of waiting," she said lightly. "It's hard to sleep when you know you'll wake up in a different world than you imagined the night before."

"Don't I know it," Elias muttered, shaking his head before he glanced at her. "It's never really going to be over, is it? All of this. We got Amira here, but that's not the end, either."

"No. Everything that was torn down over the last five years needs to be rebuilt. And after that, my lady still needs to *rule* it, no matter what comes to threaten her reign."

"That sounds exhausting. I have to admit, part of me thought somehow everything was sorted out if we just beat Bones. I guess I never really thought about what would happen after," Elias admitted.

"The world of the living and Valka are both endless paths, Elias. Solve one problem, and another comes along soon enough. Only in the Golden Land does the path ever end," Cecily said, smiling at him. "Only the virtuous dead ever know their destination. For the rest of us, it's just a matter of finding happiness in the journey."

"You're awfully optimistic for someone who thinks Valka's not that different from our world," Elias quipped, and Cecily laughed.

"It's very different, Elias. Valka is a road you can only walk alone."

The response brought Elias up short, and he turned to see Cecily looking at him.

"What do you think you're going to do from here, Elias?" she said. Elias thought for a long moment before he answered.

"I'm going to stay here," he said, surprised to know he meant it. "There's no end to what needs to be done around here. I can help out with some of it. Besides," he added quickly when he saw Cecily relax a bit, "you people seem lost without me, and I like the food here."

"I'll remind the chef that his work may be all that binds the slippery Elias Brook to our cause, then. That should please him," Cecily teased, grinning. Still, Elias could tell his answer had pleased her. She turned to go, but glanced at him again.

"Wherever the path leads for all of us, Elias, I'm glad to have you with us," she said sincerely, reaching out and touching his hand. She held it there for a moment before excusing herself, looking a little embarrassed. Elias watched her go.

It would not have been very long ago at all he would have agreed heartily with the sentiment the world and Valka were not all that different and disagreed just as strongly that people could walk on life's path together for any length of time. And yet, it was also a lifetime ago. Several lifetimes. He understood what she meant, and he genuinely believed she was right. Maybe that, more than anything else, reminded him he was not the man who had started this journey.

The man he had been would have left now, right or wrong. The debt was paid, and he would not stay beyond that. But Elias knew the man he was now wasn't going anywhere, even with the future ahead promising only more responsibility and hardship. He hadn't known anything that might make that worthwhile before, but now he did.

There was a path out there Elias Brook could walk by himself, trusting no one and trusted by no one. He'd turned from that path the day he'd accepted Mibotha's ultimatum, although he hadn't known it at the time. That path and the one that stretched in front of him now were both fraught with hardship, toil, and pain, he had little doubt. Maybe they had it in equal measure, or maybe the one before him was worse, but Cecily had been right.

He didn't have to walk it alone. For the first time in his entire life, he didn't need to face life alone. They had given him that, Boors, Blanche, Mibotha, Amira...Cecily. Elias smiled up at the sky, wondering if Mibotha could see him from wherever it had gone. He still owed all of them a debt he'd likely spend the rest of his life paying, and he didn't mind. What'd they'd given him was worth it.

Under the night sky, Elias knew in this castle, among these people, was where he belonged.

The End

Acknowledgements

I feel like anyone who does much of anything has a lot of people to thank.

First, I'd like to thank my siblings, Tyler and Kira for giving me a middle siblings sense of humor, for your support, and for knowing I could trust in your honesty and criticism.

I'd like to thank my friends, particularly Becky, Josh, and Aniek, for making getting better at writing the most fun I've ever had.

I'd like to thank Adam and Stacy for your sincere encouragement while I was writing this and for your ongoing help contacting people and promoting it.

I'd like to thank my Grandma for believing I'd go far in life, and for sharing your insight and advice with me.

I'd like to thank my Mom for encouraging my artistic efforts and being there to help me find my way forward in the world. You've always known what to say to make me feel like I could succeed, and what to ask to make me think things through. You've taught me how to look at life, handle adversity, and to always do my best.

Finally, I'd like to thank my Dad who's always known when I needed a helping hand, a suggestion, or a kick in the butt to get myself going. I owe so much of my sense of humor and my sense of responsibility to you. *Elias Brook* would not be a book at all if it wasn't for all your help, encouragement, and insight every step of the way. Thank you so much for undertaking this journey with me.

www.ingramcontent.com/pod-product-compliance
Lightning Source LLC
Chambersburg PA
CBHW060151260626
47160CB00001B/224